Mephista

Mephista

by
Maurice Limat

translated by
Michael Shreve

A Black Coat Press Book

Acknowledgements: Jean-Luc Rivera, Antoine Dumont, Philippe Heurtel., Philippe Marlin, Remy Lechevalier.

Mephista (Fleuve Noir *Angoisse* No. 166, 1969) © 2015 by The Estate of Maurice Limat. English adaptation Copyright © 2015 by Michael Shreve.
Mephista contre Mephista (Fleuve Noir *Angoisse* No. 171, 1969) © 2015 by The Estate of Maurice Limat. English adaptation Copyright © 2015 by Michael Shreve.
Mephista et le Clown Ecarlate (Fleuve Noir *Angoisse* No. 183, 1970) © 2015 by The Estate of Maurice Limat. English adaptation Copyright © 2015 by Michael Shreve.
Introduction Copyright © 2015 by Jean-Marc Lofficier.
The Man of a Million Words © 2015 by Maurice Limat & Philippe Heurtel; translation & adaptation © 2015 by Jean-Marc Lofficier.
Teddy Verano afterword © 2015 by Jean-Marc Lofficier.
Mephista afterword Copyright © 2015 by Artikel Unbekannt; translation & adaptation © 2015 by Jean-Marc Lofficier.

Cover illustration Copyright © 2015 Mike Hoffman.

Visit our website at www.blackcoatpress.com

TABLE OF CONTENTS

Maurice Limat
(photo by Philippe Marlin)

Introduction

About Editions Fleuve Noir:

Editions Fleuve Noir was founded in 1949 by Armand and André de Caro, Robert Bonhomme and Guy Krill, for the explicit purpose of publishing cheap, popular paperbacks.

They began with police thrillers in their *Spécial-Police* imprint (1949), followed by espionage novels in their *Espionnage* imprint (1950) (their two most famous series being the exploits of secret agent OSS 117, later replaced by Francis Coplan FX-18 when Jean Bruce, the author of OSS 117, migrated to another publisher), adventure novels in their *L'Aventurier* imprint (1950), science fiction novels in their *Anticipation* imprint (1951), and finally, horror novels in their *Angoisse* imprint (1954).

Fleuve Noir's policy was to rely on a steady stable of French house authors, whose pseudonyms they owned, thus ensuring both loyalty and brand name recognition.

For forty years, with its huge monthly output, Fleuve Noir came to embody the best—and occasionally the worst!—of French popular literature.

Black Coat Press has published a fair sampling of Fleuve Noir novels in translation:

- Marc Agapit: *Despair*, a screenplay faithfully adapted from an *Angoisse* novel by Jean-Marc & Randy Lofficier (ISBN 978-1-932983-06-7).
- G.-J. Arnaud: *The Ice Company*, an award-winning *Anticipation* novel, the first in a long, popular series, translated by Jean-Marc & Randy Lofficier (ISBN 978-1-935558-31-6).
- Richard Bessière: *The Gardens of the Apocalypse* (which also includes *The Seven Rings of Rhea*) two *Anticipation* novels translated by Brian Stableford (ISBN 978-1-935558-68-2), followed by *The Masters of Silence* (which also includes *They Came from the Dark*), two more *Anticipation* novels translated by Michael Shreve (ISBN 978-1-61227-297-9).
- André Caroff: The ever-popular series of 18 *Madame Atomos* novels from the *Angoisse* imprint, collected in nine omnibus volumes, the first translated by Brian Stableford; the others by Michael Shreve (ISBNs: 1: 978-1-935558-41-5; 2: 978-1-61227-018-0; 3: 978-1-61227-030-2; 4: 978-1-61227-069-2; 5: 978-1-61227-087-6; 6: 978-1-61227-119-4; 7: 978-1-61227-157-6; 8: 978-1-61227-223-8; 9: 978-1-61227-259-7).
- P.-J. Hérault: *The Clone Rebellion*, an *Anticipation* novel translated by Michael Shreve (ISBN 978-1-61227-385-3).

- Gérard Klein: *The Mote in Time's Eye*, an *Anticipation* novel translated by C.J. Richards (ISBN 978-1-935558-48-4).
- Kurt Steiner (pseudonym of André Ruellan): *Ortog* (which also includes *Ortog and the Darkness*), two *Anticipation* novels translated by Brian Stableford (ISBN 978-1-935558-28-6).
- Pierre Pelot: *The Child Who Walked on the Sky* (which also includes *What if Butterflies Cheat?*), two *Anticipation* novels translated by Michael Shreve (ISBN 978-1-61227-107-1).

For the record, we should also mention Pierre Barbet, whose Fleuve Noir novels *The Napoleons of Eridanus, The Emperor of Eridanus, Games Psyborgs Play, Baphomet's Meteor, The Enchanted Planet, The Joan Of Arc Replay* and *Stellar Crusade* were translated and published by DAW Books.

In addition to the three *Angoisse* novels by Maurice Limat featured in this book, we are presently in the process of having six more *Anticipation* novels by another "grandmaster" of Fleuve Noir, Jimmy Guieu, translated and scheduled for publication for an early 2016 release.

About Maurice Limat:

Briefly, Maurice Limat was born on 23 September 1914 in Paris and died in Sèvres, a Parisian suburb, on 21 January 2002. His literary output, which included science fiction, horror, detective and spy thrillers, was particularly abundant and often signed with various pseudonyms.

Starting in 1935, Limat's books were, for the most part, published by Ferenczi & son, who also published Jean de La Hire. After World War II, from 1959 until his retirement in 1987, Limat was one of the major authors of Fleuve Noir. In total, Limat wrote over 500 novels during his prolific career.

In his fifty-plus science fiction novels, Limat painted the epic saga of humanity, leaving its native planet and joining forces with neighboring races of

Mars and Venus to form the "Martervenux" confederacy; and from there, embarking upon the exploration of the Galaxy. Limat's universe was surprisingly reach in exotic fauna and flora, from the unicorns of Eridanus to the spiders of Aquarius; its richness and inventiveness are somewhat reminiscent of Jack Vance. The heroes of the Martervenux saga are Chevalier Coqdor, a green-eyed telepath, often accompanied by his pet *pstor* Râx (a flying bulldog with bat-wings), Interplan police commissioner Robin Muscat, and, less frequently, test pilot Luc Delta. Together or separately, they investigate cosmic phenomena of undeniable poetry, defying the known laws of science: a sun of ice, a negative universe, a mysterious beam of white light at the edge of the universe...

Thanks to Jean-Luc Rivera and Philippe Heurtel, we have included at the end of this volume a short autobiography written by Limat himself shortly before his passing, as well as articles on his non-SF heroes, private eye Teddy Verano and she-demon Mephista, whom you will discover in these pages.

Jean-Marc Lofficier

9

Maurice Limat

MEPHISTA

ANGOISSE

FLEUVE NOIR

MEPHISTA

CHAPTER I

The car was parked near the Buttes-Chaumont. It was impossible to find a place in front of the O.R.T.F.,[1] Rue Carducci, Rue des Alouettes, and the nearby streets were too narrow and congested. Therefore, Teddy Verano arrived on foot, glancing idly and sadly at the ugly walls of the huge factory where they produced billions of images intended to entertain, inform and educate the people of France.

"Studio 26?"

In the immense glass cage that served as the entrance hall, someone gave him directions as precisely as possible. He had already been there anyway, so he wasted little time in the huge aisles under the high, ungainly balconies and down the glass-walled hallways. At last, a comfortable, cheerful elevator, warm and silent, brought him upstairs.

He stepped onto the set to the disapproving looks of a great number of people who obviously had nothing to do there, and whose presence must have annoyed the director, cameramen and, especially, the artists forced to live, love and suffer before 80 pairs of eyes. However, no one asked the detective anything. He slipped into the crowd, staying out of the shot and walking quietly, out of habit, even though they were not shooting yet.

Edwige Hossegor was there. He saw her in a black, sequin dress, close-fitting to show off her beautifully slender, sensual figure (despite being in her forties), with her gorgeous, elegant face under her magnificent black hair. But this was not the right moment to approach her. The director was putting the final touches to the scene they were about to shoot.

Teddy Verano, like everyone else, listened. But his mind was elsewhere. He fingered the letter in his pocket. The note that had made him rush over to the studio. A woman's desperate call for help. From Edwige Hossegor, presently one of the biggest stars of the big and small screen. From this supple Venus swamped by admirers. From this woman who was loved, worshipped, and idolized by a huge public. A woman whose beauty was as famous as her kindness.

---

[1] The Office de Radiodiffusion-Télévision Française was the national agency charged, between 1964 and 1974 with providing public radio and television in France.

The Orange Prize [2] had just been awarded to this charming creature.

And yet the seductive, delightful Edwige Hossegor specialized in the role of vamps and cruel women, and the viewers, of course, claimed in the magazines that they did not want to see her doing anything else.

But who could say what her private life was like? Why send off this distress signal? On the surface, she looked satisfied, happy…

Weren't there rumors that the playboy she had charmed, Baron Tragny, was bound, any day now, to offer to share his name and fortune with her?

Tragny was there; Verano recognized him. Soberly elegant, around 50 years-old, he was still a ladies' man and looked bursting with health and youth. He was often photographed with Edwige, who had the face and figure of a woman no older than 35, and the readers must have sighed, "What a beautiful couple!"

Verano wondered.

Did the baron know about the note? Did he know that Edwige wrote a brief letter to a private detective in a trembling hand:

Some people told me about you. I trust them. I want to trust you. I'm scared. Come to Studio 26, O.R.T.F., Buttes-Chaumont. I have to see you right away. I'm afraid… I'll tell you all about it in person…"

Why does this beautiful, rich woman who was about to marry one of the most eligible bachelors in Paris, who had met constant success, why did she think she was in danger?

Teddy was not very convinced of the reality of this danger.

Neurosis? Overwork, perhaps. Edwige Hossegor had filmed and filmed, non-stop, for years.

But some movement was stirring the crowd. The director was backing up, starting to shout into a megaphone that was connected to microphones. The boom operators were placing the "fishpoles" that picked up the sounds, the electricians were aiming their spots, and the cameramen were at the ready. The constant murmur of the parasitic crowd had come to end as well.

"Camera!" the director yelled. "Action!"

They were "getting the scene."

Teddy Verano had taken the time to read *Télé 7 Jours*, the TV guide magazine, so he knew what the production was about. Edwige Hossegor had the starring role in a new, 13-episode series, *The Vampires of Paris*. Since the fantasy-spy genre was trendy, they had written the role for her.

In front of Teddy, in front of all the others, they ran through a short scene.

In a modern studio apartment, a man, alone, in a bathrobe, was relaxing watching the television. He smoked. He sipped a whiskey. He was at peace. He

---

[2] Annual Parisian social event which began in the 1950s. A "Lemon Prize" was awarded to a celebrity famous for his or her bad temper, and an "Orange Prize" to one famous for being pleasant.

thought he was beyond the reach of everything. Suddenly, Edwige Hossegor appeared...

—*Or rather Mephista.*

This was the fictional name the screenwriters gave her. A spy? Or some modern, entrancing witch who used occult gadgets?

Teddy Verano had read the summary too quickly to know everything. What he noticed, like all the spectators, was the undeniable screen presence of Edwige Hossegor.

She approached the man, who looked up, surprised, enthralled, and worried too. Then he tried to get up but the woman in the black sequined dress looked at him in a way that set his imagination on fire. She leaned over him... And she struck!

The knife had come out of nowhere. Blood spurted. Because, of course, it was a color film.

The scene ended, after editing, with a close-up of Edwige Hossegor.

Everyone held their breath, admiring the posture but especially the expression on her face. How could such a beautiful woman reveal so much savagery?

Teddy appreciated it like an expert. What an actress! So kind and simple, and yet she could really scare you with her pretty face all contorted and that flame of hatred burning in her black eyes.

But the scene continued.

The victim lurched and clutched the armchair. Mephista stepped back, watching his death throes with fearsome cruelty.

The poor man staggered and gasped out the name of his enemy, "Me... phis... ta..." He stumbled; he was about to fall... to die.

No! With a jolt, he suddenly plunged his shaky hand into the pocket of his bathrobe. He pulled out a 6.35 mm gun, clambered to his feet and shot.

And Mephista, who did not have time to react, cried out like a wounded animal and fell backward, arms akimbo.

In silence, the audience was dumbstruck by the fall, marvelously executed, though so difficult to accomplish.

The man, exhausted, dropped the weapon and looked, stunned, at the body of Mephista, placing his hand on her chest where the blood (stage blood) was still flowing.

"Cut!"

And the atmosphere changed in the blink of an eye.

Despite the conventionality of the scene, everyone was still under its spell because of the talent of interpretation. The actors were still in the spotlights but they were no longer playing their roles. A murmur of admiration ran through the crowd.

"Wonderful!"

"She's the best!"

"Don't you think it's a little out of fashion?"

"With her? Not a chance. All of France is going to be following *The Vampires*. Now they'll call her Mephista."

Teddy Verano figured that it would be good fun to watch the series and thought of all the people who would suddenly become unavailable during its show time, glued to their TV screens.

Jean-Pierre Max, the actor, walked into the wings. Covered with splotches of fake blood, he laughed that he needed a good shower.

"Thank you, Edwige," aid the director, "that's all for today."

A dresser came up with a comb for the star, who lay there, arms stretched out, in that incredible position after her delicate, skillfully executed fall. Teddy was listening to praises spoken about the acting of his future client.

"Very good, Edwige? What...?" And the dresser screamed, "Madame! Madame!"

The crowd rushed onto the stage. The spotlights were still on and streamed over everyone.

Baron Tragny turned pale, shouldering his way through the crowd.

"Edwige!" he shouted.

Teddy Verano felt his heart sink. By reflex, he fingered the letter in his pocket, which Edwige had sent him three hours ago.

What if I got here too late? he thought.

The baron, the director, the script girl and the dresser lifted Edwige up. Before breaking down in tears, Tragny howled:

"Dead! It's impossible..."

Overwhelmed, Teddy Verano just watched, struggling to understand.

In a modern studio apartment, a man in his thirties, alone, was relaxing watching the television. Relaxing? Not exactly. With a glass of whiskey in hand, he kept turning away from the TV screen to look at a magnificent, framed photo on the table.

Edwige Hossegor.

Edwige Hossegor, in an exquisite summer dress, radiating beauty and youth. A remarkable photo. Across the photo, the beautiful actress has written elegantly but nervously:

To Jacques Lemoulin. Best Wishes from Edwige Hossegor.

Jacques Lemoulin sighed. Yes, they knew each other. She was sweet to him. But he would never be anything but one admirer amongst many. The prize place was taken. Lemoulin, more than anyone else, knew the role that Baron Tragny played in Edwige's life, and that he would soon make her his wife. But Jacques Lemoulin still loved her. Hopelessly.

He sipped his Cutty Sark and wrapped himself in the smoke from the aromatic tobacco. He turned away from the photo to listen to the TV. Politics, wars, riots, disasters. Sporting competitions and space race. What did the world matter to a desperate lover?

Suddenly, breaking news:

"We have just heard news that will cause the film world, and especially the world of French Television, to grieve…"

Frozen, Jacques Lemoulin saw a photo appear on the screen. The same photo, exactly, that he had on his table, except without the sweet but impersonal dedication.

The voice from the speaker seemed to come out of a nightmare:

"On the stage… an inexplicable accident… *Vampires of Paris*… Mephista… heart attack…"

Jacques Lemoulin stood up, covered in a cold sweat. Before him, the images of Edwige in her different film roles marched by, then a clip from her latest telefilm. And she smiled at him, talked to him, like to millions and millions of other people.

"Edwige…"

A sob choked the young man's throat. Younger, of course, than she whom he had made his idol, in whose shadow he had lived for months.

"It's over… finished… I'll never see her again."

"Jacques…"

His name? Someone's calling him?

By reflex, he looked at the small screen. But, no, it had already changed. The news had switched to sports. Rugby players were fighting over an oval ball to the shouting of a bunch of maniacs who thought they are athletes.

"Jacques…"

Lemoulin turned around, shocked.

She was there.

Smiling, more seductive than ever, she had just entered the apartment where he lived alone and, he thought, was completely locked up.

Edwige, in her black sequined dress that glimmered with the night. He wanted to go to her, but she came first and hugged him with that irresistible movement, both beguiling and authoritative, that only she could perform.

The poor boy, overwrought and excited, as he had just learned of the sudden death of his beloved, saw her, touched her and kissed those trembling lips that the whole world knew and admired, those perfect lips pressing against his.

He savored the kiss, the ultimate caress that he had so often dreamed about, but never thought he would taste.

Then he became alarmed. Edwige Hossegor, since it was her, it was really her, slowly backed off and looked at him.

"Edwige… No, I'm going crazy… I'm dreaming or is it really you?"

"You're not dreaming, my love."

Jacques Lemoulin, with all his senses on fire, forgot about the televised news. It had to be false, completely false, seeing that Edwige was here, in front of him, touching him, suddenly bringing him the scent of paradise that fulfilled love gave to men as a consolation for their sad condition.

With a dry throat, he mumbled her name. Then everything happened very quickly.

The beautiful, gorgeous face of the actress changed. It was beautiful, yes, still beautiful, but now of a sinister, frightening beauty. Her face took on one of those expressions that came from her remarkable talent. All of a sudden, it was not Edwige who stood before him. It was...

She herself told him, in a deep, dramatic voice.

"No... Not Edwige... There's no more Edwige... I'm Mephista."

And she struck. The knife came out of nowhere. Exactly as it was filmed two hours earlier in Studio 26 at the O.R.T.F. And this time, there was no fake blood spurting out of the chest of her victim. It was real blood...

Jacques Lemoulin's face became terror-stricken. His dying eyes were stupefied by the unbelievable action. They were also clouded with contempt. She died, or at least they said she did. And yet, she'd come to him. And she killed him.

This time, it was not like in *The Vampires of Paris*. The victim did not react. He staggered backward and crashed into his television set. The screen shattered.

Slowly Jacques Lemoulin fell to the carpet.

Mephista watched him die. And a glimmer from Hell danced in her big, black eyes.

CHAPTER II

It was eleven o'clock at night. In Baron Tragny's house in Passy, rue de Ranelagh, the baron was pacing back and forth, extremely agitated. Nearby, still calm, still under control, Teddy Verano was watching him, and his hazel eyes in his serene face expressed the intensity of his thoughts.

The baron kept glancing through the salon door into the next room—the room where he had the body of Edwige Hossegor brought.

The news had exploded and spread. The sudden death of French television's number one star. But Baron Tragny was given a wild hope when the doctor leaned over her and gave his astounding announcement:

"Madam Hossegor isn't dead. She's in a state of catalepsy."

Like a madman, Tragny jumped at him.

"Doctor, is it possible? Can you assure me that…?"

"She'll survive? Of course. But it's a strange condition that I haven't seen very often. It's like… almost like a hypnotic trance."

Then everything happened quickly.

The baron had Edwige brought to his house and immediately sent for Professor Gelor, a specialist in neurology and psychiatry. Meanwhile, Teddy Verano had time to approach him. He introduced himself briefly and showed Tragny, who was getting one surprise after another, the note sent that afternoon by the star of *The Vampires of Paris*.

"Monsieur… I don't understand, but… Stay with me…"

It was exactly what Teddy Verano wanted and so he followed the baron.

The TV and radio had announced the death of Edwige Hossegor, then two hours later, the news was retracted. But nothing was explained. Edwige, for some unknown reason, was in a rigid sleep that imprisoned her like an invisible fortress.

Now Professor Gelor was with her, along with Dr. Sorbier, a friend of Tragny and Edwige. The two doctors had asked the baron to leave. Isabelle, Edwige's personal attendant, also had to go. Naturally, Teddy Verano, after catching the eye of Professor Gelor, with whom he had often worked in the past, had quietly slipped into the salon.

Tragny was smoking his umpteenth cigarette of the evening.

"Can't they get it over with. What are they doing?"

"Hang in there, Baron," said Teddy Verano. "The eminent doctors are up against an exceptional case. So exceptional that everyone, you most of all, was sure that your beloved was dead. However, in a short time, the truth will come out. If they're taking their time now, you can be sure that they have good reason. They're doing more tests, probably. They'll end up finding out what's wrong… And Edwige Hossegor will come back to life."

Tragny turned his distraught face toward him.

"You think so? You really think that…"

A commotion could be heard and it did not stop. Suddenly aggravated, Tragny called out:

"Joseph?"

The butler arrived. Tragny, in spite of the modern façade, continued to live in his house like if it was the turn of the century.

"The journalists are making a lot of noise. Please tell them to quiet down and show a little respect. There's a…" He was about to say "deceased". But he paused before continuing, "…A very sick person here."

Joseph bowed.

"I will remind them, Monsieur."

A minute later, it was silent again, relatively silent at least, because an army of journalists and photographers were waiting in the entrance hall for Professor Gelor to come out.

Tragny remained alone with Teddy Verano as the consultation went on. Presumably, Gelor and Sorbier were baffled. They were examining all aspects of Edwige Hossegor's magnificent body, noting that she was still alive, but that all her physiological functions seemed to have paused. A suspension of life is what the neuro-psychiatrist declared a little later.

Joseph reappeared in the salon.

"Excuse me, Monsieur, there's a gentleman who insists on seeing you."

"I was adamant that no journalist…" Tragny grumbled. "I let them stay in the hall… That's enough. That's too much…"

"Monsieur, he's not a reporter."

Joseph held out a card. Tragny ignored him and foamed at the mouth.

"Throw him out! Him and the others… I don't want to see anyone, you hear me, no one…"

Joseph looked very uncomfortable.

Teddy Verano, with a kindly smile and pretending not to ignore the baron's frenzy, took the card tactfully.

"Allow me, Joseph. Oh, Baron, I understand Joseph's dilemma. It would be hard for you to refuse to see this man…"

Tragny glanced at the card and jumped. He had just read: *Guy Farnèse, Chief of Police.*

"The Chief of Police… here? At this hour?"

"Exactly," Teddy Verano said. "Farnèse and I are old friends. Private detectives like your humble servant often have connections with the police. And Farnèse…"

Tragny crumpled the card in his hand.

"This is not the proper hour to launch for an investigation."[3]

---

[3] In France, the police cannot visit a suspect's home between 9 p.m. and 6 a.m.

"I'm sure Farnèse is here unofficially. Besides," Verano smiled, "a chief of police usually doesn't need to be reminded of the legalities. He knows very well that between sundown and sunrise..."

"But," the baron roared, "Edwige hasn't been murdered."

He threw the card away, paced a little with his hands behind his back, and made his decision.

"Show him in."

The Chief came in, greeted them and, on seeing Teddy Verano, held out his hand.

"I know, Chief," Tragny said, "that you know this gentleman. Very well. You will know, then, that I am in a very tragic situation and I'm..."

"More tragic than you can imagine, Baron."

Tragny and Verano were both startled. Joseph was still standing there, so the baron waved to him to leave. He obeyed, regretfully.

"Monsieur," Farnèse said, "I felt compelled to come pay you a visit, in a personal way if I may say so. Knowing that you are the fiancé of Mademoiselle Hossegor, I believed that everything concerning her concerns you as well."

"That's right," the baron replied.

"A new development has come up. I was notified while my department was starting its investigation and I thought I should notify you. Do you know a Monsieur Jacques Lemoulin?"

"Absolutely. He's an acquaintance of ours. He's an excellent tennis player and we've hit quite a few balls together."

"I regret to inform you that Monsieur Lemoulin has been murdered."

"Murdered!?"

Tragny jumped back as Teddy Verano listened with keen interest.

"One of his friends who went to invite him to a last minute party," Farnèse continued, "was surprised that he didn't answer the door since he knew he was home and could hear some music. He called the concierge who opened it with a master key... Lemoulin was dying, swimming in his own blood. He had been stabbed."

"Stabbed!"

By reflex both Tragny and Verano recalled the filming a few hours earlier and the last scene played by Edwige Hossegor before falling into the incomprehensible catalepsy which had put her beyond the world of the living.

Farnèse described the scene. The broken TV, splattered with blood, but still working, blaring the music which had caught the visitor's attention.

Tragny, overwhelmed by emotion, gasped:

"The poor boy... but who could have... and why?"

"One moment," Farnèse said. "I haven't told you the worst part. If I focus on this point, it's because I'm aware of what happened today at Studio 26 in Buttes-Chaumont and what the film is about. Lemoulin is dead. But before dying in the arms of those who found him, he pronounced one word. One name, rather..."

In spite of himself Farnèse, the Chief of Police, a practical man who did not believe in fantasy, cracked a smile.

"One name... It reminds me of the old popular novels or the comic books of today..."

Baron Tragny and Verano already understood. Farnèse said the name, but they all murmured it at the same time.

"*Mephista.*"

CHAPTER III

Baron Tragny was in a strange state of excitement.

"Chief, what am I to make of this? Mademoiselle Hossegor is already absorbed—quite so—in the character of this series being filmed. Your presence here leads me to believe there's some unfortunate connection being made... What are you suggesting?"

"Baron," replied Farnèse with an icy smile, "I think that nothing in what I said should hint at the slightest accusation of Mademoiselle Hossegor."

"That's for sure," Teddy Verano jumped in, since he liked to put his two cents worth in such conversations.

Tragny was on edge.

"I told you that in spite of the unusual hour my visit here is strictly personal," Farnèse continued. "I wanted to inform you... just to avoid any hasty, unpleasant conclusions... Reporters are mobbing your house."

Tragny threw up his arms in anger.

"If it were up to me..."

"But you're thinking of Mademoiselle Hossegor's career. She won a Prix Orange, which, if you chase these gentlemen away, will turn into a 'Lemon Prize' with the most disastrous effects."

The baron had to figure that if Farnèse really knew about the ways of show business, such allusions were inappropriate to say the least.

But Teddy Verano jumped back into the fray.

"Besides, how could Mademoiselle Hossegor have anything to do with Lemoulin's murder? For hours, she's been in a cataleptic state that made us think she was dead, for a few minutes anyway... enough for the news to spread throughout France and the world before it was retracted. And from the moment she fell in Studio 26—I was present there myself—she's been surrounded by people continually. They brought her here and, since then, the baron, Isabelle her attendant, the nurses and doctors, haven't left her side. So, how could anyone imagine..."

"There's no question of that, in fact," Farnèse said. "Mephista... Obviously, a man is committing crimes in this name, which makes for a real story..."

"A man or a woman," Teddy Verano mumbled.

"If you'd like," Farnèse held back from shrugging his shoulders.

Tragny was keeping half an eye on the room next door, but the doctors were still not coming out.

"May I ask you, Chief, what is the purpose of your... *visit*?"

Farnèse did not react to the way he emphasized the last word.

"Well, before any real investigation begins, I wanted to ask for your collaboration, since you're the man most qualified to help Mademoiselle Hossegor in everything that concerns her."

"I am, indeed, fully devoted to Ed... to Mademoiselle Hossegor."

"Great! Baron, I'd like to point out a minor detail. In the bloody wreckage of the apartment where they found Lemoulin at death's door, and where he accused this mysterious Mephista, some fingerprints were found. Slender, delicate prints, likely belonging to a woman. One hand that had been smudged with the victim's blood and touched the still working but broken TV screen..."

"We keep coming back to the TV," Verano said.

"Yes. Quite clearly. I won't be telling you anything new by saying that the dumbest criminal avoids this kind of signature."

"Therefore, Chief, you concluded..."

"You understand me, Messieurs. If they want to cast suspicion on Mademoiselle Hossegor, they have to look no further..."

Tragny burst out laughing.

"But that's ridiculous! Because Edwige has been unconscious since..." (he looks at his wristwatch) "...exactly 6:20 p.m. It's after 10 p.m. And there are plenty of witnesses, Monsieur Verano here to start with."

"Oh," Farnèse spoke calmly, "I admit how absurd the connection sounds. So, I'm going to ask you—as a personal request, I assure you—to allow me a little verification."

Tragny was getting fed up and obviously wanted to throw him out.

"And you call this a personal visit!"

But Teddy Verano gave him a quick glance to advise him to stay calm.

"I'm listening, Chief."

"I imagine that Mademoiselle Isabelle who was, I learned, at the studio because she's always with Mademoiselle Hossegor, has brought some of her personal effects?"

"Yes. With me in the ambulance that was called as soon as the doctor confirmed she was alive."

"Good. In Mademoiselle Hossegor's purse would be her identity card, in the name of Edwige Versant, a.k.a. Hossegor?"

"You want to see her ID, Chief? I can humor you."

Isabelle, who obviously had not gone to bed, promptly brought the requested document. Tragny and Verano looked at Farnèse. He examined the card, the photo of Edwige, and stared for a while at the fingerprints. Then, he took a photocopy out of his pocket. Tragny understood its significance at the same time as Verano. The Chief of Police compared the two prints in silence.

Tragny, controlling his desire to get this over with, but finding the wait interminable, could not help asking in a broken voice:

"Well?"

"Well, this print... these prints are identical, Messieurs. Mademoiselle Hossegor's finger and the finger of... let's say, Mephista..."

Tragny was pale.

"Edwige... Mephista... But come on, it's crazy, it's completely ridiculous!"

Farnèse, calmly holding out the two documents, said:

"See for yourselves. There's no mistaking it. The bloody hand found at Lemoulin's is the hand of Mademoiselle Hossegor."

"Who was cataleptic. Who still is, regrettably. And the fact has been corroborated by dozens of witnesses."

"I have no doubt about that," Farnèse said, "But..."

"But what?"

"A set-up?" Teddy Verano asked. "But it's full of holes."

"I'm drawing no conclusions yet," the Chief replied. "I'm just getting the facts."

"Well, and you call this a personal visit..." said the baron, bitterly.

"Monsieur Tragny, I just state the facts. Thank you for seeing me. I will simply say that if they really wanted to commit a crime and blame it on Mademoiselle Hossegor, in the eyes of the police, it won't stand up. It's too obvious."

"OK, so they failed," Teddy Verano said. "The real criminal couldn't imagine that Mademoiselle Hossegor would have this cataleptic fit at the very time... or at least, on the very day of the crime."

"Anything is possible. I..."

Farnèse said no more. The door of the room opened and Dr. Sorbier came out with Professor Gelor. Tragny forgot all about the police and ran up to them.

"Well? Please... Tell me..."

"Lethargy, monsieur. It's a fact. But my colleague and I can assure you, at least for the time being, that Mademoiselle Hossegor's life is not in danger. Even if she looks deceased. I say 'looks' in the physiological sense, because in appearance, one could really believe that she's really dead. No, Mademoiselle Hossegor is alive, just as the first doctor had stated. But her life is, how can I say... suspended. Very slow breathing, weak pulse, but still there."

"But, professor, can such a state... last?"

"There, Baron," Gelor shrugged, "is where we face the unknown. Her case is really very strange..."

"And the reason for the fit... for the blackout?"

The two doctors kept silent, obviously flustered. They talked for a minute. Tragny answered their questions as best he could. Drugs? It was not like Edwige. Stimulants? She used nothing like that. She led a healthy, sober life. A lot of work, of course, but nothing explained her falling into this trance, so frighteningly like death.

"Tomorrow morning, we'll take her to the hospital for more thorough testing. You understand, Baron, that there are many things we can't do here at your house."

Tragny had to give in. The doctors left. It had been decided that at 8 a.m., another ambulance would take Edwige to Dr. Sorbier's hospital. Farnèse, who had listened to the doctors, also left.

The baron decided that he would not go to bed, but spend all night with Edwige. The nurses were allowed to use one of the bedrooms. Tragny wanted to stay alone with his love.

Teddy Verano was the only one left.

"Before leaving, one final word, Baron…"

Tragny was visibly anxious to see Verano disappear like the rest. He was very tired, but too worked up to sleep. It seemed obvious that he could watch over Edwige all night without sleep.

Teddy took out the letter sent by Edwige.

"Oh!" the baron groaned. "That's right, we forgot… We should have told the Chief of Police…"

"You forgot, Monsieur Tragny. I can breathe now. The whole time Farnèse was here, I was afraid you'd remember it and say something. I even thought I said too much when I mentioned a set-up to frame Mademoiselle Hossegor. It's fair to say that Farnèse knows nothing, but he does know at least that the great star could not have murdered Lemoulin. Still, as a policeman, he worships the methods of anthropometry, so a fingerprint is a fingerprint, obvious proof, indisputable in a criminal case."

Tragny began pacing again.

"So, Edwige could have enemies… an enemy? This threat… I don't understand anything. Sometimes she'd get preoccupied, anxious, but she worked on her roles and I respected her silence, her reveries. Why didn't she say anything to me? Why this letter that sounds like an SOS?"

"Everything's there, Baron. That's why I didn't say anything to Farnèse, yet. I'm asking you to trust me, like Mademoiselle Hossegor did, and let me do my little investigation as I want. It won't last long. One or two days. Then I'll give my findings to the police."

"You'll work… illegally?"

"Mademoiselle Hossegor called on me. You can understand that I only want to work in the interest of my client."

He said goodbye and left. Tragny was too tired to discuss it any further. He was alone, so he went to Edwige. Only then did the nurses leave the room to go and lie down but remain available.

For a long time, he stayed there, alone.

The journalists, after accosting the doctors, harassing them with questions and bombarding them with flashes, had finally left the house. The servants were in bed. Tragny was alone. Alone by the bed where Edwige lay, still beautiful in her mystifying appearance of death.

"But she lives… she lives… My beloved…"

For the tenth time, he leaned over her, looking for signs that she was waking up. He was scared. Scared that she would live like this, never wake up, until she died, as it happened sometimes in certain cases that remained unsolvable.

The minutes passed. Night spread over Passy and everything fell silent for those few, rare hours when Paris seems calm. There was only a small, shaded lamp in the room where Baron Tragny watched over Edwige Hossegor…

A shadow slipped among the rhododendrons in the garden outside the house.

A woman's shadow. Tall and slender. Dressed in a sequined dress that glimmered with the night…

The stranger slipped among the flowerbeds. She reached the steps to the yard. then started climbing the stairs.

Tragny, anxious, leaning over Edwige, thought he heard something and turned his worried face. Someone had just entered the salon through the French doors…

CHAPTER IV

Tragny took a step toward the door.

"Who's there?" he asked.

He was no little boy. No coward either. At almost 50, he practiced many sports, including combat sports, and his military service was a secret to no one. Still thin, despite his gray hair, he was man enough to face any adversary.

However, in this agonizing night at Edwige's bedside, Edwige the cataleptic, threatened by who knew what menace, he felt his voice fail, his heart wrenched, and fear crept through his veins.

Nobody answered his question.

He left Edwige and entered the salon. A thought crossed his mind.

"Isabelle? Is that you? You aren't in bed? Do you want something?"

But Isabelle did not answer.

A woman was standing there in the dark shadows. He could barely make her out. Silent and motionless, she was like a statue in the dark, and he knew right away that it was not Isabelle. That figure...

A cold sweat beaded on the baron's forehead.

"Who are you? What are you doing here? Answer me..."

He approached the stranger, but as he got closer he became more frantic than ever. No, it couldn't be...

The French door opening onto the garden, through which the nocturnal visitor had come in, was still open. A dim light from a nearby street lamp contrasted sharply with the darkness on the ground floor of the Tragny house. This light allowed the baron to glimpse the features of the woman standing there. He clenched his fists.

"What's the meaning of this? I demand that you speak up..."

He was getting dizzy. He did not want to admit the truth and a flood of dark thoughts washed over him.

"Edwige?"

But Edwige was lying in bed, behind him, where he had brought her, where he had been, watching over her...

She could not be in front of him. She could not be standing up here, face to face, in the salon, a few feet away from the real Edwige.

He jumped forward and turned on the light.

"Edwige..."

It was her. There was no doubt about it. The woman he loved, whom he adored, whom he was going to make his wife. Edwige Hossegor, the television star, the incomparable actress. Edwige with her beautiful, elegant face, her brilliant teeth, her supple body and in the flesh, despite everything, highlighted by the shiny black dress...

Mephista's dress.

"No! It can't be true!" he screamed. "Tell me the truth!"

He made a move to leap at her, but she challenged him with an ironic flame in her eye that he had never seen. At least, in real life. Because this look, both ironic and threatening, cruel and playful, was what Edwige wore in more than one role as a *femme fatale,* a sorceress, a she-devil, everything that had given her fame, fortune and glory. It as the very look that she had on her pretty face while filming *The Vampires of Paris.*

Faced with this look, Tragny backed away.

He was sure, however, that this was not some cheap costume. The woman standing before him, awe-inspiring by the sheer evil that she exuded out of every pore, was really Edwige Hossegor.

Tragny gulped, barked something, and gave up the idea of grabbing this Edwige. He turned around and ran into the next room.

"Edwige…"

Edwige was still there, motionless, frozen, with no sign of life. An Edwige whom the doctors were taking care of, even though they did not understand the reason or nature of this strange lethargy.

Tragny wiped his sweaty face with a trembling hand. He ran to the bed, leaned over and touched the impassive face of his love. As if to be sure that it really was her, as if attempting an exorcism, he put his lips on her cold cheek. On Edwige's flesh…

And once again, he spun around. Through the doorway, in the salon, he could see the other Edwige, Edwige number two, Edwige exactly the same, Edwige whom he had sworn on his eternal salvation was really Edwige Hossegor, not a twin sister, not a woman who resembled her, not the caricature of some dreadful imposture, but really Edwige.

And Edwige, this Edwige who walked (as opposed to the other who did not move) was watching him, leaning over her double.

"You just kissed Edwige to be sure that it's really her, Baron," she said "To be sure that the woman lying in the bed is the one you love. Well, come to me… Don't be afraid… It's ridiculous and unworthy of man like you."

The champion Tragny and ex-Captain Tragny were quivering in the heart of Edwige's lover. It was fiendish, of course. But he had to know. He walked toward her.

Edwige number two held out her hand and, with a graceful movement of her neck, was already tilting her head up for him, her lips parting open.

Tragny felt like he was on the edge of some unknown abyss. He was going to cave in; he was going to break down under the mysterious kiss that was calling him irresistibly. He was captivated, but inside himself, he was battling silently like a lost man who is about to lose everything, who has, perhaps, already lost everything, but who still wants to fight because he is, above all else, a man.

He kissed this woman, yes. To know.

Edwige number two suddenly turned off the light and, in the dark, dragged the baron away, whispering:

"There's no reason for her to see us…"

Her… Edwige number one. Sleeping Edwige in the bed, in her death-like slumber. Edwige who was not supposed to see him kissing the other Edwige.

Tragny was about to embrace his fiendish mistress when someone burst into the salon like a cannonball. He barreled up to the couple, snickering.

"Excuse me for interrupting such a sweet rendezvous."

The other Edwige backed away swiftly so it was Tragny who was bumped into. He reacted with his usual force and the intruder stumbled to the side.

Since the salon was dark again, they could not see much and Tragny could not make out the face of the staggering individual who crashed into the divan that cracked under his weight. Clenching his teeth, ready for a fight, Tragny marched up to the stranger, ready to strike again and put an end to all these mysteries—with violence, since there seemed no other way.

The man struggled to stand up. Tragny was about to grab him by the throat.

"Ro…bert!" Someone called him by his first name. And he could recognize the voice among a thousand. It was the voice of Edwige.

Dumbfounded, he ran back into the room. He believed he understood and he wanted it to be true.

"Robert, Oh Robert!"

"My love."

Edwige was awake. In the dim light of the bedside lamp, he saw her beautiful face trembling, her eyelids fluttering, her lips, straining to pronounce his name.

"Edwige. Don't worry… I'm here… I love you."

He took her in his arms and covered her with kisses. She was coming out of her lethargy. She was waking up. Was the terrible nightmare finally over?

But he got hold of himself and, in spite of the intense joy erupting inside him on seeing that Edwige was not dead, that the doctors were not wrong, he still had to fight against the harrowing mystery.

"But then… the other?"

Edwige did not seem to understand. She held onto him tightly and, instinctively, he called for Isabelle and Joseph…

And this man who was there? And the other Edwige?

The man reappeared, wiping his bleeding lip with a handkerchief.

"You! What are you doing here?"

"Compliments on your right hook, Baron. You live up to your reputation. Unfortunately…"

Tragny grabbed Teddy Verano by the arms and shook him furiously.

"Talk… Talk… That woman… Who was that woman?"

"Calm down," Teddy Verano said, "you've already wrecked half my jaw and though I wanted to get my hands on her, I couldn't. The result is... she's gone."

"Gone?"

Tragny wanted to run into the garden but Verano stopped him.

"No use. I looked... but I don't understand. She was there, that's a fact; she's not there now. Where did she go? Damn me if I understand a thing." Then he muttered, "Bloody Hell, there's some devilry involved... because, really..."

Joseph and Isabelle came running in, half-dressed.

"Quick, Isabelle, take care of your mistress. Joseph, call Dr. Sorbier."

He took Edwige's hands, as she smiled weakly, and covered them with kisses.

"My dear... Don't be scared... It's over... You were ill, that's all."

Joseph ran to the telephone and Tragny left Isabelle to attend her mistress. He went back to Teddy Verano.

"So, what are you doing here?"

"My job, Baron. I was keeping watch. Yes, I work like that sometimes, without anyone knowing, not even my clients. I wanted to get an idea of things. In this situation, it was very easy. These little houses in Passy, so close to the studios at the Maison de la Radio, still have that old-fashioned charm in their yards and gardens. You can hide there very easily."

"And what did you think you would find?"

"I don't know. But you have to admit, Baron, that I was very close to finding a solution, if not *the* solution, if it wasn't for your marvelous right hook..."

"I'm sorry. I..."

"Ah, those are the hazards of the job. And that's not the problem. There's this woman..."

"How'd she get in? Did you see her?"

Teddy Verano shook his head.

"To tell you the truth, I only saw her in the middle of the garden, walking toward the steps, then up and into the house."

"Didn't you want to stop her?"

"Of course, but you stopped me first."

"How could I know that it was her and not me that you were after?"

"The misunderstanding is logical, but it's unfortunate."

Edwige's voice could be heard faintly pleading:

"Robert..."

Isabelle came over.

"Baron, Mademoiselle is calling for you."

Tragny ran to Edwige and Teddy Verano followed him casually. Edwige was sobbing into Tragny's chest and the detective heard her stammered out:

"My dear... I feel... like I'm crawling out of the grave... I dreamed... it was awful... I wanted..." She took a deep breath, made an effort and continued,

"I dreamed that I wanted to kill you... No... that Mephista wanted to kill you..."

"It's nothing, my love. Nothing but a nightmare."

Reluctantly he looked at Teddy Verano.

They said nothing to each other. They both felt the terror lurking around them, made more dreadful by being beyond comprehension.

CHAPTER V

Three days passed. Professor Gelor and Dr. Sorbier were in agreement. Although Edwige had come out of her lethargy as quickly as she had fallen into it, a serious examination was in order, as well as a period of confined recovery.

Starting the next morning, after the devastating day followed by the eventful night, Baron Tragny had, consequently, given in to the medical authorities. An ambulance had taken Edwige to the hospital and, for three days, guarded her jealously from prying eyes, while Tragny along with Edwige's aunt, her only family, and two or three close friends, could only see her through a window.

They said it was for her mental health, for her sanity in short. The Baron gave in.

He had slept little and talked long with the private detective whom he already considered a new friend, whom his fiancée had contacted in her moment of distress. That was what united them: to know the reason for her call for help.

Tragny knew nothing at all about it. Edwige's aunt, having seen little of her, was not much help. Eva Mellion, a journalist friend who did public relations work for Edwige, did not seem to know anything either. Finally, there was Isabelle, her attendant, young and very devoted to Edwige. She, too, gave no useful information.

"And yet," Tragny repeated for the 100th time, "Edwige felt threatened, since she called on you."

"And," Teddy Verano replied, "it might not have been an idle threat..."

"You think her fainting fit—which is a poor term—might have some criminal action behind it?"

"I've seen so many things like that, Monsieur..."

"Yes. They call you the 'ghost detective,' don't they? I guess because of all the investigations that you've made into the Occult. This is all very well, but with regard to our situation here..."

"I don't want to make any formal statements yet, seeing that I haven't been able to question Mademoiselle Hossegor seriously, but I've already got the feeling that there's a will, an extraordinary power, that's involved in this affair."

"You mean that Edwige had... how can I say it... a spell cast on her?"

Tragny was a realist. At least, he claimed to be, like everyone else who believed only in what was right in front of their face. But he was too smart to laugh at such things as magic, and Edwige's condition, so far being scientifically inexplicable, was starting to make him listen more closely to Teddy Verano.

Chief Farnese had come to pay another visit. He was investigating the Lemoulin affair, which was going nowhere. But he gave in also and had postponed Edwige's hearing while admitting that she would likely provide no pertinent information. Like Tragny, he easily saw that Edwige Hossegor's guilt could only come out of the wildest fantasy, because when their poor friend was murdered, she was in that awful coma amongst a crowd of witnesses.

And yet, there was the bloody fingerprint…

On the morning of the fourth day, the baron called Teddy Verano early.

"I'll be right over," the detective said.

He was barely awake. He dressed hurriedly and gulped down the coffee that Yvonne, his wife, had lovingly prepared for him.

"I'm sorry, dear, but this morning, we've got authorization to talk to our great star, to examine her, make a battery of tests and all sorts of medical nonsense."

Half an hour later, he and Tragny entered the white room where Edwige smiled at them. Dr. Sorbier was there. He whispered a few words to Verano, leaving Tragny to greet Edwige with a flood of passion.

"Not too long, Messieurs, Mademoiselle Hossegor is still very tired."

The two men sat on either side of the bed. They started by introducing Teddy Verano, whom Edwige had contacted without knowing him, trusting in his reputation.

Tragny, who was dying to know, came right out with it:

"My dear, we have little time. The doctors are adamant about this. You know what happened to you… and it was so surprising… well, nothing at all is clear… when you woke up you told me about a nightmare…"

Edwige's beautiful face tensed up.

"The baron is right to remind you of this, Mademoiselle," Teddy Verano added. "Because there's a lot of things that you have to know. So let's take them in order. You wrote to me asking for my help. It wasn't without reason."

"Oh no, although…" Edwige sighed. "I wonder if you'll think I'm crazy."

The two men tried to assure her.

"No, no," Edwige cut them off. "Listen to me… No, I won't even try to tell you right now… my fear is so ridiculous, so unjustified. Oh, Robert, Robert, I don't know what to think… I'm scared."

The baron took her hands tenderly.

"Edwige, we're alone. You can talk in total confidence. Since you trusted Monsieur Verano, you can't stop there. He's been by my side for three days and I can assure you that I, too, have learned what kind of man he is."

Teddy bowed slightly to thank him. Edwige was about to talk but there was a knock at the door.

"Well, well," Tragny said good-humoredly, "what's this then?'

A nurse entered with a huge bouquet of red roses.

"Ah! More flowers! And *him* again…"

"I thought I should bring them," the nurse said. "Mademoiselle told me…"

"It's true," Edwige interrupted her. "It's… *him* again, as you know, Robert. It touches me and I asked that they bring all the flowers in here."

The nurse put them in a vase.

"If you accept all the flowers sent by your admirers..." the baron grumbled. "For three days at your home, at mine, here in the hospital, it's an avalanche. Bouquets and bouquets, always more flowers, bunches and basketfuls... Oh, you are loved, Edwige!"

She held out her pretty hand that was a little thin and weakened by the past few weird days.

"Don't be jealous, dear. You're the only one... Really, Robert..."

When the nurse left, the baron ran to the door and shouted after her:

"Please don't disturb us. Especially no journalists. Except for Mademoiselle Mellion. But she won't be here until this afternoon."

Edwige looked at the red roses with melancholy. Maybe more than mere melancholy, and Teddy Verano was startled.

"These roses... Excuse me, I'm being indiscreet, but it's my job."

"Oh, you have the right to know. We should tell you everything," the baron spurted out.

"But Mademoiselle Hossegor should first explain the reason for sending her letter without anyone knowing, if I understand correctly. Not you, Baron, not her aunt, not Eva Mellion and not Isabelle."

The two men turned to Edwige, questioning but silent. She was obviously uncomfortable but ended up saying:

"I'll tell you about these flowers after telling you why I'm so touched and troubled by them. No, Robert, don't go imagining things. You know very well that I don't know who's sending them..."

"Yes, I know."

"And don't sulk, my love. He wrote that he's hopelessly in love with me, and he's 20 years old, that's all I know. Do you think I'm the kind of woman who would choose a boy over you? That would be unworthy of Edwige Hossegor..."

"Let's get back to the letter," Teddy Verano said, trying to stay on track and stay away from the baron's petty jealousies.

"I called on you, Monsieur Verano," Edwige Hossegor said, "because I was scared."

There was silence. Tragny looked worried.

"A threat?" Teddy Verano pressed on gently.

"Yes."

"Someone wanted to hurt you? Someone in the movie industry?"

"No. Absolutely not. I can say that I've got nothing but friends. A lot of friends. But there must be some people who... well, who are a little bothered by my success."

"So, jealous rivalry?"

"No," she smiled sadly. "No colleague ever threatened violence toward me because I got a role they thought should be theirs..."

Tragny was getting upset.

"Edwige, you're keeping us waiting. What happened? What did you think you had to keep to yourself and tell no one about?"

"Not even you, isn't that right, my love?"

She broke into tears as Tragny became frantic.

Teddy Verano let the crisis pass and then, with his own kind of gentleness, a strong and persuasive but mellow voice that could be very charming, he asked:

"This threat... it seemed shameful to you?"

Edwige nodded her head. Tragny thought he understood and cried out:

"Blackmail then? About me? Someone wants to extort money by threatening you... to reveal to me some past... or imaginary escapade and..."

"No, no... Listen to me, Robert. And you too, Monsieur Verano. I told you, I'm going crazy. The threat... it really exists... but it's not from the outside. Nobody wrote to me, spoke to me, or called me. It's inside of me that everything happened... inside... inside me..."

Suddenly, she dropped back onto her pillows, biting her lip so she would not start sobbing again. The baron stood up to look for the bell to call someone, but Teddy Verano stopped him.

"One moment please. Mademoiselle Hossegor, you're worn out. Isn't it normal in your line of work? And the kind of roles you play..."

Edwige suddenly stopped looking nervous. She sat up and grabbed the detective's hand.

"Oh, I knew you'd understand. My roles... the characters I play... The vampires... Mephista... Yes, I think so. Everything comes from that. But I don't want to any more, I don't want to play criminals, evil women... That's what's disturbing me."

"Have you told your doctors about this?" Teddy Verano asked.

"Yes, of course."

"They said nothing to me about it," the baron snarled. "They just said something about a little depression..."

"First of all, they kept their professional confidence," Teddy Verano observed. "And Mademoiselle Hossegor must have asked them not to tell you."

Edwige nodded.

"It's all very well and good," Teddy Verano continued, "but they were still unable to understand the fainting fit that lasted for hours and during which... a lot of things happened."

Edwige looked at him with surprise and anxiety.

"Yes, you have to know. We'll tell you about it afterward. For three days, we've purposely kept you away from everything. Tragic events took place... which were obviously connected to your condition."

Edwige was deeply moved.

"Let's get back to the facts" the detective went on. "This threat... from within. Did you find an enemy inside you somehow?"

"Yes. I was scared... for a while... scared of my dreams... scared of my thoughts. The role... this diabolical role... after so many other roles of same kind. I felt like I was Mephista all day long every day lately... and I was scared of..."

"Yes, finish what you want to say."

She fell back onto the pillows.

"I couldn't go on. I was worn out. I dreamed that I killed... yes, that I did evil things, that I was a demon incarnate... like... the other night, Robert... I dreamed that I was going to kill you... I told you..."

"Yes, my love, I know."

"This has happened to more than one actor," Teddy Verano commented. "Professional conscience, an actor's high sensitivity, the fact that they embody the characters they play so completely that they can't tell where reality ends and the fiction begins."

"Also," Edwige spoke sadly, "if I understand correctly, the doctors were thinking of neurosis... Oh, I remember the case of Duquesne in *Madame Sans-Gêne*, playing Napoleon and ending up really thinking he was the Emperor for a while."[4]

"Mephista is obviously something different. But it's only a role. Not reality."

"Then why am I so scared? Scared of being Mephista? And all the monsters along with her, all the witches that I played?"

Tragny was dying to tell Edwige what had happened in his house the previous night, but he let Teddy Verano lead the conversation. He was taking it step by step.

"And these roses? Why are you so nervous when you get them, even though you let them in, but not all the baskets that friends and unknown admirers have been sending you since... we got so worried about you?"

"Since you thought I was dead, you mean?"

Teddy nodded.

"Well, along with all the people who say they adore me, I receive these roses... and letters... kind of naïve and clumsy... A young man who says he's 20 years old and in love with me..."

"Like so many others," the baron said.

"Yes, you jealous, naughty man. But he's touching. I laughed a little about it with Robert. He sulked on principle because he knows very well that it's not

---

[4] Actor Edmond Ducuesne played Napoleon in the 1911 film adaptation of *Madame Sans-Gêne*, an 1893 historical comedy-drama by Victorien Sardou and Émile Moreau, about Cathérine Hübscher, an outspoken 18th-century laundress who became the Duchess of Danzig. The play was revived many times in France and toured in the English provinces in 1897. It was also adapted as an opera, in 1915, and several times for film.

serious. This kid is young enough to be my son, you realize that…Except his silent admiration is a breath of freshness, though of course it's hopeless, so that I feel like it's a protection for me, a kind of good luck charm… Excuse me, I don't want to sound vain, but in my work, a woman is exposed to love… I mean to all kinds of compliments, sometimes very inappropriate, but often very touching. That's why out of the hundred, the thousands of flowers, I accepted his… and Robert's of course… and sometimes," she added simply, "those of another friend of ours, very discreet, but also certainly in love with me. His name is Jacques Lemoulin and…"

The two men turned pale.

"My God, what's wrong? What happened?"

They looked at each other. Teddy Verano, in a slightly different voice, said:

"We mentioned a tragedy… during your mysterious slumber… You have to know everything now since you have to tell us everything… Be strong…"

Edwige listened without saying a word. She too turned pale on hearing of the death of Lemoulin, murdered in his apartment in front of the photo signed by Edwige Hossegor. When it was all told, when she knew the truth and that Chief Farnese had showed them that the bloody fingerprint from the smashed television was from her own hand, she cried out in a fit of horror:

"He accused Mephista! He's right… it's her… she killed him. Me… me, Mephista… like I want to kill Robert… like I want to kill that poor boy who sends me red roses… kill them, kill them… all my admirers… everyone who loves me… because they are love… because I am hate… because I am evil… I am death…"

An hour later Edwige was resting, pumped full of tranquilizers. Doctor Sorbier spoke to Tragny and Verano.

"Typical neurosis, Messieurs. Mademoiselle Hossegor thinks she's the character she's playing. Overwork. Rest. Nothing else."

Tragny plainly wanted to believe the doctor. Teddy Verano was telling himself that it was not by talking about neurosis that they would explain the murder of Jacques Lemoulin or the apparition in the middle of the night of a second Edwige in Baron Tragny's house, just a few feet from the bed where the real Edwige was lying in apparent death.

CHAPTER VI

"Thursday, 3 p.m., at 116bis Avenue des Champs-Elysées."

"OK, Mademoiselle Eva," replied Teddy Verano. "I'll make a note of it. And... how did the rest of the shooting go?"

"Very well. Maybe it's hard to believe. We were all scared: the baron, the director, the technicians and me, of course. Unnecessary fears. Now back home, Edwige is back to herself. And we can finish the last episode of *The Vampires of Paris*, which has been on hold since... well, since the day she fainted."

"But this isn't the episode we're going to see?"

On the telephone Teddy Verano heard Eva Mellon's little laugh.

"Oh no! I see you're no technician, Monsieur Verano. The film has to be developed and edited, synchronized with the sound and the music that's been composed separately, add in the credits... it takes weeks. But don't worry, when we show the finished film you'll be invited at the premiere."

"I don't doubt it, Mademoiselle, since you're in charge of invitations, right?"

"Exactly. So, Thursday at 3 p.m."

"OK. As long as Mademoiselle Hossegor doesn't need anything from me in the meantime."

"Let's hope not," sighed Eva. "And you..."

"Nothing yet. Anyway, I'll keep you up to date."

After hanging up, Teddy Verano flopped into the armchair in his small office on Rue d'Enghien and calmly lit a cigarette.

While pursuing the usual leads: suspicious husbands, unfaithful wives, parents kidnapping their own children from separated spouses, disappearances that might or not be elopements, he had made two things his priority.

First, he was training his stepson, Gerard, Yvonne's son, despite some argument from his wife. Secondly, to get Gerard "on the prowl," since he was getting more and more interested in the detective business, he gave him the Edwige Hossegor case to study, patiently and thoroughly. For the moment, young Gerard was "doing" the florists, trying to find a clue that might lead them to the young stranger in love with Edwige. He was still bombarding her with extravagant bouquets and sweet notes of tenderness that were getting on Robert Tragny's nerves.

Teddy wrote in his notepad: *Thursday 3 p.m. Paris studio Showing of the first part of* The Vampires of Paris.

He thought of Eva Mellion. A charming girl, dynamic, very pretty at twenty years old, slender with blond hair cut like a tomboy and clear, kind eyes that expressed a strong character that was not at all unattractive to a man like Teddy Verano.

Being absent on the day Edwige had her first crisis, she had arrived the next day, coming from Berlin where she had been dealing with a publicity contract for her boss. She had always had a lot of affection for and devotion to Edwige, and Tragny seemed to be very fond of her, just like Isabelle who was also very loyal.

Teddy was thinking about all this. He saw a clear difference between the real Edwige, the adorable woman who could connect with those around her, who was appreciated on the set where she had none of the tantrums or animosity of sophisticated stars, who could so kindly receive her admirers while keeping a distance (like with Jacques Lemoulin), and the monster Mephista, the fictional creature spawned not only from her latest role, but also from all the more or less diabolical characters whom she had played so far and who had made her famous.

Who could have it in for her? he thought.

He got sent over the file of letters from admirers and requests for autographs. He went through them but a lot of them looked the same, some courteous and considerate, others more passionate, most of them naïve and clumsy. A few (it was rare) were bitter. And, as often happened in letters to famous people, there was no lack of obscenities and threats.

Teddy Verano, who had some experience in what a pen could reveal, found in these rivals, as scathing as they might be, no sign of aggressiveness that could lead to hypnotizing or bewitching Edwige.

The comedienne had learned everything now, that an unknown woman who looked exactly like her had entered the Tragny house at night. There was, therefore, another Edwige Hossegor, another Mephista.

"A woman who imitates you and who might commit crimes…"

Edwige had shuddered in thinking that the woman who had murdered Lemoulin (if it really was a woman) must have looked like her. She wept over this friend whose feelings she was aware of.

"Stabbed… and thinking that it was me…"

Tragny would have preferred to keep the truth from her but Teddy had insisted on telling Edwige everything.

"She has the right to know. Besides, it'll shock her into fighting her neurosis. She would end up believing she's guilty, identifying with Mephista. That's what Gelor and Sorbier are afraid of. But now, knowing that there's an impostor who acts and looks like her, she'll break free, understanding that she has nothing to do with it."

Tragny gave in and the two doctors agreed: Yes, they supported such a method.

Edwige, in fact, was a little calmer and admitted that her fears could have been imaginary, a result of overwork. It was no less true that the fainting fit on the one hand, and the presence of a false Edwige on the other, remained hard to explain and defied all logic. As for the death of Lemoulin…

The investigation was going nowhere. They had found absolutely nothing to help the police. Chief Farnese, in spite of the too blatant bloody fingerprint, was courteous enough not to harass Edwige, and was satisfied with going through his friend Teddy Verano to let her and Tragny know that he would inform them of any new developments.

"A police chief who finds a bloody fingerprint, who knows the victim pronounced his murderer's name before dying, and who still doesn't incriminate the person in question, pointed at twice, that's what's funny. Farnese really does see how silly it is. How can he accuse Edwige Hossegor who was in a coma at the time and among I don't know how many people... including me?"

Teddy Verano scratched his chin.

"Yes, but... what about the other one?"

An idea, still vague, was forming in his mind.

Edwige unmoving, Edwige cataleptic, Edwige dead. Seen and confirmed by dozens of witnesses including police officers, nurses and doctors, not to mention all the technicians from the O.R.T.F.

And Edwige as Mephista (even while under watch in that incomprehensible coma) had gone to kill poor Jacques Lemoulin, then that night had visited Tragny's house.

Teddy Verano had worked on too many occult cases to make the decision that the rationalist Farnese had to make: there is a woman who is playing the role of Edwige Hossegor and committing crimes as her.

"No, there's something else... but what?"

Edwige was doing much better. She had finally finished shooting her television series. Dr. Sorbier was following her case closely and found her normal. Two or three times, she had met Teddy Verano, but he had to admit that, in spite of everything, she was not calm. The nightmare was coming back, hazy, in the distance, but troubling.

"Mephista won't let me go," she said. "After the premiere, I'm going to leave Paris. Tragny is taking me on a cruise. It'll be our honeymoon."

Teddy Verano wondered, would everything go back to normal? Without knowing why, he was sure of the contrary.

With Gerard's help, he was looking for the young man of the red roses, but he apparently changed florists every time, which stalled the investigation. His letters were also mailed in an untraceable manner. Real shyness? Cleverness?

Teddy Verano was itching, even just out of personal curiosity, to solve this mystery, a minor event in the drama looming over Edwige/Mephista.

Farnese was still ignorant of the truth about the nocturnal visit of Edwige number two. Eva Mellion, too. Tragny and Verano had only told Edwige in the interests of her mental health.

On Thursday at 3 p.m., Teddy Verano was right on time for the appointment. There were only around ten people there: Edwige, Tragny, Eva, the director, Jean-Pierre Max, Edwige's co-star, three technicians of both sexes without any artistic claims, but who are usually found at these events where they have nothing to do. No journalists. A showing must have been scheduled for them later, when the last episodes would be wrapped up.

Teddy Verano, like the others, sat in one of the armchairs facing the huge, bare, dark room. The sound engineer went up to the projection booth with the metal boxes of film and, a minute later, all the lights went out. In the back of the room, bright flashing lights appeared at floor level. They were synchronizing the soundtrack.

Edwige was sitting between Tragny and Eva. Teddy Verano was next to the pretty public relations girl. In spite of her usual friendliness, Edwige appeared nervous, but everyone in her entourage, obeying an unspoken order, tried not to upset her in any way. Everyone, apparently, feared a relapse of her alarming crisis.

On his arrival, Teddy Verano had thought he had seen her eyes implore him, as if to say "I want to talk to you." Yes, that must have been it. But there was the baron and Eva. He knew that neither one had known of the letter sent to the detective by Edwige herself, who usually had all her correspondence go through Eva Mellion first.

She's afraid again, he thought. *This screening?*

He had thought long and hard about it, and had mentioned it to Tragny, as well as Dr. Sorbier, who was now more than ever determined to protect the health and sanity of Edwige Hossegor.

"She's going to see herself, like millions of viewers will see her a little later, as Mephista. Will this be positive or not?"

Edwige was obviously suffering from her split personality, half-woman, half-actress. The fact of knowing that an impostor might have killed Jacques Lemoulin, and had certainly come to Tragny's house, had given her some peace of mind since she knew that she had nothing to do with her good friend's murder.

Now, she would be a spectator. What she would see on the screen, like the others present, would be the fruit of her artistic efforts, the temporary incarnation of a fictional character, undoubtedly evil, but only fictional.

Teddy Verano wondered what her reaction would be this time. Just an actress judging herself fairly, thanking her director or, on the contrary, would she make a scene because the music drowned out her voice or the lighting technicians left an ugly glare on her left nostril?

Or maybe, new terrors, a neurotic fit, the horror of seeing and hearing Mephista, of being frightened by the crimes she sees herself committing on screen?

Jean-Pierre Max, an excellent actor in his own right, had whispered to Teddy:

"You'll see; she's fantastic up there."

And Teddy had thought:

As long as her great talent doesn't have a negative result...

The atmosphere felt heavy, nerve-wracking. The private screening, in its way, was going to add a new element.

From the projection booth the operator asked through the microphone:

"Can we start it?

The director answered for everyone:

"Yes."

They settled down.

The lights flickered off.

There was an instant of absolute blackness.

Then, without credits (which had not yet been made), on the wall that formed a screen, they saw the first images of *The Vampires of Paris.*

CHAPTER VII

There was the usual silence of the first few moments. In this kind of private screening, the audience has only one thing in mind: to critique at all costs; to nitpick; to find any real or imaginary faults so that they can tell the filmmakers, with an aloof and superior attitude, what they saw, what they "wanted" to see, so as to prove their expertise.

The only sound was a soft buzzing, a little annoying, from the projector in the booth above the room, and, with the first scene, some background music chimed in. The first adventure of *The Vampires of Paris* came rolling out.

Given what had happened to Edwige Hossegor, Teddy Verano thought that all the privileged spectators at the screening were waiting with bated breath for both Mephista's appearance and Edwige's reaction.

A shadow passed over, excused itself, and sat down. It was the sound engineer. After leaving the projectionist alone, he had come to watch the film, seeing that everything was adjusted to his liking.

The dramatic elements captivated the audience for a long while. Although there were several episodes of the famous *Vampires*, they were not showing them all, but with the interruptions to change the reels, it was still going to take a good two hours.

"Cigarette?"

"We can smoke?"

"Of course. We're not in a public theater."

"Then, gladly."

"A cigarette... Hold on... Give me a light..."

"Yes my dear... Here you go."

"Thank you. But Monsieur Verano has kindly offered me..."

These few words were spoken in the dark, but Edwige's gesture did not escape Teddy's notice. And he was sure that it was so obvious that everyone noticed.

Edwige had not hesitated to stand up, walk by Eva and with the feeble excuse of getting a light from the detective, she had found a way to sit next to him. Right away, quite naturally, she said to Eva:

"Excuse me, dear. It was rude of me to just walk in front of you. Keep Robert company."

The baron, two chairs down, clearly had nothing to say. It was so obvious that Edwige wanted to talk to Teddy Verano alone that the girl got up without saying a word, took Edwige's seat and started whispering to the baron.

An empty armchair now separated her from Edwige, who was sitting next to Teddy Verano. The film was playing again. In almost total silence. This kind of audience generally never expressed their disappointment except by the simple and rather rude pleasure of "going along" with either a shudder or a laugh.

She wants to tell me something... again, Teddy Verano thought.

But Edwige did not start talking and the detective figured it was better not to test her trust, since her reaction might shock Eva and upset Tragny.

In the dark, they could barely see anything but the red tips of the cigarettes, as everyone had started smoking. Sometimes, there was whispering, but it was rare, and the huge, bare room echoed, rather unpleasantly to be sure, with the soundtrack booming it out a little too loudly for a film meant for the small screen. They used the standing ashtrays in front of the seats.

All of a sudden, Edwige leaned forward to crush out her cigarette and at the same time whispered:

"I'm scared."

Teddy Verano did not even blink an eye but spoke in a flat voice:

"Do you want to meet together... a little later?"

"No... I'm scared of what's going to happen."

"Before leaving, we need to make an appointment."

In the shadows she grabbed his arm.

"What's going to happen... right now."

"Here? You think so?"

"I know so. Don't ask me how, I can't explain it."

The show was reaching a climax with one scene of violence after another on the screen. The sound was getting louder and louder. Screams, gunshots, a car chase like a real race.

Teddy Verano knew why Edwige Hossegor had chosen this moment to speak to him. Since the episode was really noisy, it was the perfect time to whisper her worries into the detective's ear. The others were a few feet away and heard nothing of what she said, even if they were not paying too much attention to what was happening on the screen.

"What are you afraid of? If you think it's inevitable, we should get you out of here fast..."

"Oh! It's starting again. This inexplicable anxiety, this desire to hurt someone that I feel inside me... Oh, look there!"

She turned away suddenly and pointed to Mephista on the screen. Teddy Verano, who was starting to understand the exquisite, the sweet, the spiritual Edwige, watched and was struck by the frightening expression that crossed her pretty face.

Weapon in hand, she was protecting the hideout of a gang of villains and shot one of the heroes of the film, with a scream of hatred and rage that made everyone, despite looking passive and unconcerned, shiver in their seats. This was not Edwige Hossegor. This was definitely Mephista.

Rarely, no doubt, had an actress incarnated such a diabolical spirit. She was really scary. And Teddy saw how scared Mephista could make Edwige. Because, despite everything, she was herself.

Once again, she whispered to him in the dark.

"She's in me... I feel it... another crime is about to be committed..."

"Who's under threat? Do you know?"

"No."

"Is it the baron again? Or..."

"I don't know, but there's going to be another victim. Oh, Monsieur Verano, I've thought so much about it... I don't always tell Robert everything, or the doctors..."

"Or me?"

"Am I wrong?"

"Do you doubt it?"

"I'm just so scared... that you will all think I'm crazy..."

"Not me. Or Tragny, who loves you. Or Gelor or Sorbier, who have a great deal of respect for you. Talk... if you really feel a tragedy is coming."

"Yes, I wanted to avoid it. Listen to me... I came to a strange conclusion. I must not pass out again."

Teddy Verano said nothing for a moment, as they listened to the dialogue from the film. In the dark, he could feel Tragny and Eva looking at him, turning away from the film to try to find out what Edwige and he were talking about.

And he was thinking that she was right. Because it was when she had fallen into a cataleptic state that Jacques Lemoulin had been murdered. And also during that fatal time that Edwige number two, the mysterious person resembling the actress, had dared to show up at Tragny's house.

"Speak. Say something."

"Calm down," Teddy Verano said. "There's no reason to suspect that another accident can happen."

"There is. It was the same the first time. I was scared. That's why I called you."

Teddy was puzzled. There was no doctor present since Sorbier had been called away. Should he get Edwige out of there? Interrupt the screening? Or what? Because he agreed with her: what seemed particularly dangerous was that sleep of death that had taken hold of her. Wasn't it at that moment when they could assume (or at least suppose, with respect to poor Lemoulin) that an independent Mephista, so to speak, had struck, apparently having nothing in common with the human version of Mademoiselle Hossegor.

And yet, Teddy Verano told himself, *there's a connection between Edwige and this Mephista coming out of the screen, entering life and taking action, killing...*

Yes, the more he thought about it, the more certain he was that it was this monstrous, this hideous phantom, this double of Edwige/Mephista, who was guilty of Jacques Lemoulin's murder. The fingerprint, of course, was too obvious, too unmistakably planted to attract attention, as Chief Farnese had said. But it is no less true that everything happened during the time when Edwige was sleeping.

He heard her mumbling:

"Don't fall asleep…"

There was an intermission to change the reels. The lights were turned on and some conversation started up. Teddy Verano noticed, as he expected, that Tragny was surly, clearly furious that Edwige was putting her trust in the detective, a trust that he would have given anything to share. As for Eva, she obviously frowned on it too, but, always the professional, she talked with the director to discuss a press conference for Edwige.

The sound engineer came back from the booth and said they could restart. Neither Tragny nor Eva, nor anyone else, dared to sit next to Edwige and Teddy Verano. They understood that the two of them needed to be alone to talk, which must have annoyed them all.

A new scene started. In no time at all they saw Mephista commit another crime. Menacing, she had a young, naïve, blond girl under her control. The girl was sweet, in a very touching way, and being threatened in a despicable blackmail. The scene would have been boring, if it were not for Edwige Hossegor's incomparable acting.

"You'll obey me. You'll do what I tell you. Otherwise the man you love will die! I know how to hurt people. I am hatred. I am Mephista. I am death."

There was silence while they watched the pretty face of the little heroine. They had cleverly filmed the girl's eyes in a close-up shot, zooming in so that the twin reflection of Edwige's face was etched on her corneas. The effect might have been simple, but it was striking.

Then, all of a sudden, Teddy Verano heard a voice near him, a woman's voice saying:

"I know how to hurt people. I am hatred. I am Mephista. I am death."

Although he had listened to the actress' voice on the soundtrack with interest, now he heard the same words with a kind of horror. Because it was Edwige who had just spoken them in her seat.

He felt more than he saw Eva turn her head and Baron Tragny, a little farther away, lean over to get a glimpse of Edwige in the dark. Among the spectators around them were a few reactions.

"Mademoiselle Hossegor…"

Teddy Verano was suddenly in a panic. What was happening?

In the shadows, in the dim, flickering light coming from the screen, he saw Edwige sitting stiffly next to him and then fall over backward without a word.

"Mademoiselle Eva… Baron… Quickly… Let's get her out of here."

Tragny cried out and rushed over. Eva was already at Edwige's side, slapping her hands. But they were ice cold. Her entire body was also ice cold, lying in the upended seat.

There was a lot of noise, deep sighs and screams, and useless comments. They lifted Edwige up and laid her on a couch. But it was hard to see. The director and the sound engineer were calling up to the booth to turn on the lights.

"Doesn't that idiot hear us?"

"He's busy with the projection!"

"Daniel! Stop the film! Lights! Turn on the lights!"

Everyone was standing around Edwige and, despite the low visibility, there was no doubt about it. For a second time, she'd become the victim of an incomprehensible cataleptic fit.

"Eva, call Dr. Sorbier. Quickly! I'm bringing her back to the house," said the baron.

Eva disappeared. Tragny was upset because it was still dark.

"Really," Teddy Verano said, "is there no way to stop the film and give us some light?"

"I'm going up there," the sound engineer said. "He's so immersed in his projector that he doesn't realize what's going on."

He left the room.

Tragny kissed Edwige's cold hands.

"My poor sweet love... Oh, what's happening?"

A scream answered him coming from the projection booth. Almost immediately, the engineer came scrambling down the stairs. The film was still rolling and the people were caught in the stream of images, in the soundtrack of the movie, in the luminous brushstroke of the projector.

They were scared, calling out, screaming, bumping into each other, looking unreal, with the film that would not stop, that seemed to never want to stop, with the flow of weird images that made shadows on the big screen, with the ranting and crying of people in two dimensions...

"Speak... Say something!" Teddy Verano yelled.

"Up there... in the booth... Daniel..." sobbed the sound engineer.

"What? The projectionist?"

"Dead... Murdered! Blood everywhere!"

Teddy Verano rushed up the stairs like a madman. The film was still rolling.

A little later, they noticed that the first reel had disappeared.

CHAPTER VIII

"And do you know, Gerard, what they found in the projectionist's wallet?"

"Uh… I don't know. There're so many things…"

"Put your little brain to work. If you want to work in this field, you'll have to learn to think. Come on, it has to have some connection with the Hossegor affair. OK, what are we focusing on right now?"

Teddy Verano's stepson suddenly lit up.

"Ah, hold on! A list of admirers. But nothing's come of it."

"Not yet."

"I've got it. A photo of Edwige."

"Exactly."

"With a dedication?"

"No. The poor boy had just told the sound engineer that he was keeping his precious photo for the end of the screening when, as shy as he was, he planned to ask Edwige to sign it." He let out a sigh. "Another one. Just like Jacques Lemoulin… Even Tragny, since it was on the night of Edwige's first fainting spell that the strange creature—let's call her Mephista—came to his house around midnight."

"Do you think she went there to kill the baron?"

"Listen, my boy, I said so at the time, and I still say so: everything is unfolding around the circle of Edwige Hossegor's fans."

Gerard looked slyly at him.

"Well, Teddy, I don't want to go bursting through open doors playing Sherlock Holmes… You must have thought of it before me… that the cause of all this is a jilted lover."

"Not a bad notion, my boy. Except the hitch is that all three times—here I'm taking Lemoulin's dying testimony as accurate—it was a woman, the spitting image of Edwige, who was present."

"By the way, any news from Farnese?"

"Yeah, right! We're a long way from his 'personal visit' of that first night. He is, of course, still avoiding the ridiculous accusation of Edwige herself, but who could deny that this affair, or rather these different affairs, involve her intimately? So, we saw him again at Tragny's house since that's where Edwige will be residing from now on."

"She and the baron aren't married yet?"

"You have to admit that there might be a little wrinkle in their plans. Besides, they figure on legalizing it when the investigation's over, and then they'll run away… somewhere where they'll have some peace. All the contracts with the beautiful Edwige Hossegor have been suspended for three months. She needs rest. Just between us, I think there'll be an extra guest on their honeymoon... Dr. Sorbier."

"Is she doing better?"

"Like always after a crisis—since this is becoming a habit, a regrettable habit, with crimes every time—Edwige is fine. This catalepsy also lasted a few hours and we had to tell her about the murder of Daniel, the projectionist, found stabbed to death... with his blood-splattered photo..."

"Any fingerprints this time?"

"No. Neither Farnese nor his men found anything. And those boys know their job. He's convinced—and me too—that the first time—the Lemoulin murder—the fingerprint was left on purpose. But since Edwige was obviously out of commission..."

"No twin sister?" asked Gerard, thoughtful.

"Why not a Siamese twin? Of course not! Besides, that wouldn't explain the fingerprint. There are no two alike, you know that."

"I would really like to know what they're thinking down at the Quai des Orfèvres."[5]

"Farnese is in a rage. They've got nothing on the death of Lemoulin."

"And Daniel?"

"You've already forgotten?"

"The receptionist's testimony? Of course not. She thought she saw Edwige leaving the studio with a package under her arm."

"What did the package contain?"

"I'm not an idiot, Teddy. The film reel. The first part of the film that you were watching. When they'd put on the second reel... when Daniel was killed... the projector kept running until the end. But didn't the receptionist find it odd?"

"The star leaving alone during the screening? Yes, it seems she was a little surprised. But she was busy, you know, with the switchboard. With all the calls, she didn't pay too much attention. Stars in this building are coming and going all day long. The girl's kind of blasé."

"And yet, there's no mistake. A second Edwige."

Teddy Verano stood up and suddenly dropped his usually relaxed and often smiling attitude.

"Yes, Edwige Hossegor number two. Mephista. The one who kills." His voice became softer. "Who kills when the real Edwige is sleeping. Sunk in catalepsy. Just after she got scared, after she sensed that something horrible was going to happen... after she called me and..."

He made a fist and struck at an invisible enemy in the air.

"And I was powerless to protect her and to prevent the murders. I couldn't do anything!"

Gerard was troubled.

---

[5] Parisian headquarters of the Police Judiciaire.

"But, Teddy, mother told you yesterday: nobody, not even Chief Farrese and all the police could prevent such crimes... unless they watched everyone who got near a woman like Edwige Hossegor. In her profession, with her fame, they are legion..."

Teddy Verano sighed. Gerard offered his pack of cigarettes. They smoked together in silence in the detective's small office at 77 Rue d'Enghien.

"So, where are we with the flowers?" asked Teddy Verano. "Any progress?"

"Now I've made some progress. Three florists—I followed up on the deliverymen and women—got a visit from a young man. Around my age. Not bad looking. A big guy, tall, and polite."

"Shy. I see. And sweet... or dangerous, depending."

"I took a map of Paris and located the flower shops. I'm sure that he lives around the Place de la République. He likes to change florists every time, so he won't get caught. He loves in secret."

"Yes, my boy. Lover or not, he's complicated."

"He intrigues you. He's important to you."

"Yes."

"Do you suspect him of being involved in the crimes?"

Teddy Verano stared hard at Gerard.

"Yes. He plays... or he will play a role. But not necessarily that of a criminal."

"A victim?"

"Why not? The guy's escaped the murderer so far... This murderer who appears to be a woman who lashes out at Edwige's more of less openly declared admirers... Because he's anonymous, that discretion that has saved his life... so far..."

"What? You think he's in danger?"

"Like the others."

"Luckily," Gerard laughed, "I'm not in love with Edwige... I've got a crush on Gina Lollobrigida."

"You've got good taste. But an actress on the television screen is more accessible."

Gerard started looking nervous.

"Say, Teddy, this guy with the red roses... it's like he's acting almost as if he understood all this. He shows his love while staying behind a veil of mystery... Maybe he's waiting for them to catch the criminal so he can come out?"

"Possible."

"Teddy, there's something else. A minute ago, you said something that really struck me..."

"I'm very flattered that I can have such an effect on you."

"Teddy, no kidding. When talking about the murderer, you said that it *seemed* to be a woman. Now, Lemoulin accused Mephista with his dying words, and you saw a woman at the baron's house, and only because you were hit (Teddy Verano rubbed his chin remembering) you couldn't stop her... Finally, Daniel was clearly killed by this twin of Edwige who was seen by the receptionist at the studio on the Champs-Elysées..."

Teddy Verano did not respond, so Gerard continued:

"...A woman who looked like Edwige... You've seen so many things in the field of the Occult. Me too, since you married mother, since we've all been together... You've taught me that there's more to the world than what we think we see. What are you thinking really, Teddy?"

Teddy Verano lit another cigarette.

"In the field of the Occult, my boy, we need more than this to assume something. We've got no clues..."

"The fingerprint?"

"Even Farnese thinks it's a hoax."

"What about you?"

"Me... I don't know... Not yet..."

"But you've got an idea?"

"Yes. And you're going to figure it out. Follow me on this. When Lemoulin was murdered, who was accused? Edwige?"

"Yes. I mean, no. Mephista."

"The fictional character. The role. Not the real woman, the woman of flesh and blood, who uses all her talent, all her spirit, and, above all, who is a friend. OK, that night Tragny and I saw who? Edwige?"

"Ah, I see. No, you saw a woman who looked like her—Mephista again. *And who was dressed like Edwige when she became cataleptic.*" Gerard's imagination was in full swing. "But... I see... at the studio... the woman who left with the package, who stole the reel... She was dressed exactly like Edwige on that day, clearly."

"You're making progress, my boy. So, your conclusion?"

Gerard looked at Teddy Verano, not wanting to go all the way.

"OK, you're forcing me to say it. It's as if the murderer, this diabolical Mephista, jumped out of the screen... that she's the character Edwige is playing, her double, her ghost. A ghost murderer. I don't know... Edwige's ectoplasm, a materialization of her subconscious. I'm totally with you, but you're going to have a lot of trouble getting your friend Farnese to swallow that!"

"Also, going along with Tragny, I haven't kept the Chief up-to-date on our little drama—the least possible anyway. Edwige's anxiety still has no part in the investigation. Neither does Mephista's apparition—let's call it that—at the baron's on the night of the first crime."

"And the stolen reel, how does that fit in?"

"In this whole affair, there's certainly some kind of connection with Edwige's work. Her roles. Her image as an actress playing these astonishing characters. Lemoulin knew what she was filming and had seen her in costume.

Therefore, he didn't see Edwige but Mephista—the woman who killed him. I'm sure it was the same for Daniel the projectionist. Now…" His face clouded over. "I wonder who's next?"

He thought for a moment before adding:

"Don't waste any more time on this. Keep searching for the kid with the red roses."

"I'm on it, Teddy. I think… well, since I'm not there yet, I'd rather not tell you."

They left each other. Teddy Verano went to Tragny's house, while Gerard went back to the long, monotonous, often nerve-wracking legwork to find the stranger in the city who as sending roses to Edwige. This involved making more visits and having more conversation with florists and deliverymen. He bought flowers, as cheap as possible, and often got loaded down with them so he brought them back to Yvonne, his mother, in the evening, or gave them to pretty girls in the streets, who were surprised, but not altogether very excited by the gift, their generation seeing them more as hippie symbols than tokens of genuine sentiment.

Once again, when Teddy Verano arrived at Tragny's house, he was welcomed with: "Any news?"

He had to admit that there was nothing new, except that his best sleuth (he did not confess the family ties) thought he would soon discover who the charming stranger of the red roses was. It turned out that said stranger had, in fact, struck again, to the baron's great annoyance.

But Edwige, who was already sad enough, kept saying that his discreet passion was like a kind of fetish, and that Robert Tragny had no reason to worry about a gentleman from whom they undoubtedly had nothing to fear.

Mademoiselle Mellion was keeping the journalists away. No one was admitted inside the baron's, except the doctor and the private detective. It was cocktail time, so Eva diligently and silently offered Teddy Verano a bourbon.

Sorbier arrived a few minutes later. Edwige approached him right away.

"You've given me too many tranquilizers, doctor. Today, I'd like to ask you for the opposite."

"Really?"

"Yes. There are drugs that keep you from sleeping, aren't there?"

"Of course. So, you don't want to sleep anymore?"

"Mademoiselle Hossegor," Teddy Verano interjected, "is obviously afraid of another crisis. Since the crimes happen during her fits…"

"But that has nothing to do with normal sleep."

"Doctor," Edwige pleaded, "I'm begging you…"

Teddy Verano and the baron made discreet signs to Sorbier.

"OK," the doctor said. "I'll write a prescription. But allow me, my dear to be worried. Not to sleep… it's dangerous. How long do you think you can keep it up?"

51

"You don't understand. I want to be able to drug myself... when I feel a crisis coming on."

"That's right," Teddy Verano agreed. "In the screening room, just before she fell unconscious, she whispered, 'Don't sleep'."

Joseph the butler entered.

"Telephone, Joseph?"

"Yes, baron. It's for Monsieur Verano."

"You can take it in my office."

The detective complied. Gerard's voice echoed on the other end of the line.

"I think I've got him, Teddy."

"Our boy?"

"Yes. Boulevard Voltaire. Near the town hall of the 11th arrondissement."

"Give me the exact address. I'm on my way."

Gerard gave the address of a Patrick Florent.

"Great. Are you following him?"

"He's got a beautiful studio apartment. I'll work up the nerve to approach him."

"OK. I'll be staying here for another minute or so, then I'll see you soon."

He hung up and headed back to the salon, smiling. But, upon hearing a crash, he rushed in and saw Sorbier, Eva and Tragny holding onto Edwige.

Feebly but firmly, she was struggling against them and had just knocked over her glass of Old Crow. On purpose. To break it.

She grabbed a piece of glass and slashed her arm in a terrifying fit.

"I don't want to! No! I don't want to! He's going to die! The roses... I can't fall asleep... Torture me! Kill me! Stick needles in my flesh... Burn me with a branding iron! Robert, Eva, help me! Doctor... doctor..."

They fought a frenzied battle against her horrifying state.

"An injection... quickly... get her on the bed..."

"No!" Edwige screamed as they snatched away the dangerous shard of bloody glass that had, luckily, made only superficial wounds, although quite dramatic ones. "I don't want to! No sleep! Mephista is coming back! If I sleep... I..."

They carried her away still struggling.

Teddy Verano made a snap decision.

"Boulevard Voltaire. Right away. Patrick Florent is in mortal danger!"

CHAPTER IX

A scene from a film that was repeated again and again, right now in Paris, but perhaps, some day, all over the world...

A little like what happened that one night, that horrible, final night with Jacques Lemoulin.

A young man sat alone at home, in a comfortable studio apartment. It was already evening. He was relaxing in shirtsleeves, without a tie. The television was droning on, but he barely watched the screen. He sipped his Americano, all alone, while casting meaningful glances at a framed photograph. Near it stood a vase with red roses.

Red roses that Patrick Florent—for it was him—replaced every day.

Every time he sent a dozen of these same roses to his idol, Edwige Hossegor, he kept three or four for himself. For his photo. For his dreams.

He savored their scent, thinking that, at that very same time, maybe at that very minute, the incomparable Edwige Hossegor was smiling as she inhaled the perfume of her flowers. Her flowers from him.

And maybe she was reading his letters, whose naiveté he was fully aware of.

Soon, surely, he might get over it. He was 20 years-old. He studied law. His parents were well off in the country, giving him enough money to live comfortably in Paris while he finished college. Later, he might pursue more tangible, less idealistic loves. Maybe at school, he might find a girl more spirited than the others...

But Patrick Florent was a dreamer. Withdrawn. He was in love with a woman out of reach. But he had no illusions. He sent her flowers and wrote to her, knowing full well that a star of her caliber received countless letters and untold bouquets.

What did it matter! The countless, relentless red roses, the unsigned but identical letters, all of this had built enough of a personality for her to know that he existed. And she did know, without a doubt.

More than one young man dreamed of Edwige Hossegor. Or Rachel Welch. Or another woman just as unreachable. Some souls felt so much need for love that they focused on a beauty that was out of reach, and all the more beautiful in that no reality will ever match it. At least, for these poor hearts.

Patrick sighed.

He had changed florists again. That way, he was sure of throwing off any suspicions...

If she tried to find out who he was...

But no. That was just an illusion. Edwige did not care about him.

53

It was he who was using the unknown, anonymous gift of romantic roses to play out his immature sentiments. To enrich his life.

He would eat dinner later. He had to work. A huge law book was on the table, begging for attention.

Someone rang the doorbell. Patrick had no girlfriend except for his ideal. Few friends. And his family was far away. So who might it be?

He went to open the door, naturally, and found himself face to face with a young man who could not be much older than himself, and who was smiling kindly.

Patrick Florent did not smile. He was not pleased with being bothered in his den of a shy student, of a lonely lover.

"What's this about?"

"Are you Patrick Florent?"

"Yes. But I've never seen you at the Univer…"

The possible mistake was already being corrected.

"My name is Gerard Parmier. I work in Public Relations for the O.R.T.F. (All this was rather vague, but the other was unlikely to check.) I'm doing a survey about the popularity of our actors amongst the student population…"

Patrick turned slightly pale, which did not escape Gerard's notice.

Nevertheless, he did not invite the visitor in.

"What does this have to do with me?"

"Would you mind answering a few questions for me?"

"I don't really know…"

"Listen, it's my job. We're the same age. We could be friends."

But Patrick was not convinced.

"You want me to say what exactly?"

"What you think of our stars. Look, for example, you watch T.V. I can see from here that you have a set. What do you think of Edwige Hossegor for example?"

Patrick was no longer white. He turned red.

"I don't give a damn about Edwige Hossegor. Who do you think you are…?"

Gerard had got lessons from Teddy Verano. He knew that he wasn't supposed to ever lose his cool, and had to put his pride in the closet when necessary, so not to scare away the " punters"—as Teddy called them.

"That's not very nice of you… I'm just doing my job."

"Who's stopping you?"

"Right now, you."

"I've got work to do, too. Leave me alone."

Gerard kept smiling, inspired by his step-father's mocking attitude. He looked over Patrick's shoulder at the apartment.

"Hey, hey, you sly fox… There's her photo… You told me you didn't care for her."

"Get out of here!"

Abruptly, Patrick got mad. He straightened up and confronted Gerard with the kind face that hid nothing of what was happening inside him.

The apprentice detective kept smiling—although a little forced—but did not budge an inch.

"Come on, don't get angry…"

"Leave me alone, or I'll punch you in the…"

Gerard hesitated. Keep talking? Go away? His hesitation was costing him the battle, he knew it.

With an apologetic look he gave in.

"OK. Sorry if I said anything…"

The door slammed in his face and he found himself alone on the landing of the building on the Boulevard Voltaire, the very building where the guy with the red roses lived, the guy he had been looking for so long.

And he was not too proud of himself.

He thought about what he should have done. Prove his authority, first of all. Enter by force, perhaps. Or find a more convincing line. It was a stupid thing to say, he told himself. The survey thing was weak. What an idiot.

He called himself all kinds of names, which did not make things better. And he just stood there, in front of the door. On the other side, he imagined Patrick was furious. He heard the television that Patrick was probably barely listening to.

Teddy would say to me: you've acted like a kid… You should have taken control of the situation… You should have…

Gerard bit his lip. He had, however, done a pretty good job noticing some key details. Seeing the tags on the bouquets sent to Edwige, he had visited all the florists in the arrondissements around the Buttes-Chaumont studios. After checking and cross-checking, he had ended up with a description, then a neighborhood, then an address. Now, he had found his target. And he had seen Edwige's photo. No mistake about it.

This might amuse Edwige. It would certainly interest Teddy. Gerard finally made up his mind. He was not going to stand there like an idiot (which he felt he was). He would go back and report everything to Teddy. His stepfather would tell him what to do next.

After all, his mission had been to find the guy with the red roses and the crazy letters. Mission accomplished.

With his conscience somewhat appeased, Gerard headed downstairs. Suddenly, the lights went out in the staircase. He was about to press the button, but, a split second before him, someone else turned on the timer. Someone in the building. Someone either coming up the stairs, or going down.

They were coming up.

Gerard, now beginning to display some of the reflexes of a professional sleuth, leaned over the banister to see who was coming.

He jumped back and had to choke down a weird sort of cackle. No! It couldn't be! He must be dreaming...

He quickly turned around and, instead of continuing down, sprinted back up the stairs, making the least noise possible. He was agitated and his heart was pounding in his breast. On an upper landing, leaning over the banister, he took another peek and couldn't believe his eyes.

It was Edwige Hossegor!

Troubled thoughts spun wildly through his overwrought mind.

Edwige Hossegor? Edwige, here, at the home of the boy who sent her red roses? How could she know where he lived? She couldn't have sent another detective on the trail of her mysterious lover. Besides, this was really of little concern to her. Right now, she had far more pressing concerns, a lot more serious problems... She had told Teddy Verano about the roses and the notes. And it was Baron Tragny who had insisted that they should find out who was behind it. Yes, he was jealous, but it wasn't him coming up the stairs... But if it wasn't Edwige either, then it was...

Gerard felt a lump in his throat. Teddy Verano had told him everything. At least everything he knew about the baffling mystery. Meaning, he knew a lot more about it than Chief Farnese.

No, this was not Edwige Hossegor. It was the other. The woman who had killed Jacques Lemoulin. Who had snuck into the baron's house at night. She who had murdered Daniel the projectionist in cold blood at the screening to steal a reel of the series in which Edwige starred. Poor Jacques... Poor Daniel who both also had a photo of Edwige...

Edwige... Always Edwige... The photo... and death followed...

Mephista was here!

She had come to kill this silly Patrick Florent, just as she had killed Jacques and Daniel.

Gerard's entire body started trembling. Not in fear—he had seen plenty of scary things in Teddy Verano's shadow—no, with emotion.

The sound of the doorbell drilled into his ear. She was ringing Patrick's door.

He leaned over, trying to get a better look. But from his vantage point, although he was almost falling over the banister, he couldn't see her anymore. But he knew she was there.

Patrick did not answer the ring. He must have thought it is the pseudo-pollster from the O.R.T.F. But she kept ringing.

Finally, he opened the door. Gerard heard it, then a kind of muffled cry from Patrick Florent.

Patrick, crazy in love with an unreachable princess. He found her standing there, on his landing, ringing his doorbell. What would happen?

The door closed. Gerard scrambled down the stairs. No one was on the landing, but him. The timer switched off. He stood there, in the dark, in front of the door. On the other side was Patrick, the poor fool, a worm in love with a star, who must be believing that he had just been transported to fairyland. Patrick who was locked in not with Edwige, but with Mephista—his would-be killer.

Gerard was tempted to ring the bell, to bang on the door, to break it down screaming, "Patrick, watch out! She's not Edwige!" But he would be the one who would look crazy. A scandal would not solve anything. He had to…

Yes. He had to do something. And fast.

Being who he was, he started by doing something completely stupid. He crouched in front of the door and looked through the keyhole. What luck! The key wasn't in it. He could see a little. Too little…

The woman (the side of her dress, the line of her hip, it was her) stood in front of the law student. They were talking. But Gerard couldn't hear what they were saying. He waited there a long time in the dark, praying to Heaven that nobody would come by. Fortunately, all was quiet in the staircase.

Oh, if only he could hear them. See them. Understand.

The couple's whispering seemed more intimate. Then the two silhouettes suddenly left his (very limited) line of sight. After a short minute, the light changed. The table lamp had been turned down, no doubt. Gerard expected to hear the quiet but characteristic creak of the couch.

This Patrick must be completely stupid, he thought. He, the forlorn lover, could believe that it was really Edwige Hossegor who had come to him, like in some children's fairy tale, with the swipe of a magic wand, to assuage his (until now) hopeless passion? He did not see the imposture? He did not understand the danger?

Gerard saw nothing anymore, but a small, dimly lit slice of the room. Knock? Ring? Interrupt the intimacy? That would almost certainly be dangerous. It might also hasten the fatal blow, the murderous blow that the diabolical creature was preparing, in one way or another, to deliver.

Gerard made up his mind.

He took something a lock pick of his pocket.

"I've got myself into this crazy situation… I have no choice!"

CHAPTER X

The door creaked after a little nudging. Gerard, after some efforts, had picked the lock and quietly opened it.

He entered Patrick's apartment, fully aware that he had just broken into it as illegally as possible. He put Teddy Verano's lessons to full use. There was one piece of advice in particular that he remembered, amusing at first, then proving its real value: nothing is more like a thief's bag of tricks than a detective's bag of tricks.

He had used a simple but effective skeleton key and his relatively easy victory surprised him. The door had opened and now he was standing inside the apartment.

He looked around.

It was not hard to imagine what had just happened.

In the dim light of a single lamp, Patrick Florent, bedazzled, on the heights of ecstasy, wasted like a drug addict, had dragged himself (or been dragged) to the couch, captivated by the enchantress who had shown up so suddenly, so mysteriously, on his doorstep. Apparently, he had had no time to ask himself questions, to wonder how she could know his address in the huge, monstrous city of Paris.

Whispers... a look... a caress... that's all it had taken.

They were both there, kissing passionately, feverishly.

Gerard saw this and was obviously not surprised, but clearly embarrassed. Despite the fact that he was acting in a good cause, that he was sure that this woman was not Edwige Hossegor but really Mephista, that this poor Patrick Florent was about to be murdered by this siren from Hell, he realized how this must have looked.

Ten seconds later, someone else realized it too.

Patrick Florent's head was spinning, and with good reason. He had just fallen into the arms of his unreachable love, wondering if he was dreaming; he was starting to get excited, and then this clown barged in on them.

Even in the meager light he recognized the intruder: the alleged poll-taker. He thought he had chased him away for good, but not only was he still around but he had just broken in!

Patrick was in a rage. He stammered an "Excuse me!" directed at this woman whom he believed to be Edwige Hossegor and who, in a gesture more savage than bashful, had just pulled the straps of her dress over her shoulders, after it had slid off under his passionate kisses.

Gerard had none of the experience or composure of Teddy Verano. He stood still for a few seconds, feeling more and more awkward, even though he knew he had acted correctly.

Patrick came up to him, his eyes popping out of his head, his fists clenched. But Gerard was not looking at him, but over his shoulder at the strange creature lying on the couch, propped up on one elbow, glaring at him...

Those eyes...

Gerard would never forget them. He felt like two rays of fire burning into him. Twin thunderbolts of hate. Like everyone who watched television, he knew them; he had seen them before; they were the eyes of the beautiful Edwige Hossegor in her roles as an evil woman. Except, this time, it was not a movie. She was looking at him. Only him. And she was not playing a role.

Edwige... or Mephista? Gerard shuddered, felt pierced to the bone by the grisly look from this monstrous woman. So frozen he as by her bewitching eyes that he barely heard Patrick cursing at him. And he got smacked hard in the face. He reacted right away because his lips hurt badly and he could taste the blood trickling into his mouth.

Nonetheless, he tried to talk, to clarify the situation.

"Listen to me! You don't know what's really happening. This woman..."

"Shut up, you bastard!"

Patrick socked him again, deaf to Gerard's appeal.

What could not last was Gerard taking it passively. After all, he was well built and, although he did want to straighten things out, to save Patrick in spite of himself, he also had his dignity, which suddenly exploded and fought back with force.

So it was with force that he responded to his aggressor and hit him back while yelling:

"Listen to me! This is not Edwige Hossegor! It's not..."

An uppercut cut him off, and took a little piece of tongue as well. Stronger than before, he tasted blood again.

In the next second, Patrick's eye became half-swollen, shut by an unexpected left hook after a fake jab with the right that would have frozen Marcel Cerdan himself.[6]

The two of them, evidently, were not going to talk things out anytime soon, because Patrick, now seeing out of only one eye, jumped on his opponent and rained a series of blows on him. They tumbled into a bookshelf. All the books fell out, a small vase broke, and the bookshelf fell over into the front door, slamming it shut and blocking it. The two young men were not done and the fight went on as viciously as ever.

Shouting, spitting blood, with a split lip and a sliced tongue, Gerard was aware enough of the situation to try to talk to his opponent, to block the punches more than throwing them. But with the rage of a wild animal in heat, torn away of from his lover's kisses, Patrick was completely oblivious to everything out the fact that he had just been snatched from realizing his most cherished dream.

---

[6] Marcel Cerdan (1916-1949) was a French world boxing champion.

The young dreamer writing tender notes of hopeless love and spending all his money on blood-red roses was long gone. There now was only a maniac flailing away at Gerard.

By chance, Gerard managed to twist Patrick's arm behind his back. Teddy Verano, who thought of everything, had given him lessons, not only in French kick-boxing but also in judo and karate. Patrick suddenly howled out, not knowing how he got himself pinned. For a moment he had to stop.

Face to face, noses almost touching, he saw the wounded face of his enemy, panting and sputtering.

"You have to listen to me, you bloody idiot..."

Gerard was swearing like his stepfather, who would have loved to hear it.

"Listen to me," he continued. "Your life is in danger. This woman is not Edwige Hossegor. You're the victim of a cruel and horrible imposture. This woman kills. She's killed Jacques Lemoulin and the projectionist Daniel. Now she wants to kill you."

Patrick Florent was stupefied, literally. He tried to move, but Gerard had his arm bent behind him so strongly and so skillfully that trying to escape would have broken it. And what he heard was so baffling...

He sobered up. The rush of excitement followed by the stream of violence was melting away.

"What... what did you say?" he asked.

They suddenly realized that they had fought and wrestled each other halfway into the bathroom. Gerard loosened his grip. Patrick reacted and tried to hit him again, but Gerard did not let him and punched him in the gut so that Patrick staggered back into the living room, bumping into the furniture.

Running after him, Gerard barked:

"Watch out! She's going to escape!"

Because, seeing Patrick in trouble, Mephista had rushed for the door. Patrick made a move. Gerard hit him again, not so hard, but enough to keep him quiet.

Then he approached the woman.

"I've got you, Mephista!"

What a pleasure to shout this out... A wonderful, melodramatic statement, straight out of the movies.

Gerard, still at the start of his career, believed he was a great detective and played up the drama. Because Mephista couldn't leave. There was only one door and the collapsed bookshelf was blocking it. However, there was one thing he was scared of: the creature's eyes. But he fought against it. He resisted. He laughed out loud to break the spell.

"Don't try to leave. Fate has done its job."

Edwige (or Mephista?) suddenly ran over to Patrick and cried out:

"Help me... Defend me... Is this how you love me?"

Patrick, out of breath, turned a swollen but savage face to her. The words of this incomparable beauty stirred him. He straightened up and advanced toward Gerard. The duel was going to start up again, and God knows how it would end.

"Gerard!"

Where did this voice come from?

Gerard suddenly lit up with joy.

"Teddy! Teddy! I've got her. She's here!" he screamed.

He took a step forward, but Mephista, without a word this time, pointed to him with a severe, irresistible gesture.

Patrick was urged on; he took a gulp of air and lunged forward. Gerard was worn out. His energy was gone and he was in no shape to start another fight. But he had to face up to it. This time, as if possessed by the diabolical influence of Mephista, Patrick jumped on Gerard with such force that he knocked him down and the two of them fell on the carpet.

They wrestled, rolled around, hit each other, bit each other, tried to grip each other's throat... their breathing was fast and ragged.

"Gerard! Bloody Hell! What's going on in there?"

Teddy Verano, who stood on the landing, tried to get in. With his skeleton key, of course, because the door was locked. But it only opened an inch or two since the fateful bookshelf that kept Mephista from getting out was also keeping the detective from getting in and helping his stepson.

Gerard received a blow that made him see 36 sunlights when his head hit the sharp edge of the couch where, a few minutes ago, Patrick Florent thought he was tasting sensual paradise when it was really death lying in wait for him.

Patrick did not take advantage of his victory. He was at the end of his rope too. He took a gulp of air and, with his heart pounding hard in his chest (this time not from romantic passion), he collapsed on top of Gerard's barely conscious body.

Teddy Verano, with all his strength, tried to break down the door, but the damn bookshelf, fragile as it was, was lying exactly across the threshold and couldn't be moved from the outside.

The sound of his struggle could to be heard throughout the building, alerting the neighbors and the concierge. So much noise, plus all the yelling and the fighting, had disturbed the peace of this comfortable apartment building on the Boulevard Voltaire.

In any case, Mephista was still not able to escape.

Gerard realized this in his red fog. Stars were dancing before his eyes and there was a constant ringing somewhere in the depths of his aching head.

"Ted... dy... I've... got... her..."

Patrick huffed and puffed, painfully, trying to get up. He coughed. So did Gerard, crushed under a weight that felt mammoth—as it should, since Patrick had collapsed on top of him. They coughed together and their eyes stung. It was hard for them to see, even though the table lamp had miraculously escaped destruction.

Teddy Verano, now surrounded by people on the landing, started coughing as well. And the scared neighbors coughed, too, one after another, because of the smoke starting to filter through the narrow opening of the door.

"Gerard, I can't hear anything! Gerard! Are you hurt? Oh, bloody hell, if they've hurt you..."

The detective thought of Yvonne who was surely going to hold him responsible for her son's fate.

Everyone was coughing now and Teddy suddenly understood why.

"Fire! There's a fire!" he cried, horrified.

Patrick was jolted, on hearing this through the door. He stood up, freeing Gerard, who struggled to sit up before Patrick helped him off the couch. Both of them started yelling together:

"Fire!"

Something was burning in front of them. Or rather *someone*. A huge flame shot up to the ceiling and licked it eerily.

Frozen in horror, thinking that the nightmare would never end, the two brawlers forgot all about their fight. What was burning there... before their eyes... no... they couldn't believe it...

Teddy Verano finally managed to shoulder his way through the door with the help of a strong neighbor who'd guessed that something had gone terribly wrong—he'd come with an axe to break down the door. The detective wanted to help his stepson, but stopped at the unexpected sight of the blaze between him and the two young men who were squeezed together before the frightening vision.

An already unrecognizable form had caught fire, spontaneously, for an unknown reason, and the flames were consuming it, devouring it, eating away its contours, deforming its shape.

A strong odor caught in everyone's throat and the smoke made it too hard to see exactly what was going on. In the bitter haze, the spectators coughed like mad. Some started spitting; others backed away, still screaming "Fire!" calling for the firemen... But all of them, for an instant, thought that they had seen the shape of a woman at the heart of the blaze.

Gerard and Patrick had no doubt about it. It was over her that they were fighting; she who was burning up in this inferno that had come out of nowhere—Mephista!

CHAPTER XI

In no time at all, a plan of attack was formulated. Teddy Verano was not the type to accept adversity passively, either from natural stubbornness or speculative philosophy. Therefore, while bawling out the neighbors, who were busy panicking, he managed to find two or three reasonable men and one or two energetic women who, with no better alternative, formed a human chain to carry water in various receptacles to contain the weird fire before the firemen arrived. On seeing this, after being shouted at by his stepfather, Gerard ran into the bathroom and grabbed a bowl to use against the terrible blaze.

All this took several minutes. Meanwhile, Patrick Florent, completely stunned, was of no use at all. Huddled on the edge of the couch, gaping and wild-eyed, he stared at the disaster through the smoke that became thicker and more irritating than ever.

"The window! Gerard, open the window! We're all going to suffocate!"

Gerard, who had not thought of this, quickly obeyed. A fresh breeze cleared some of the air in the apartment and the landing, where the improvised firemen were helping Teddy Verano. Without him, they would have given in to dumb panic and done nothing. At his urging, they had, in no time at all, saved their building. Because, in Patrick Florent's apartment, it was a real disaster.

The walls, ceiling and door had been licked by the flames and were covered with ominous black streaks. The carpet was destroyed, as well as the drapes and upholstery. On the floor, just a few feet away from the entrance, lay some unspeakable thing that Teddy Verano was now examining with curiosity.

Water was dripping everywhere, ruining the furniture and knickknacks, damaging what the fire had not wrecked, or had barely touched.

Most importantly, in the middle of the room, lay the remains of the presence of Mephista. This was what Verano was examining, and what Patrick was staring at, dumbfounded.

Now that the smoke was clearing, after the flames had died down under the bucketfuls of water, Gerard was also looking at the thing with growing bewilderment.

Teddy Verano now walked around the huge, thick, dark puddle, almost choking on the smell that emanated from it. Of course, after fighting the fire, the neighbors were in no mood to leave the place, so everyone had gathered on the threshold, trying to see inside. Especially since the detective himself was already inside, trying to walk around (as best he could) the huge, shapeless, liquefied, still smoldering, fire-blackened thing on the floor.

The panicky concierge shouted that the firemen were on their say. Teddy Verano spoke calmly, thinking of something else:

"It's a little too late."

"I also called the police."

"Excellent idea."

Then he stared down at the remains of the evil seductress and murmured:

"I wonder how I'm going to explain this to my friend Farnese?" He laughed. "Explain what? As if I understood a thing myself..."

The gooey puddle was starting to harden. There were gallons of it. That was what had spontaneously combusted as often happens around a fire. Gerard said a little later that he had seen a kind of spark at the very beginning and heard a faint crackling. But he wanted to know the truth as well. Teddy was like his soothsayer, and so he went to him.

"What does all this mean? What does it really mean, Teddy?"

Teddy Verano looked at him for a minute without answering. Then, he took a deep breath and said:

"My poor boy, if only I knew."

He opened his mouth to say something else but Gerard waited in vain. Teddy Verano's hazel eyes had just sparkled.

"Did you see something, Teddy?"

Teddy Verano had left Gerard's side, kneeled down and taken out his handkerchief. He picked up an object.

"A knife," he stated. "It's still hot... damn, with this blaze..."

"A knife, Teddy? Do you mean...?"

The detective's face wrinkled a little.

"No doubt about it, my boy. This knife was meant to kill this young man. And it's this same weapon that killed Jacques Lemoulin and Daniel the projectionist."

"The fingerprints..."

Teddy held the knife in his handkerchief, stood up and faced his stepson.

"We'll give it to Chief Farnese. He'll do what's necessary."

"But what about the fingerprints... What if they belong to..."

"Hush!"

Teddy Verano slipped the wrapped weapon into his pocket, but Gerard was not done asking questions.

"While waiting for the firemen... and the police... tell me what might have happened here."

"You know better than I. You were here."

"Me? Yes, of course... but then... What does this mean? Where is she? I'm sure she didn't go out through the door. Besides, you were on the other side. And she didn't jump out the window..."

The other tenants, one by one, invaded the apartment, offering a thousand theories about the origin of the weird fire that left behind a huge puddle of black wax, now almost completely hard and even cold.

One lady whispered that it must be Martians. A serious gentleman blamed some fifth column of the far right.

Teddy and Gerard were conversing by the window. All of a sudden, Patrick snapped out of his stupor and started swearing at everyone for being in his home, a home that was, now, almost inhabitable. He yelled and screamed. Teddy and Gerard came over as a neighbor who seemed to know him spoke kindly, trying to calm him down. She might have succeeded had he not seen Gerard.

He became livid and jumped at his throat.

"You wretch! You're the one who killed her! She was here... my beloved. You burned her. You..."

"Help me, quick!"

Patrick was on the verge of a breakdown. He howled and foamed at the mouth. Teddy, helped by Gerard and a strong neighbor, carried the poor boy into the bathroom. Quickly, with the help of his assistants, he pulled off Patrick's shirt and bent his neck under the bathtub faucet. The ice-cold water poured over the young man, lashed him, stung him and cut off his mad ranting.

Two minutes later, they felt him droop in their hands. They sat him on a chair and Teddy Verano rubbed his face hard and fast with a towel. He let him breathe a minute, then what he was expecting happened: Patrick Florent broke down in tears.

Some of the men frowned on this, believing that "real men don't cry." The women, however, were more sympathetic.

"I want you all to leave us alone," said Teddy Verano to the crowd. "I need to ask this young man some questions."

The concierge squeezed through the crowd.

"Say, fella—what right do you have to give orders around here?"

In the distance, they could hear the wailing sirens of the fire engines.

"Look," Teddy Verano said with his charming smile, "you go and explain everything to the officials. You called them so you can be the first to talk to them. The police will be here soon, so I advise you to do what's necessary."

He spoke with such authority that the concierge, concerned by the approaching sirens, let himself be pushed out of the room. Teddy Verano remained there, with Patrick still sobbing, Gerard, and the helpful neighbor.

"Stay with us, Monsieur," he asked the man. "You can be a witness that I'm doing no harm... while waiting for the police chief who will certainly arrive soon. OK, now, it's just us, Patrick."

"Edwige... Edwige," the young man mumbled, "She... she burned."

"Of course not, my boy, not a scratch. Rest assured your idol, the beautiful Mademoiselle Hossegor, is at home right now, and I believe she's fit as a fiddle. Well, at least she has no burns."

Patrick looked up and shouted:

"But she was here... she burned. I saw her!"

"No. There really was a fire, but Edwige Hossegor was not in it."

"But she was here, I tell you! I saw her. I was..."

He stopped short, sensing the indecency of what he was about to confess.

65

"Go on," Teddy Verano said cheerfully. "You were holding her in your arms. You were kissing her, fondling her... and she responded. Even more remarkable, she was the one who seduced you. Don't tell me it's not true."

"Yes. So, you knew..."

"I knew that this woman was coming here. Lucky for you, Gerard here arrived on time to save your life."

"Save me? You mean to ay... Edwige Hossegor would have killed me?"

"That was not Edwige Hossegor."

"It was another woman," Gerard explained.

"You want in on this. Go right ahead. Explain to me and to Patrick and to this gentleman, our witness, where this woman went, since you think there was a woman here."

Gerard was stunned. He swallowed hard.

"Come on, Teddy, I'm not a complete idiot..."

"You say there was a woman here? And she burned? OK then! I'm going to tell you, my boy, when you burn a body, whether Edwige Hossegor's or any other, it leaves traces... and not traces of wax. Do you understand?"

"Yes... It looks like wax... I know."

"Another thing. Her clothes. If they went up in flames, where are the remains? Because, as you know, even the synthetic tissue that women wear, nylon and stuff, leave traces. And I'm sure that we saw nothing but something that looks like wax in this apartment."

"Teddy... I'm afraid of understanding... Do you think that, maybe, it was a wax doll?"

"Why not?"

"But I saw her. She walked, she talked, she... Go on, ask Patrick. When a guy holds a woman in her arms, he knows perfectly well if she's a real woman or a doll."

"Yes. Under certain conditions. I'll explain later."

"What are you thinking? A hallucination? An illusion? OK, Verano, I'm going to ask you if what you put in your pocket to give to Chief Farnese was an illusion or not."

"Bravo! Gerard, you're making progress in logic. So we agree. The knife, right? It's real. And it would have killed off this young man on the spot... like the two other victims of Mephista."

"So it *was* Mephista and not Edwige."

"Have you ever doubted the duality of this person?"

"No, of course not."

"At this moment, Edwige Hossegor is sleeping. Or rather, she's in a cataleptic state at Baron Tragny's house."

"I understand less and less. Hold on... You mentioned a ghost, a kind of vision of Edwige..."

"Here we go."

"Ghosts—characters like that, which seem to come out of a movie, right off the screen, should have trouble wielding a knife."

"And yet, this knife exists."

"Ah Teddy, what a pain! You don't want to tell me what you know…" said Gerard, waving his hands in frustration.

"Only if I knew more."

"I thought of something else. I saw her enter the building."

"The woman or the ghost?"

"Look, have you ever seen a ghost turn on the light to go up the stairs?" asked Gerard, perking up. "Well, Mephista, since there is a Mephista, did exactly that."

"A very real, even realistic action. Like she did, quite convincingly, to prove her femininity to Patrick Florent. And to kill him, in an equally realistic way. We're becoming very rational folk now, don't you think?"

"If I get anything in all this…" the neighbor, who was still present, started.

"Don't worry yourself, Monsieur," said Teddy Verano. "We've been tracking Mephista since her first manifestation and we still don't understand the truth about her. At least, not yet. But it'll come. Anyway, Gerard, I notice that Mephista is always acting like a real woman, even though she's not. To fool anyone she meets. She didn't come up the stairs in the dark, although I'm sure the light was completely useless for her."

"Ah-ha!" Gerard shouted. "So she's not a real woman?"

Their conversation was interrupted because there was suddenly a lot of noise in the apartment. The firemen had arrived. The police showed up soon afterward. Teddy Verano and Gerard had to make long reports on the strange events that had played out in Patrick Florent's apartment.

The detective eventually managed to whisper to his stepson:

"Woman or not, here just like at Tragny's house, like at the Champs-Elysées, like at Lemoulin's, I'm absolutely sure that she didn't come alone."

CHAPTER XII

"We thought it'd be good," Chief Farnese began, "to keep you up-to-date."

"As it should be," Edwige Hossegor said sharply.

She was very pale, still feeling the effects of her unconscious hours that were as inexplicable as the earlier ones. Dr. Sorbier had practically not left her side since Eva had telephoned him the day before.

Edwige had woken up in the middle of the night. She had described her nightmare in which there were a lot of flames, a sharp knife and—she had admitted rather reluctantly—a clearly erotic aspect.

The next day, around 5 p.m., at Baron Tragny's house, Teddy Verano and Chief Farnese had talked together for a long time. The detective and his stepson had given Farnese a detailed account of their adventure in Patrick Florent's apartment, which was, at least for the moment, inhabitable.

Patrick was also supposed to make a statement, but his good faith was doubted by no one, and the game he had been playing, sending the clumsy, tender notes with the red roses while staying anonymous, was explained perfectly well by his youth and sensitivity that pushed him to focus his budding amorous passion on Edwige, the unreachable actress.

What was not explained, however, was what had happened later. Farnese was still trying to figure out. He had called Tragny, who had talked with Edwige as well as the consulting physician, and given his approval for the meeting.

In the big salon, surrounding the star of the O.R.T.F., several people had gathered. There were, of course, the two hosts, Robert Tragny and Edwige Hossegor. Two other regulars to the house stood nearby. First, Eva Mellion, public relations, and Dr. Sorbier, who was working with Professor Gelor to find a way to prevent any future fainting fits that were so dangerous to the star. Farnese was there, obviously, as well as Teddy Verano. Gerard Parmier, officially introduced as his stepfather's assistant, had also been asked to join them. Last but not least was the young man being confounded by one surprise after another, Patrick Florent.

The poor boy was staying in a furnished apartment near his ruined studio and looked very embarrassed to be present there with his idol. Because, this time, there was no mistake possible; the terrible imposture was over. This really was Edwige Hossegor, in flesh and blood, who had given him the sweetest welcome, putting him at ease with a smile and enough kindness and simplicity that he was no longer so unhappy.

Sometimes, he blushed when he looked at her. Could he forget that, only the night before, under pretty extraordinary circumstances, he had held her in his arms—or so he thought!—and she had spared no affection, which, according to the secrets dragged out of him by Farnese and Verano, bordered on indecency?

For the two detectives, it was one more piece of evidence. There had been the fake Edwige, a fake that left no trace but a pile of wax, according to the laboratory analysis by the police.

"Mesdames and messieurs," Farnese began, "I brought you here so we can try, all together, to get to the truth. I'll tell you right away that our methods as police officers are a little different than those of my friend Verano. He believes in things… let's say, things that could be qualified as impossible…"

"Or invisible," the hazel-eyed detective corrected kindly.

"As you wish. But in my line of work, I can't waste time on nonsense. My job is to catch criminals. To track them down and put them behind bars. That's the case… well, it will be the case with this outlandish Mephista who recklessly pretends to impersonate Mademoiselle Hossegor."

He paused, coughed.

"What I've just said will come as no surprise, but it's serious. Very serious. Even more so because it's inexplicable. No, Verano, don't laugh. Inexplicable now doesn't mean inexplicable forever. There is always a time in these mysterious investigations when a rational explanation clears up what at first looked completely baffling."

"I never said, Chief, that the mysterious forces that influence the world are irrational. They just are, period."

Farnese snapped his fingers in annoyance.

"Please. I respect the work you've done, very often outside our investigations, but sometimes it's been quite nonsensical."

"Thank you for the 'sometimes'," Verano mumbled under his breath.

Farnese inferred more than he heard.

"So, what was I saying? Ah, yes! The drama… From the pretty ludicrous drama last night, there are two pieces of evidence. First, the pounds of melted wax being analyzed, but whose initial examination appears to conclude it's pure beeswax."

"Interesting," Teddy said.

"The second piece of evidence is more troubling. I'm referring to the knife."

An "aaah" went around the room.

"My friend Verano picked up this knife… and like any good policeman, he did it without wiping off any fingerprints…"

There was silence, charged with the oppressive weight of expectation. Tragny took Edwige's hand affectionately so as to reassure her, to protect her from what was coming.

Teddy Verano looked at the star with compassion; Gerard with interest; and Patrick with all the love that was churning him up at the idea of the strange martyrdom that this woman was suffering, this woman whom he had placed on such a high pedestal…

"The fingerprints, without a doubt, belong to Mademoiselle Hossegor."

Eva and Dr. Sorbier made a move to help Edwige, but she stood up, very straight and very firm, and said:

"So, Chief, there is no doubt about it: this knife is the same weapon that killed Jacques Lemoulin?"

"Yes, ma'am. And David the projectionist. I should add that in all three cases—the third murder being premeditated but aborted thanks to Gerard Parmier—the deadly weapon was wielded by a woman who looked exactly like you. And not only looked like you, but who *was* you."

"Chief..."

"Excuse me, baron. You know that this time, like the others, I'm not accusing Mademoiselle Hossegor. However, you have to admit that this smells like witchcraft..."

"I did not make him say that," Teddy whispered.

Farnese shot him an angry glance.

"OK, Monsieur the ghost detective, please explain it to us."

"First of all," Teddy Verano said, "there was no woman involved in any of the three murders. We're back to this idea that was brought up yesterday. A wax doll, or maybe a robot... That's a bit far-fetched. Still, given what happened, especially what Patrick Florent here can tell us..."

Patrick turned red, feeling very uncomfortable. Edwige tried to help him with a little smile full of kindness.

Teddy Verano noticed his discomfort.

"Monsieur Florent, do you think that the woman who came to see you last night could have smiled like Mademoiselle Hossegor is doing right now."

Patrick stammered. They encouraged him.

"No," he finally admitted, "it was... something else... it was... Mademoiselle Hossegor, but more... more savage... (he lowered his voice) more seductive... Oh, I'm sorry to say such a thing... in public..."

"We're not in public," Farnese said, "and you must speak without embarrassment. We have to clear this up, don't forget. And above all, above all, I insist on this, we must figure out how to stop these crimes."

"You think she'll strike again?" Edwige cried out.

"I fear so," replied Farnese, nodding.

Edwige started fumbling for a cigarette. Eva offered her one.

"Doctor... doctor... I know no more than the rest of you about what's happening... but whether you're watching over me or not, I feel a terrible responsibility in the matter."

Everyone tried to protest.

Edwige cut them off with a wave of her hand.

"No! Listen to me, all of you. I fall asleep... or rather I fall into a cataleptic state. Oh, I can feel it coming on, but I can't stop it. Afterward, I feel like I'm coming back from the dead."

She spoke so sincerely that everyone in the room shuddered.

"I slept. Let's accept this. Because in spite of everything, I pass into a dream world while I'm in this second state that affects all of you so strongly that, during my first fit, you thought I was dead, and not figuratively. Then what do I learn on waking up, on returning to consciousness? That Mephista, this Mephista, a fictional character, a creature born on paper, the work of screenwriters, to be built, molded, revised, touched up, destroyed and rebuilt as needed, like all the leading roles for a television series, this Mephista, who has no face or flesh or life, but whom, in the end, thanks to me, Edwige Hossegor, exists, this horrific demon materializes and kills or wants to kill. And two men are dead already. A third, last night, almost lost his life in the arms of this imaginary, detestable fictional incarnation of mine…"

Patrick Florent was shaking all over. Edwige walked over to him. He lowered his head as she approached. She raised his chin up, gently, then forced him to stand up. He looked more awkward than ever. She kissed him firmly and sweetly on the cheek. He could not have blushed more. Then he turned pale with joy.

"There's no more doubt," Edwige said. "And I am grateful to you, Gerard Parmier. Thanks to you, I don't feel like a criminal for the third time."

They protested again but Teddy Verano indicated he wanted to speak.

"Go on," said Farnese, "since you don't like this, or only partly, but you usually let other people talk and you just look and listen."

"I want to come back," Teddy said, "to a detail that will undoubtedly relieve Mademoiselle Hossegor of her completely imaginary feeling of responsibility. I told you about it, Gerard, and I mentioned it to you, Chief. We can't forget about Mephista's clothes. I say Mephista. Woman or doll, illusion or robot, maybe a little of all that... Every time Mephista shows up, she's wearing the same clothes as Mademoiselle Hossegor. Patrick and Gerard's description of her appearance yesterday is again in perfect agreement. Now, we found no trace of clothing in the pile of wax, which is the only remains of her visit. There was only wax, beeswax as the police lab says. Which caught fire in the most incomprehensible way…"

"What's your conclusion?" Farnese asked.

"Nothing yet. I'm searching. Just like you, Chief."

Farnese tried to hide a little shrug.

"It's also true that Mephista only appears when I'm unconscious," said Edwige. "I fear there's a demon inside me… A lethal demon who comes out of me… to commit these horrible crimes…"

She broke down in tears. Eva was kneeling near her and Tragny was also upset. This meeting was exhausting Edwige and he did not care for it at all.

"Mademoiselle," Farnese said, "the monster who committed these crimes does not come from inside you. It only borrows your appearance. There's a lookalike, a dead ringer for you, unknown until now, but a lookalike."

"Now we're starting to agree," Teddy Verano said.

Edwige stopped sobbing and looked at them.

"A lookalike, you say? What's the difference? Mephista... or the entity, the power that makes her act, comes from me... Not from my body, since I know that I'm in caring, friendly hands every time... But from my appearance... and especially from my soul. Oh, that's it, my soul is stolen! I'm thrown into a world of horror... like I told you, I feel that something horrible is coming, then I pass out... and then, after I wake up, I remember."

She pushed Tragny and Eva away.

"I told you all, I can't live like this anymore... My life is impossible. I want no more murders, no more blood spilled, no more inexplicable phenomena... I feel like I'm damned, yes, that I'm going to be cursed for being mixed up in all this, as if this Mephista, who started as make-believe, is now another Edwige, the other part of me, a nocturnal, blood-red, evil Edwige."

"But, Edwige!" Tragny shouted. "You're here, you're sleeping, you're never at the scene of the crime."

"It's me," she repeated, "I know it's me... I can't go on... no more... I don't want to live like this..."

She was frightening to look at, her nerves so frayed. She trembled convulsively.

"If it starts up again... if I feel a crisis coming on... I won't sleep..."

She ran over to Sorbier and shook his arm frantically.

"Doctor, listen to me... I must stay awake... I have to ... I mustn't not fall into *that* again. Not have those blood-red dreams to find out, when I wake up, that during my temporary death, I somehow participated in a murder."

"I promise you. But you have to calm down, my dear.'

Tragny shielded Edwige with his body.

"Messieurs, I think you can understand that this meeting has exhausted Mademoiselle Hossegor. Isn't that right, doctor?"

Doctor Sorbier motioned to Eva to take Edwige away but she spoke again:

"Rather than start up again... Death! I'd rather die..."

An instant later, she excused herself and left the room.

Farnese and Verano left the house, shown out by the baron who was not very friendly and was visibly angry with them for not having freed Edwige of her fantasies. Gerard and Patrick followed behind them. They were no longer thinking about arguing or fighting, and what was strange was that they were becoming fast friends.

Teddy Verano whispered to Farnese:

"Considering Edwige Hossegor's nature, she played the scene wonderfully."

"A little overacted, eh? That's my opinion too. Actresses are often outdone by their acting. I have to admit that this Mephista is very dramatic, but maybe a little exaggerated."

"In any case, we've been privy to quite a unique and never-before-seen episode of the adventures of Mephista. A real hit, as they say in the business."

"So tell me, Verano, what are you thinking? I'm sure you have an idea."

"Uh... Chief... maybe a little later. Oh, by the way, I want to ask you something. Can I go back with you? Yes, to the station. Department: parking tickets."

"What a funny idea. What do you want there?."

"I want to check if by chance there were any interesting vehicles parked in the vicinity of Mephista's various crimes when she showed up."

Farnese looked at him curiously.

"An idea in the back of your head?"

"Can I look through the fruit of the meter maids' work?"

"If you'd like."

Farnese brought Verano to the department in question. *Decidedly*, he thought, *private detectives have very peculiar methods.*

CHAPTER XIII

On recognizing her husband's voice, Yvonne knew right away what was going to happen.

"You're going to tell me that you're not coming home for dinner again tonight."

She heard Teddy Verano's quiet laugh.

"My dear, I pay my respects to your insight. But don't worry, I'll be home later this evening."

"Let's say later tonight." Yvonne Verano sighed before asking, "Any news?"

"Oh yes. Well, maybe."

"About... which case?"

It must be explained that Yvonne, caught now between her detective husband and her son learning the trade, had no choice but to stay up-to-date on their investigations.

"It's about... You know..." Teddy Verano whispered.

"Oh!" Yvonne exclaimed.

"Be quiet, dear. Has Gerard come back?"

"Not yet. Do you want... to take him with you?"

"No. I'm going to pay a little personal visit. Outside of Paris. Yes, I found something in the files that good old Farnese let me look through at the station."

Yvonne felt worried. This was not the usual, harmless affair that Teddy Verano generally dealt with. Besides the shadowing, the pre-marriage spying, staking out adulterers or investigating shady businessmen, there were often enough elements that were related to the Occult, which Teddy Verano had made his specialty.

And now, for a little while, there was the great adventure of Mephista. From the start Yvonne could see, with the heart of a wife and mother, that Teddy and Gerard were confronting an incomprehensible monster.

"Don't worry," Teddy Verano said, "I assure you, at least for tonight, that I'm taking no risk at all. A little detour in the countryside, that's all."

"Far from Paris?"

"Less than 100 miles. In the Loiret. An area in which my investigations seem to take me a lot, I don't know why..."

Another sigh from Yvonne. A mysterious premonition was making her anxious.

"Darling," Teddy Verano said, "do you want to write it down?"

"Yes. Hold on, I'll get a pen... OK, I'm listening..."

"Write: Monsieur Verrier, Jules. Beekeeper. Cerisiers—that's the name of his town. Not far off the highway, near a maze of ponds."

"Why so many details? Oh, Teddy! You know there's danger. You're risking your life…"

"No, my love. It's just that… whether we like it or not, Gerard is now my assistant, my right arm man—please don't sigh like that again—he has to stay informed."

"So, that's where you're going?"

"It's around 3 p.m. now. I'll get there around five. So you see, if I say I'll be back this evening, it's completely reasonable with the Citroën DS."

"And then? What should I tell Gerard?"

"To telephone Tragny. Yes, the baron. And tell him what I found. Edwige Hossegor made me promise to keep her informed of all my discoveries." There was his quiet laugh again. "Whether true or imaginary. But I'm thinking that this particular find might prove interesting. If I'm wrong, too bad. The weather's not bad and I'll be taking a nice little trip. There's the sun, the flowers… it's the ideal season for bees."

"Teddy, what if I were to go with you?"

"Don't think of it, honey. What about your son? He needs to contact the baron as well as Edwige."

"Why don't you do that yourself?"

"Women… eternally curious."

Yvonne's voice became nervous.

"Teddy… you smell danger and you want to keep Gerard away from it, don't you?"

He had some trouble convincing her. In the end, he explained what it was all about and Yvonne admitted that it might just be a lead to follow.

Ten minutes later, Teddy Verano's DS passed the Porte d'Italie and cruised onto the southern highway at almost 90 miles an hour. He was more and more convinced that a criminal, like everyone else, used a car since it was difficult to live on the planet today without getting around in one.

His reasoning was simple. Mephista—be she woman, wax doll or robot—had to have been taken to the scene of her crime by… someone. He got the idea of searching through the parking tickets given around Tragny's house on the Rue de Ranelagh, around Jacques Lemoulin's apartment, then around the Champs-Elysées and Boulevard Voltaire at the time when the demon killer showed up. He had spent hours and hours at it. Listing, classifying, comparing and contemplating. Relying on detective's luck, especially when something clicks all of a sudden, for no rhyme or reason, and all the pieces fall into place.

He had passed over the clue without looking twice the first time, but the second time…

There had, indeed, been two tickets given for illegal parking to the same van during both Lemoulin's murder and the night of Patrick Florent's attack, when Mephista, or what stood in for her, had ended up combusting spontaneously and incomprehensibly, leaving nothing but a pile of melted, charred wax.

When he read the name, address and profession, for the second time Teddy Verano jumped.

"Can it be..."

False hopes, very often in such cases. Such a thin, superficial connection. But it could hold up. After making the necessary call to Yvonne, he was on his way.

To the town of Cerisiers, with which he was vaguely familiar.

To the home of Jules Verrier, beekeeper.

He drove at such a good pace that he arrived, in fact, in the sunny afternoon well before five o'clock as planned.

At Cerisiers, a few miles off the highway, among the stretches of flatland where fishponds stagnated and a still vibrant wildlife had escaped human massacres, Teddy entered the small town and became what he usually was on these kinds of trips: Theo Verdier, salesman.

Just in case, he had changed his look slightly with the help of a false moustache. He always kept the necessary materials in the DS, so when he got out he looked a little heavier, walked a little slower, smiled a little wider and spoke more loudly, which was unlike him. A briefcase engraved with T.V. and appropriate business cards—everything was ready for the show.

In rural country like this, there was usually only one store for food, drink and tobacco. There the fake Monsieur Verdier bought cigarettes, drank a glass of white wine with a hazelnut aroma, and talked a lot, explaining that he was on the lookout for beekeeper's honey, etc.

The grocer/bartender/tobacconist told him about two possible suppliers: a young lady named Farmond, who was very well known in apiculture, and, of course, Jules Verrier.

"Mademoiselle Farmond? Yes, she's the one they told me about." He consulted his notebook. "Does she live far from here?"

These towns are usually very spread out, made up of hamlets and large properties like farms or castles. He got a little information on Farmond and was about to start in on Verrier when two guys burst into the shop.

"Look," the friendly owner said, "these guys can tell you where the gentleman you're looking for lives."

"Monsieur Verrier?" the two of them asked together.

"Exactly. Monsieur here is looking for honey."

"Ah! OK," one of them said, "we thought it was for the movies."

The comment was so unexpected that Teddy Verano, despite his usual cool-headedness, was stunned.

"The movies? Does Monsieur Verrier have a movie theater? Here? In Cerisiers?"

"Of course not, M'sieur. Well, yes, kind of, I mean..."

The misunderstanding was quickly cleared up. Teddy Verano learned that the Monsieur Verrier, a jolly good sixty-year old if ever there was one, had established a little film club in his house (a big old manor house) where the young people from Cerisiers and the area would meet.

For a long time, he had belonged to the Federation du Cinema Amateur and was passionate about everything concerning movies and cameras, including television, radio, really everything that modern physics had brought to man in the world of images and entertainment.

Teddy felt his interest grow the longer they talked about him. Mysterious connections started forming in his mind about things that had, in fact, been very vague before arriving in Cerisiers. So, he bought himself another drink and talked some more.

Jules Verrier had a real workshop going the all the kids from town who wanted to learn about radio or similar technology could go and work there whenever they wanted. He even gave courses, helped the newcomers, improved their skills and organized screenings where all the kids apparently had a good time, not to mention the prominent local figures. They watched classic silent films and some avant-garde productions reserved for club members. A strange character, for sure, but considered a little like a philanthropist.

"It's his mania," the shop owner concluded. "That and his bees."

"Besides," the owner's common-sensed wife added, "he's not hurting anyone. He's even helping out the kids."

Teddy left the café a little dazed accompanied by the two young men who would not leave him before giving specific directions to Verrier's house.

The DS took off down a sunny road winding between two ponds. He drove slowly, looking for his way, not very comfortable in this pleasant but sometimes dangerous country.

He looked at the incredible abundance of wild flowers. The meadowsweets and buttercups, marjoram and daisies, brooms and reeds, all enveloped in a humming cloud. And bees, bees everywhere.

One of them flew in through his open window and buzzed around his face. He shooed it away, thinking of other things.

On the other side of the pond were some little woods that hid the house of the beekeeper/film buff. Teddy Verano parked the car so that it could not be seen, got out and took a few steps smoking a cigarette, concerned, trying to organize his thoughts.

It was too good to be true. If it really was.

Get to know the guy as soon as possible, he thought.

He hesitated. Was he going to be found out? Even playing to the hilt the role of Theo Verdier, salesman for a company that was eager to buy the most delicious honey directly from savory source?

The sun beat down; the ponds sparkled with light. Teddy Verano's head felt heavy in spite of the pure air.

How far he was from Mephista and Edwige Hossegor, from all the inexplicable crimes and the strange wax creature who had melted into a shapeless heap from a spark that came out of nowhere.

Nature, here, was so cheerful, so charming...

And the bees...

He watched them for a moment as they alit on the wild snapdragons, dipped into the calyx that swallowed them up like a weird throat, then reappeared and left, laden with pollen... Was the solution here?

He made up his mind, walked around the woods and towards the gate described by the considerate young men who had every reason in the world to be nice to a visitor to the local benefactor.

Teddy rang. Nobody answered. Jules Verrier must have been out.

He noticed that not even a dog was running around the yard enclosed by a low, ivy-covered wall that surrounded over two acres of land. Through the greenery, he could see what they pompously called the manor.

Second Empire style, a little hybrid, dilapidated. Just one story. But three television antennas. Quite large.

These could obviously be explained by Verrier's passion. He had to receive broadcasts from far away, and this, thanks to certain methods that the boys had implied were, if not invented but at least perfected by him, to make the most of them. The antennas were attached to some of the huge oak trees that surrounded the house. Thus no storm could knock them over even though they were each around 50 feet high.

"Yeah... yeah... yeah..." Teddy mumbled. A world of thoughts bombarded him.

He walked around the property. All of a sudden an idea came to him. *Say... I don't see any beehives.*

He made up his mind. As agile as a young man, in spite of the ungainly appearance he gave to Theo Verdier, he scaled the wall and jumped into the yard. He walked to the manor, looking for beehives but still could not find any. However, he did note the presence of countless bees.

Close to the house, he kept near the bushes, trying to approach it with more caution. Verrier might be home.

Then, coming from the ponds, was the sound of a motor. A small van. A Citroën 2 CV.

A moment later the vehicle (but not the engine) stopped in front of the gate. Someone got out, opened it, brought in the van, closed it, and finally arrived before the tiny manor. A van on which was painted a pretty sign: a dazzling golden beehive and the business name of the philanthropist/film buff of Cerisiers: Jules Verrier - Beekeeper.

Jules Verrier, a short, thin, frisky man with white hair jumped out without seeming to suspect that anyone was on his property, because Teddy Verano had remained out of sight.

CHAPTER XIV

It was not the first time that Teddy Verano had to sneak around in the dark. His career had already got him used to night vision.

Of course, he had no supernatural powers, as opposed to the monsters he sometimes had to confront, but he had trained himself for a long time to feel his way around, to trust his instincts, to maneuver in tight spots without any light at all and develop enough finesse so that he was not handicapped by the dark. Once again, he was grateful for that training, which he sometimes forced on Gerard.

On hearing Jules Verrier's van, the so-called Theo Verdier had not stayed long in the park. He wanted to spy on the residents of the manor. He had quickly scrambled over a railing onto a kind of small terrace that had attracted his attention, because it was there that he could see the three huge antennas that looked too big, even for receiving long-distance transmissions.

While the van was almost in sight, the detective had finally found what he was looking for: a way in. At the base of the antennas, firmly tied down, were the cables connecting them to their appropriate equipment, which must have been either on the ground floor, or, more likely, in the basement that Verano had just spotted.

A cellar window (whose lock he forced a little) was his way in, so that the beekeeper/ radio ham could not suspect the presence of an intruder. Teddy Verano, therefore, slipped into the unknown and the very dark basement. It was pretty big and, he vaguely realized, stretched out behind the house through some rather long shacks that he had noticed looked very recently built.

It was dark. It was cold.

Teddy Verano could not see a thing, but he moved forward following the metal cables from the huge installation, which was so unusual in such a place.

Two things struck him as weird and piqued his curiosity. First of all, the strong odor in the dark air. Not a foul smell, but very fragrant, sometimes sweet, even too sweet, but mixed with a more offensive staleness. Secondly, there seemed to be a background sound in this kind of underground passage. A muffled hum, a constant purring...

He had slid through the window so fast that it had closed behind him and he was now a little lost. He had a hard time getting his bearings and figuring out exactly what could be surrounding him.

He heard, very faintly, the sound of the van that the beekeeper must have been parking in the garage. And he thought that the whole space must be sound-proofed, that this weird man had really built something bizarre down here.

The farther he advanced, the louder the muffled humming became. And, little by little, his eyes got used to the dark. He found metal objects, cables and electrodes, film reels and a camera that, for an amateur, was quite an investment, both in money and time.

In this workshop the kids from town go and work whenever they want... They take classes... improve their skills... but if they told me that good old Jules Verrier gets something out of this work, that he gets done for free, I wouldn't be at all surprised.

A door. It was open. And it was even darker in the room before him.

He listened. Still the constant humming. But not a sound from the lord of the manor.

Teddy took a chance and groped around for a light switch. He turned it on and, to no surprise discovered the room of the tiny film club. A dozen seats, more or less. Walls hung with black velvet. A small but respectably sized screen at the back. Next to him was the projector. Teddy took a minute to look at everything.

The Cerisiers film club... that follows the training where they work all together, or almost, on everything dealing with the film industry... Great, but...

He had a strange smile on his face.

I guess I'm only finding out what anybody can find out. What everybody in Cerisiers already knows. What Jules Verrier wants to show everybody.

He grinned.

I'd really like to find out more than Monsieur Everybody is allowed to see... like, maybe, Jules Verrier's secret.

He jumped, alarmed by a noise in the distance. He quickly switched off the light and stood in the dark. He did not want to use his small flashlight instead of coping with the dark. He did not move for a minute. No, Verrier was not coming down, at least for the moment.

To be on the safe side, Teddy Verano did not turn the light back on. He groped along the wall until he found another door hidden behind the black drapes.

The mystery starts here... Too bad Gerard isn't with me... This is where it really gets interesting...

While talking to himself, he took out his lock tools, the ones that he got Gerard to use, and the padlock did not last long. He went through the door into a third part of the basement. Then he stopped and kept silent.

Still the humming. But it seemed louder. And the smell, even stronger and more pungent from the sweetness, more nauseating too. Suddenly, he thought he understood.

The source of the first was the source of the second. Except that around him, he thought he felt something moving.

Or someone?

In the dark, very dark, in this room, probably also lined with velvet, but more mysterious, more secret, reserved for the initiated or who knows? For Jules Verrier alone? Were there... human shapes?

This premonition was becoming annoying. He could have sworn that he was not alone in this part of the basement. And yet, he did not really know if there was a living thing—or things—around him.

Oh well... I'll chance the lights...

This time, listening in case Verrier decided to show up, he turned on the flashlight. And the circle of light started to roam through the black space.

He saw Edwige. Edwige Hossegor.

A photo. A magnificent poster. A well-known picture, already widespread in the trade.

Edwige—or Mephista—was all over the walls. One. Three. Ten. Twenty. He looked in vain for other stars, other faces. It only took a few seconds for him to be sure that in this room, there were nothing but images of Edwige Hossegor.

So, he was not mistaken. He was at the heart of the problem. But what was the solution? The unthinkable solution?

He threw caution to the wind and searched everywhere. He found more and more photos of Edwige in all her roles, in all attitudes, with that indiscretion, that kind of indecency that belongs to women who are in the public eye and who, since they are everywhere on the small screen, seem to be part of everyone's home.

Shelves with round, metal cases whose contents were obvious. Plus, these cases were marked. With no surprise, Teddy Verano read the titles of Edwige Hossegor's films, for both the big and small screen: *Lucifer's Daughter. The Witch of Paris. Infernal Passion...*

And naturally, a brand new reel was lying in the last case, shiny, polished: *The Vampires of Paris.*

The first episode. The reel stolen from the projection room on the Champs-Elysées... for which Daniel was murdered.

He was startled to find a bunch of photo plates neatly classified and arranged on wooden stands.

Enlargements... Hands...

He figured that the slender, delicate hands must belong to Edwige too.

So this is what he used to create his Mephista. Farnese got these finger-prints off the T.V. set of Jacques Lemoulin, stained with blood... and they were also on the knife that I found in Patrick Florent's apartment.

Edwige haunted the strange Monsieur Verrier. But this was still not a solution.

Thinking he heard a footstep, he turned off the flashlight and was again plunged in darkness, even darker after the light had disappeared. He listened. It seemed to him that, this time, Verrier was rummaging around, not too far from him. Probably in the first room of the basement where the workshop had been set up.

Better to get out of here before running into this guy. I'll have plenty of time to come back later.

Teddy Verano moved away, but bumped into something. It felt hard and cold, but with pleasant curves. His hands examined it and glided over an unquestionably feminine chest.

A mannequin.

The fragrance was heady. He turned on the flashlight, risking everything, knowing that Verrier might, at any time, come into the film club room.

This time, he was disappointed. He could have sworn he was about to see the face of the mannequin, and this face would be the marvelously recreated beauty of Baron Tragny's beloved. But there was nothing.

The head of the mannequin was totally blank. It was just a shape with the nose, eyes and mouth barely formed, without the slightest identity. But the feel of it and the smell...

Wax. A subtle, hard wax of incredible delicacy. Wax from a beehive. That pure, marvelous wax that bees make. The same wax that had been used for centuries for spells and for crafting the human dolls of their future victims. A wax doll, yes. But life-sized. An Edwige Hossegor fantasy. And Verrier could only be a staunch enemy of Edwige, or one of her secret admirers turned even more dangerous.

Teddy Verano had handled a few occult cases where sorcery had played a major role, so this was not the first wax doll he had run into. Still, he had never seen one of this size or this quality.

With his little light, he examined the mannequin. It was only sketched out, but so finely that the form of the star was undeniable. However, he searched in vain for the legendary signs that cursed occultists put on their statues to "baptize" them in fiendish ways. No pricks in the heart. There was no trace of blood, or nails, or hair.

Well, this is a rather odd kind of magic...

In spite of himself, he was thinking of magic. He was reaching the point where the ghost detective, the spiritualist fighting against the evil forces from beyond, and the rational man from the 20th century, had joined forces to search for a synthesis of the various elements, to connect the dots, to piece together the mysterious puzzle that had come out of both the visible and the tangible and the invisible and the intangible.

Magic or physics... But magic came before physics. It's an unexplored branch of physics, that's all.

He shuddered. There were footsteps next door. Now Verrier had unquestionably entered the projection room. Teddy Verano thought he heard him coming to the door.

He's going to see the padlock opened, the door ajar...

He pointed his circle of light all over, saw hundreds of Edwige's different expressions flash by, until he finally found what he was looking for. There was another exit behind a huge poster of Edwige in the role of Mephista.

Teddy Verano jumped on it, pushed and felt no resistance. The door was not even locked. No doubt Verrier felt safe in this area that he kept secret from his appreciative volunteers. The detective went in, and shut the door behind him.

He found himself in the dark again, suddenly gasping for air. He had just seen, or rather glimpsed, a brighter basement that opened onto the outside, not with windows but only with a bunch of slits cut into the whitewashed wall. In front of him were at least 30 beehives in two rows on either side of the room.

And the bees ruled this place. It was their home. They were buzzing, causing the hum that he had stupidly not recognized before, being preoccupied as he was with all the other problems. Bees everywhere. Two swarms buzzing around and with him being without any special protection, he would not last long in their company.

Moreover, Teddy Verano had seen that the bee room had no exit. No other door, but the one to the room full Edwige/Mephista pictures.

The insects left and came back with their load of pollen through the slits. Here, they were totally protected from bad weather and accidents. Verrier could take care of his " guests," collect the honey for his business, and the wax for his weird hobby, completely safe and secure. But it would probably be better not to venture further into the beekeeping zone without the suit, gloves and helmet that friends of the royal jelly always wear.

Teddy Verano was almost scared. He was panting in the dark and heard one or two bees buzzing around him. Apparently, during the brief time that the door had been open, they had flown through and were now lost in the darkness, flying around, searching in vain for a way out.

For a very short minute, Teddy Verano wondered what he should do.

Then, behind him, the door to the projection room opened up.

CHAPTER XV

Because the absurdity of the situation, Teddy Verano wondered for a split second if he was going to tremble in fear or break out laughing.

He was in the dark after turning off his flashlight and the shape that entered was cut out of the bright backlight coming from the film club in such a way that he saw a fat, grotesque monster with a swollen head, the color of burnt sienna, something like a diver's suit to explain the obesity of the little man blown up like an advertisement for a tire company.

And this strange little man stopped, looked at him in plain sight, because the light shone on the detective, and he mumbled:

"I knew there was someone here. They told me... They were disturbed, naturally."

He flipped the light switch. The room lit up and, from every inch of it, Edwige Hossegor smiled, leered and kept watch from her beautiful, expressive, incredibly fascinating face. Teddy Verano was more affected by not analyzing them, but he was struck by the arrangement of the posters, carefully classified, not random, so that everywhere in the room, the observer was dominated by Edwige's personality emanating from the pictures.

"Who are you? What are you doing in my house?"

Jules Verrier—since it was him, of course—was in no hurry to talk. Thus, he gave Teddy Verano some time, very little to be sure, but enough so that the detective could pull himself together a little.

"Go on, answer me. And don't try to run away. They told me you were here. They helped me out. They're strong allies and they can defend me... attack you if necessary."

"Who are you talking about, Monsieur? Your bees, I guess?"

Verrier did not have time to answer. Teddy Verano continued right away:

"You can be sure that I mean no harm to your charming tenants. It's not for them that I let myself in here... while you were gone."

"So you're not a thief? Well..."

Teddy Verano thought twice about saying he was a salesman, but rejected the notion. Instead, he blurted out:

"I'm here... for her."

He waved his hand around the posters, the hundreds of Edwiges and, in the middle of the room, the weird wax figure sitting there like a phantom of a naked woman, impersonal and a little scary.

Verrier was really a strange man. He started talking, apparently accepting the unusual intrusion.

"For her," he did not sound surprised. "So, you too..."

Teddy Verano tried to play along. He lowered his head and tried to look devastated.

"Yes, me too."

He made a quick examination of Verrier's costume. Just the overalls, the helmet and the gloves, the armor of a man working with beehives to protect himself against the stings, which had made him look so weird in the backlight.

Behind the helmet's grill, Verrier's beady eyes scrutinized the detective.

"If I understand correctly, you're in love with her?"

Teddy Verano figured it was best to play the ashamed older man who had fallen into the love trap of a younger woman.

The beekeeper/film buff grinned.

"And you thought… that I was also in love with her? The kids in Cerisiers told you that, didn't they? That's a good one!"

Teddy Verano was astonished by his attitude and was already convinced that he was dealing with a madman. But he lied straight off:

"Yes, the kids. The fans of your film club. All of them, deep down, have a crush on Edwige Hossegor. All of them come here… to work a little, to be with you, but especially for her…"

"In love? At my age!" Verrier snorted a laugh. "That's fine for the poor little morons. Oh, I'm not criticizing… Without them and the volunteer work I get them to do, I couldn't have created what I did. And my inventions wouldn't be finished. One man alone could never have installed my antennas or developed my 3D cinemascope. My invention… Yes, my little lover of Edwige Hossegor, it *is* my invention… that no one, get it, no one has seen working yet..."

He laughed again but this one rang out like a bell.

"Except the idiots who… OK, that's enough. They won't be talking."

Teddy Verano made a quick association of ideas and his heart froze. Verrier stepped forward. The detective stayed on guard. But the weird man in his costume passed by without making the slightest move and he did something very simple. He opened the second door of the room covered with pictures of Edwige. The door going to the beehives.

Teddy Verano shuddered but all he said was:

"My Lord, Monsieur, please be kind enough to close that door. Your tenants are lovely, I'm sure, but we must be careful around beehives. I saw a couple of swarms buzzing around and if one of them came in here…"

"You're right," Jules Verrier said. "But I need the bees. Without them, she wouldn't exist."

He pointed to the wax woman, the woman whose form resembled a naked Edwige Hossegor but without a face, which intrigued Teddy Verano.

"Thanks to my bees, I was able to… sculpt in the purity of their impeccable wax."

"I can appreciate that. But if you closed the door…"

"You're scared? I understand. But no, I won't close it. Though I feel your anxiety. Come and follow me."

He walked into the film club and Teddy Verano followed him rather nervously. This man worried him a little, but he had often fought, even with bare hands, against criminals and madmen. And Verrier certainly belonged to the latter category.

But what could a man do, as strong and determined and clever as he might be, against a swarm of deadly bees?

He would have sworn to it that Verrier was capable of all kinds of treachery and the most dangerous actions. However, the man seemed to have lost interest in him. He was going to one of the drapes and lifting it to uncover a closet door. He opened it and Teddy saw several overalls of different sizes, helmets with thick veils making a grill of the face and pairs of gloves.

He held out some gloves and a helmet.

"Start by putting these on. You won't be in any danger in a minute. Wait and I'll look for your size."

Teddy Verano breathed more easily. After all, things were not turning out so badly. But he was wary nonetheless.

"Ah! That's the one I was looking for. This should fit. Pretty much at least."

"I'm sure it will do fine," Teddy Verano said in a hurry to put on the protection as he could hear the faint but characteristic buzzing coming from the poster room. The bees, slowly but surely, were filling it up.

He put on the helmet. Verrier had to tell him:

"Not like that."

He adjusted it and gave him the gloves. Then he held out the overalls.

"I'll help you."

Very quickly, Teddy Verano experienced the feeling that he should not let Verrier do it. When a man goes behind you, even to help put on a special suit that you are not used to, all kinds of dirty tricks are possible.

But he pretended to stay calm, in spite of the general fear looming over him from the strange personality of this man and from the vibrations of the light, graceful, harmonious wings that smelled sweetly of honey but were as dangerous as dozens, hundreds of little poisonous darts. A painful poison that at high dose could cause serious, if not lethal, reactions.

Everything happened in a flash. Verrier adjusted the overalls.

"There, that'll do."

"I can't find the arms. Oh…"

He could not avoid the impact; he staggered under the blow that he had felt coming, but could not avoid. Everything started spinning. Verrier, although not a big man, had taken the man he had just subdued, pushed and shoved him, taken advantage of his semi-consciousness to get him back into the poster room and throw him into a metal chair.

Teddy Verano gasped inside the helmet. His hands were still protected by the gloves. Doubly protected, because he was also closed up inside the loose-fitting and undoubtedly tampered with suit that worked like a straightjacket, binding his chest and arms and putting him at the mercy of his captor.

There was light coming from both the lamps and the open door of the beehive. The bees flew in, one after another, and they swarmed together, their constant buzzing getting louder and louder.

Teddy Verano, who had been hit at the base of his neck, rattling his spine, was aware of his blunder. He wanted to see how far the other would go and he had let himself be outmaneuvered. With his head in a fog, he thought vaguely: *Gerard wouldn't have been so stupid... Less stupid for sure.*

Verrier was watching him now, rubbing his gloved hands. He started laughing again. Then he stopped and screeched:

"Idiot! You're an idiot if you take me for one! I know you don't give a damn about the bees. Or the film club. And you're no more a salesman than I am. Yes, yes, I saw my little friends from Cerisiers. They told me. I knew you were here... and then the bees were acting funny... You'd disturbed them... I know... I talk to them. So, tell me, is this what you're looking for? My machine? You, too, want to recreate, wherever and whenever you want, the woman you desire? The marvelous, wonderful creature..."

He pointed to the wax woman, the faceless woman standing there, looking graceful, lascivious and disturbing all at the same time.

"But you don't know... you don't understand... nobody knows or understands... except me, alone... how to animate her. You have to take her soul!"

Teddy Verano had dealt with these kinds of monsters and geniuses before, these mad scientists, fiendish inventors halfway between scientific realism and the depravity that comes from excessive occult practices. He was seeing one more of them here, he was sure. But what kind? And what was Verrier trying to say with all his talking.

The bees were still entering. Verrier decided to close the door.

"No... Go away... It'd be better for me to give you a little demonstration..."

Teddy Verano did not move. Should he jump up and ram into his belly? Or better yet, kick out at him? He could have done it. Verrier was not young and probably not very strong, even if he had a wicked chop, as he had proved. But he had heard the word "demonstration." Now he had to know.

This kind of madman loved to show off his knowledge. Or his perversion. And Teddy Verano had already paid to find out that Jules Verrier's secret was not a fantasy, but that he really had invented something fantastic.

He waited. He knew that he was about to see the true secret of Mephista.

CHAPTER XVI

Jules Verrier's beady little eyes sparkled in a weird way behind his protective grill.

A show-off? Teddy Verano thought. *Engineer? Or what? Obviously an extraordinary man, but also a megalomaniac... who can't resist the sadistic pleasure of showing what he can do.*

Verrier was watching him. He must have feared some kind of trick and was on his guard. But he was talking, talking, talking as he moved the drapes to reveal other photos, sketches, drawings, all of them representing the beautiful star of the O.R.T.F. and also some projectors, spotlights and cameras, obviously "rigged."

And the monologue went on.

"In love? Me, in love? That's for others, Monsieur. Idiots get a crush on a woman, dream of her all the more passionately as she seems both close to them and very far away. Never, I'm sure, since the invention of the television has such madness in a man's brain been as strong..."

He arranged his projectors with precision derived from long practice. Teddy Verano noticed that everything seemed centered on the wax figure, gloomy and cold, faceless and soulless, the pale, sad specter, the opposite of his fiery speech.

"Edwige Hossegor is both the intimate friend and the distant princess. She visits our houses... and you know that such artists are pretty much inaccessible. But there are still crazy men who create a whole romance around her. Me, I knew the real Edwige. Not the one everyone thinks... Not the one those close to her, her family and friends, know or think they know..."

He laughed sneeringly.

"Even her lovers. That idiot Tragny. You can sleep with a woman and not know anything about her soul... and it's her soul that interests me. A soul that I wanted, that I want, that I succeeded in pouring into the wax, the pure wax, the fine, malleable and living wax from my dear little bees..."

He was still keeping busy. Four projectors were now pointing at the wax doll. And countless spots that he was adjusting one by one. Teddy Verano, now determined not to react before learning everything, could not figure out what all this would be able to do.

Verrier hooked up some wires.

"A woman! Ha! Call her an actress to tell the truth... Edwige Hossegor... Always the roles that reveal her... She hurts, tortures, kills... That's her, the real her... The killer, the she-demon..." With a theatrical wave of his hand, glorified, he shouted, "*Mephista!*"

Here we go, Teddy thought, who had not missed a word though he was pretending to be groggy, in pain, still not recovered from the blow to the neck.

"The heart of the problem is the soul of that woman. Mephista reveals it… But it's all a show, on T.V., not reality… So, I wanted it to be reality…" He waved some more. "Some men have seen the real Mephista. She came. She killed. They won't tell. ."

His hands were shaking, clenching at empty air.

"In love with her… Stupid boys… One guy named Lemoulin… A projectionist, a boy too… But this other one…"

Teddy really wanted to try to focus his speech by asking questions, but he chose to stay quiet after the reference to Patrick Florent.

Jules Verrier looked calmer. For a few seconds, he checked all his machines. Then he announced:

"You're going to see the true Mephista."

Fascinating, Teddy thought, but did not say. He saw a vicious enough smile on the face of the beekeeper, who had not bothered to take off his suit, or Teddy's for that matter.

Verrier continued:

"You understand that you won't be able to tell anyone about this. You will see Mephista, and then… it's over… She is death… She kills."

Teddy Verano trembled on hearing this. A monster, yes. And what had this monster invented?

Verrier had also closed the door to the film club.

"We're almost ready. You're about to see."

He looked jubilant. He turned off the lights and everything disappeared. Teddy Verano sat in the dark. He could not see the posters, nor the machines, nor the wax figure, nor Jules Verrier. But he heard the latter moving around in the shadows. And he also heard the buzzing of a few bees who could not return to the hives. One of them hit his grill, that luckily protected his face in the dark.

He broke out in a cold sweat. He waited.

And, all of a sudden, he could not hold back a cry of surprise, almost of awe. Edwige Hossegor was standing in front of him, emerging from the darkness.

At least, her face and her head. Just a head, motionless, floating in the dark, at the same height as a human. And Teddy Verano guessed that she was exactly the same height as Edwige.

Jules Verrier seemed satisfied.

"You see, what did I tell you? It's really her, isn't it?"

Teddy Verano could barely see him, standing in the shadows by his machines.

The detective understood right away. It was a very meticulous and, no doubt, very sophisticated focusing system of a projector in color and in relief. Three-dimensional rays, apparently, casting on the neuter, impersonal wax head a series of photos, of superimposed images, expertly arranged to create the relief, the color, the exact features of Edwige Hossegor with such accuracy that covered every pore of her skin. It was her, unquestionably her. To die for.

"There you go," Verrier said. "Nice work, isn't it? Except, in the end, nothing extraordinary. Henri Chrétien's process,[7] cinemascope, synchronized with I don't know how many techniques... See, Monsieur, it's others who invented it. Not me. I took their ideas. I made my little idiots work, my little fans as you say. All the kids from the village who are crazy about movies and radio. And we arranged all this. To create Mephista."

Teddy Verano saw his hand—he had taken a glove off to adjust the machines—come out of the shadows and caress the face of the apparition.

"Pretty Mephista. But only a wax doll, a mannequin. Not much. Anyone can do the same." He groaned suddenly. "Except, what the others don't know how to do is how to animate the statue. To put into this lifeless puppet the soul of Edwige Hossegor—the soul of the true Mephista. Do you know what a spell is?"

Teddy Verano figured it best to give him a toneless, muffled "Yes."

"My invention, my real invention... is this machine."

In the dark, he tapped on a metal box that the detective could barely see.

"A machine to cast a spell. It's tuned, permanently, on Edwige Hossegor. A hyper-hypnotizer, you might say."

The craziest ideas were dancing through Teddy Verano's brain, but were now starting to line up.

"Edwige. Mephista. My rays activate the doll. And my hypnotizer works on her, on the woman whose spirit has to be transmuted into the robot. Are you following me?"

Teddy Verano was listening, but remained still, fascinated by the immaculate face that was still emerging, like a phantom, a seductive phantom, and frighteningly real.

The grotesque hands of the madman were twirling around the waxen head on which the projectors were building the mask that looked so much like the actress.

"You see... she's lifeless. Suppose I got my robot working. Oh, don't even try, it's my secret. A subtle molecular action on the atoms of the wax. And it moves, it walks, it seems alive... I have made the perfect television that transmits not just the image but *the soul itself!*"

---

[7] Professor Henri Chretien (1879-1956) is known for his telescopes as well as the Hypergonar lenses for anamorphic movies. In December 1952, 20th Century Fox acquired his device and created the name of CinemaScope for it. However many years before, a few anamorphic movies had been produced with his Hypergonar lens in France and, at the Expo 1937 in Paris, Chretien presented two movies with a similar concept to Cinerama.

A mocking laugh.

"My kids built a wonderful antenna for me. I promised them I would use it to receive broadcasts from all over the world. What they don't know is that, in truth, it's not just a receiver, but a transmitter as well, that they built according to my directions. They're not smart enough to understand. Apprentices. Very nice, very devoted, but..."

He walked around the wax figure whose nudity was draped in darkness under the glaringly bright head.

"A robot that walks, that has Edwige's face, that can kill, if and when I want... It's not enough. It has to be her who strikes, who kisses, who kills like she seduces. And that's where I have reached the sublime."

Teddy Verano heard him panting hoarsely in the dark.

"It wouldn't be complete if it was just a mechanical toy. No, I wanted to go farther. That it really be Mephista who kills, one after another, all those ridiculous admirers. A wonderful adventure, isn't it? The monstrous spider, the praying mantis devouring its lovers."

He walked around the wax figure.

"An ordinary body... nothing but a mannequin... but by infusing Edwige's soul in it, everything becomes real. And whoever sees her coming, walking, approaching, will die under her spell. Because they see Edwige, they expect Edwige, they feel like they're embracing Edwige... when it's really Mephista.'

All of a sudden, he flipped some switches and Teddy Verano was surprised to see a small screen appear. Verrier fiddled with the television machine that Verano guessed was tuned to very specific transmissions. The images were blurry at first, but quickly cleared up. The detective was not surprised to see Rue du Ranelagh, the Tragny home, then the salon and Edwige's bedroom.

"I stay in communication," the engineer explained smugly, in the throes of ecstasy. "That's why I recognized you, Monsieur. So let's see... you found my trail. That's very good. And now, I'm going to give you to Mephista. Mephista will kill you." In almost a whisper he muttered, "I mean, really, Edwige Hossegor. Your friend."

For a minute, he stopped talking. Teddy Verano heard a machine humming. Probably the metal box he had called the mechanical super-hypnotizer.

It acts on Edwige's brain and captures her brain waves, deduced Teddy Verano. *Then, it creates an illusionary aura around the robot, coming from Edwige herself, that fools the people who see it by showing her as she is at the moment of transmission... like Lemoulin and Daniel... like Tragny and me that night... like Gerard and Patrick Florent... How nice, how crazy! That's why we found no trace of clothing. There's nothing but a bunch of animated wax and an extraordinary film in color, in 3-D, without a screen... that casts a spell on those who view it...*

But Verrier was getting upset. The screen was flashing through the different rooms in Tragny's house. They saw only two people: Isabelle and Joseph finishing their dinner.

"Hold on… So, she's not there. Well, I assure you, my machine is perfect. I'll find her."

It took some time. Verrier looked lost as Teddy Verano watched confused images roll by and heard muffled, indistinguishable sounds. And then, finally, Edwige's face appeared. Very hazy. In the dark.

There were two people at her side and all three looked squeezed together. The view tracked out, showing two more faces, a little farther apart.

Teddy Verano gasped. He was seeing a car. Baron Tragny's Caravelle that the diabolical inventor had just spotted. Edwige was sitting in the back between Eva Mellion and Patrick Florent. Baron Tragny was in front, driving, with Gerard next to him.

Teddy Verano understood right away. Verrier, too, because he laughed and shouted:

"I was looking for her and she's coming here! She's coming here! With her entourage, her defenders…"

He turned a knob and Teddy saw some lights blink.

"I'll get the hypnotizer working. In three minutes, Edwige Hossegor will pass out. In three minutes, her soul will be here, imprisoned in the wax figure. And once again, it will be time for Mephista to walk the Earth!"

CHAPTER XVII

React... Act... Fight... Do something...

Everything flew by insanely fast in Teddy Verano's mind. Now he knew. A fiendish inventor. An extraordinary genius. An occultist to boot. Very clever. Very crafty. And totally insane.

Teddy Verano knew enough about the scheme. He knew not only the basics of the system that only experienced physicists could have explained and pieced together, but also the particular process used by the gifted but evil bee-keeper.

Mephista, his Mephista, was only the material support of the demon he had unleashed against the poor men who were only guilty of falling in love with Edwige Hossegor.

Edwige, whom he chose for her acting, for her roles in which he found an inherent personality, infernal and evil, that seduced him by was is the exact opposite of natural feminine seduction.

At the same time, he had built the artificial likeness of Edwige/Mephista with photos and films. He collected posters, pictures and films, stole what he had to and succeeding in getting the image of the O.R.T.F. star in thousands of copies in every pose. He worked in the shadows, slowly and patiently, to build up this perfect likeness of the woman. But even projected onto the wax robot that he brought to life with some unknown, unimaginable, terrifying process, it still was not enough.

So, he cast a spell upon Edwige. Mechanically. Certainly by using the grimoirs of the ancient sorcerers who, over the centuries, had already performed this remote control over human beings, long before the discoveries of Hertz, Branly, Marconi and Ferrié. Because these ancient wizards knew how to use brain waves, which they could not see nor understand, but they could feel and bend to their will and whim.

A machine to cast spells.

A special "television" that showed Edwige and her friends in the Caravelle speeding toward Cerisiers in search of Teddy Verano, in pursuit of the monstrous Mephista. Because Yvonne had alerted Gerard who had told Tragny and Edwige. Edwige who always wanted to know the truth about her situation. They were coming.

To know how far away they were was impossible. Teddy Verano only saw the potential danger. The monster was going to capture Edwige's soul, perhaps permanently, animate Mephista, arm her and take hellish pleasure in murdering all her friends, whom he thought would soon be at his mercy.

Teddy Verano's arms were tied, tightly, flat against his body, but he was wound up, ready to pounce.

"Watch this!" Jules Verrier says. "And watch out!"

All of a sudden, just when the detective was about to jump and use his head as a battering ram, he saw a shower of sparks flash in front of him. It crackled for a second before disappearing, leaving behind a strong, awful smell.

Verrier choked on his laughter.

"You don't know everything yet. I can also strike from a distance. I can destroy. Once before, you tried to capture Mephista and I destroyed her like this. I can unleash the same fires against you…"

Teddy Verano became frozen stiff. He was stunned by what he has just learned. Verrier's science went farther than he thought. On seeing Gerard, Patrick Florent and Teddy Verano corner the animated monster in the apartment on the Boulevard Voltaire, the mad genius had used this process to hit her with his bolt of sparks. He did not destroy her, only melted the wax so it became nothing but a shapeless mass.

Teddy Verano felt lost for a moment. He was still sitting there, tensed up, trying to figure out what to do next. Verrier was fiddling with his metal box. On the screen, the detective could still see inside the Caravelle.

The inventor let out a cry of triumph.

Edwige collapsed in the car. Eva and Patrick were in a panic. Tragny and Gerard turned around and the baron stopped the car.

"Now, we won't be disturbed for a while," Verrier said.

Teddy Verano, whose heart was pounding, pulled himself together but he felt the other watching him closely.

"Don't move now… you haven't seen everything yet. Here's my master-piece… Mephista… Mephista alive… Mephista with the spirit of the woman whom all men love to love…"

Other spotlights were suddenly turned on. It was not just the miraculous face, but Edwige Hossegor's entire body that now appeared.

Edwige in a tailored dress. *Edwige exactly as she was right now in the Caravelle.*

Edwige, whose soul this infernal machine had just captured in order to infuse it into the wax robot. And it was radiating life, as if this wretched puppet with its halo of visible waves, was really Edwige. It was fake, as fake as could be, but Teddy could have sworn that it was really her.

Mephista looked at him.

Mephista, coming out of the surrounding darkness, the only thing lit up in the darkened room, like a dazzling ghost. Mephista, who gave him a seductive, frightening smile that belonged to the actress of *The Vampires of Paris.*

Jules Verrier came up from behind her, holding something out to the robot, which grabbed it.

A knife.

The blade sparkled in the spotlight.

Mephista started to walk.

Teddy Verano was horrified to hear her speak to him:

"Dear friend, what a joy to see you again."

It was all here—even her voice. Totally real.

Mephista, falsely alive, but maybe alive nonetheless, even though she was just a pile of wax energized by a physical process, carried Edwige's soul in her, or rather the artificial soul of the actress who had made up all the diabolical roles she had played so well.

Although Teddy Verano had his hands tied, and serious cramps in his shoulders from the tightened suit, his lower body was still free. He made his move, and threw the powerful kick he had been keeping in store for Jules Verrier straight at Mephista.

Verrier cried out in anger as the she-demon was thrown off balance, fell over and broke apart. The mad inventor went berserk, seeing his masterpiece damaged. He lost his head, rushed forward and got kicked in turn. Right in the shin, which threw him to the ground howling in pain.

Teddy Verano, his arms still tied up, jumped over the body and headed for the machines. He kicked them all over, trying to cause a short circuit and break the dreadful installation. Sparks flew. Then a flame leaped up.

The detective had time to step back. And right at that moment, he looked at the television screen. He still saw Edwige with Eva trying to wake her up. But the three men were not in the car. Had they already arrived?

That was when Verrier got up, groaning, and stumbled to the back door that led to the hive room and disappeared. What was he doing? Teddy Verano heard him, figured it out and rushed over...

In a mad rage, Verrier was knocking over his beehives and, in the half-light of the basement coming from the setting sun through the slits, the detective saw the whirling swarms, the spinning bees, the panicking, confused insects in living clouds.

Verrier had sensed the threat of intruders already nearby, who were about to invade his property, and was playing his final card.

Gerard, young Patrick and the baron... If they came in... If they ran into the angry bees...

Verrier in his beekeeper outfit was safe. Teddy Verano, too, was protected by his gear. But he knew that he had to stop his friends from coming in, not only because of the bees but also the catastrophe in progress.

The fire in the machines!

He kicked over the wreckage of the wax robot to duplicate what had happened in Patrick Florent's apartment. The fire began to consume the pile of wax, which melted and started smoking.

Verrier returned and ran at Teddy Verano. With one last effort, the detective barrel headed first into his stomach and threw him back into the hive room.

Verrier tripped over one of the hives.

The fall broke the grill on his helmet.

There was a loud cry, an inhuman cry, which echoed through all the rooms. An angry swarm attacked Verrier, flew into his clothes, devoured his face, penetrated everywhere, now that his suit was no longer protecting him.

Meanwhile, Tragny, Gerard and Patrick had entered Verrier's property. They had begun to search all over, running around like madmen.

Suddenly, a smoke cloud appeared and they saw an armless monster running toward them. A weird, clumsy thing with a big head that looked swollen, yelling at them, "Run away! Run away! The bees! The bees!"

Edwige woke up slowly. Once again, she had fainted. She had been Mephista. Now she could remember terrible, confused, frightening things.

They surrounded her. Friendly voices saying soothing things.

Baron Tragny hugged her and covered her face with kisses.

A little later, they would tell her the whole story, since she wanted to know everything. What Jules Verrier did. What he built. The danger that an actress might face when playing wicked characters.

The mad inventor was in sorry shape. He would pull through, undoubtedly, but the bees had wreaked havoc on his body. The doctors wondered whether his reason would survive.

The smoke had spread everywhere and got the better of the bees. Specialists came to pick them up and save what they can.

Verrier's fantastic machines, however, had been destroyed, short-circuited, burned to rubble. No one would get much out of them. None of the mechanical spell casting survived the destruction of the laboratory. Teddy Verano thought it was better that way for everyone.

He looked looks at Edwige Hossegor's beautiful face. What might lie, sometimes, deep inside a woman's spirit? For, in the end, the mysterious Mephista, as different as she was, was still born from within the secret depths of the actress' soul...

Maurice Limat

MEPHISTA
CONTRE MEPHISTA

ANGOISSE

FLEUVE NOIR

MEPHISTA VS MEPHISTA

CHAPTER I

Martine woke up with a start. She shuddered right away. It was past 6 a.m. She must have gone to sleep an hour earlier after staying awake most of the night.

Olga was not back. Her twin bed was still made.

The sad, dingy morning light struck the tiles so that the room, in spite of the two girls' efforts, looked gloomy. They had never been able to do a thing about it since they'd come to Paris, since the two childhood friends had pooled their hopes together. Bad luck had been hounding the girls from Lille for a year now.

Martine, the more prudent, more reserved, of the two, was trying to make a career as a secretary, with the secret hope of getting into public relations with a big firm someday. Her degrees, she believed, were perfect for it. And she believed her job ideal. Unfortunately, after six months, her boss, a dynamic young man and a bachelor, who had begun to look upon her as more than just an employee, had been killed in a stupid car accident. His replacement was more ambitious and he had let her go.

Two or three jobs later. All failures…

Olga was also struggling. The tall dark-haired girl with deep, dark eyes and a rather severe beauty, had a strange, troubling effect on the male sex. A few days after their arrival in Paris, she had unveiled her secrets, which she had never revealed to Martine before. She wanted to act on the stage, or in movies, or television.

Martine was not the kind to believe in such things and laughed at first. But Olga was serious, and, right away, enrolled in one of those famous acting classes where the professors, usually failed actors and not always honorable, would exploit the true or supposed gifts of an unbelievable number of young men and women seduced by the mirage of the spotlights.

However, Olga appeared to have some talent. Moreover, her physique seemed to interest some directors. Alas… after a few months, not much had come out of all this. She had been an extra in one or two films, but then came the union fees to pay, the waiting in producers' offices, the beginning of disillusionment.

Martine was bravely looking for work in more reasonable, less fanciful occupations. With her noble character, she swore she would never abandon Olga, all the while lecturing her and criticizing her for wasting her time on such nonsense. Olga shot back that, even though Martine was involved in nothing artistic, she was having no better success.

In fact, the two girls, face to face, had to admit that their bad luck, at least in part, had a common source: their strict honesty.

Neither of them had ever been willing to give in to the self-serving propositions of certain men. Proud Olga and pure Martine had been able to keep their independence, only looking at boys whom they could trust. No compromise of any kind.

Sometimes, in spite of their sad days, they could still take each other by the hand and comfort each other.

"No, it'd be too stupid, too pathetic. We're not hussies. A boy, yes, with all our heart, when we can open our arms to him for the simple joy of being with him, with pleasure. But to accept this..."

Offers of thinly disguised prostitution disgusted them and, in their mutual respect, they forged a stronger bond that joined them together and helped them live, and survive the bad days.

But the bad days went on and on. Neither of them earned any more money. Rent went unpaid and, the night before, a glum-looking, ashamed employee had come to seal off the electric meter.

November was gray and the cold rain did not help matters. The refrigerator, now useless since there was no more electricity, was empty. Martine was shivering as she remembered that there was still some coffee left...

She was worried, very worried. Olga had still not come home. This never happened, at least not without her friend telling her. She was deeply, sincerely attached to Olga, and she thought the feeling was mutual.

Crazy ideas flashed through Martine's mind. An accident? Paris was a fertile land for traps, for all kinds of incidents... And for a young woman alone...

Of course, Olga, although slender, was not a weak woman; she looked older than 24, which only made her more attractive. Martine was scared for her.

Over the last few days, she had not seemed herself. She went out a lot, claiming to be doing the rounds of the studios and agents for bit parts, a nice euphemism for being an extra. She had dropped off countless photos, snapshots that had bankrupted her. One of the photos was framed on a small table.

Martine, the blonde, the sweet Martine, looked at Olga's beautiful face. With its tinge of femme fatale, it should certainly have caught the attention of movie producers.

It was now 6:30 a.m.

Blinking her eyes a little wildly Martine got up, shivering in her pajamas. Just to be sure, she glanced outside. The sun was struggling to break through. The surrounding fog added another gloomy aspect to the season.

Martine was starting to miss her home in the north. She had come to Paris. Why, she now asked herself? Return to her family? That would be to admit failure and face the ironic smiles, the phony courtesies and the hostile climate that would grow around her.

Olga had told her: "I'll never go back."

And now... after she had been gone for the night...

A romantic adventure? Possible. That would be the least bad.

Martine began preparing her coffee.

All of a sudden her heart froze. She could not even do this simple thing. There was no electricity. The electric bill had not been paid and the power had been cut off.

Martine was dazed for a minute. Then the situation appeared to her in all its horror. She was almost willing to drink a little cold coffee, but it made her sick to her stomach and she refused.

She went back to her room and flopped onto her bed, feeling all the misery weighing down on her, thinking that maybe she would never see Olga again.

She gave up. Tears rolled down her cheeks and sobs convulsed her frail shoulders. Her hair veiled her haggard face that her weeping only ravaged more.

Images popped up that she could not chase away. Olga falling in the metro. Olga kidnapped by some human traffickers. Olga as a corpse, floating in the dirty water of the Seine.

A knock at the door made her jump.

She sniffled, looked around for a handkerchief, and tried to straighten out her hair.

Someone was knocking. But why not ring the doorbell? Then, she realized: no more electricity. They could not ring.

She got up but the door had ready opened.

"Olga! At last!"

In her distress Martine had finally found something to be happy about.

Olga stood very straight, holding her key.

"I knocked to warn you... Stay calm..."

Without thinking, Martine ran to hug her friend, but instead ran up against a kind of chill from pretty Olga.

"What's wrong with you?" she asked.

"Nothing, sweetie," said Olga. "Everything's fine."

Olga came in, threw her hat on her bed and took off her coat.

"Could you make me some coffee?" she inquired.

Martine looked like a schoolgirl caught red-handed.

"No more coffee... There's no more gas or electricity."

Olga did not look troubled at all. On the contrary, a kind of flame shone on her pretty face and in her dark eyes. To Martine, it looked like defiance.

"Sweetie, this will all be over soon."

"What do you mean?"

"I'll explain... later."

Olga flitted about, making herself at home. Martine started to get worried again.

"Olga, I was so scared... You didn't come home last night... I didn't sleep..."

"Poor baby! Forget about it."

"Tell me... Maybe you don't want to tell me, but..."

"Yes, you want to know where I was. I understand. I'll tell you... later... when the time's right."

She was in front of the dressing table, letting down her beautiful black hair. Martine watched her, having a hard time understanding her casual attitude. There was a long silence. All of a sudden, Martine sniffed the air.

"Olga..."

"What is it, sweetie?"

"Do you smell something? There's an odor..."

"An odor? You're imagining things."

"No, really, I swear. It's like... Oh, that's funny... It smells like sulfur... yes."

"You're tired, kitten. You should go back to bed."

"I don't want to sleep. Besides, you're here now."

Olga smiled in the mirror. But Martine did not see the usual tenderness in this smile of her friend whom she thought of as a sister. Olga kept combing her beautiful hair. Martine approached her, feeling uncomfortable.

"Say, Olga..."

"What is it now, honey?"

"Are you..."

Olga cut off the question with an ironic look, still through the mirror.

"Yes, sorry," Martine bit her lip. "I'm being nosy."

"No, really, you're being stupid."

And Olga turned around, pulled Martine to her and kissed her, putting an end to the conversation. Martine accepted the kiss, said nothing, but she still thought that a weird smell was wafting through the room... ever since Olga had come back.

After straightening out her hair, Olga suddenly turned around again.

"You've suffered, sweetie. You're unhappy. You can't even make a cup of hot coffee. Martine, you know how much I love you... Listen to me, the bad days are over."

"What do you mean?"

"They're over for me. Well, that means for you too. You'd better believe it. My good fortune will be yours."

"Your good fortune? Oh, Olga, have you found a job?"

Olga did not answer right away. She got up, grabbed her handbag and took out a lighter, which Martine did not recognize, along with a pack of cigarettes.

She offered one to Martine and started pacing the room, smoking nervously, looking suddenly exhilarated.

"I can't tell you. But it won't last... Well... Just tell yourself that I did what I had to... Success, fortune, glory... I want it all. I was born for it. And you'll be by my side, as always. You'll see how happy you'll be!"

"Olga, you're scaring me."

Olga's eyes flashed fire.

"Yes, me too, I'm scared," she said in a weird voice. "Scared... I was wrong. I'm sure I was wrong. Now everything's going to change. And I'm going to succeed. I'll rise to the top. I'll be an idolized star, loved by the public... Men will fall at my feet... I'll marry... I don't know who yet... But I know that I'll be the most beautiful, the most powerful, the richest woman..."

"Olga!"

"You'll marry too. Happiness has to be bought, you know."

"Olga, you didn't... accept to...?" Martine shrieked.

The would-be star laughed loudly, almost offensively.

"Accept what? The dirty, vile propositions of a man? Me, a prostitute? Ah, no, sweetie, we swore to say no to that sort of things, and I've kept my word, believe me. No, it's... I can't tell you. Just understand that I know, get it, I knew for sure that success is coming... in one day, maybe two, there will be news... They'll offer me something... and I'll be off for a new life. Don't worry, I won't forget you in my bliss."

Martine looked at Olga, understanding less and less.

Olga started talking, going back over all her projects, all her dreams, the same as all poor girls who surrender themselves to the dangerous occupation of being an actress. For a long time, becoming more and more excited, beguiling Martine with her crazy promises, trying to drag her along into the gilded country of happy daydreams.

An hour passed.

Olga smoked non-stop. Martine was floored and did not know what to say, wondering if her friend had not genuinely lost her marbles. At a certain point, she shouted:

"You don't realize, do you, we've got no more money and neither of us have any prospects for work. We owe two months' rent. We haven't paid the electric and the gas bills We have other bills. And the pawnbroker loaned me 30 francs. But I've got to pay him back in two days... Come on, Olga, please, pull yourself together... Or else, you've got some amazing job you don't want to tell me about. I have to wonder why..."

"I haven't got anything yet. But I know it's coming. Very soon."

"But how do you know?"

Once again, Olga kept silent, only to restart, an instant later, her muddled speech about her marvelous projects.

At 8:30 a.m., someone knocked at the door. It was a small man delivering a telegram.

"Mademoiselle Olga Mervil?"

Olga ransacked her purse and threw him a coin before ripping open the telegram in front of Martine's anxious eyes. Martine, who would never forget the look of wild triumph that washed over Olga's face, so that, for a second, she looked terrifying.

"Look here... Read... Teleor Productions. You know them? The ones who only make movies for international television... They're offering me to double for Edwige Hossegor... Oh, it's not a fortune, but with what they pay, it should tide us over for a while."

"Olga, is it true?"

"Look."

Martine took the telegram and started reading. But looking up, she saw, in the dresser mirror, Olga's face, since her back was turned to her. Her beautiful eyes were glaring strangely and she seemed to be staring at someone, or rather talking to someone.

Martine was scared. She thought she could read Olga's sensual lips repeating two words feverishly, in a whisper:

"Thank you... Thank you..."

Who was she talking to?

And why did Martine kept smelling the weird odor of sulfur lingering in the room?

CHAPTER II

"Take off your clothes, Mademoiselle."

Olga obeyed without a second's hesitation in front of the cold eyes of Eva Mellion, who they had said would meet her at Baron Tragny's house. It was there, on the Rue du Ranelagh, that Teleor Productions had sent Olga after their first interview.

Everyone knew, Olga as much as anyone else, of the tender relationship that linked Edwige Hossegor, the star whom she was supposed to double, with Baron Tragny, an ageing playboy whose fortune could hardly be counted. They had talked a lot about him in the papers and on the radio a few weeks earlier when Edwige had been the victim of a very strange adventure during the filming of the television serial, *The Vampires of Paris*.

In professional circles it was rumored that the beautiful actress' health had not improved much since the sinister affair. However, they were now publicizing a movie. For the big screen this time, and, breaking with custom, Teleor was in charge of the production.

What did all this matter to Olga Mervil?

She had wanted to get lucky and she thought she did. She did not want to think too much about the price she would have to pay...

For the last few hours, things had been very busy. There had been her return to the cold, miserable room where Martine was waiting for her. Then Teleor's message. Then the meeting at the production office. Then, after a simple phone call, she'd been asked her to meet with Eva Mellion, Edwige Hossegor's right hand woman, since a double could only get the final approval from the actress herself.

And before all this, there had been that weird night...

No, she must not think of it. Olga could already see big changes in her life. She had no regrets. She did not want regrets.

Everything was going fast, very fast. At Teleor, everything had seemed positive. They had called on her based solely on the photos from her file they had held for months. Now, she was at Edwige Hossegor's house and Eva Mellion was preparing to take her measurements.

Of course, Olga was a lot younger than Edwige, but she was certainly cut from the same mold. She looked like her and seemed perfect for the modest, thankless, but very lucrative role of "double," which meant staying in the shadows vis-à-vis the public and standing in for the star in the scenes about to be filmed. It was still not the coveted glory she sought, but Olga had good reasons to believe that all this was only a prelude to much greater success, the kind that exalted the likes of Brigitte Bardot, Sophia Loren and Marilyn Monroe.

Eva Mellion took a tape measure and walked up to Olga, now in her bra and panties. It was obvious that Eva admired the beautiful body standing before her. Although she stood still like a statue, with her pretty blonde hair cut like a boy's, framing her emotionless face, Olga could see the impression her natural beauty was making on Edwige Hossegor's public relations agent.

Olga obligingly let herself be measured around her chest, waist and thighs, the length of her legs, etc. It was clear that Eva Mellion had already had had several opportunities to measure and filter out, for some reason or other, minor actresses whose ambition was reduced to "doubling" Edwige. Eva did not say a word; she just made notes in a small notebook. It was important, in fact, to verify that Olga's measurements matched the star's, an indispensable detail for the rehearsals in front of the camera.

Olga was lost in a world of thoughts. Thus, then, she had not wasted her time. She had not been mistaken. The incredible experience that she had been bold enough to venture on was already producing results. In a few hours...

Maybe she was a little disappointed. Only a double...

Even just a supporting role would have been a lot better for her. Just a shadow in a film would have been more profitable for her than this sorry role where she had to disappear when the filming started and give her place to the "real actress."

But she must not think of such things. She was already sure she would be accepted. She would get paid a great deal. She would have the satisfaction of helping Martine by pulling her out of poverty.

Afterward... she would climb up through the ranks, she was sure of it. She was committed to this. Bitterly. One had to pay one's dues, then, later...

A "later" that Olga did not want to think about.

Eva Mellion got up off her knees and stepped back, silently observing the beautiful, almost nude, statue of flesh before her. A smile crossed her face and, from now on, the businesswoman was gone, replaced by the woman, plain and simple. And Olga saw then how pretty she was with her masculine haircut.

"I think, Mademoiselle, that you're lucky. Your measurements are exactly what we've been looking for."

Olga found her very nice. Besides, as a woman, first of all, she was happy to see another woman admire her, having no choice but to admire her. Her beauty... she was going to use it to her full advantage. This beauty that only the night before...

No, she must not think about the night before. She had to live through this day that was destined to be momentous, that was starting off so well.

Olga was very comfortable with what she was wearing and was in no hurry to get dressed. She was a girl who enjoyed being nude, or almost nude, figuring that she was spreading joy through the pleasant vision she offered. But one question was burning on her lips.

"Will I be meeting Mademoiselle Hossegor now?"

Eva Mellion's fresh face clouded over.

"You should, indeed… But I don't think it will be possible today. Mademoiselle Hossegor is not feeling well."

Olga expressed her disappointment. Her enthusiasm was already curbed. With Edwige sick, this visit may have been a waste of time. Even if she was hired, the film might be delayed, which was always bothersome.

The two women exchanged some small talk before Olga, trying to hide her disappointment, thought of getting back into her clothes.

"No, please, Mademoiselle," said Eva, "could you stay like this for a minute?"

She trembled with surprise as she saw Eva Mellion's eyes turn to the door. Two men were there, standing in the doorway, very politely in spite of the impression that Olga must have made in her underwear, an impression that no one of the male sex could escape.

Of the two men, Olga recognized at least one. All actors, well known or not, knew who he was: Marcel Trempont, Edwige's favorite director. He stood next to a gentleman in a handsome suit, very elegant, with silver hair, whom Olga assumed must have been Baron Tragny, Edwige's fiancé.

It seemed to her, all of a sudden, that this impromptu entrance was going to prove invaluable.

"Could you walk a little, Mademoiselle? Forward, yes… now turn around… that's it… a smile… Thank you." The director walked up to her. "I'm Marcel Trempont."

Olga was not flustered at all. It seemed to her that everything was now going to happen it had been foretold, and no bad surprises were going to pop up. At least for the moment. Because she knew perfectly well that she was on borrowed time after last night, that terrifying night she had dared to live through…

Very casually, she revealed her beautiful teeth.

"I recognized you right away, Monsieur Trempont."

"But I didn't know you. I'm very glad to meet you."

Another smile from Olga. But Trempont was no longer smiling. He turned to his companion.

"What do you think, my friend?" he asked.

Tragny—it was him, for sure—made a sweeping gesture.

"There's nothing to discuss. She's Edwige. Exactly like she was a few years ago. Another Edwige… but younger."

"I think you're right… Still, you know what we need… She must be perfect…"

A wave of thoughts flooded Olga's mind. What does this mean? What was she going to hear? What was happening?

"Mademoiselle," Trempont said, glancing at the notes that Eva Mellion gave to him, "I'm not in the habit of making snap decisions lightly, but in your case, I believe… I say: I believe… that you fit the bill."

"You mean, to double for Mademoiselle Hossegor?"

"No."

The statement amazed Olga, but her surprise did not last long. Marcel Trempont continued:

"What we need is more than just a double. We must replace Edwige Hossegor."

Astonishment. Dizziness. The room was spinning. The vases and wall hangings, all of Baron Tragny's furniture, was dancing around. Replacing Edwige Hossegor... But then...

"Yes. Let's not drag out the torture. It happens that, because of her pressing health problems Mademoiselle Hossegor had to quit my next film, *Horror at Midnight*. Everything was ready and we had to stop. This is costing the producers a lot of money. So we've started looking for the right double to replace our star. And we've just found her. I mean, found you. Looking at Mademoiselle Mellion's notes, you look suitable for this difficult and, er, amazing role. Obviously, Fate will ultimately decide, Mademoiselle. I don't want to make any formal promises right now, but I'm pretty sure I'm not mistaken—you can fill the role previously assigned to Mademoiselle Hossegor perfectly."

Olga hid her excitement behind a smile, but a weird flame lit up her eyes.

The director saw it and immediately turned round.

"Did you see that?" he asked Tragny and Eva Mellion. "Did you see that flame in her eyes just now? Bravo, Mademoiselle! But I'm babbling... We'll let you get dressed and wait for you in the salon—if Baron Tragny doesn't mind. (Tragny nodded courteously). Then I'll give you some instructions for your screen test. Afterward, if it goes well, as I believe it will, there won't be any problem The part will be yours."

They left.

Olga stood motionless, thunderstruck. So, it was true. Everything was true. *Everything. Everything the night before had promised.*

The chain of events was incredible. Called up just to be a double, and now she was about to be hired in a starring role with the unspoken approval of Baron Tragny, whom everyone knew was the money behind his fiancée's films.

So Edwige Hossegor was sick. The famous actress, specialized in horror roles, would not be filming *Horror at Midnight*. It would be Olga, little Olga, unknown Olga, the extra, who would take her place and play the leading role in this new production. One of those impressive roles in which Edwige had excelled.

Wasn't she the one who had personified it all with her tragically famous character of Mephista?

"Great!" Eva smiled. "I understand if you're a little overwhelmed now, but you must get dressed."

Olga snapped out of her reverie and apologized.

"I assure you that I'm with you 100%," said Eva. "Such an opportunity… it's extraordinary. But then, that's life and I'm happy for you…"

In the salon, the producer and director were talking. Marcel Trempont repeated:

"I'm sorry for your dear Edwige, but really, you've got to accept that, in spite of her courage, it's impossible to start filming with her under the present circumstances. We can't risk a delay. Think of the money already invested… So we need somebody else and you don't find a Mephista on every street's corner… or in every studio."

Tragny wrinkled his nose.

"Please, Trempont, stop talking about Mephista. You know that, after what happened, just mentioning her name makes Edwige sick… She doesn't need this anymore."

"But, my friend, there has to be a sequel to *The Vampires of Paris*. More adventures of Mephista."

"I doubt Edwige will agree to film them. When she's back on her feet, I'll find another script for her. As for Mephista…"

"Well then, I'll use my beautiful nobody! What's her name? Olga Mervil… ten letters. Excellent. Theater and movie people are superstitious, and believe in the magical power of numbers. Look at these examples: Gaby Morlay, Alain Delon, Serge Lifar… I forget the others…"

He took one of the photos from the file that Eva had left with him.

"She's magnificent. But especially what you saw just now… That flame in her eyes…"

"I admit, it was impressive."

"Look, this doesn't have to take anything from your marvelous Edwige… But you must admit that with a girl like that, we can…"

Marcel Trempont paused to daydream a little.

"She impresses me. I can't say how much… She's not like Edwige, the perfect actress for the roles of diabolical women. She's not an ideal Mephista. She's more than that…"

All dressed now, Olga appeared before them.

Trempont managed to mutter:

"She's Mephista herself."

CHAPTER III

The thick fog was drifting everywhere and the nearby Seine remained invisible. Through the café's window, Martine tried to see something, but only the lights from the cars speeding by pierced the dark. The silhouettes of passers-by were ghostly. They hurried, rushing to escape the desolate night.

The small café was pretty run-down. The walls were still decorated with paintings by an artist long since disappeared, who had left nothing to posterity but these gloomy landscapes that ironically conjured up sunny fields.

People came and went in to get warm at the bar. Regulars. Probably most of them worked in various jobs at the nearby studios. More than one gazed at the pretty girl alone, but she knew how to cool the enthusiasm of eager eyes by veiling her ruby red lips and pert nose behind her blond hair.

It's taking so long, my God!

She was still jobless, but the atmosphere had changed over the last three days, thanks to Olga. Since her visit to Tragny's house, she'd been waiting to do the screen test for Marcel Trempont. Two days later, they had called her back and asked her to come to the Boulogne-Billancourt studios at 6 p.m.

"You'll come with me, honey."

But Martine was scared for some unknown reason, intimidated by all the weird coincidences, and she had refused.

"No, I'll wait for you," she'd said. "I'd rather not go with you into… that world."

Olga had insisted, but Martine, normally timid, remained obstinate. Therefore, they had agreed that she would go to Boulogne and have a drink while waiting for Olga.

6 p.m. was the time of the meeting. It was now past 8 p.m. Martine felt awkward being stared at by the owner and the waitress, pretty rudely it seemed to the girl waiting for someone who was not coming, sitting in front of her glass in which the withering lemon festered in the cold rum.

Olga had left her a ten-franc bill, but still feeling shy, a little hung up, lovely Martine had not dared to order another drink. There was so little money in their shared purse that it seemed outrageous for her to have another grog. If she had any cigarettes left, she would have felt better.

A few tables away, a couple had their arms around each other and were whispering. She thought they were talking about her, making fun of her.

She did not know how to act. She was feeling more and more uncomfortable. A newspaper boy had walked by earlier. To buy a *France Soir* would give her something to do. But she had no money, nothing but the bill left by Olga. So she did not dare buy one.

Martine was not the type of girl to take risks, which was another reason why she was afraid of the adventure that Olga had just embarked on.

Why was she late? What could have happened?

She imagined something horrible.

Olga took risks, yes. But what had she risked?

Martine thought it must have been something totally shameful. A bunch of details came rushing back in her mind about Olga's look, certain comments with a double meaning, and sentences Olga had not finished, as if she were afraid of saying too much. Martine tried to tell herself that Olga was free, after all, and owed her nothing. But she also knew that you could not wipe out such a deep friendship after so many months of hardship.

And Olga certainly did not lie when she had said she would include her friend in what she was already calling her promising future.

The lovers burst out laughing. Martine blushed. And yet, they must have had other things to talk about than this poor little girl waiting alone (probably for a man). She wanted to remove all doubts by screaming out that her friend was coming, that she was not being stood up like an idiot.

Annoyed by the couple she turned to the window that dripped with steam on the inside, and mist on the outside. She was sitting right next to it, having chosen the seat so that she could see Olga coming without thinking that, at this hour, at this time of the year, and with the ugly weather, it was hard to see the people walking by.

Then, in the crowd she saw...

...Not Olga, not her elegant form, but someone standing rigidly by the window. Someone who seemed to be looking at her.

It was a man. Tall. Taller, probably, than natural, but it must have been an illusion from the fog. Martine could not say what he was wearing. She was also unable, if someone had asked her two minutes later, to describe him. But he was disturbing enough to strike terror in her with the only thing that she could make out in the fog. His eyes. Eyes that glowed strangely, abnormally, because all the other faces passing by were shadowy masks.

It was so sudden, so unexpected, that Martine stifled a cry. She realized right away the disastrous effect that her reaction was causing.

The two lovers looked at her strangely; the owner behind the bar stared at her while drying a glass; the waitress, who was busy with some new customers, had whirled around; there were caustic looks from the two guys in overalls lingering over their drinks at the bar.

Martine froze, but still blushed.

She did what she could to fool them. She grabbed her handbag, took out her compact and lipstick, and started redoing her makeup, as if to prove to all these people that everything was all right, that she was not scared, that they were all wrong.

While putting on her lipstick, admittedly with a trembling hand, Martine turned the little mirror so that she could see (if anything could be seen) the street, the foggy riverbank where the washed out missiles of headlights shot through almost continually.

Nobody.

Was I dreaming?

No, she would have sworn to it. *He* was there a second ago, gazing at her through the grimy window. His fearsome eyes bore into her.

But the tall figure was gone.

Martine brightened her face and her mind as well. This could not last long, she thought, as she followed the movement of the outdated wall clock stuck between the bottles filled with multi-colored liquids on the shelf. For the umpteenth time, she compared the verdict of the hands with her own wristwatch. In about two minutes, they would confirm that it had been two and half hours since Olga had headed out for the studio.

A screen test... It should only take a few minutes to film...

Martine was imagining things...

She almost screamed with joy when Olga entered the café. An Olga whom she had not seen coming, too absorbed as she was in her sad thoughts. An Olga whom Martine had no need to question.

"Olga! Is it done?"

"Filmed. Developed. Signed, honey."

"Signed? You mean, a contract? Really? Truly?"

"Yes, it's crazy. I'll tell you all about it. Let's go."

Martine did not have to be asked twice. She called the waitress over and threw the ten-franc bill at her, dying to know more, but not wanting the good news to be spelled out in these abominable surroundings. She left a big tip. Olga also looked anxious to leave, so the two of them left behind the curious eyes of the audience, whose male part seemed very interested in Olga's strange beauty.

"Let's walk a little... toward Paris. I'll tell you on the way."

Martine needed to get some air, even if it meant this foggy night air. She said nothing else as the two girls began to walk arm in arm along the riverbank.

"We'll take a taxi a little farther up."

"But... you have money?"

"Of course. Don't worry. We'll go back home, get dressed, and go celebrate with the men..."

"What?" asked Martine, astonished.

Olga explained that the director and the producers (Tragny plus two others) had invited her to a nightclub around 11:30 p.m. Olga had mentioned her dear Martine and "the men," being anxious to please their new star, were quick to invite her close friend along.

"Me... me... but I wouldn't dare..."

"Silly girl! You'll see. Wait, listen..."

She told in detail the story of the screen test in the private room, the obvious satisfaction of Marcel Trempont and the production managers, and even the opinion of a woman who must have been the script girl. All the way to Eva Mellion who was there and congratulated her.

They promised her a wonderful career. They were counting on *Horror at Midnight* to be a hit and were already talking about another production, for television, which would be a sequel to the famous *Vampires of Paris* and Olga could play Mephista, the diabolical heroine.

"But," Martine was surprised, "I don't know much about all this, but shouldn't Edwige Hossegor play that role?"

"Of course. But listen, some things I heard... Edwige is still sick.. or there's something else they're not telling me... In short, even Tragny, her lover and her backer, is okay with it. She wants to leave these kinds of roles behind her."

"But that's what made her famous, like Barbara Steele or Maxa, when she was the star of the Grand-Guignol."

"Yes, but Edwige Hossegor wants no more of it. I don't know why. I just know I arrived at the right time."

"You're lucky," Martine said naïvely.

Olga grabbed her arm and squeezed it so hard it felt like it was breaking.

"Hey, you're hurting me!"

Olga loosened her grip and spoke to Martine in a weird voice, a voice that was not usually hers, but had popped up at certain moments over the past few days.

"Luck... Chance... that's for idiots, my little Martine. For everyone else— listen carefully to what I tell you: it has to be bought."

Martine was taken aback. Oh, she certainly guessed (it did not take a genius) that Olga must have agreed to some big sacrifice in order to "force" her destiny like this. But she could not figure out what.

They started off again in silence.

There was practically no one along the Seine. Only the cars rushed by on an endless, haunting carrousel, as if the passengers were in a hurry to flee these foggy gulfs.

The two girls walked along the Seine and barely saw it. They sunk deeper into the cold, thick fog that seeped into them insidiously. Martine shivered, but she felt Olga next to her burning with a strange fire.

"You see," the future star said a minute later, "when I got the message, when they offered me to be her double, I was a little disappointed, I admit. I was expecting more... at least a small part. Later, I realized that it was all wonderfully orchestrated, and what people call 'luck' had just arrived. Everything fell right in step, a natural course of events. You're right, I came at the right time."

"It was a godsend," said Martine.

But she did not expect a reaction from Olga after such a trivial comment, or so she thought. Olga let go of her arm and growled:

"Don't ever say that word."

"What word? Oh, you mean 'god'?"

"Hush!"

"But why, Olga?"

"I can't tell you."

Silence again. They walked on, but no longer arm in arm. Suddenly, Martine, more troubled than ever, swung around.

"What's wrong with you, now?" asked Olga, annoyed.

"Someone's following us."

"I don't see anyone."

"Yes, yes... I'm sure of it. Oh, it's *him* again!"

"Who are you talking about?"

"That man... at the café..."

Feverishly, like dropping baggage that was too heavy, Martine described her vision and the mysterious apparition of the man with the glowing eyes.

Olga listened in silence while walking. Almost in spite of herself, Martine kept turning around, more frequently, afraid to see the man she had just described.

"You must have been day-dreaming," Olga finally said. "Besides, sweetie, how could you see a man's eyes in a fog like this?"

"Exactly, Olga. I wonder... if they weren't the eyes of a man..."

"Oh, be quiet... be quiet..."

Once again, their conversation was cut off, stopped short. A taxi was passing by and Olga left Martine to rush into the fog. She managed to get seen by the cab driver, and called out for Martine who joined her with a sigh of relief. She was more than happy to escape this oppressive evening. She was cold and she was scared.

A minute later, the two girls were sitting in the back of the taxi, being driven to their small apartment in Montmartre, the address of which Olga had given to the driver. At the moment the taxi had taken off, it had seemed to them that there was indeed someone on the riverbank. A tall man, who looked unnaturally big in the night and the fog. A man whose eyes, despite the distance and the dark fog, looked like they were glowing.

But the girls said nothing to each other, as if the vision was unimportant, or as if it was just some unimportant wanderer in the night.

The taxi took them away.

CHAPTER IV

"What exactly are you afraid of?" Teddy Verano asked.

Edwige Hossegor did not answer right away. She laid her cigarette in the beautiful, emerald green ashtray, stood up and went to the small bar.

"Red or *bianco*?" she asked.

"*Bianco*," the detective replied, smiling.

Edwige Hossegor started measuring out the Americanos. Teddy watched her pouring the Cinzano silently, skillfully and elegantly.

"My dear friend, why are you delaying your answer? What you're doing instead is certainly a pleasure, but it's really only a cover for you?"

Edwige came back holding out the glass with dancing liquid.

"Teddy, you're not here to pester me. I'm miserable and you know it."

"Of course. Otherwise, you wouldn't have called me."

She went away again and came back to sit down. She was very beautiful in her flattering, sweeping dress, a beautiful, brocaded, electric blue.

"Teddy, in my eyes you're not just someone who gets paid to investigate. After what you did for me, you're a friend... Do we call friends over only when things are bad? I've proven to you the opposite happens often enough already. And I haven't forgotten what you did to free me from that monster who had put me under his spell... or the part that your stepson, Gerard, played in that awful ordeal."

"Don't tell me that it's starting all over again."

Edwige nervously crushed out her cigarette and clasped her hands together.

"Well, yes, it is."

"Come on!" Teddy Verano objected. "Like all cases of sorcery, the spell ended when the sorcerer was destroyed. And the sorcerer, in your case, was not really the man who started it all, but the evil machine that he built, that used cameras to perfect what occultists call the *volt*, the wax figure representing the person targeted..."

"I know all this, Teddy. Before this encounter with Mephista, I didn't pay much attention to what you call magic, but because of it, I was forced to look into it..."

"So you know that you're free from Mephista's control."

"No, I don't think so."

"But the machine, the spell caster, was destroyed. The *volt*, that monstrous wax robot in your image, was also demolished, twice in fact. All that's left is the mad genius that was behind it—that film buff cum physicist, Jules Verrier. As you know, he's safely locked up at the Henri Rousselle Insane Asylum, and only death will get him out of there."

Very clearly, with that beautiful voice that had done so much to make her reputation as an actress, Edwige Hossegor said::

"And yet, Teddy, it's not over."

Teddy Verano sank back a little more comfortably into the armchair.

"I'm all ears, Edwige."

"You know that after filming *The Vampires of Paris*," the actress explained slowly, "after the crimes committed by this Mephista wax-doll in my image, after the cataleptic fits during which Verrier's evil machine took hold of my spirit and my appearance, and after our victory over that damned madman, I had to take a few months off to rest. Tragny took me to Switzerland, to a remote castle. I have to say that he was, as always, the perfect friend, discreet and devoted. Our marriage had to be put off once again... But what did that matter! The premiere of *The Vampires of Paris* was a hit and I kept up on reading the trade papers, my fan mail... In short, when I got back to Paris, a new contract had already been signed on my behalf..."

"Yes. For *Horror at Midnight*," Teddy Verano said. "I read about it. Teleor, for business reasons, temporarily branched out of their television production, to make a big budget feature film. Baron Tragny, the main partner in the firm, gave his approval."

"Yes. I liked the screenplay. The role was... But you know the kind of role which I usually play..."

"And in which you are unrivalled, incomparable."

Edwige Hossegor stared at him for a moment. In a slightly different voice, she continued:

"That's right... Well, this time, I think there's someone who will be better than me."

"None of your many admirers would allow it."

"Everything changed, Teddy. Anyway, what happened is this. I was about to start shooting principal photography; everything was ready to go, and just when I thought I was healed, free, the nightmares started again."

"Don't tell me you've been fainting again."

"Not this time, no. I had dreams... Or rather, nightmares: scenes of battle, of murder, of torture, and all kinds of horror... That's all I dreamed about, with my poor, tormented spirit..."

"May I ask you a question?"

"Yes, go ahead."

"Before... before this Mephista business, were you plagued by these kinds of dreams?"

"Never."

"When you filmed all those horrible scenes in the past, did you ever dream about them afterward?"

"No, never. I was never disturbed by them at all. I was simply doing my job as an actress, honestly. And I was happy because I loved it; yes, more than anything I loved playing these roles... Anyway, this time, when I started on *Horror at Midnight*, I was seized by fear. I felt like this new role was going to bring me trouble, that bad luck was looming, that..."

She lowered her voice, instinctively, to finish.

"...I felt like Mephista, the physical Mephista, not just the character on the screen, was going to start up her crimes again."

Teddy Verano listened attentively. He did not respond right away, but asked if she had a light. Edwige held out a huge lighter.

"Isn't it just anxiety after a few months without working?" he remarked. "You're starting over again, in a way. It's a little bit of stage fright, like they say in the theater."

"No, no. I see where you're going. You want to reassure me no matter what. Listen, Teddy, I know stage fright; I've had enough of it in my career. I think it's innate in every real actor, and you never dive into a new role without some fear of the outcome. Before every film, before every series, I was afraid. But it was purely professional."

She got excited as she spoke. She stood up and lit her own cigarette.

"I never saw myself surrounded by so many ghosts," she concluded.

"It's obviously the memory of Mephista acting up."

"The memory... No, Teddy, it's not the memory."

"What then?"

She approached him, graceful and still seductive despite being in her forties, which was no secret to anyone. She sat right next to him. He could smell the mysterious scent that some women's bodies give off, that aura that makes men's heads turn.

"Teddy, I'm not scared of my memories. I know perfectly well that the spell-casting machine was broken and all the scientists were at a complete loss trying to find its secret."

"Let's hope it stays that way, that they never find it."

"I hope so too... I also know that Verrier went totally mad after his dirty little tricks all failed and he's locked up in a padded cell. No more wax women walking around in our world, looking and sounding like me, thanks to some strange mixture of sorcery and physics... And yet, I'm scared. No, wait, let me finish, Teddy... I'm scared of what's coming."

Teddy Verano took a hit off his cigarette and a sip of the Americano.

"Very well. In sum, you're not dreaming of Mephista or of your past roles. What you're scared of is a kind of premonition. You're seeing things ahead of time, that haven't happened yet."

"Exactly."

"What sort of things?"

"New crimes, all kinds of crimes, accidents, disasters... and Mephista is mixed up in it every time."

Leaning toward her, his hazel eyes sparkling, Teddy Verano asked:

"In these visions, are there memories either of the tragic events a few months ago, or of scenes from *Vampires*, or even earlier films?"

"No. It's all scenes, so to speak, that I have never seen before. Everything is new… But I know they're bound to happen…"

"OK. So you say. You're positive about it. But if everything is only happening in your imagination…"

"You think I'm crazy, but…"

Teddy Verano cut her off and protested loudly, but Edwige did not listen.

"Can you guarantee that nothing will happen? Listen to me, Teddy, I've already talked to Doctor Sorbier, who cared for me with so much dedication and competence. He now thinks that I'm a pretty good medium."

"That means that your special sensibility—are you not a marvelous actress?—allows you to latch onto images of past or future deeds… I know… Likewise, it's thanks to this particular disposition of yours that that wretch Verrier could affect you and snatch away your personality to animate his awful wax puppet, that mannequin. A mannequin that, unfortunately, looked exactly like you and acted like a normal woman."

"A mannequin that killed," Edwige's voice had suddenly turned hoarse.

There was a moment of silence.

Edwige lit another cigarette and continued:

"So, I'm scared. I haven't said anything to anybody except the baron and Dr. Sorbier. My first thought was to quit the film."

"Quit acting? But that's crazy."

"Hold on, I didn't say that. My career is important to me. It's everything to me. It's my life. But these damn roles are starting to scare me. I tell myself that I should've stopped playing them a long time ago. I tell myself that it's insanity, after what happened, just to think of becoming, if not Mephista, at least some other diabolical creature…"

"They're only fictional creatures, characters from novels and screenplays."

"Yes, but who live, whose ghosts are projected onto all the screens in the world, big and small; characters who influence millions and millions of viewers, Teddy… Imagine the consequences… If I were dead—don't interrupt me—if I were gone for good, which will happen someday, since I'm just a woman like any other… something of me will remain… not Edwige Hossegor, who always tried to be as kind as she could be, not I, who wanted, as far as possible, to work well with others in the studio, but that horrible image of me will remain… Mephista will remain… she and her demonic sisters… who are all Mephista."

"I think," Teddy Verano said, "that you're exaggerating. If you were right, nobody could make films, write books or put on plays unless they were sappy romances. The world needs something besides taffy and cotton candy. André Gide said that you don't make literature from good intentions. Nor with bad, for that matter. But I think that, for a work to be worthwhile and have a certain moral impact, it needs a minimum of realism. If you want evil to be punished, don't hesitate to show this evil in action, with all its dire consequences. I would even say that certain films, certain novels, which are not sappy, have had a positive influence on some perverted individuals and shown them the difference between good and evil."

Edwige Hossegor smiled.

"Thank you, Teddy... You're the kind of friend who knows how to make someone feel better. Seen in this light, the thing is, in fact, somewhat appealing. You're almost making me believe that, by portraying these mean, cruel, demonic women, I'm doing charity work..."

"Yes. Since all the films show the ultimate downfall and defeat of these vile heroines."

Edwige thought about this for a moment before saying:

"Certainly... I'd like to believe... but I'm too scared, Teddy. I told Tragny, but he threw up his hands. Because he loves me, you know. And because he knows what my career means to me. Also, it's a little funny, but that's how it goes—he's invested a lot of money in *Horror at Midnight*. In short, when I told him about my decision, it was catastrophic to him."

"But I see that he's accepted it."

"Yes, because Dr. Sorbier told him that my health, my mental balance, was at stake."

"I understand all this. That's where Olga Mervil comes in."

"Ah, that woman..." said Edwige, sighing deeply.

"She's replacing you in the film. It's her first role, it seems, except for some really minor parts. But if the photos don't lie, she's very beautiful... different from you, but very beautiful."

Edwige handed him copies of *Cinémonde* and *Ciné Revue*.

"Different? You think so? Trempont and Tragny are of the opposite opinion. They chose Olga Mervil because she looks just like me. And believe me, the make-up artists are going to accentuate the likeness for the sake of the production."

Teddy Verano read an article illustrated by many photos that reported Marcel Trempont's latest discovery.

"Yes, I can see the similarities... But her eyes... No, they're different..."

"Teddy, Teddy... look closely! Aren't those Mephista's eyes? Not mine, not my interpretation, or the imitation created by Verrier... These are *her* eyes... Trempont calls her the perfect Mephista."

Teddy Verano put the magazine down.

"So, let's be clear. You think there's danger here?"

"Yes. But I can't put my finger on it."

"In any event, you seem to be out of harm's way."

"Am I?"

"Yes! Because someone else is playing the role that scares you. And by the way, it's not even Mephista."

"No, it's a very similar character. What I fear—oh, you're going to think I'm crazy—is that Verrier has hatched another dirty trick, that all these pictures are oozing evil."

"Edwige…"

"Teddy, don't tell me I'm being stupid. I'm scared. That's all. So… what should I do? And don't talk about taking another vacation to the mountains. No, no, I can't do nothing. I need action."

Teddy Verano stood up.

"All this might just be in your mind, but we have to free you of it."

"How?"

"By looking reality in the face. After all, maybe you're right and burying our heads in the sand won't solve anything. Therefore, I propose that you… and I…"

Edwige looked at him questioningly.

"They're filming right now, aren't they?"asked the detective.

"Yes. For another two weeks. Trempont is delighted. Olga Mervil is keeping her promises and it seems that the whole studio is thrilled. Some even say they're a little frightened… because they don't often see an actress take her role so seriously."

"Except you, my dear."

"Thank you, my friend. So, what do we do?"

"We're going to go to the studio and watch this new Mephista filming. And we'll find out if it's only your imagination working overtime… In which case, you'll drop this obsession in a heartbeat by seeing the truth…"

He paused briefly.

"Or else, your instincts are right, and there is something evil at work here… and we'll be better off knowing what."

CHAPTER V

Laughter broke out around Henri as the stagehands of the Teleor studio outdid themselves teasing the young man.

"Watch out, it'll bring you bad luck."

"You never know, maybe you'll end up marrying her."

"She's built pretty nice…"

"We can't say that… But for a pretty little mouse, she's a real fox."

"She's not my type. I prefer Claudia Cardinale."

"Anyway, Henri, don't kid yourself, she's way out of your league."

"Besides, I'm telling you, I'm sure she's got the evil eye."

Everyone exploded. Some complained, others shook their heads. The world of stagehands, just like the actors, also had its superstitions.

The stage manager called out:

"Break's over, let's go!"

The men left the counter and went back to their various posts. The cameramen to their equipment, the boom operators to their "poles," and the others to their various jobs.

Robert, the chief cameraman, tapped Henri on the shoulder.

"Come on, my boy, they've poked enough fun at you. Put it all out of your mind. Listen to an old man's advice."

Henri sighed and, deep in his pocket, fondled the photograph. It was a photo of Olga Mervil, the new star of *Horror at Midnight*, who was performing to everyone's satisfaction. A few malicious people whispered that Baron Tragny was becoming secretly interested in her, and that beautiful Edwige Hossegor was on her way out.

"It's normal," they said. "She's the same kind of woman, but 15 years younger."

Others claimed that there was nothing to it. Besides, Tragny seemed to be faithful to Edwige, although they never saw her at the studios anymore. Anyone could see that, from the start, since the cocktail parties at Teleor, after the press conferences given by Marcel Trempont, and all the interviews of the new star, the playboy was not fluttering around his new star.

They saw her in nightclubs and some parties, but if Tragny was there, so too were the director and the screenwriters. Olga's attitude also left no room for ambiguity. She remained alone, in the middle of everyone.

They all knew that she lived with a friend. Some had smeared her for this "friendship," but here again, the wagging tongues were cut short when they saw Martine, who now worked as Olga's secretary. Her charming smile and beautiful pure eyes silenced all the vicious gossip.

All this created something of a mystery. Despite the many romantic trysts the journalists had invented when Olga had met Jacques Brel, Yves Montand, or a few other celebrities (married or not), everything was swiftly set straight. Olga remained alone and seemed to live only for her work, for her first starring role, to which she brought her undeniable presence and unquestionable talent.

The men in the studio had seen many other new stars before; however, one after the other, they all paid homage to the exceptional professionalism of Olga Mervil.

The film would be a hit, no doubt about it. Photographers were having a field day, and articles flourished. More than one journalist had said of her, who was, after all, just a beginner, that she "had it in her blood." She was just starting out, and already they talked and wrote about her as if she was a new Jeanne Moreau.

It must be said that luck seemed to be weighing heavily on Olga's side. Tragny himself could not get over it. As much as he knew what it usually cost to launch a new star, i.e.: to throw them onto a public that has not chosen them, he had to recognize that Olga Mervil was easy money, what with all the demands for photographs and autographs flowing in, and her fascination with both the journalists and the crowds promoting her in the trade journals.

Among her admirers was young Henri, a cameraman at the studio, only 20 years-old, full of energy and innocence. He dreamed of her, of beautiful Olga, which had made him the butt of the more or less crude jokes of his older colleagues, with the exception of Robert the cameraman. After 30 years in the field, this veteran of the cinema had his own opinion on the subject, and he was the one who had said that Olga probably had the evil eye.

Be that as it may, Henri had got himself a unique photo of Olga, thanks to a photographer whom he knew, and gave access to the studio near the actor's dressing rooms. He was careless enough to say that he wanted to ask the budding star to sign it, and naturally the jokes had rained down on him. Young Henri was good-natured and took it all in stride. He had his little blue flower, his secret garden, so he just told himself that he had made a mistake in opening up to his rude colleagues.

His plan was simple. After all, Olga was not going to gobble him up. He would go and ask her to sign the photo after they finished shooting the scene. He would go to her dressing room. Normally, this was forbidden, but Berthe, her dresser, knew his grandmother's concierge (this made a connection) and would open the door for him.

"We're shooting!"

Marcel Trempont was worked up. He had just given his instructions to Olga and Jean-Pierre Max, the usual co-star of Edwige Hossegor, who had agreed to share top billing with Olga, along with two supporting actors.

It was a scene in a salon. The heroine, a dangerous and mysterious creature, was surrounded by police officers who suspected her of being the leader of an occult evil organization, replete with evil spells. Olga was supposed to capti-vate them, baffle them, and escape their trap by making them fall into her own.

The cameras gleamed under the spotlights after everything was in place. Marcel Trempont was nervous; the production manager was still running around, shouting orders; old Berthe was putting the final touches to Olga's make-up. He as dressed in the a tight-fitting, very low-cut, black dress and sat in an armchair that had been cleverly positioned by the art director.

The director was watching the face of his star with one finger on his mono-cle. Old Robert adjusted a spotlight and nudged Henri.

"You're in love with that girl? Look at her... take a good look. Do like Trempont. And tell me she doesn't scare you. I never want to see her in my bed, I'm telling you."

Henri laughed a little. He knew Robert was a good guy. He was not mak-ing fun of him, just giving him sound advice.

But Henri held a vision of Olga in his heart. He saw her; he lived with her every day. Her photos were barely on sale, and he was happy to already have a gorgeous one. He was thinking only of his little dedication. Curving his finger, however, he took Robert's advice, but after "framing" his idol like this, he found her more beautiful and more fascinating than ever.

"Camera!" Trempont yelled.

Some spotlights went out while others were turned on. The studio fell si-lent.

Jean-Pierre Max (playing a chief detective) started in and confronted the strange character that Olga incarnated. The camera recording their scene hummed almost imperceptibly as Trempont watched over the different angles

Two people tiptoed into the studio.

Of course, everyone respected the rule of silence and said nothing. But their eyes spoke volumes as they fell upon the couple coming in. It was Baron Tragny, the producer, accompanied by Edwige Hossegor herself.

Everyone was stunned.

The renowned star was coming to watch she who could only be called her rival, and whom they said was going to steal away the good graces of both Tragny and the public.

Here was something that would cause some noise and affect the nasty comments that had been circulating for a while.

Someone else was coming in behind the couple. A man who looked like a journalist. He stood off to the side with his hands in his pocket, looking amused. A man who was already familiar with the studio environment, but who still en-joyed it, and was interested in seeing a movie shoot. He observed and nothing escaped his hazel eyes. Not even the presence of the young, unassuming blonde girl who was sitting behind the script girl taking notes.

Teddy Verano stood behind with Edwige Hossegor. After suggesting they come to the studio to get a closer look at this Olga who scared her, in order to fight against the anxiety that was coming back with new symptoms, he had asked the Baron if he wanted to come as well, and Tragny had said yes.

The detective spotted everyone, starting with the ravishing Olga, who looked to him like she was in a halo of electric light that showed off her beautiful but somewhat hard features, and especially her extraordinary eyes, that one would have said, could mesmerize the whole world; all the way to sweet, unassuming Martine, who looked a little dumbstruck being dragged along by her childhood friend, who refused to abandon her and had sworn to make a place for her at her side.

That girl is wonderful! They weren't exaggerating.

He saw someone waving his arms, pointing at something up above, on a steel beam hanging over the set. No one seemed to be paying attention, except for old Robert who saw everything.

One of the lights was overheating. It as a spot placed a few dozen feet over the scene, to cast a particular shine on half of Jean-Pierre Max's face, while Olga's remained in full light.

Teddy Verano saw a small young man take up a ladder among the booms, climb over the beam toward the spot, and delicately rearrange the wires. Robert had sent Henri to the fix the minor problem without disturbing the director.

Just then, there was an interruption.

The director made slight changes to the position of the actors. Everyone relaxed and started talking again. Now, of course, they looked at Edwige Hossegor, who smiled, cheerfully, as Tragny introduced her to Olga Mervil.

Henri was finishing up his repair on the beam, but Marcel Trempont did not want to lose any time and was already calling everybody back.

"Camera... Action!"

Silence again.

The actors were in position; the "weird" lighting was on... The words of the dialogue floated through the silent studio, words that mysterious machines recorded and that would soon be replayed thousands of times to millions of spectators. Millions of spectators who would be struck by the savage beauty of Olga, by the dark melody of a voice like no other, and especially by her frightening eyes full of wickedness, eyes that opened onto the abyss...

Teddy Verano bit his lip. He was so used to strange things that he could feel something was not right with the girl. He felt as if she was not from this Earth, that she bore within her one of those curses that he had spent his life fighting against.

Oh, come on, I'm being stupid. I, too, am going to let this dark beauty put a spell on me... Really, Teddy, you're too old for this. What would Yvonne say if I fell in love like a teenager?

They were filming. Teddy watched pretty much ever thing. Then came another scene. This time, a full shot of Olga facing the policemen, who walked out of the shot. She as creepy, standing there like a creature of the night, as beautiful as the darkness; she had a few menacing, eerie sentences to pronounce.

Up above, Henri was still straddling the beam. He stayed put on Robert's orders, so as not to disturb the shot; the old cameraman had asked the young man to stay overhead in case of another breakdown so that he could fix the spot without interrupting the scene.

Teddy Verano then looked at Edwige Hossegor. He saw her in the shadows. The beautiful star looked peculiarly stressed, although she had seemed relaxed when she had shaken the hand of her replacement. Edwige, too, had to be under the evil spell emanating from that girl.

Now Henri changed position; he was still sitting on the beam but leaned forward, glaring down, devouring with his eyes the girl he was attracted to, fascinated by, enraptured with...

Olga was wrapped up in her role. She talked and let out some weird tonalities. Her voice became hoarse, but with a strange, luscious tone, that captivated the audience:

"You think I'm guilty, detective, but I'm innocent. At least, I have committed no crime. But I'll tell you the truth... I bring bad luck... Worse yet... I'm not just a deadly talisman that causes disasters, *I am bad luck incarnate...*"

A silent shiver ran through the studio.

Overhead, little Henri was stunned.

Why did Teddy Verano look up at that moment? Because the young man intrigued him. Because he felt that, die to his precarious situation, the poor kid was destined to become the victim of everything that Edwige Hossegor, the sensitive, the medium, had foreseen...

Feeling unsteady Henri tried to get a better grip. His hand slipped and he touched the burning spotlight. A sudden movement, a reflex, but too late... he was off-balance.

Olga, standing there in all her frightening splendor with her bare shoulders under the spots, cried out once more time:

"*I am bad luck incarnate!*"

Someone screamed in the studio; followed by more cries of terror.

Too late! Henri the stagehand had fallen. There now was a body lying crushed at Olga's feet.

Blood had splattered all over her.

The camera had caught this unrehearsed scene, the most horrifying in the history of film-making.

When Olga screamed, "*I am bad luck incarnate!*" audiences would forever see on film the moment when the poor boy had fallen, still twitching, limbs broken, his skull cracked open, a pool of blood spreading out like a sinister pool, enveloping the feet of the actress of *Horror at Midnight*...

CHAPTER VI

The flashes sizzled.

The photographers were having a field day. Sensational articles would be published, even more in the daily press than in the trade journals.

The police arrived. The studio doctor did nothing but declare the victim dead on the spot. They had lost no time. Now, Henri's body was being carried away on a stretcher, covered under a tarp. All the studio personnel stood there, upset by the tragedy.

Teddy Verano, being respectful like everyone else, noticed a curious thing: poor Henri had fallen right between Olga and Edwige.

Both of them now looked on, frozen stiff.

Olga was like a statue. She looked really strange to the detective. He saw her eyes sparkling, but not a muscle in her face twitched.

Edwige, on the other hand, was very upset, and did not try to hide it. The famous actress who had played Mephista, the vamp of all vamps, the great femme fatale of the screen, was, in her private life, a woman like any other: decent, sensitive and compassionate

It all would make for some weird photos... What a sensation in the evening papers, seeing Olga Mervil, "the new star of the year," facing Edwige Hossegor, the venerated actress, with a bloody corpse between them!

Rumors were already spreading. Some whispered that it was going to make great publicity for the movie, the director, and the budding star, Olga.

Others shook their heads, voicing the opposite opinion. There was blood on the film and this was never good—it brought bad luck. Furthermore, everyone could still hear Olga's last recorded words: "*I am bad luck incarnate!*"

Edwige grabbed Verano's arm.

"Edwige? Are you feeling ill? Of course..."

"Teddy, take me home, please. This is too hard for me, and Tragny must stay here."

A minute later, Teddy Verano's black Citroën DS was carrying Edwige Hossegor and her improvised knight in shining armor.

During the trip, which was not long, they spoke little. They were both choked up. Edwige saw in the tragedy the confirmation of her ominous feelings. Teddy Verano, as always, was trying to probe the arcane depths of the human soul, the abyss that holds the key to so many enigmas.

He brought Edwige back to Eva Mellion and Isabelle, her attendant, and waited around for a while, accepting a glass of port and smoking with her. Edwige was still nervous and quite pale. She was clearly dying to ask some questions, but did not seem to know where to begin. The detective guessed as much, but did not want to push her. He knew that he had to take it easy on the beautiful actress. Since her previous adventure in which Mephista had materialized so bizarrely, she was very fragile, psychically.

"Teddy," she suddenly spurted out, "tell me the truth..."

Teddy Verano looked up innocently from his glass of Cintra.

"What truth, my friend?"

"Oh, don't play innocent. It's not your style. Teddy, a man just died, horribly. A poor boy... In his pocket was a photo of... that girl. The police took it away, all stained with his blood..."

"I see," Teddy Verano said softly. "But you shouldn't worry, since it's not about you anymore. You gave up the role. And. Let me remind you, her role isn't even Mephista, if that's what you're thinking of."

"Didn't you feel anything... frightening?"

Teddy Verano took a puff off his cigarette, hesitating.

"A connection to your dreams, your nightmares, your fears? But, it was just an accident."

"No, Teddy, it was something else, and you know it."

"And what is this something else, please?"

"A force... Forces are being unleashed around me, by me, by all the films, all the images of evil incarnated in the woman I personified..."

"OK, but since you're not filming *Horror at Midnight*, you just have to change the type of roles you take; play a nice grandma, although it might be a little too soon for that, or a nun... basically, all the heroines of generosity and self-sacrifice..."

Edwige looked discouraged.

"I was counting on you and you're making jokes..."

"Truthfully," Teddy Verano said, "in my opinion, they're just coincidences. Unpleasant, to be sure, in this case. You lived through a tragedy, but it's in the past. Today, a young man—and the gossip's already out that he was head over heels in love with Olga Mervil—fell from the studio ceiling and died while gawking at this idol. Where's the connection?"

"I wish I knew."

"Me, too," he said, still speaking softly, but a little jabbing.

Edwige Hossegor raised her eyes.

"What do you mean, Teddy?"

He stood up, leaned over, took her hand and placed a delicate, elegant kiss near her wrist.

"Do you know where I'm going now? To the studio, but please don't tell anyone. I want to check out something..."

She gave him a long look of gratitude as a goodbye.

Did I do the right thing? he asked himself on the way back to the Teleor Studio. *I shouldn't give her something to worry about, but Edwige is one of those hyper-sensitive people who think you're scoffing at their fears if you con-*

tradict them, that you're making fun of them, or giving up on them. Telling her I'm going back to the studio for a little private investigation lets her know that I'm on her side, and hinting that I smell something fishy, as mysterious as it might be dangerous, will make her feel better...

He avoided a cyclist, turned right at a green light and concluded:

After all, my job is to protect people. Especially people being threatened by invisible, unusual forces. Tragny pays me generously to protect Edwige ... We've become friends... I have obligations... I'll see this through to the end.

In fact, he was excited about this new mystery. Edwige's statements had set him thinking, and Olga's personality intrigued him. She looked like Edwige, but there was a huge difference between the two women.

Teddy Verano knew Edwige's true nature: considerate and generous, although able to become a monster on the screen. Olga was something else. A kind of legend was already forming around her. Journalists were talking about her odd personality, which nobody could figure out, and her secretive life, which foiled all public gossip. And it was not young Henri's death that was going to clear up these mysteries, quite the contrary.

When Teddy Verano got back to the studio he found a group of journalists still fishing for information from the personnel. Tragny and Marcel Trempont were surrounded. The director was declaring that the filming would continue the next day, and that this was just an unfortunate accident.

Teddy Verano waved to Tragny, but the baron didn't see him and got lost in the crowd. Then he spotted Ginette Madison, a journalist for the morning edition of *Le Parisien*, whom he had known for a long time.

"Ginette! Always looking for some new scoop?"

"Teddy Verano! What are you doing here?... I remember now! You're Edwige Hossegor's bodyguard, right?"

"My friend, I need to stay incognito."

"Oh, oh! Teddy Verano on the trail! A murderer in the studio?"

He rolled his eyes melodramatically.

"Worse than that: a ghost. Ginette, I swear to you that I'll tell you what I know, and your article will be sensational. But help me out. Give me that camera you're slinging around."

"What?"

"I don't carry one around all the time like you."

"I see. Monsieur Verano wants to blend in."

"Exactly. With a camera, they won't notice me. You can take notes and I'll look like I'm chasing after photos. If need be, I'll take one now and again."

"Don't use up too many flashes."

"You're a beauty. Put it on my tab."

The ploy, as simple as it was, allowed him to walk around for a while in the studio. They barely paid attention to him. There was still some feverish activity under the spotlights, most of which had been turned off. On seeing a blonde head near the dressing rooms, Teddy guessed that it was Martine, who was always following Olga. Thus, he knew that she was in her dressing room

Abruptly, off to the side, he gave the camera back to Ginette, slipping it around her neck.

"With this, I decorate you for services rendered... to me. Thanks and I'll see you later."

Ginette smiled but said nothing. Even better, she covered him as he left discreetly, sneaking behind a backdrop.

A minute later she bit her lip when she spotted him.

"That sly fox... he'd gone right to where Henri was when he fell."

But undoubtedly, in the hectic crowd, she was the only one to notice the detective overhead, coolly overlooking the studio. The technicians had all deserted the upper posts. Along with most of the stagehands, dressers and junior personnel, they were glad to talk to journalists, dishing out fanciful stories that would become even more fanciful in the evening and morning editions.

For sure, Teddy told himself as he advanced carefully along the metal passageway, *beautiful Olga is on her way to stardom now. This girl, who was completely unknown a few weeks ago, has had incredible luck. They say that everything is working for her. Everything...*

He stood there for a moment, staring. He saw, far below, between the presently abandoned cameras, a huge spot of sawdust. It was the sawdust they had spread around to soak up the technician's blood.

Everything... even a young man's death...

But he kept moving, agile as a cat, as silently as possible, in the direction of the dressing rooms.

Like all studio dressing rooms, at Teleor, they had no ceiling. They were just partitions set up to form cells that they made as cozy and comfortable as possible.

Teddy Verano, now far from the crowd of journalists, studio people, and even policemen, was slowly approaching the actors' area. He could see that most of the dressing rooms were empty with their lights turned off. But Martine was there, he recognized her, speaking with old Berthe, the official dresser.

Hold on, where's Olga? These two women ought to be with her.

Moreover, Berthe was agitated. The detective kept moving and was soon within earshot. They did not see him and did not dream of being overheard by someone on the beams above. Besides, even if they looked up, they would have had a hard time seeing him in the shadows among the darkened spotlights.

"Yes, Mademoiselle Martine," Berthe was saying. "She asked me to leave, saying she was expecting someone else."

"Good, Madame Berthe, you have to listen to her."

"You, too. She said you have to wait here."

"Well, me, you know, I'm used to it."

"You're going to stay here? You should get the script girl's folding chair so you don't have to stand up the whole time."

"Thank you, Madame Berthe. Don't mind if I do. I'm quite upset."

"Who wouldn't be? That poor boy, can you believe it?"

Berthe suddenly lowered her voice and looked toward Olga's dressing room where Teddy saw the light from above.

"And her... Mademoiselle Mervil... Did you notice? Of course, since you know her so well. It's unbelievable. She didn't look disturbed. Me," the dresser turned dramatic, "if a man died for me, that would certainly do something..."

Teddy Verano leaned over further, hanging onto the cables so that he wouldn't miss a word.

Martine looked uncomfortable and he heard her mutter:

"Olga's like that. Don't try to understand, Madame Berthe. Look, why don't you make us some tea. I need to pull myself together... after this tragedy... and the police... and the journalists. Luckily, it's starting to calm down."

"Tea's a good idea," the dresser said. "I'll do that."

"Wait! Since Olga wants to be alone, I'll go with you."

And the two of them went to the back of the studio.

Teddy Verano took the opportunity to make some agile leaps to get from one walkway to another so that he was swiftly near Olga's dressing room.

The young woman was alone, sitting in front of the make-up table, almost naked in her underwear. She had let down her beautiful black hair and, with her head in her hands, seemed to be meditating.

A little while passed. Teddy wondered who she was waiting for, and why she had kept out the faithful, charming Martine.

From his vantage, because of the angle, he could only see part of the room. The door, in particular, was barely visible, and he was now on the opposite side of the hallway. Thus, he could not see the "visitor" arrive. Or leave.

Is she waiting for a lover? No, it has to be something else. Otherwise, Martine would know about it. Who the Devil could it be?

And this thought struck him. *Who the Devil...?*

All of a sudden, he had a weird feeling. He leaned over as far as he could to see into the dressing room. But no, the walkway was situated so that he could not see any better. But at least, now, he was happy to see the radiant vision of Olga. Clearly she was waiting.

Suddenly, after looking at her watch, which was resting on the table, Olga stood up, went to get a pretty negligee (paid for by Teleor), all pink and frilly, put it on a chair in reach and, thinking she was alone, started undressing. She was not wearing much, so it did not take long.

Teddy's throat went dry.

Like every time he faced temptation in the course of an investigation he had this funny little thought: *What would Yvonne say if she could see me now... seeing what I'm seeing?*

Olga was really very beautiful, in her uncensored beauty, all pink with delicate brown flecks.

Teddy Verano, even though he felt little attraction to a creature who seemed so dangerous, was breath-taken.

Olga looked at herself in the mirror. Clearly, she was satisfied with herself and, with a very feminine movement, starting from her thighs, she moved her hands up over her hips all the way to her breasts. As if she were offering herself, so beautiful that it was not even indecent in the mirror's reflection.

Almost out of regret, she stopped posing, smiled strangely at her image, and Teddy saw her reach out for the negligee. With her right hand. Because, with her left, she made a surprising gesture. She brought her hand, pointing with the index finger, first to her heart, then her two shoulders and finally to her forehead while her eyes stared weirdly at nothing. She froze for a few seconds.

Teddy Verano was stunned, but his mind was hard at work.

Following the old peasant custom, being naked she crossed herself... But, God in Heaven, Olga Mervil had crossed herself backwards!

He shivered. The ghost detective, the enemy of witches and vampires of pseudo-mages and false occultists, knew what this sacrilegious gesture meant

At that moment, someone knocked at the door.

CHAPTER VII

Teddy Verano desperately craned his neck, trying to see more, but, unfortunately, from his position, he could get no closer. Hanging over the walkway, holding his breath, able to do nothing else, he listened. At least, he should consider this worth the effort.

He still saw Olga, who was standing in the same position. And this struck the detective. Because the naked woman did not even have the reflex to cover herself with her negligee. This was a strange show of immodesty, and Teddy Verano told himself that Olga Mervil was, without a doubt, like no other woman.

All she said was "yes," in a flat voice, like "enter."

Because of all the people coming and going in the studio, there were any number of different individuals who might be knocking at the young star's door. Knocking and entering, since she had invited the person in so simply, while being so scantily dressed.

No, Teddy told himself, *this girl is not normal. Even if she knew who was knocking... and how would she know? Second sight perhaps? Hmm...*

It was so extraordinary irrational. Olga's dazzlingly swift debut, shot up like an arrow, the publicity she got that seemed to come spontaneously, and now the technician's death that brought in the journalists—wasn't there something rather unnatural about it all?

Teddy saw a man's shape now. He saw him from the back and only above the shoulders. At an angle. It was hard to see enough to be able to identify him later.

Olga still showed no shame. She had not blinked an eye. She watched him close the door behind him with her big, black eyes, which resumed that occasional sparkling stare that was so characteristic of her.

There was a long moment of silence.

Olga watched the visitor, this visitor whom Teddy could not see well, and who was standing face to face with Olga, enjoying an exclusive show, a show that thousands of men would have given their eye-teeth to see.

And although Teddy was in a bad position to judge, he would have sworn that this man had not come with lewd intentions. Moreover, Olga's beautiful body showed no signs of excitement, nor did her calm face, poorly lit of course, but whose strange beauty was still striking.

At last the man talked.

"Olga... you were expecting me?"

"Yes."

The answer was curt with no sign of emotion.

Another silence, then the conversation began. Their voices were quiet, but clear and surprisingly cold. Under the apparent iciness, however, Teddy Verano thought he felt strange currents flowing.

"Do you know why I came?"

"Yes, I do."

"Did you forget your promises?"

"No, not at all."

"You will prove it?"

"When I'm asked to."

"What have you done for the one who is helping you?"

"Nothing yet. I haven't had the opportunity."

"The opportunity will come, Olga. Very soon. Do you feel strong and ready to succeed?"

"I won't fail."

Again silence. What was strange was that neither of them had moved. They stayed in the same position face to face. Olga, still naked and showing no embarrassment, had not asked him to sit down. Teddy Verano, understandably, was starting to feel dizzy.

The visitor continued:

"Olga... are you satisfied?"

"How could I not be? Ever since... since I said yes, luck has smiled on me."

"You've recognized the fortunate chain of events?"

"How could I doubt it? I've got it all... All of a sudden, I've got everything I wanted with all my heart..."

"You can say 'with all my soul,' Olga."

Here, she looked slightly troubled for the first time since the conversation began. The little gloom did not escape the perceptive eye of the hidden spy but undoubtedly not of the mysterious visitor either.

"Say it, Olga... *with all my soul.*"

Olga was clearly nervous. But she pulled herself together and in voice that broke a little she said:

"With all my soul."

"Why the hesitation, Olga? It's your soul that's at stake. And thanks to it, you are becoming, day after day, in ways unknown since the invention of the cinema, a superstar, which even the most famous achieve only after years of struggle."

Olga nodded but said nothing.

"Thus," the man continued, "the One who must not be named has given you proof of the power. You know it and that's good. Furthermore, today, just now, right here, you got further proof, Olga."

This time, the naked woman shivered.

"In what way?"

"Let's see, Olga… On your clothes, on you, is there not blood? The blood of that boy who was gnawed away by his love for you?"

Olga got uncomfortable and reached for her negligee.

The man stopped her.

"Oh, Olga! Modesty… What a foolish sentiment! It's unworthy of you."

After a pause, the words that the man spoke hammered into Teddy Verano's ears:

"…Unworthy of the servant of the One who must not be named."

So, Olga stayed naked, motionless, icier than ever, after a brief show of emotion.

"Olga," the voice went on a little more passionately, "the fate of that boy is a guarantee for what awaits you. Hundreds, nay, thousands of men will be at your feet. You will be worshipped as a goddess. They will kill themselves, they will die for you. Women will be in agony and tear themselves apart out of desperation because your beauty, multiplied on all the screens across the world, will bring discord, debauchery, desire and jealousy… all the passions. Oh, Olga, our master will be so proud of you!"

Olga listened to this crazy speech that wrapped around her like a demented, magnificent and intoxicating aura.

"Henri's blood, my beautiful Olga, is the gruesome baptism that you have accepted, that you have to receive… Don't tremble. It had to be like this. Isn't this what you desired?"

"I still desire it," Olga said forcefully.

"Excellent! That will please our master. We'll be asking you for proof of your loyalty very soon."

Olga did not say anything, once again, but Teddy, who had good eyes, saw that she accepted by blinking her eyes.

"Are you ready?"

"Yes."

"Do you know what is asked of you?"

"Yes, but…"

"But what?"

"I don't know the name of the… the victim…"

"Hush! The name cannot be revealed to you yet."

"But I'll need to know it so I can act."

"You will be notified in good time. Today, I'm only here to see how you are doing."

A brief silence. Then Olga asked:

"Can you just tell me… when I'll know?"

"Soon, Olga. When? Even I don't know. I or someone else will come to tell you. All you have to do is obey."

"I will."

"Whoever is the person?"

"Whoever it is," answered Olga, stiffening up.

Teddy Verano never knew how it happened, but he suddenly had the feeling that Olga was now alone again in the dressing room. The man had disappeared, secretly, closing the door behind him without a sound.

You'd swear he had vanished into thin air.

Olga did not budge. She stood there, absorbed in thoughts that the detective imagined were terrifying, but that remained hidden to him.

At last, the young woman came out of her trance, slipped on her negligee and cracked open the door of her dressing room. She called out:

"Martine... Martine... Come here!"

Teddy Verano, who was about to leave his perch, decided to stay a minute longer.

The blonde Martine did not take long to run up.

"You called me, darling?"

"Yes, kitten. After all, you're my 'public relations' girl now. Have you seen Tragny? Or Trempont?"

"Yes, just now. Say, Berthe was wondering if you want some tea."

"Yes, I'd love some. So what's new?"

"The investigation is going to stop. It was an accident. Oh, the poor kid. I feel horrible."

"Don't think about it too much, sugar."

"You know he had a photo of you on him?"

"Yes, I know. Soon there will be many others with my photo."

"Oh, Olga," Martine was shocked, "how can you say such a thing?"

"Martine, sweetie, I'm becoming a star. This isn't the time to get sentimental... What's wrong?"

Martine was sniffing the air.

"What is it? Do you smell something?"

Martine's face suddenly dropped.

"No, nothing." And right away, she followed up with, "Tonight at 11 p.m. at the *Blue Parrot*. With Trempont. It seems they have to see you there... There are a bunch of stars coming."

"Well, that's where I belong now. Along with my public relations girl, right?"

Olga hugged Martine just when Teddy Verano decided to climb down from the walkway. The studio was clearing out and he could leave without anybody asking anything. They took him for another journalist.

He went back home with a troubled mind, thinking about everything that had just happened, not only the technician's death, but also the weird things said by the stranger paying Olga a rather secretive visit.

If I'd seen him leave, I could have followed him...

He laughed a little to himself.

135

Another time... I'll see him again. In the meantime there's the rendezvous at the Blue Parrot *tonight.*

He had dinner with Yvonne and his stepson Gerard. But his mind was elsewhere, and they let him know it by ribbing him kindly. Gerard asked him if had fallen in love with the new superstar everyone was talking about.

Teddy Verano snapped out of his reverie and replied:

"Instead of saying stupid things, why don't you get the news on the radio? I'd like know if they're talking about the tragedy at Teleor."

They did indeed talk about it after sports and politics.

"Olga Mervil's glory is getting bigger every day. We've just learned that the French discovery of the year has received a very special offer from Hollywood... A 7-year contract for two films a year... We congratulate her, especially since those watching consider her success absolutely unique in the annals of film and..."

Teddy Verano was not listening any more. He was starting to think that such luck, such unnatural luck, must have come with a high price to pay.

And something that rarely happened to him occurred: he got scared.

CHAPTER VIII

The ambiance, with its false glitter, was like in all the nightclubs.

At first, one saw nothing, but a jumble of humans, a mass of intertwined couples, clustered together, gliding slowly to the sound of the music, which drifted in waves through the smoke-stuffed, perfumed-plagued, sweaty atmosphere that gusts of air-conditioning tried in vain to purify, creating nothing but cold, unpleasant drafts for those in its path. The lights were placed so strangely that they only cast vague puddles when they fell upon a face or a shoulder.

At one of the tables near the stage, a young man sat alone in front of a glass of whiskey, leaning on one elbow, smoking and scrutinizing the darkness with a deeply interested gaze. He had spotted *her* a little while ago.

She was not dancing. She sat at a table with several very lively people. A table, moreover, at which the eyes of the customers in the *Blue Parrot* were almost constantly staring. A beautiful woman sat in the middle and they had masterfully positioned the parrot-shaped lamps (after the name of the establishment) to flatter her. It was Olga Mervil, surrounded by Marcel Trempont and several actors, including Jean-Pierre Max.

But Michel Roz, sipping his Cutty Sark, lost in thought, only had eyes for the young blonde girl at the table of celebrities, who looked a little embarrassed, a little out of place in this ambiance that ill-suited her. She sat apart, rarely laughing at the jokes of witty Bob Andair, the TV actor. She spoke even less.

Since everyone was looking at Olga Mervil, Roz was probably the only one interested in Martine. He, too, was not dancing. He did not feel like it tonight.

At 30 years-old, well built and slim, he was one of those young men not lacking distinction who wander into this kind of nightclub sometimes, seldom participating in the general fun, but looking abstracted, always in search of that special girl or of his own dream. Michel Roz, however, thought he was seeing his dreams come true.

This young, discreet, blond girl who looked so charming and intelligent. . .

He saw that she was out of tune with her circle of actors who are always a little superficial. Like everyone, he knew about the hype around Olga Mervil and was fully aware of Marcel Trempont's talent and reputation, the discoverer of stars, and he wondered what the delightful girl was doing there.

Nearby two women were chatting, giving him inviting looks as often as possible. In spite of the darkness (the girls were lost in shadow much more than the stars), he could only see that they were young, pretty and carefully preened. But Michel Roz was not interested and ignored their advances. He was watching Martine.

The melancholy in her eyes and her sober outfit clashed violently with the joy being flaunted by Olga, whether a true or false joy, this and many other things made him create a novel, make up a whole story around the stranger, build up a screenplay where he only wanted to play the romantic hero.

The crowd suddenly heaved. The music stopped and while all the parrots turned on at the same time, a group entered the room carrying small cameras, tape recorders and portable spotlights.

"Television…"

Michel Roz lit another cigarette, listening to the girls next to him in spite of himself.

"It's for Olga Mervil."

"The luck of that girl… it's like she gets all the breaks…"

The trivial comments of the dolled up girls brought a smile to his face. But the two chatterboxes babbled on, expressing all the envy, all the jealousy of all pretty girls faced with one whom they judged "not bad, but no better than the rest," and on whom fortune had smiled lavishly.

Olga was very relaxed, as if she had had ten years of stardom, welcoming the reporters and posing for a ¾ shot with Marcel Trempont.

Then the dance struck up again and, this time, they filmed Olga waltzing in the arms of the handsome Jean-Pierre Max. They set up the tape recorders for the interview to follow.

One of girls next to Michel had just been asked to dance and left with her new partner. The second girl, seeing him stand up, thought it was for her, but she was disappointed when she saw him walk away. She started powdering her nose fiercely.

Michel Roz had made up his mind. While the TV people were setting up or taking pictures, he had noticed that the blonde girl was left alone at the table. She, too, was freshening up.

He would never have dared to ask for a dance at a table with Olga, Trempont, and all the famous people, but suddenly, seeing her by herself, even more alone, he plucked up the courage.

"May I have the pleasure, Mademoiselle?"

Michel Roz would never forget the sweet, piercing eyes that looked up at him. No, this girl was not a regular at the *Parrot*. She looked more like a shy kid lost in a room full of adults. More than ever, he had the feeling of a troubled child.

Martine's gaze lasted only a second, but the examination must have been positive because she accepted with a nod, and stood up.

They waltzed together for a while, in silence. He was thoroughly happy with her being with him. This girl, seen for the first time, was definitely having a surprising effect on him. Nothing compared with those spicy, exciting girls for whom the first dance is but one step closer to the bedroom.

The waltz ended. While walking her back, he asked quite humbly, almost shyly (which was not his style), if they could dance again. She said "yes" kindly, not at all like a "celebrity's friend."

A little later, they played a tango. Olga stayed at the table this time, pouring into a microphone some totally pointless words, punctuated by that weird laughter that had become her trademark, a laugh of wild joy that made the listeners shiver.

"I have to admit," Michel Roz said, "that I never would have dared to approach you…"

"Why? Am I so intimidating?"

"You? No, absolutely not. But you're part of her entourage …"

"You don't like it?"

"It's not that, but when you aim too high…"

She laughed, graciously, and they started talking, very quietly, swept away in the throng of dancers where they had turned the lights back down. Olga's table remained the only lighted place in the *Parrot*.

After some small talk, Michel learned that Martine was a friend "almost since childhood" of the new star, and she was in charge of her PR. With charming naiveté, Martine admitted that the title was purely honorary, because she knew pretty much nothing about the role she was supposed to be playing.

"Olga is so good to me…"

"Oh. And yet, she seems so daunting."

"Don't say that. She's beautiful."

"I don't deny that. But a fierce kind of beauty… Anyway, they say she's going to specialize in horror films, that she's going to replace of Edwige Hossegor, the famous Mephista."

"They say a lot of things," Martine sighed.

"That aren't true?"

Her beautifully clear eyes looked up at him. They passed under a spotlight and, all of a sudden, he saw a dread fear in her eyes.

"What's wrong?"

"Nothing… nothing."

"You looked worried."

"Excuse me, Monsieur, I… no, it's nothing."

"Do you want to go back to your table?"

"Oh no! I want to stay…" she blurted out.

"With me?" he whispered, softly, very affectionately.

She snuggled against his shoulder so that he would not see her face and maybe also seeking his manly protection.

Carrying her away to the rhythm, he teased quietly:

"You seemed… scared of the Devil… Or a witch… Your friend Olga must be a little like a witch…"

"That's a stupid thing to say."

"Her success is like black magic."

"Oh, be quiet!"

They were silent for a while before he spoke again. His voice was full of charm like an incantation.

"There are some girls who need a knight to come to their rescue and fight off the demons."

He felt her tense up against him. Her slender hands were shaking and he suddenly knew that she really was scared and his jokes were not just jokes—there was some truth behind it all.

"What a pity," he said, "that you're with all these people."

"But I owe so much to Olga."

"Not at all!"

Once spoken, she seemed to regret her words. Even in the shadows of the dance, he thought she had blushed. Finally he took the leap.

"Listen, mademoiselle... Mademoiselle... what?"

"Martine. And you?"

"Michel. The name of an archangel. Well, I don't have this honor... but you know..."

"The one who brought down the Devil." She giggled. "The Devil and his demons..."

"You're going to say I'm pretentious. But those who fight never fight better than for a pair of beautiful eyes in distress."

"Why do you say that?"

"Because... it seems to me... you're afraid."

She did not answer.

They played the tango again, and this cut short their conversation. She fell back into his arms but, this time, he knew that she was terrorized. Looking up, he realized that, while dancing, she's been looking over his shoulder at a point in the room, next to the bar.

Michel turned around and saw, among the darkened crowd, a man, rather tall, standing still, who was not drinking, not smoking, just standing at the bar, on the edge of the dance floor, looking at Martine.

He was really struck by this, and stopped for an instant. He apologized but she, as if mesmerized, did not respond. Then, with the instincts that belong only to chivalrous, headstrong men, he grumbled softly into Martine's ear:

"If you're scared of that man over there..."

"Oh, be quiet! I'm sorry..."

She tried to wriggle away from him but he held her.

"No, please... Stay. With me you have nothing to fear."

Once again she looked up at him and, for a minute, they danced slowly, without saying a word, barely seeing each other in the poor light. For Martine, it was a relief to see this face that was still young, so open, and so full of energy, that seemed so different from all the other faces that were always "performing"

140

around her, all the actors that Olga had been rubbing shoulders with over the past few weeks.

She cast another nervous glance at the stranger before letting herself be swept away in the dance. But he was turning closer to the bar. He was leading her there. Slowly. Because all the dancers were moving in slow motion to the languid rhythm of the tango as their bodies mingled together.

Michel had no sexual thoughts although Martine's alluring body was hugging him tightly. He realized that he was protecting her, that he was born and put into this world to save her, like a heroine from the legends, and he felt possessed by the spirit of romance, by a knight's soul lost in the middle of the 20th century.

They reached the bar. The stranger was gone.

Martine, without saying a word, was looking for him and seemed relieved by his absence.

Michel felt the need to tell her:

"He's left."

"Yes, I... No... Perhaps I was mistaken..."

"I know I'm being forward, but I'd like to help you."

"Oh, I'm so glad you said that!"

"You know, I think I can."

She put her cheek on his shoulder and said very softly:

"I believe you."

The dance finished and he brought her back, greeting the people at her table, although they paid him no attention. The reporters continued their interviews.

He left as the band started a jerk. Then there was another tango. Michel needed nothing more. Martine watched him coming back, happy without really knowing why. This time, it happened fast.

The scary man popped up at the edge of the dance floor right when they passed by. Michel tried to look into his eyes as he stood there, obviously on purpose in a patch of shadow to hide his face. He felt Martine trembling in his arms. He was fed up. He stopped dancing right there. Martine stiffened up and tried to hold him back.

Michel turned to the stranger, grumbling:

"Are you done watching this young lady?"

The other did not budge.

Michel walked toward him, still not able to see his face clearly.

"Did you hear me? I'm talking to you!"

"Please..." said Martine, grabbing onto him.

"Come on, this guy is harassing you. As if I can't see it."

The guy in question stood as still as a statue. The people around could see Michel's anger. Nothing would stop him now.

141

"Are you going to answer or not? I'm telling you to get the hell out of here."

He took one step closer. He went no farther. All of a sudden, he felt a shock. Like a punch in the stomach. But an electric charge. He fell back onto the floor, bumping into the other dancers. After being dazed for a second, he stood up, furious, not even thinking to apologize. He ignored the men's sarcastic remarks and the ladies' cries of alarm and shouldered his way through the crowd, looking for the stranger, but he had vanished, who knows how.

The incident was already forgotten amidst the bass beats as the orchestra started in on another jerk, completely different than the tango.

Michel spotted Martine at a distance. Bob Andair had come to get her and he saw Olga, Trempont, J.-P. Max and the others standing up. They brought Olga a fur coat. The reporters were packing up.

"She's going…"

He felt like she was searching for him in desperation, but the group of film stars were surrounding her, carrying her away.

Michel was bewildered by the whole evening and could not move. A man was standing next to him. He jumped, but saw clearly that it was not the mysterious stranger who was terrorizing Martine and had taken him out…

And how had he done that anyway? Michel could have sworn that his adversary *had not even touched him.*

He was surprised to hear a kindly voice whispering to him:

"Don't worry. You'll see that charming girl again. Because she could very well need you, a brave man, to protect her. Excuse me, can I buy you a drink? I'd like to have a few words with you. I admired your attitude just now. Only idiots would laugh at your fall." A pause and then, "Idiots… and those who do not know." He led Michel to the bar, adding, "But I should introduce myself. My name's Teddy Verano."

He said his name and in the glow of the bar lights, Michel saw his hazel eyes sparkle.

CHAPTER IX

Will I see him again? thought Martine.

It all felt like a dream, like Michel had just appeared and then disappeared forever...

And yet I'm not crazy. It was real.

But do I know what is real or not, what is tangible or not, after these last few, frightening weeks in Olga's shadow? If only I'd known... Of course, I'd hang onto him...

But no, I'm turning into an idiot, with all that's happening. How could I literally throw myself into the arms of someone I'd known for only half an hour, maybe a little longer? But I felt something strange when I was with him.

It's not the first time men have flirted with me. In Lille... and then in Paris... And even more, since I started playing secretary to the stars... Well, a future star, but already on her way thanks to the well-orchestrated publicity, the clever hype...

And then things got scary with the bloody death of that poor young stagehand.

The papers will get hold of it and make some bizarre connections. They already are. Olga, covered in the poor boy's blood. And at the same time, she gets a wonderful offer from Hollywood.

No, they'll say whatever they want. They'll make thousands of conjectures. I have my own idea. I say, it's not natural.

It all started... one morning. After a sleepless night, worried crazy, I was waiting for Olga. She wasn't the same after that night. I've thought of all kinds of things. I'm sure I'm wrong, that it's something beyond my understanding.

Something dreadful...

But what?

I tried asking Olga about it several times. She loves me, I'm sure, and she constantly shows me proof of it. She treats me like a sister and forced the production people to give me this job, even though I'm totally incapable of doing public relations. "I'm just happy to be her faithful little secretary. Others do the work with the press and the public...

I'm stubborn. I want to know. I drop hints. But I see that I annoy her, that she doesn't want, or can't, answer me.

Her whole attitude has changed. Oh, she's still alone, of course. If she had a lover, I'd know. Because we still live together, but in a beautiful apartment now, on Avenue Paul Doumer. Our little studio in Montmartre is long forgotten.

Who is paying for all this? There's money... where does it come from? Advances for films... What else?

I'm dizzy. I'm scared. I have to admit it.

Despite Olga's generosity, I'm scared of her. She's got a fire constantly burning inside her, and sometimes she stares at me. I don't know if she's seeing me or not, but it burns me...

Can I continue to live like this? I want to run away, bury myself in a simple life, boring but normal.

I know what I'm missing. The arm of a strong, healthy, sincere and open young man. I have no interest in those around me at the studio. Men and women in search of one-night stands. For a lot of people in this business, nothing is important, not even marriage... Maybe I'm old-fashioned but I dream of a quiet happiness, a happiness that lasts. Getting married in order to divorce—that's not the life for me!

So, there was Michel last night... Out of the blue, I was starting to trust him, to talk to him. Was I being stupid? I don't know anything about him. But there are people we meet and feel like we've known them for years, forever...

Dare I give a name to these feelings? It'd be crazy...

But then the other *showed up.*

I recognized him. In Boulogne, in the rain, at the café window, when I was waiting for Olga... Again, following us down the Seine in the fog... Olga pretended that I was wrong, that it wasn't possible... But I saw him.

And it was him again last night. Him... and his eyes... Eyes that glowed.

There was Michel's aggressive reaction, and then the fall. After that, I was separated from him, and Bob Andair came to take me away. I was back with what they're already calling "Olga's gang." We left the Parrot *and didn't see Michel again.*

My God, I'm crying. Yes, I'm crying. Will I ever see him again?

It's my fault. Silly goose, I should have pushed Bob Andair away, told him that I wanted to see the young man who so gallantly defended me instead of running away like a coward. But I'm shy, timid, passive. No, I must rebel! I shouldn't have such an attitude anymore.

What happened to him? What does he think of me?

Martine, you're becoming a romantic. Forget about this man...

In my confused state, far away from my family, alone in Paris with Olga, alone because Olga isn't the same, I have no one to trust...

I would have liked to trust Michel.

Olga...

She's here in her room. No more little twin beds like in that wretched studio where we used to live. I have my own room now, not too big, but in her house, it's worthy of a star...

Four o'clock in the morning. They brought us back. We're alone. But what's that? She's talking... to whom, Good Lord?

I'm cold. I'm scared. I'm shivering. Someone is with Olga. Who?

Do I have the right to know? Is there really a man here? Of course, it's her right, absolutely, but still, I wonder if...

I want to know. I can't stand it. And I'm doing something that's not nice at all. I'm listening at her door, trying to see through the keyhole....

Olga is there, dressed in a see-through nightgown that shows off the beautiful creature that she is. She hasn't gone to bed yet. She's standing with her hands in front of her, like she's praying, and talking with... with someone invisible.

She's talking... I can't hear what she's saying. I press my ear against the door, not trying to see for the moment. I listen carefully, with my full attention.

"No, not her! I can't. That would be dreadful!"

I heard this—or almost. What does she mean? And it's not the first time I caught her like this, talking to no one with her big eyes wide open, eyes that are worse than scary...

Olga... She's talking... I have to listen... I have to know...

"No, all-powerful master, don't make me... It's awful. It's atrocious. She's innocent. Oh, yes, I understand, that's why..."

Olga seems to be suffocating under some terrible weight and she gasps:

"It's because she's innocent... A pure victim is needed and that's how the sacrifice will be completed."

What does all this nonsense mean? Olga's going crazy...

Often since... since that infamous night when she didn't come home, I've wondered about this. Has she lost her mind?

But in her professional, life she's completely the opposite, very reasonable, cold, impenetrable; she argues well, stands up for herself, and intimidates the filmmakers as well as the journalists. I never would have thought she could become such a remarkable businesswoman.

What a contrast between this girl who, according to one reporter, already knew how to sell her talent and beauty so well, and this poor thing in a state of delusion, almost nude, holding dreadful conversations with god-knows-who.

Who indeed? It's as if Olga is talking with someone from another world...

She's groaning now, and I try to see again. I see her begging, wringing her hands, asking them not to touch... Touch who? Who is the innocent victim she speaks of?

Then, since the other *seems unrelenting, in a desperate gesture, she turns her hands against herself and, with sudden madness, claws at her breasts.*

Blood spurts...

"Olga! Olga! Please!"

I cannot take it anymore and I rush into the room.

Olga snaps out of her hypnosis and looks at me with pure horror in her eyes, as if I were a ghost. It stops me cold.

Nude and beautiful, bloody and tortured, she is magnificent and frightening.

She screams as if an invisible hand is strangling her:

"You... you... I don't want to... Get out... Go... You don't understand..."

She backs away and pushes me away. I want to help her, not to leave her like this, I run to her and try to take her in my arms.

"Martine, no!"

"Olga, please..."

What is happening to her?

She pounces on me and her hands, those beautiful temptress hands that they said were made to caress or to kill (a journalist's phrase, but true) grab me by the throat.

She's strangling me... I'm going to die... Help! Michel...

Everything is spinning around me. I struggle. And I hear a voice, a different voice, dark and hoarse, a voice that is unnatural, a voice that says:

"Don't kill her, Olga. She must live. The sacrifice has to follow the rules. When the red mass is celebrated, when you are who you want to be, nothing else will be refused you..."

But Martine did not hear this. She had passed out. She was nothing but a poor little body, a young girl fainted in her nightshirt, as delicate as a crumpled flower, at the feet of beautiful, bloody, terrifying Olga.

CHAPTER X

A human meteor shot into Teddy Verano's office on the Rue d'Enghien. The detective was on the telephone, trying to calm a woman who had hired him to follow her husband whom she suspected of having an affair.

"Calm down, Madame. I'm going to send you a detailed report. But I can assure you, right now, that there's nothing in it and your husband is simply hiding from you to play the horses... I will admit that he bets big. Yes... Are you sure? I understand, Madame... yes... understood... with the little note, OK... my pleasure, Madame."

While talking, he made signs to his untimely visitor to stay calm and sit quietly. In vain. The newcomer was flushed from running and out of breath. He fidgeted constantly and looked like a man with news of the utmost importance.

Two or three times, with the telephone to his ear, Teddy Verano had to furrow his brow and point fiercely at the chair. But the other paced around like a lion in a cage, desperately wanting to speak. Verano, however, could not just drop a client.

When he finally hung up, he started to say:

"What the hell! Can't you wait a minute...?"

"Monsieur Verano, it's horrible!" said the visitor.

"What is?"

"Martine's disappeared."

"What? Disappeared? When?"

"Three days ago."

Teddy Verano jumped out of his chair.

"Three days! Bloody Hell!"

"Three days and three nights."

"Since that night at the *Blue Parrot* then?"

"Yes."

This time, it was Teddy Verano's turn to press his visitor.

"Come on, talk... Tell me what happened!"

Michel Roz flopped into an armchair. His voice was strangled by emotion.

Three days ago, Teddy Verano had met the young man when he had invited him for a drink at the nightclub where Olga Mervil, Marcel Trempont and their gang were holding court, along with pretty Martine.

They'd met next to the dance floor, where the brave and generous Michel had tried to confront the man who was terrorizing his maiden (Martine in this case). Michel had just been knocked down in some inexplicable way. The detective had reassured him, explaining to him that the girl was in no immediate danger, at least for the time being, and anyway—this seemed to make Michel happy—it would be easy to find her again if the need arose.

After all, didn't she live in the shadow of Olga Mervil, the up and coming star? She was her secretary, her confident, or something like that.

They had talked for a long time. Michel Roz was overwrought and his budding passion for Martine had been sparked by their unusual encounter.

Teddy Verano had seen right away how to make good use of this attitude. Since Michel was looking for Martine, and she was deeply interested in him, he only had to bring him into his camp.

The next day, spurred on by the detective who had told him what he was doing, and hinted that weird things were involved in Olga's unusual success, Michel Roz had hit the streets, neglecting his own affairs to conduct a little personal investigation.

Teddy Verano had guided him, providing the necessary information. Michel Roz called him every day. So far, he knew that Olga kept filming every day in Boulogne, but her blonde friend was nowhere to be seen.

Led to the Avenue Paul Doumer, where the future superstar was living, mingling with the journalists, who were all over the celebrity's neighborhood, he did not succeed in spotting Martine.

Finally, he had worked wonders to get in touch with a housekeeper who worked next door to the two women. The servant was a repatriated woman from Algeria. Michel Roz, who had an uncle in the same situation, had bonded with her, and found out what had happened three days, or rather three nights, earlier.

A little before dawn, which meant the day after the memorable night at the *Blue Parrot*, the concierges had seen a car—an American or Italian limousine, she wasn't not sure—park for a moment. Olga Mervil got out with Martine and a man whom she did not recognize. The car sped off into the night and returned only after daybreak.

It was cold. It was raining.

This time, Olga was the only one to get out of the car. She went back home and, the next day, life went on as normal for her. She went to the studio and had many visitors, but Martine was nowhere to be seen.

Michel Roz had learned this one hour earlier, after he had managed, after a long, hard build-up, to "seduce" the housekeeper. Without a second to lose, he had jumped into his car and rushed over to the Rue d'Enghien, knowing that, at this hour, he would probably find Teddy Verano there.

The detective bit his lip listening to Michel's story. Had he been completely wrong? He had guaranteed that Martine was not in any immediate danger. Had he missed something?

Of course, he had not told Michel Roz everything. He was particularly secretive about the weird conversation he had overheard at the studio. While Michel was talking, Teddy Verano was reviewing the facts and broke out in a cold sweat.

Olga, he suspected, was playing a dangerous game. Wasn't the man in the limousine the same person who had come to ask the star to keep who knows what promise? He had even mentioned some future victim. Could it be Martine?

Scared now, Teddy Verano asked himself this question, but did not want to say too much to the young man who was falling in love. Hadn't he proven this, first by standing up to the guy who had such a strange effect on Martine, and then by searching patiently for her for three days on his own?

And the man from the *Blue Parrot*, could he be anyone but the very same person Teddy Verano had barely seen at the studio?

Some of the things said, or hinted at, and some of Olga's gestures, had brought out some strange suspicions in the ghost detective. Being around witches, sorcerers, ghouls, vampires and other creatures from beyond, often mixed up with criminals and charlatans who exploited both the gullibility of men and the invisible, mysterious, undeniable forces that could take on frightful forms in evil hands, all this had given him a remarkable education in the Occult.

Michel Roz, for whom he had just poured a glass of whiskey to keep him in the office for a moment longer, looked at him and said:

"My God, Monsieur Verano... you're sweating!"

It was true. The detective was really afraid. He was building up a dreadful scenario in his mind. He thought he understood Olga's role, and the other role, that of the innocent, the unaware, was the one she had made poor Martine play.

Whoever the *Other* might be, the designated victim they were talking about in the studio had to be Martine. What infernal power was demanding that Olga sacrifice her friend? For what unthinkable purpose? In exchange for what reward, what benefit for the future star?

All of a sudden, after a moment of silence, of thoughtful concentration that Michel Roz dared not interrupt, Teddy Verano decided:

"Finish your scotch. We're going. No, hold on a minute."

He jumped on the phone and dialed a number. Michel sipped his Cutty Sark and watched his every move.

"Hello. Mademoiselle Mellion? Teddy Verano here... I need to talk to Mademoiselle Hossegor... Yes, it's urgent. Is she there? The baron's not there either? It doesn't matter. It's her I have to talk to... Yes!" He paused a moment, then said, "Say it's about Mephista..."

At this name Michel Roz perked up but said nothing. Teddy Verano was already saying hello to Edwige Hossegor and asking to see her immediately.

"OK, we'll be right over," he said, hanging up.

Roz swallowed the last of his whiskey.

"Quickly, we're going to Passy."

"We can take my car."

"No, mine."

They hardly talked during the ride, which was slow going with the red lights and all the traffic at that hour.

"When you hear what I have to say to Mademoiselle Hossegor, you'll know everything," said the detective.

More traffic around the Pont Mirabeau.

"Michel, you've got guts, I know, but I need to ask you, before going any further... how much do you care about Martine?"

"It's stupid, I know, and crazy. I saw her for barely an hour, but after we danced together... she was telling me secrets... and then, that man... she's in danger, I feel it..."

"Yes, but what kind of danger?"

Michel Roz was about to ask more questions but Teddy Verano shot off between two trucks.

Shortly thereafter, with no more time to talk, they were being welcomed by Edwige Hossegor. Eva Mellion had made a discreet exit.

"Edwige," Teddy Verano began, "this is Michel Roz, who should hear what we have to talk about. You know that I don't want to disturb you for nothing. You also know that I take your intuition, your premonitions seriously... I still don't know what's happening, but it seems that you were right on target."

Edwige lifted her beautiful head and her eyes sparkled.

"Mephista is at it again?"

"I'm afraid so."

"And Mephista... is... that girl?"

"In this case... yes."

Michel Roz was quite intimidated. Being from the business world, he was not used to being close to a famous actress like Edwige Hossegor. But Teddy Verano was talking, and he was listening, scared, to the conclusions being drawn by the detective's reasoning, as he acknowledged Olga's weird behavior, the incident at the *Blue Parrot*, and what nobody but him knew so far: the mysterious conversation in Olga's dressing room.

The longer he spoke, the paler Edwige became.

In playing her diabolical roles, she had slowly become familiar with the world of the Occult. Her professional conscience compelled her to get information about mediums, prophetesses, sorceresses and other creatures that she played. Then, there had been her own adventure with Mephista, the evil wax robot who looked like her and committed abominable crimes in her name, Edwige Hossegor, the great star of the screen.

Michel Roz was horrified. A realist by nature, he knew nothing about these things that had once made him shrug his shoulders. But now, things were different. There was Martine. He did not yet understand much, except that he was so suddenly passionate about her, and that she, happily, seemed to feel the same about him, but she had disappeared and was threatened by unusual dangers.

Teddy Verano had finished talking. There was a short silence that Michel Roz dared not break. Edwige stood up.

"Teddy, you were right to come here. We have to go to the studio."

"That's exactly what I was hoping you'd say. I'm not the police, and it's hard for me to break through the front door. Besides, Olga doesn't know me and, until we hear differently, she hasn't committed any crimes."

Michel Roz admired Edwige's triumphant smile when she said:

"So, we agree. I told you that it'd be better to know. Well, let's all go to the studio together."

She straightened up, magnificent, always the performer, even in her natural movements.

"I want to know... I will know... And this girl, I'll rip off her mask. Yes, Teddy, you can count on it... I'll rip it off her..."

CHAPTER XI

They started over. They started over and over again.

In the movies, they figure that a day's worth of film equals one minute on the screen and, most often, the public knows little of the enormous work of the director and his many collaborators.

In spite of the difficulties of the scene, of the cold violence demanded by the character, Olga earned everyone's admiration. Each time, she was able to put on (gladly, they would say) the frightening face of her character.

It was a particularly dramatic scene during which the heroine of *Horror at Midnight* was having a young man tortured. Marcel Trempont's art was to highlight the melodramatic aspect of the scene, to keep the brutal visions (which were sometimes farcical) in the background, so to speak, and stay focused on the faces of the protagonists.

They saw, one after another, the tortured look of the patient, the faces of the torturers, half-hidden by scarves, and, finally, Olga's face. The cold cruelty, the sparkle of sadistic joy in her eyes, the sensual ferocity sketched on her lips made for passionate kisses—that was what editing would give to the sequence of captivating images.

Marcel Trempont was sweating blood and tears, but the technicians thought that this scene would be one of the best of what they had already filmed. And everyone, unanimously, stood in admiration of the art of Olga Mervil.

Was it even dramatic art?

You would swear that "you were there," as the stagehands said.

In the shadows around the set, surrounded by black velvet, where the skillfully lit faces were captured one by one by the cameras, more than one of them was whispering, "This girl is really scary…"

Olga's legend was taking shape, solidly, and nobody could forget that, a few days earlier, a few feet from where she stood now, they were filming another scene, during which the body of young Henri had just crashed down to the ground.

But time had passed.

The work day was over and Trempont's assistant was politely pointing to his watch, while the director talked about another shot. Trempont was about to push him away, but quickly held back.

"Right. It's too late. OK, thank you all. See you tomorrow, guys."

And straightaway, the silence in the studio was broken. The incredible, almost religious, respect that surrounded filming gave way to all kinds of private conversations. Lights were turned on almost everywhere, while the huge spots died out. The black velvet background suddenly lost its magic and the actors walked off.

It was then that Marcel Trempont noticed the three visitors who had quietly entered during the last few minutes.

"Oh, my dear friend, you're here."

He kissed Edwige's hand and, with one of those elegant and vague gestures of a star, she introduced her two companions simply as "friends." Trempont shook Teddy Verano's hand (whom he remembered seeing before around Edwige), and then Michel Roz'.

Edwige explained that, with Tragny gone—traveling abroad on business—and being terribly bored at home, she wanted to see the production up close. Neither Trempont nor anyone else at Teleor could refuse Baron Tragny's beloved anything, so the director offered to take the visitors to the bar.

"Later, dear," said Edwige. "I'd like so much to congratulate Mademoiselle Mervil. My friends are also ardent admirers."

Trempont bowed and, in no time at all, Edwige with her two companions were standing in front of Madame Berthe.

The dresser was playing her role well. Sometimes, dragons spit fire to keep away unwelcome visitors from the dressing rooms of the actors who were so often assailed by people who had nothing to do there.

But she knew Edwige very well, having dressed her, and she babbled while smiling:

"Mademoiselle Mervil... Of course! She'll be so pleased..."

Olga was in a bathrobe and had let down her beautiful black hair. Berthe introduced Mademoiselle Hossegor and, naturally, the future star gave her most beautiful, stereotypical smile to the "successful" star who was paying her such an honor.

"Berthe, some chairs... and some port for everyone."

"You're as nice as you are beautiful, and as beautiful as you are talented, for sure," Edwige said as she sat down.

Teddy Verano sat off to the side with Michel Roz, and admired the ease, the manners, and the apparent confidence of Edwige.

At Tragny's house, and during the trip over to the studio, they had talked and compared their notes to come up with a battle plan.

Teddy Verano was well aware of what trouble had been dwelling in Edwige's soul. And yet, he was pleased to see that she seemed to have taken back control of herself. Had the actress made up her mind to stop being the victim of demons like Mephista? Or was she playing another role?

This was possible. Her sizzling career might allow her to appear relaxed, smiling, very comfortable in the dressing room of an actress who could become her rival tomorrow, if not her replacement. But if a duel was bound to take place between these two, Teddy Verano was sure that it would not be only on the artistic plane.

Devastated by her roles, scared by the evil projections emanating from the characters she had embodied, Edwige Hossegor had turned down *Horror at*

Midnight and graciously, it seemed, left it to the debutant who was uncommonly lucky. Therefore, she had no apparent reason to be jealous.

Teddy Verano even knew that, on hearing about the tragic death of the stagehand, Edwige had almost sighed in relief, thinking that such a tragedy might have happened to her.

But now, there were too many odd things surrounding Olga Mervil's debut. A bloody aura was forming around her face that looked so pure—but a purity disturbed by her glaring eyes.

In the up-and-coming battle, Teddy Verano believed he could find no better support than Edwige Hossegor herself. Better still, it was Edwige, she who had once been Mephista, who said that she was ready to stand up and attack.

Berthe poured the port. Smiles flashed all around as they exchanged "star" talk about how dull the scary scenes were, how interesting to be directed by an *artiste* like Marcel Trempont, and whether or not the screenwriters were worth what they were paid.

Michel Roz wondered where all this was going. They were wasting time, he thought. He was thinking only of Martine. What had become of her? What was going to happen to her?

Michel knew all about the mysterious person who had come into this very dressing room to remind Olga of some terrifying promise she had made to seal some even more horrifying pact...

Suddenly, Edwige changed the conversation to Olga's acting. Since no actress in the world is impervious to this kind of subject, it was easy to start in after a little small talk.

"Just now, my friends and I were admiring you. Really! To reach such a degree of cruelty for such a beautiful woman is great art, if I may say so."

Like a real star Olga took it in stride.

"Coming from you, Mademoiselle Hossegor, it's the highest compliment... I must tell you that I have often admired you, on both the big and small screen. Your acting in diabolical roles was the height of perfection. No one will ever equal your exquisite creation of Mephista."

"That's kind of you to remind me... But playing those scenes exhausted me. It's true, I must have pushed myself too hard... because I'm really not such a monster in real life... and can I say, without offending you of course (she had that tinkling laughter of a woman of the stage), that I admire your nature even more."

Michel Roz and Teddy Verano both saw very clearly, though fleetingly, Olga Mervil's reaction.

"It's true. I'm pretty relaxed about it."

"As if all this was so simple for you," Edwige continued, "...or so straightforward."

There was a brief silence. One of those heavy silences before the storm.

Edwige furrowed her brow. A little too soon, perhaps, for Teddy Verano, but Olga had felt the attack.

"I've worked a lot on these kinds of roles."

"Really? I thought you were just starting out?"

Olga gulped her Cintra and put down the glass.

"You can work... without filming anything at all."

"Very true, Mademoiselle Mervil. But to reach such a degree of realism takes either a lot of experience in acting, or..."

Edwige paused and took a drink herself. The two men waited for the clash of swords in silence.

"Or... what?" Olga asked with a smile that suddenly betrayed all the nastiness boiling up inside her.

Edwige still sounded cheerful.

"What was I saying? Ah, yes... that to prepare for such a role without acting experience, it would take... let's say, great knowledge of the world. At least, of a certain kind of world..."

She kept smiling. Olga too. And these smiles on these two pretty women were full of poison. Neither Michel Roz nor Teddy Verano could find anything to say. They could not interfere in a duel like this.

Now Edwige attacked more directly.

"Aren't you upset by that awful memory? That poor stagehand who fell off the beam and crashed at your feet, splattering blood all over you... What a horrible baptism for an actress just starting out."

Olga, in spite of her tremendous self-control, looked like she had seen a snake. She could feel not only Edwige's searing eyes on her, but those of the two men as well. Her feminine instinct sensed a danger that she could not yet determine, but that was growing stronger.

"You mean...?"

"Just what I said."

Olga was curiously pale, but she reacted:

"It's horrible, I admit, but it was only an accident."

"Was it really?"

"What else could it have been?" Olga said, with a furtive smile. "Don't tell me you think it was murder?"

"Murders," Teddy Verano spoke for the first time, "are not always committed in simple, natural ways."

"Sorry, but I don't understand, Monsieur."

"Oh," Teddy Verano said, "maybe it's too much for you, but Mademoiselle Hossegor, if I understand correctly, means that there's a difference between the movies and reality, between drama and life, between real blood and stage blood... The boundary that separates us humans from the world of the dark, of the beyond, is not so clear-cut... and when one is involved in certain roles..."

Olga pulled herself together.

"Are you saying that, somehow, someone can bring bad luck?"

Teddy Verano smiled. A mischievous flame burned in his hazel eyes.

"I'd go further... even bringing good luck. Well, relatively good luck... Like for great artistic success, for example... You know that there are people, women, who back away from nothing to get what they want. Especially in the movies. And sometimes, they use frightening methods. Although this brings them 'good luck,' which is only a relative term, it's also true that bad luck can fall upon other people around them."

Olga looked uncomfortable as she fumbled around for a cigarette. Michel Roz offered her one and Teddy Verano held out a light. With a triumphant smile, Edwige stared hard at the girl. But the three of them were up against a formidable adversary.

"I have to admit that this is all a little too hazy for me. So, who are you really? Journalists?"

"Please... we're investigating the mystery of a new star's sudden, meteoritic ascent to fame."

"I'm not a big star," Olga smiled.

"But you will be soon, if..."

Olga shuddered at these words.

"If... There's an 'if'?"

"Maybe. Some methods, in fact, can backfire."

Olga suddenly stood up, wrapped in her bathrobe.

"Excuse me, I forgot. I've got an urgent appointment. I have to get dressed."

"Oh," Edwige said, "you still have a few minutes. By the way, I was surprised not to see that young friend of yours... you know, that ravishing blonde who works as your secretary, I think, and who hasn't left your side since Marcel Trempont and Teleor found you."

"My friend Martine. She's gone to see her family."

Edwige looked at her not hiding her skepticism.

"I don't know her, but I'm worried about her."

Olga, too, sounded sarcastic.

"She will appreciate your concern, I'm sure, Mademoiselle Hossegor."

"Don't you agree that things are kind of messy around you, Mademoiselle Mervil," Edwige pressed on. "Like the bloody death of the stagehand we were just talking about. You never know... if some bad luck had struck that young man..."

This time, Olga could not hold back. Her stunning face twisted in anger and it was as stunning as it was scary. Marcel Trempont's cameraman had gotten the same sensational shot with this look on her face during the pinnacle of the torture scene.

"But who are you?" she barked.

"And you?" Edwige shot back.

She was standing up now and walking toward Olga.

"Who am I? I'm Olga Mervil... A woman... An actress..."

"Let's go!" said Teddy Verano, trying to grab Edwige's arm.

Olga looked like she was starting to panic.

"Who do you think I am?" she stammered.

Edwige, leaning forward, beautiful as well, but more impressive because more of a woman, more mature, more solid, spoke again, in a soft but broken voice that contained all the terrors and all the passions that she had lived through:

"You're something more than that, Olga Mervil. You're something coming from me... You're one of my roles... You're all my roles mixed up together .. Everything horrible and scary and breathtaking that I ever portrayed... You're the demon and the witch, the vampire and the murderess... incarnated into one... I know it... I feel it... You can't fool me... One man has already died because of you and a young woman has disappeared... Since you walked into this studio, I can feel dark forces prowling about... Can you deny it? Can you say it's against your will?"

"Get out!" Olga yelled. "All of you, out! Leave me alone!"

"Not quite, my charming Olga."

Quick as lightning, so swiftly that Teddy Verano, who had been trained in such reflexes, admired the movement, Edwige had opened her handbag and pulled out a small revolver and pointed it at Olga.

"Let's stay calm, OK?" said the detective.

Teddy Verano figured that Edwige's skillful maneuver was due to some scene she had once played.

Olga was trembling now, backed against the wall. Staying a safe distance away, Edwige spoke in a tone such that one could not tell where the tragic actress ended and the woman ready to fight began:

"Olga Mervil, you're the woman I hate because she was born from me .. She's a projection of all the evil women I brought to life in my career... Olga Mervil, you are Mephista."

Michel Roz was dumbfounded. He saw only one thing: although the situation was completely absurd, Olga did not deny it; she accepted Edwige's surprising accusation without even a shrug. He understood that he had just walked into a frightening world that he was obviously not expecting to find in a movie studio.

Above all, he was wondering what dangers might be looming over Martine, the exquisite girl he knew so little about and who, minute by minute, was growing dearer to his heart.

But Olga, shaking like a demon sprinkled with holy water, asked:

"What do you want from me?"

"You're going to get dressed and follow us."

"Where?"

157

"We won't hurt you, Olga Mervil. On the contrary, we want to exorcise the evil inside you... and find out what's become of Martine."

"Get out if you want me to get dressed. I'll call my dresser."

"No need. These two gentlemen will leave, but I'm staying."

Teddy Verano waved to Michel Roz and they left the dressing room. They said nothing. In silence, they were absorbed in their thoughts. The detective was thinking that Edwige was a beautiful fighter, and her career as a femme fatale had been good for her firm, aggressive qualities.

Soon the two women reappeared. Olga was tense. As for Edwige, she was pretending to play with her scarf, but they guessed that she was still holding the revolver. Olga/Mephista was under control. At least, for the moment.

But a few journalists and photographers who were still in the studio had been waiting for the two actresses to leave. Teddy Verano and Michel Roz instinctively flanked the two women.

Edwige could be heard whispering to Olga:

"Smile, Olga. When there are photographers around, women like us have to smile all the time... That's part of the job."

And Olga smiled, along with Edwige.

They left the studio in a barrage of flashes that hit Teddy Verano and Michel Roz as well.

They climbed into the black DS and the detective took the wheel with Michel Roz sitting next to him.

The car sped out of Boulogne going toward the center of Paris, carrying Olga to an unknown destination.

CHAPTER XII

A red fog... a veil, maybe, but red...

I wake up from some kind of nightmare...

The feeling of intense horror, of icy cold.

Where am I? What happened?

The events of the past few weeks have shaken me up. Everything since that awful night when I was so scared for Olga, when I waited up for her until dawn... Her coming back and her strange attitude...

And then, the whirlwind of her sudden success began. Her faithfulness to me, her kindness in wanting me to share her astonishing adventure... The movie, the studio, Marcel Trempont, the miraculous offer from Hollywood...

New, different, surprising faces... But only one happy face, only one ray of hope in this chaos that scared me, filled with other, hostile faces.

Michel.

Michel seen so briefly. Michel, who showed up as if to protect me. Michel, who was separated from me in the flurry of the crowd in the nightclub where I saw that man who looked so menacing. That man with the glowing eyes...

But is he really a man?

I often think he doesn't even belong to the world of the living... that man whom I've now seen several times. He's the one who separated me from Michel...

Where am I then? It's so cold... I slept. My bed feels very hard and cold. And yet, our apartment on the Avenue Paul Doumer is cozy...

Where's Olga? What time is it?

Oh, all this red around me... I feel nauseous... and I see hands, hands, more hands, thousands of hands... hostile hands, menacing hands, hands reaching out for me...

Help! All these hands in all this red...

Olga... yes, it's Olga. I see her. I recognize her. She's like a bird, a huge bird. A bird of prey...

Olga, my friend forever, my soul sister. Olga, who was never poisoned by her sudden rise to fame, who always thought of me and demanded that I be by her side...

This bird with wings spread out... with sharp claws...

Olga, what is this monster in the red fog? It's another Olga, a demoniacal Olga, an Olga with the body of a raptor, with threatening claws, and I don't know any longer if her face is a woman's or some awful bird of prey...

Olga's pouncing on me...

No, I don't want this! No, the claws are sinking into my flesh, digging into my chest, tearing out my heart...

I think I screamed. I'm awake now. The nightmare is over. I'm sitting on my bed. I'm feeling around for the knob on my bedside lamp, but I can't find it. Nothing but a rough, wet wall. How did this wall pop up near my bed?

My bed? This hard, cold bed... where I am lying down dressed in a wrinkled dress and lose stockings... with my hair let down...

I'm scared. I look into the darkness. I don't understand what's happening to me but I know that I'm no longer on the Avenue Paul Doumer.

A basement... Yes, that must be it. I'm in a basement, lying on some kind of cot. My God... what's happening to me?

Martine, poor little Martine, make an effort... Think... Remember... I can't...

I want to scream, but my voice is caught in my throat. Olga...

A jolt shakes me. All of a sudden the veil, the big red veil enveloping my memories, tears away...

I see her again, lusty, hysterical, fighting with ghosts... I see her suddenly walking toward me, menacing, horrible. Another Olga... An Olga like the character she plays in her new role... the sinister Olga from Horror at Midnight. *No more sweet, charming, faithful friendly Olga...*

Suddenly, an awful question crosses my mind like a streak of fire: What if this was the real Olga? What if over the years I knew her, I was cherishing a monster?

No, I'm crazy. There's something frightful in all this that escapes me... I want to, I have to, understand... I will find out.

I stand up. I feel my way along, trying to picture my prison. Because it is a prison.

I'm starting to remember... Yes, that awful night! Olga's hands around my throat... Oh, I can still feel her terrible grip. And it's not an illusion, not a nightmare. It was, dear me, real! Very real!

I know that I must have cried out instinctively:

"Help me, Michel!"

And then, there was a vision of that man... Him again... He was talking, saying:

"Don't kill her, Olga."

After... After, I don't know... I woke up here. But where is "here," Lord?

I feel a light switch. I press it with a trembling hand. Click! A yellow bulb lights up behind a grill in the wall. It is a basement.

The humidity seeps out of the walls. In a corner is a metal bed with a mattress. That's where I woke up. A wooden door, but framed in iron and, of course, locked tight from the outside. Nothing I can do.

A small window... it's too high for me to reach. Besides, it's reinforced and they sealed it shut. Everything was prepared for me.

And it's cold. The walls weep. I can't hear a sound. I stagger around... No, I'm not dreaming. I was dreaming, but now this is real. And what a reality it is!

Let's see, I'm Martine, Olga Mervil's friend. Last night (but was it really last night?) I was at the Blue Parrot with that festive bunch of movie people and journalists, everyone very real, very "in." There, I met Michel. I danced with him. He held me tight and we talked. We told each other a few secrets. It was like a source of freshness washed over my heart...

Today... but what is today? Day? Night? How can I know in this tomb? Time is passing. I'm shivering from the cold as much as from fear...

I cried out. I screamed. I don't really know if my voice "got through" .. I lost my voice. No one answered me. Still no noise, not the slightest vibration. I feel like I'm dead, like I've been wiped out from among the living.

Michel... Michel.. Oh, sweet and manly face barely seen! Why is this man I barely met so important in my eyes, the eyes of my heart?

From time to time... I have no notion of time... I don't have my watch .. I don't know...

They dressed me because I remember that I was in a nightgown when Olga jumped on me and that spectral voice rang out. And they brought me here. Was I awake? Sleep walking? Hypnotized? How can I know?

I don't know anything. I don't even know if I'm still alive... But I am alive. I'm a girl of flesh and blood. And to prove it to myself, I bite my wrist and dig my nails into my neck... A little bit of blood...

Yes, I'm very much alive.

But imprisoned, buried, in who knows what grave... What's happening to me is horrible... under this ceiling crawling with spiders...

Eternity... an eternity is opening before me... I'm going to stay here... I'll never leave... never... never to see a living soul again... never to see Michel again, to live and to love...

Maybe this is hell. My God, what did I do to deserve this fate?

A sound. They're coming.

There's a crazy hope in my confusion, but then again, I'm seized by terror right away. Who can it be if not him, or them, who are keeping me captive, who kidnapped me and stuck me in this abominable place?

I'm right. The door creaks open. A man is entering. I'm scared not knowing. And I'm scared when I see him. I'm disgusted...

He is thick, short and ugly, with the neck of a bull, a shaven head and a brick-red face. The face of an alcoholic, of a degenerate. Those eyes... I know those eyes, and all girls like me know them all too well... The eyes of a perverted man whose pupils light up in a weird, disturbing way before a pretty girl... Eyes that grope and molest...

The man is carrying a tray. A tray with a bowl, a glass and a chunk of bread. He walks in. A bunch of questions bubble up in me, but I can't make a sound. Still looking at me, he puts the tray at the foot of the bed. He sighs and hesitates. I'm trembling, but I want to control myself.

He has to talk. He has to tell me... What is this story out of the Middle Ages or of some bad soap opera where the poor heroine is locked up like this? And yet I'm in the middle of the 20th century. Through Olga, I belong to the world of movies and television... and things like this can't happen.

He looks at me and it's this look that keeps me from talking. What frightful desires reside in those eyes! He leaves, as if regretting it...

The evil spell is broken. I rush to the door but it is locked. I bang on it, bruising my fists. I scream:

"Talk to me! Tell me the truth! I want to know! I want out of here!"

I scream the same things over and over.

He's gone. Silence again. I have seen only one human being. And I'm scared again.

Where did he go? Who is he? That brute could not be behind my abduction. So who is he working for? Who is he holding me for?

Minutes of anguish creep over me. I cry. I yell. But I'm cold and hungry...

Oh, the tray. I go back to my cot. Soup and a glass of wine. Bread. That's all. I swallow the wine, then the soup, which I had let get cold. I nibble on the bread. And then... and then, nothing. Hours in my tomb.

The horror...

He came back. Twice. He brought me the same meager, tasteless meal. I tried to talk to him. He answered, barely, in a lowered voice, but that horrible, lecherous look in his eyes that terrified me.

"I can't tell you anything. I'm nothing. I obey. The masters command..."

I begged him. I threatened him. I don't remember everything I said. He came closer and fear came over me. I knew what monstrous desires were rumbling inside him.

His lower lip hanging down, his eyes shot with blood—he was an awful sight. But I saw what an effort he was making to hold himself back. He feinted a move toward me and I screamed. He stopped.

"I don't want to hurt you. You're so pretty." *He repeated again and again,* "so pretty... pretty." *In a tone of voice... It made me sick.*

But the woman whom a man desires has control over him. I took a chance.

"Please, tell me what's going on. Where m I? Why did they bring me here? What's going to happen to me?"

"What's going to happen?"

He looked at me. He was about to talk. He gulped hard, in a disgusting way.

"I can't tell you."

"So you know."

He nodded and I begged him to talk.

"If I told you... No, it'd be terrible for you. It's better you don't know."

He left and looked back one last time from the doorway. And with a sigh of regret he said:

"Such a pretty girl. What a pity."

Here I am alone again. With the horror.

It's better I don't know. But is what's going to happen really so terrible?

I can't sleep. I'm scared. I turn off the light but the chill darkness makes me so scared... and I'm afraid of the spiders.

So I stay there with my eyes wide open.

I'm cold. I'm scared. I try to exorcise my horror by thinking of Michel. Michel whom I desperately want to see again.

And Olga? Olga the she-demon... Olga the bird of prey... Olga who tried to strangle me...

"Don't kill her, Olga."

I have to live. Olga has to let me live. To live for... For something that man knows about. Something so horrifying that he didn't want to tell me.

Oh, when he comes back I'll jump on him, I'll fight... he has to tell me.

He came back. I was waiting for him. I had the fever. I was ready for anything. I asked him again and he refused to answer. So when he was about to leave I gathered all my strength and jumped on him, screaming, trying to bite him.

He lost his head.

I understood what a stupid mistake I had just made. When I touched him, as violent as it was, I unleashed all the lechery that he had repressed. He howled like a wild beast and, with no regard for my nails scratching his face, searching for his eyes, he grabbed me with his strong hands. He lifted me like a feather and carried me to the cot.

I understood. I yelled, fought, begged...

"No, not that, not that!"

He said nothing. He was panting like a beast. He threw me on the cold, hard bed and tried to rip my clothes off.

No, I'd rather die...

But he's strong and I'm just a young girl. I can't go on...

Michel... Where is Michel?

I feel his disgusting breath on my face. His heavy, hairy hands are tearing off my dress...

And everything stops. I hear a voice. A voice that I recognize. The brute lets me go, backs away, his head lowered. He takes refuge in a corner of the cellar like a guilty dog about to be punished.

I raise myself up a little and see him. Oh, that ghostly face... No, he's not a man, not a living being...

He's the one I saw in the café in Boulogne, who followed us along the Seine, who separated me from Michel at the Blue Parrot... *the one who told Olga,* "She has to live."

His pale hand lifts up and slaps the brute.

"Stupid moron! Don't you know she has to stay a virgin, she has to stay pure?"

What does he mean?

He continues in his monotone voice, a voice that sounds like it comes from another world.

"Purity... Our master demands that her purity remain unmolested, that pure blood flow in homage to the impure... The red mass gets all its power when the victim is unspoiled."

He looked at me. And I was scared, more scared by his ice-cold eyes of death than by the eyes of the hysterical madman who had attacked me.

I'm alone again. I'm cold. I can't even eat. Everything makes me scared. In the yellow light, I tremble in horror... A horror that staggers me, that I don't understand, that I don't dare try to understand.

CHAPTER XIII

The whiteness of the pillow and the sheets brought out the jet-black radiance of the beautiful hair that the nurses had let down and the black fever that burned in the eyes. Thus stripped of all artifice, back to her natural state, Olga was still curiously seductive, with that disturbing aura that gave her all her charm.

Her charm that tomorrow would spread all over the world through the big and small screens, would reach the average man, bewitch the older man, the energetic young man, the teenager who called himself free and was always a romantic of some sort.

Olga looked around. The shot had immobilized her a little, struck her nerves. But she was lucid, very lucid. She realized that they must have driven her to a hospital and locked her up, closely guarded. And these people around her...

There were four of them. The nurses had left. Olga figured that they are not exactly friends, that they had brought her here by force, that they were bold enough to kidnap her right in front of the studio personnel and journalists, and that the battle was about to begin.

They had the upper hand. Would people be suspicions? But who would suspect Edwige Hossegor? Anyway, Olga knew what they would say in this case: "Just a publicity stunt. A trick played by a couple of stars on the media, nothing more..."

Despite her disorientation Olga was aware of her delicate situation. She saw them: the man with the hazel eyes, spirited but always a little sarcastic, and, in spite of everything, with that look on his face that his mysterious nature forced him to occasionally deny: kindness.

The other, younger man looked athletic, determined, with unfriendly eyes and no regard for her beauty. Had she seen him before? It seemed that he had mentioned Martine... It was she who was on his mind. He felt nothing of the spell that Olga's flesh gave off. Because of this, she could not expect any mercy from him.

This other man with gray hair, whose eyes were hard behind the frameless glasses. She heard his name. Gelor... a doctor... yes, that must be it.

Finally, sitting at the foot of the bed, staring hard at her, a woman. More beautiful than ever, in spite of her 40 years plus, and maybe because of her dazzling maturity. Edwige Hossegor. From her either, she could not expect pity or weakness. Olga knew this from the start.

But Professor Gelor was talking.

"Can you hear me, Mademoiselle Mervil? Yes... I know that you hear me. We've just given you a tranquilizer. The nurses put you in bed because, in my opinion, you're not an enemy, not guilty but sick. So, please consider your condition as such, and treat me only as you would your doctor."

They others said nothing. Olga did not respond. The silence was heavy in the room. Olga watched them. She drew on all her strength. She knew that she would have no room for error.

Gelor enunciated every word:

"You're not in your normal state. You're under an evil spell, probably of a demonic kind. Our task is to free you from it. But you have to help us. Are you ready to give us this help?"

Silence from Olga. But a momentary twitch in the corner of her mouth.

Neither Gelor nor Teddy Verano were fooled. It meant: "Don't count on me. You're dreaming. I belong to the world beyond that you deny. I know what I know, and you can't do anything about it."

Calmly, the doctor approached her and took her wrist. Olga appeared passive but her eyes were glaring harder and harder.

"Mademoiselle Mervil, you wanted to become an actress. Everyone knows that, in order to succeed in such a field, and to avoid one disappointment after another, just to give up in the end, or hold on until you're poor or commit suicide, there are four things that are necessary..."

He counted them off, probably Edwige Hossegor had helped him to draw up such a list.

"Talent... Beauty... Wealth... and Luck. You're beautiful and you have talent, but you lacked wealth and you needed luck to replace it and provide it at the same time. We know your impeccable past. You always refused the sad compromises that so many girls succumb to. Therefore, this luck... you somehow helped it along.... Brought it up... I just want to ask you a simple question: How did you do it?"

Silence. Four pairs of eyes posed on Olga, but she did not answer. Gelor, who was probably expecting this, jumped right back in.

"Let's say, if you prefer, what price did you pay to buy your luck, that crazy chance that takes an unknown today and turns him or her into a big star tomorrow, in demand from Paris, or Hollywood, even before finishing his or her first film, whose face is on TV and on the front page of newspapers and more... Mademoiselle Mervil, we're well aware that this came after, er, let's say, a pact that you signed, some kind of agreement that you made. Will you tell us what kind of pact it was?"

Olga did not budge. Now she was looking beyond them, at something or someone unseen.

Gelor pressed a button. A nurse entered with syringe at the ready. She prepared to give the injection. Olga reacted in a flash. She tried to jump out of bed, but screamed out in pain and rage and fell back onto the pillow.

Gelor had moved quickly, but someone had been even quicker yet: Teddy Verano. He knew judo, karate, and all kinds of clever moves to immobilize the strongest adversary. The nurse took advantage of this to stick the needle in Olga's enticing flesh before retreating.

Olga writhed in anger. Gelor stepped back.

"Mesdames and messieurs, it will take a minute."

The scopolamine would work and put Olga at their mercy. She cried out her powerlessness. The breakdown of her will. She knew that, in the altered state her enemies had created, she would be forced to answer their terrible questions and give up, in spite of herself, even more terrible answers. In a few minutes... or hours. Olga did not know.

Everything around her grew blurry against the light blue paint on the bare walls. She saw nothing but all these blazing eyes trained on her. Then, with her last bit of strength, she called out, mentally:

"*O powerful master, don't let me give in... Help me, help me, in the name of Evil...*"

And the voice came to her, hard, unshakeable, as Gelor's eyes seemed to cast steel darts that wound her.

"Olga Mervil, did you sign..."

"Yes."

"A pact? A diabolical contract?"

"Yes."

Now it was a mere whisper. She struggled not to answer, but it was too hard.

"Who dragged you into this?"

The unshakable voice repeated the question until she grumbled:

"Him..."

"What is his name?"

"I.|. I don't know."

"Where did you meet him?"

"At night... the fog... I was cold and hungry... it was all over... he came out of the shadows... he said, 'I know who you are,' and he knew my name, my situation..."

"You were with Martine?"

"No. He didn't talk about Martine."

"We'll get to that. Now, tell us about this man."

"He... saw me again... made me a proposition..."

"What kind?"

"Success. To be a star... The queen of the '70s...wealth... fame... to be the prettiest, the richest and most admired..."

She became excited, talking in spite of the drug. Her face lit up with an inner fire that was frightening to behold, even with all her seductiveness. But none of this told the questioners much. Teddy Verano said he suspected much of this already.

Gelor waved to the detective to continue his questioning.

167

"Who taught you how to cross yourself backwards?"

Real terror came over Olga's pretty face as she mumbled:

"Him."

"Where did he take you?"

"To... the mass... the red mass..."

"Where?"

She struggled not to talk, but the question was repeated.

"In a house... in Paris."

"What area?"

"Near one of the Portes... In a house that will soon be demolished."

"Where, Olga Mervil? You have to tell us."

"I don't know."

"What was around the house?"

A pause before she stammered.

"Water... tower."

They looked at one another.

"Maybe the Porte des Lilas?" guessed Teddy Verano.

The detective and Gelor patiently continued questioning the poor girl who was starting to drool a little. But, bit by bit, they wrestled the secret out of her.

The man. The leader of the inner circle of a dark cult, made up of people who had devoted themselves to evil in order to become rich and powerful, to climb the ladder of politics, or control the one they desired, to satisfy their vices... They celebrated the red mass, the cursed mass, the bloody mass, the horrific sacrilege. Blood was spilled and it always ended in an orgy.

Teddy Verano and Gelor were experts in demonology, so they were not surprised. They knew all the secrets of the black and red masses, the ploys of blasphemers devoted to the Devil, the products of an aberration whose origins was found in the twists and turns of the human brain, so subtle and so fragile.

Olga had gone there. Olga had denied Love and Truth. Olga had—at least, she believed it—sold her soul to the Devil.

From these madmen, these dark, lunatic sorcerers, these bloodthirsty monsters who did not understand the dreadful consequences of their awful rituals, the poor girl had believed that she would get the gilded future she had dreamed of. And events, at least at the onset, seemed to prove them right.

It was a frightening story, but by no means original, except for Edwige Hossegor who, despite being tormented by thinking about all the evil characters she had played, had never imagined that such perversity truly existed.

And it was frightening for Michel Roz, too, strong and healthy, a sportsman, an athlete, to think that in this Space Age, right in the middle of Paris, there were men and women backward and evil enough to worship Satan.

But like a parrot, Teddy Verano kept repeating a question that had already been asked by Professor Gelor, and that Olga had so far refused to answer.

"What was the price of success, Olga?"

"My eternal soul," she finally groaned.

"No, Olga. That's not enough. The Devil is not satisfied with vague promises for the future. The Devil, or at least those representing him here, always requires more. We know that, in a true pact with the Devil, there's always a clause that demands proof—a gift—a sacrifice. You were supposed to bring an innocent victim to the red mass and hand her over to these monsters reeking of sulfur... No, don't writhe in denial... Sulfur! A feature of Hell's presence on Earth! Or perhaps they just buy some at the chemist's to impress people like you... No more nonsense, Olga! You promised to sacrifice a 'lamb,' something to serve as a guarantee of your good faith to the master to whom you gave your soul... What's the name of the victim?"

Olga struggled, groaned, tried not to talk.

"Her name?" Teddy Verano barked.

He knew it, of course. They all knew it. But they wanted her to admit it. Finally, in a frightening wheeze, Olga panted out:

"Martine..."

"Good. And where's Martine now?"

"At their house."

Michel Roz looked like he wanted to pounce on Olga, but Teddy Verano stopped him. They had to find out the location first. A house that was going to be demolished... Near the Porte des Lilas perhaps... But there was also an entire area scheduled for renovation right next-door the Porte de Bagnolet... Old houses stagnating amidst new high rises and motorways popping up on all sides.

They had to know... it was a question of hours, maybe of minutes.

Martine was in the hands of these demented maniacs. Martine would soon be carried alive to the altar of the red mass...

Olga had stopped talking. Suffering a fit, she was foaming at the mouth, twisting and drooling. The star discovered by Marcel Trempont, the one Hollywood was waiting for, had turned all of a sudden into a wretched madwoman.

All four of them, leaning over her, understood that she would not say anymore—not today.

Nothing more for hours and hours.

CHAPTER XIV

"What could she be thinking of?" the nurse on duty at Olga's bedside wondered.

In spite of every possible discretion, the news had leaked out and the hospital personnel now knew the identity of their strange patient. Besides, her photo had been published everywhere over the past few weeks.

Professor Gelor and his partner, Doctor Sorbier, had been closely following Olga's case for the last two days. What illness was affecting her? Obviously, it had to be psychological, but despite more sessions with her, they could not get anything out of her.

At Teleor, everything was going very badly. The filming had stopped. Baron Tragny had been informed told and planned to return quickly. Marcel Trempont was tearing out his hair. They had promised him that his star would soon be back on her feet, but the director was not at all reassured and wondered whether he should start refilming Olga's scenes. But first, he would have to find another girl like her to use as his Mephista. An almost impossible task!

Olga did not move, did not talk, looked like she was always sleeping and asked practically nothing. One nurse. Then another. And another. Olga could never be left alone.

It was the end of the third day. It was dark and drizzling outside. The nurse had to stop reading. There was not enough light and she was forbidden from turning one the electric light, except for necessary care. Olga had not moved. In spite of the darkness, the nurse saw that her eyes were closed. But perhaps she was only pretending to sleep? If only she could pierce the secret of that beautiful face...

Olga knew what was happening around her. Olga waited. The Cult needed her. They would not leave her in enemy hands. They would come and get her.

In the twilight, in that obscurity that enveloped the world, the nurse dozed off. Like all her colleagues, she was vaguely disturbed, realizing that this patient whom they were watching so closely, who was really little more than a prisoner, might pose a real danger for those guarding and caring for her. Like everyone, she had followed the strange adventure. They had mentioned Olga's illness to the press, but the address of the private hospital, located in the western part of Paris, had been kept secret.

Everyone knew, however, that Police Chief Farnese had launched an unusual investigation because of some strange and secret information private detective Teddy Verano had given him.

They whispered about this in the hospital corridors, but what the nurse did not know was that the police was on full alert and the search in the Porte des Lilas and Porte de Bagnolet sectors had not turned up anything.

Therefore, the nurse knew some of the story, but for the rest of it, her imagination ran wild. She had the vague feeling that she was playing a bit part in a drama that was far bigger than her, and for this, she was proud.

The door of the room opened, so quietly that the nurse did not notice it and she remained motionless in her chair.

A man entered. Olga's eyes were still closed, but she *saw* him. She knew who he was.

The nurse started because Olga moved on her bed.

"Do you want something?" she asked.

Olga did not answer. The nurse stood up and approached... No, nothing. The patient was not moving anymore.

Reassured, the nurse went back to her chair to wait patiently. One more hour until the end of her shift, which had seemed particularly tiresome. When she turned around, she saw a man walking toward her silently, after closing the door. Her cry became caught in her throat. Because in the darkness she had seen the glare of those two incredibly intense eyes that seemed to shine like a cat's

For a moment, she did not move. It was like 200-pounds of lead were weighing on her, on her limbs, keeping her from showing the slightest move of defiance. She felt exhausted, very exhausted... Those eyes...

The man stood like a statue, dictating his mental orders. The poor girl backed away, farther, farther... She bumped against the window and stopped, only half awake, only half understanding, so surprised by her sudden fatigue that she thought that death was coming for her final rest.

The man turned his head toward Olga. His lips did not move but he talked and she heard him.

"*Get up, Olga. Get dressed. You have to leave this place and come with me. They're waiting for you.*"

Olga obeyed and took her things from the small metal cabinet. The man watched her and when she was ready, he turned back toward the frozen nurse, as if to consider what he might do with this poor thing under his invisible control.

The nurse opened the window and, like a nightmare, unable to fight against the forces unleashed against her, started to climb on the ledge. They were on the third floor.

Olga and her mysterious guide left, still wrapped in silence.

A loud cry of horror and of death followed them as a white shape fell to the ground below...

Outside, people screamed and called out for help. Straightaway, a huge commotion spread through the hospital and the grounds. They ran to help the poor girl, but it was too late. In the meantime, two shadows slipped through the corridors, passed by the reception desk and left, sneaking through the bushes.

Emotions ran wild. They were expecting anything but this at the hospital. Was it an accident? A suicide?

For a while, everyone ran around, neglecting their duties. Two shadows hiding in the bushes took that opportunity to sneak out the back gate. A car was there with its lights off. The man had the key and was followed by the woman. Quickly, it whisked them away.

At the hospital, they were trying to understand. A stretcher carried away the nurse's broken body. On the police frequency, a dispatch was sent out:

"*Falcon calling Delta. Falcon calling Delta.*"

Upon learning of the attack on the nurse (for, what else could it be?), Chief Farnese swore like a pagan. Teddy Verano was immediately informed. Edwige Hossegor and Michel Roz (the three of them were almost always together now) were at his side when that happened.

"What's going on?"

"The bastards... They threw a nurse out the window. But if they figure that it's so easy to escape a hospital under guard, they're in for a surprise... The police are after them. And if we don't find the house about to be demolished, as Olga called it, it's likely that they'll lead us there."

Michel shuddered.

"As long as we get there in time. Oh, Martine!"

Teddy Verano patted him on the shoulder.

"You want to bet that nothing has happened to her? Yet... I repeat, as long as Olga isn't there, they'll wait. And you don't know Farnese as I do. He let them get away on purpose... It was a trap that he set for them!'

"What can we do?" Edwige asked.

"Well, I intend to prowl around Belleville and Bagnolet. My friends in the police will keep me informed and I want to be there when they throw the net over those madmen who think they're Satan's little helpers. Plus, I've got my own plan."

"I'm going with you," Michel said emphatically, thinking only of Martine.

"Me too," Edwige Hossegor joined in.

The cars took off into Paris. Walkie-talkies were turned on. Eventually the police spotted a suspicious little car in the evening rush hour traffic heading for Belleville. They made sure that it did not look like it was being followed. The passengers thought they'd gotten away scot free. However, police eyes were trained on the car and those inside.

Three women dressed in black entered. Martine was startled to see these new apparitions.

Instead of the perverted brute who regularly brought her meals, but now barely looked at her, just putting the plate down and scurrying out as if he was afraid of his own desires, these three creatures had entered her prison.

They were three women who were still young, with beautifully done-up hair, but whose exquisite make-up could not hide the weird wrinkles, the odd sags marring their faces, which had not yet suffered the assaults of old age. Three women no doubt affected by some mysterious depravity.

Martine examines in a daze their weird black dresses. They were covered from head to toe, but with a bold, obscene design slashed out in places that a woman, even scantily dressed, normally hides under even the flimsiest clothes.

Martine did not have much time to scrutinize the dresses. The three women came up to her. They surrounded her.

"You're coming with us," they said in a monotone voice, with no emotion.

Martine, without knowing why, was more scared of these women than of her lecherous jailor. She scooted back on her cot, where she usually stayed, lying down. Small but strong hands grabbed her and dragged her off. She struggled, yelled, but the long hours of captivity in the horrible cell (several days and nights no doubt) had worn her down.

Another voice, as impersonal as the first, murmured:

"Don't be scared. We're going to make you beautiful, even more beautiful."

And the third almost chants:

"You have to be beautiful, more beautiful…"

Half-conscious Martine left her evil dungeon with them. She could not say where they went. Dark places, other basements probably, and then, the blinding light of a very modern, very comfortable bathroom.

She had no strength to resist. The three women, with slow, methodical movements, in no hurry, steadily but forcefully, took off her wrinkled clothes, stinking of her captivity, and put her in the bathtub. The warm, scented water felt good and the women's hands dipped into the blue water, massaged her, relaxed her…

After the pleasant bath, they dried her with spotless towels before putting a white dress on her with no underwear. A very decent dress, the opposite of the shameless outfits of the three strange women. A dress that was plain, buttoned in the front with a belt around the waist.

They sat her down and fixed her hair. She breathed in heady perfumes but barely reacted. Was this a dream? Was the nightmare continuing? Evolving?

A hidden fear was gnawing away inside her but she could no longer fight back.

These three women… Their wilted beauty, their distant, gloomy eyes, it was all so hideously frightening…

One of them spoke, still in a dead tone:

"It is time."

And the two others repeated:

"Yes, it is time."

They surrounded Martine again, after examining her with eyes that show no reaction. Obviously, however, they judged her ready since they left the bathroom, leading Martine like a well-oiled robot.

Martine walked. She thought she heard some muddled whispering. She couldn't see well because, after the bright, clear light of the bathroom where they had given her that weird preening, she was now in the dark. The hallway seemed endless and totally black. But at the end was a hazy light, reddish, cloudy…

Martine arrived with her three guides who stuck right next to her.

A curtain. A black curtain, but the eerie glow filtered through an opening. The three women made Martine go through and the procession came out in a big room with a fairly low ceiling, its walls entirely covered with the same black curtains, shiny like nylon. A black hanging covered the ceiling and gave the gigantic box the appearance of a vast coffin.

There were people here, lots of people.

Men with bare chests wearing nothing but tight, black pants. Women with the same outrageous, immoral dresses as Martine's three guardians. People of all ages. All of them staring with gloomy eyes.

But when Martine entered, there was a kind of shiver that ran through the eldritch crowd. Then silence. Total silence.

Martine, almost being carried by her three companions, approached the back of the big, black room, noticing that the reddish glow came from huge, queerly twisted candelabra, all holding thirteen candles. Thirteen black candles.

The air was heavy and perfumed, with a mixture of sulfur and incense, probably coming the night-colored candles.

Before the fixed stare of the motionless, mute audience that had now stopped its constant whispering, Martine arrived at the back, between two huge candelabra also with thirteen branches and black candles, but these were absolutely enormous. Between the candelabra was a kind of platform, also covered in the shiny black nylon.

Three steps. A cube covered in black, like everything else. Or something like an altar.

Martine looked in outraged shock at the crucifix hanging above the altar. Hanging *upside down.*

An irresistible nausea washed over her. She stepped back. She felt something evil was brewing… something beyond abomination.

But the three women in their prurient robes grabbed onto her. Martine cried out in horror as they dragged her, indelicately now, up the steps to the altar and lay her down on the black table, holding her tightly as they tied her down with silver cords.

The candelabra diffused their hideous red glow.

And the half-naked crowd, stricken with a sudden tremor, exhaled a ghastly rumble, a muffled, menacing rumble like a cursed caress…

174

CHAPTER XV

It was like a flood of flesh and night, menacing and sensual.

Martine, stretched upon the altar, did not see the people. She sensed them without yet realizing anything, except that she would have to experience the deepest depths of horror.

But a man had just shown up, parting the group of adepts of the foul sect. He went to the steps and the three women separated, though remaining there, standing solemnly. He was completely draped in a kind of black gown, different from the other men present.

The gown made his pale face stand out more hideously with its sunken eyes, thin lips and bird-like nose. He was ugly, the kind of ugly that evokes phantoms. Martine knew him, even if all she could see was the dark ceiling—the frightening person who had popped up several times in her life over the past few weeks.

He made a sweeping gesture and everyone became quiet. In the funereal chapel, enwrapped in the smoky red glow, all that could be seen was a confusion of shadows and naked skin in suggestive and pale blotches.

Marcel Trempont and his team could not have done better. But maybe the filmmakers would have balked at the ridiculous, outdated aspect that must have totally escaped these fanatics in the creepy crypt.

Now the formerly empty eyes became strangely lit up. Men and women squeezed together were getting excited, eager to see the weird ceremony they had been waiting for begin. And all of the them, especially the men, were staring avidly at the white figure of Martine, literally posed on the altar and whose white robe showed off her curves, making her more desirable than all the shameless women huddled there among the half-naked men.

The man started speaking.

He spoke about the dark days before men walked the Earth, mixing up spells gleaned from old grimoires and verses from ancient Hindu texts. Even though nothing had yet happened between the adepts, the crowd was more fit for the vice squad than any other department of the police. A healthy, balanced mind would have promptly called it the worst gathering of crazy people anywhere.

But those present believed in the power of the evil entities they worshipped.

"The grand moment is here... the time when all of you will worship our Dark Master, when you will not be satisfied with harmless gatherings where only animal blood is spilled .. Tonight, we are going farther than ever before. The ultimate sacrifice. The promises of the red mass will be fulfilled. Then all of you will receive the reward for your loyalty to our Master... and your success, thanks to the Prince of this world, will be certain. Nothing will be refused you, and all joys on Earth will be given to you."

A ripple went through the crowd and the groping began in the shadows of red and black.

The priest of Satan suddenly raised his arms toward the back of the room.

"The priestess is going to appear… Opposing forces have mobilized to stop our sacrifice. I was able, thanks to the powers of Evil, to free her and bring her here. Nothing can stop us now."

He paused. Then in a solemn voice, he said, '

"Appear, daughter of Satan! Come forth, Mephista!"

On the altar, the poor little body of Martine shook with a violent trembling. She was slowly starting to understand, to imagine she understood. And the many strange things she had noticed in Olga's behavior were now seen for what they really were.

Under these madmen's control, what wouldn't she risk?

Olga stepped forward. Wearing the same black gown as the priest, she walked among the faithful. Everyone was looking at her and more than ever, their eyes shimmered like garnets, reflecting the red flames dancing on top of the black votive candles.

Walking stiffly, majestically, more beautiful than ever, Olga came to the altar, climbed the steps, but did not even look at Martine before turning to face the crowd. In one, quick movement, she dropped her gown and appeared in her statuesque nudity, highlighted by the weird lighting that cast copper, blood, unforgettable tones on her skin.

A murmur ran through the adepts, which the priest stopped with a raised hand.

"Mephista, tell us who you are. Tell us what the Evil One is expecting of us."

With her beautiful voice that the Teleor microphones had recorded for the world's screens, the new star spoke. She told of her gloomy youth, her coming to Paris, her fruitless efforts, her outdated honesty and her pointless virtue. Then she had met the Evil One, learned out about the diabolical cult, and had been called upon by the Infernal Powers.

She found out, she stated, where the road to Truth lay. In the well-being from riches and free love, in the intoxication of glory. Trampling underfoot the years of poverty, she accepted the sinister pact, sold her soul one night during one of these red masses, where the priestess was another woman who had preceded her on the paths of renunciation, and who had won the hand of a billionaire. Olga could verify that she had got her wish, and was now one of the richest women in the world.

In turn, she was pulled out of the rut. In one day, almost, her wishes became reality.

Then the black priest smugly brought out Olga's contracts, talked about the movie she was filming, all the interviews, and the offers from Hollywood.

Finally, Olga said that she was thankful to everyone who had got her where she was, indicating that her sacrifice was a small thing: renouncing virtue and denying Christianity...

But what a reward! What a triumph! A golden future was opening before her, and she was inviting everyone present to imitate her. She was getting more and more worked up, intoning the words they had whispered to her in place of a liturgy.

"I am Mephista! I am Evil! I have been baptized in blood, by the body of a boy who desired me who came crashing down at my feet and the scarlet wine of death splattered me... I am Satan's Daughter! Through my image, spread across the world by the millions, I will stir up all desires, I will break up true love, I will build up impure ones, I will set man against woman, man against man, and I will ascend a throne of gold and blood to reign like the women whose bodies inflame and corrupt all men on Earth..."

She talked and talked, boasting of all the monstrosities that she hoped for, that she wanted to see come forth on her path to becoming the perfect femme fatale, the woman who gives nothing, loves nothing, who is pure, cold delight and whose eyes and kisses are lethal poison.

Finally, trembling, she thundered:

"Tonight, for you, before you, I will celebrate the sacrifice and this will be the supreme red mass. I will sacrifice what I hold most dear to me..."

The small frame in the white dress did not move. Drowned in horror, disgust and the dizzying nonsense, Martine realized that the awful comedy was going to turn into a bloody tragedy and she fainted—which spared her from hearing this:

"I have to sacrifice the person I hold dearest... I have no parents, I have no lover. I have no child, but I'd throw it on this altar if I had one. I do, however, have this young girl by me. One of those girls who are crazy enough to want to remain pure, to believe in love... It was decided that she would be my red offering to the Prince of this world. Therefore, it is to him I pay homage by offering up this pure blood..."

Hysteria broke out among the audience. Among all the men facing the altar, there were two who were bare-chested and in black stockings like all the others, but they looked at each other, and a flame lit up in their eyes that had nothing to do with the demented perversity that shined in all the others.

No one paid particular attention to them. All the worshippers were too absorbed in the exalted words of the naked priestess and in thinking about the atrocious act that was about to be committed.

Olga cried out:

"Do not back down! Do not tremble! All together with me you will stick the knife into this fresh, young throat. All of you will drink the cup of life and death! You will delight in sin, you will reach the plenitude of the Unfaithful..."

A kind of panting, a gasp rose from the crowd where the caresses were already becoming more focused, more daring.

The black priest led the next stage with gestures. One of the three women in black brought a cushion with a silver knife that shined eerily. Another approached Martine, still unconscious, and started opening her dress, specifically buttoned in the front for this gesture. The ambiance in the room became surprisingly tense. The lunatics gathered in the black, coffin-like crypt, had showed self-control so far, but were now quivering in anticipation of the hideous spectacle promised to them, which would be, according to Luciferian tradition, the signal to unleash their basest, most bestial passions. A storm of debauchery and blood was looming.

Two men in the crowd were sweating profusely, like the rest, obviously, but for different reasons. They did not share the vile desires of the gathering. These women, lower than dogs, and these blinded men, this whole audience waiting for the Devil's gifts, made these two men's hair stand on end, and froze the blood in their veins, despite the sweat seeping out of their skin.

The black priest was now off on an infernal prayer punctuated with arcane words borrowed from the kabbalah and even older texts. The hermeticism of the speech brought the hysteria to a peak for this crowd that, like all crowds, was impressed by what it did not understand.

The three wanton priestesses who were starting to quiver, like everyone else, surrounded the victim whose throat had been laid bare.

The priest growled hoarsely and Olga, Mephista, she who had sold her soul to mount the artificial heights of fame, grabbed the knife lying on the velvet cushion.

She raised it up, offering her perfect nudity to the crowd and presenting the weapon like a sacred object.

Then, she spun around and stood next to the altar where Martine was still motionless, still passed out. All eyes were on Olga. The storm was waiting to break out. These lunatics, these depraved creatures, this whole group of monsters, were holding their breath for the final gesture, the crime that would unite them in infamy, that would earn for them, through the blood-thirsty figure of Olga, the good graces of the Prince of Darkness.

But the knife did not strike.

A shrill whistle rang out under the black ceiling. Shouting broke out on all sides and a mad scramble erupted.

A voice like thunder shouted into a microphone:

"Police! Nobody move!"

Two of those present were not willing, it seemed, to obey such an order. Together, they rushed to the altar and charged at the priest and priestesses. Olga's wrist was broken by a judo chop and she collapsed, dropping the knife, which stuck the altar only a few inches away from Martine's immobile face.

The black priest tried to target his frightful eyes, his hypnotic eyes, on his attacker but a taunting voice said:

"Oh no, pal, not on me."

And the villain got such a hard punch in the stomach that he fell backward into the huge candelabras that stood on the altar, knocking them over. The thirteen black candles tumbled onto the black nylon curtain and it caught fire.

Screams and shouts echoed through in the crypt where the panicking, frenzied crowd was quickly surrounded by the police, who were jumping through the openings in the black curtains.

The curtains themselves were spreading the fire at breakneck speed, reaching the ceiling so that now it seemed like some punishment from on high was striking those who dared to deny Heaven and who could already feel the devouring fire descend upon their heads…

It was one of those weird Parisian landscapes of the late 60s. Giant buildings springing out of the ground among muddy lakes and oceans of churned up dirt. Here and there, a few feet away from the circular boulevard, amidst the ultra-modern houses, near the motorway, a few ulcers were still attached to Paris, run-down shacks, old homes surrounded by gloomy gardens, clinging to the ground as if out of remorse, withered shrubs and stunted bushes.

The police cars were here, in the rain, grouped around one of these old houses, not far, as Olga had said, from the water tower of the Porte de Lilas. The wailing fire engine sirens could be heard. Fire was spreading through the house's basement that had a whole network of tunnels that extended rather far, but that the police were guarding well after the plan had been set up in record time.

There was an endless line of policemen, both in uniform and plain clothes, coming and going, in and out of the basements, dragging off characters in cultish outfits, men in black stockings, women in obscene dresses, half-nude, disheveled, some burned, others prey to epileptic fits, many of them crying and begging or yelling that it wasn't not supposed to happen like this, or that it was all a big mistake…

The whole crazy cult was thrown into the paddy wagons.

One man seemed to be directing the operation. He put himself on the line, had risked his life in the burning cellars, despite the fact that the air had become nearly unbreathable because of the fumes given off by the nylon in flames…

"Chief! There're burn victims… casualties… The fire is spreading all over the house!"

Chief Farnese gave orders, but the firemen were already on the job and barging through.

Near the policeman's car, a woman was pacing back and forth, holding a cigarette that she barely smoked. She threw it away just to light another.

"Madame Hossegor," Farnese said, "I understand what you want, but this is no place for you."

Beautiful Edwige Hossegor was not here out of vain curiosity. Bravely, she wanted to see the job through to the end and she was the one who had informed the police chief of Teddy Verano's reckless plan.

"Nothing surprises me from him. He'll end up biting the dust one of these days," Farnese had grumbled.

He knew the private detective, the ghost detective, who at least once in his life had wanted to attend a red mass. And Michel Roz was right behind him, his mind made up to do anything to see Martine again, who had come into his life like a meteor, and for whom he was ready to risk his body and soul.

Edwige Hossegor was terribly nervous. The police had discreetly invaded the hideout of the Devil worshippers, but Edwige she knew that Teddy and Michel had plotted to slip in amongst the cultists to be near the altar at the critical moment. What had become of them?

The firemen, it seemed, had a lot to do; the suffocating smoke from the fire was already being contained. The police officers were pushing and pulling even more people in their bizarre clothes.

One solid young man came out gripping a woman's body wrapped in a white tunic. She struggled and screamed something.

"Why, it's Michel Roz!" Edwige Hossegor cried out.

He had scorched hair and a few burns on his shoulders and arms. He let go of Martine whom he had yanked off the altar of blood. He yelled for someone to take care of her and they brought over an oxygen mask.

Another man among the prisoners was protesting. It took Chief Farnese himself to free him and give him more decent clothes by tossing an officer's cape around his shoulders. Through his coughing, he told Farnese briefly how he and Michel Roz had intervened just in time.

The Chief bit his lip. Could his men, given the same opportunity, have stopped the final gesture? Of course, they had been able to locate the damned house, raid the basements, and surround the maddened gathering. But to save Martine, this was hardly enough. Without Teddy Verano's help...

"What about Olga Mervil?" asked Farnese. "The vamp playing her movie characters in real life?"

A police officer approached.

"She's not in the wagons, Chief. She must still be down there with a few others."

The fire chief announced that they were having a hard time bringing up some the burned, disfigured bodies.

180

CHAPTER XVI

Quai de la Rapée. Two days later, early morning. It was drizzling. Everything was gray, gloomy and forlorn.

Two men left the Morgue where Chief Farnese had asked them to come and at least try to identify the bodies: Teddy Verano and Michel Roz.

The day before, other witnesses had come, including the director Marcel Trempont and various employees of Teleor. All the people who knew Olga Mervil. Farnese had likewise thought of Martine, but in her condition, they had spared her this gruesome glimpse of death.

In any event, all results were negative.

Five bodies, three of which were women, had been recovered from the basement of the diabolical house, from the ruins of the sinister chapel where the monstrous, bloody red mass had taken place and ended in a torrent of flames. Charred, unrecognizable bodies. Impossible to identify. Moreover, they still did not know the exact number of devil worshippers, or the exact identity of all the fanatics.

Olga Mervil... What had become of her?

One of the bodies, as far as the burned remains could be identified as a woman, certainly seemed to be approximately the same size as the beautiful girl who wanted to become the new Mephista. But neither Marcel Trempont, nor his collaborators, neither Teddy Verano nor Michel Roz, could say for sure. It might be her, maybe, but maybe not...

Michel Roz and the detective were walking slowly along the Seine. They were heading for the parking lot where Teddy Verano's beloved black DS was waiting for them. They still had not said a word. They were haunted by the frightening vision of the ghostly faces, horrible to see, and the twisted limbs partly eroded by the fire.

"The Devil used them," Chief Farnese said as a funeral oration.

Teddy Verano, however, was determined to snap the young man out of his reverie.

"Farnese won't be satisfied. I think he'll want to ask Edwige Hossegor to come down, but it won't do much good."

"Plus, the last I heard, she's going to be very busy. Do you know that since Tragny returned, there's been a big meeting at Teleor. Millions have been lost; all the scenes of *Horror at Midnight* shot with Olga Mervil are now useless, since they can't finish the film without her."

"I know. They're starting over. At least, with everything the heroine was in. And they end up where they should have started." Teddy Verano snickered, but not out of meanness. "Dear Edwige! Her career's got the better of her again! She's agreed to take on the role... I think that, when all's said and done, she's still convinced of her moral innocence. An actress can play a wicked role to perfection without spreading evil. She just simply can't have the abominable state of mind of Olga Mervil who believed she was summoned to success in order to sow destruction in the minds and hearts of others."

"Sure. Marcel Trempont must have sighed with relief when Edwige agreed to play the part. Olga Mervil would not have lasted. She'll soon be forgotten. Another starlet will replace her."

"But no one's going to replace Edwige Hossegor anytime soon. Whether she wants it or not, she's still the perfect Mephista. On the screen. While in real life, she's the best of women. But let's talk about Martine. I imagine it's a more interesting subject for you."

Michel Roz lit up.

"She's doing better. Professor Gelor is sure that the emotional shock won't have any harmful after-effects. When I see her, she has this smile... Oh, I know she's going to be fine."

Teddy Verano put his arm around the young man's shoulder.

"The worshippers of the red mass never imagined such an outcome. With their hypnotic powers, their sacrilegious rites, and all that ridiculous mumbo-jumbo, they still gave you a happy ending; that, I believe, is positive."

Michel Roz relaxed and began to forget the dark hours spent in the Morgue.

"Yes. I can breathe. And Martine is going to live... far from this nightmare."

Teddy Verano stopped by the river to take out a cigarette while Michel Roz offered his lighter. The detective mused for a minute.

"What a bunch of idiots! Devil worship! They must have been crazy!"

Michel Roz suddenly looked more somber.

"Excuse me, Monsieur Verano, you seem to think that this whole thing was mostly an illusion; a few exploiting the gullibility of a bunch of perverts..."

"That's right."

"I always refused to believe in the stories of a world beyond ours, but in this circumstance, there's something that troubles me a lot."

"What's that, my young friend?"

"Olga Mervil did sell her soul to the Devil. You'll tell me she came to a tragic end... assuming, of course, she's really is dead, like the others... But what about the other girl she mentioned during the red mass, the one who wanted to marry a rich man and become a billionaire and *who actually did*?"

"What are you getting at?"

"These women, just two examples among many, got what they wanted, at least to some extent. I'm sure that the investigation will show that among the Satan worshippers, many were in very high, desirable positions..."

"If I understand correctly, you're trying to convert me to devil's worship by saying that, after all, if you have ambition, you should take a chance on it..."

Michel Roz started laughing.

"No, a hundred times no, and you know it. If Martine feels the same as I do, which I believe, her love will be enough for me. And I can work hard to provide for her and make her happy. I don't see myself going back to those silly caves where we managed to interrupt the evil sacrilege... But it's a fact that Olga was getting successful and it all happened... let's say miraculously."

Teddy Verano threw his cigarette into the Seine.

"What if I told you, my friend, that there are others, many others, who also denied Heaven and who were not at the red mass, at least not the one we broke up, but who are living today, living well, even better than well? Wealth and honors. Piled with money and glory and all the pleasures of the Earth..."

"I'd almost believe you."

"And you should. Because there are. They signed the pact with their Master, the Prince of Evil... Except that sometimes, like in the old legends, he comes to demand a payment that costs so dearly."

Michel Roz tapped his foot.

"But who nowadays, except for lunatics, can believe in the Devil? You know it's stupid."

"I agree with you."

Michel grabbed Teddy by the wrist and squeezed tightly.

"So? So? This is troubling me, making my mind spin. Success... so desired and paid so dearly for, they've got it, you yourself admitted it, only to end up, sooner or later, in tragedy. And if the Devil doesn't exist, who gives it to them? Who prepares it, builds it, directs it, so that events are always so favorable to them, like with Olga Mervil's incredible rise to stardom? Who?"

"Who?"

Teddy Verano started walking again slowly toward his car with Michel Roz next to him.

"Who? But there's an order to the world, and we know who created it. A godsend can also be a trap, especially for those who don't recognize it. Be careful! It's terrible and they're not atheists—who could deny something one doesn't believe in? Their crime is much more dreadful. Do you believe that the riches and fleeting pleasures of the world destined to horrible ends in such cases are really so desirable?"

He took another cigarette as he climbed in his car.

"And what a sucker's deal! The Devil, if he exists, could, in fact, give everything on Earth. Everything. Except what he himself is refused: Love. Everything, except love. So, between you and me, to sell your soul to the Devil isn't worth the trouble."

Maurice Limat

MEPHISTA
ET LE
CLOWN ECARLATE

ANGOISSE

FLEUVE NOIR

THE SCARLET CLOWN

CHAPTER I

"Hang in there, pal"

The father heard this for the 50th time this day. A phrase he was sick of, because it was corny, a cliché. But he told himself, or rather would later tell himself (if he still had the strength to analyze things), that, in their place, he would have said the same thing.

He, too, when his friends and family were grieving, had left them like this after the wake, painful and tedious. One of those chores one cannot avoid. He did not even know who had come. There were so many people…

In small towns, where everybody knows each other, when the grim reaper came knocking, one found friends one never knew. Friends who, a few days later, would once again turn as cold, distant and uninterested as always. But everyone felt obliged to come, to say a few words, always the same, to make the usual gestures. And after they have sprinkled the body with a little holy water, and made the customary sermons, they left. You would see them again at the burial.

The father, overwrought, greeted them. It was too much for the mother. Their only comfort was Agnes. She was there, kind and quiet. Claire's best friend. The same age as her. Agnes, with her big, blue eyes, her reddish hair, her adorable face with a few freckles. Agnes, the loyal friend, who cried her heart out over Claire, and did not say or do the same things as the others.

She was there. She was able to be there. They had given her the day off at the factory so she could be with the parents. They did not have much family, just some distant cousins who only came for the funeral procession.

Agnes, in her great sorrow at having lost Claire, wanted to stay with these poor folk. Now, it was over. Done. It was late. The wake was finished.

"Phew!" was all the poor man could say. "Are you having dinner with us, Agnes?"

The mother, scurrying around with red eyes in a pale face, was making soup. They were not hungry, but they had to eat, to keep going.

Softly, Agnes accepted their invitation.

"If you'd like," she said. "I know that you're both very tired. Do you want me to stay the night?"

"My child," the mother said, "thank you, but I won't be able to sleep." She looked suddenly irritated and pointed at the window. "Listen to them... It's starting again."

The father shook his fist, threatening the place of simple joy and cheap pleasure.

"As if this was the time..."

He did not even realize the absurdity of the phrase. But Agnes slowly nodded her head.

Yes, she understood them. Was it not cruel that, although they had just lost their only daughter Claire, she was still there, forever motionless in the next room, by the coffin that they had brought in a short time, lying on her little girl's bed among white flowers, with that open box next to her while the party music struck up again?

"Though, it is the time," the father admitted.

They sat at the table with no appetite. But they still ate, their minds elsewhere, talking little and with little sense to it. Things like, "Your parents are lucky to have a daughter like you."

And Agnes gave standard answers; she, too, annoyed by the hum of carousels, the shouting kids, swaggering boys, trying to be clever in front of the girls, dragging them around on their crazy scooters or on the dizzying rides.

Agnes used to love the fair. The last time it had come, she had gone with Claire. They had had a great time and there were some boys, not so bad, who had offered them ice cream cones. Now...

Time marched on. It was night. It was cold, but this did not seem to curb the public's enthusiasm. They heard them crowding around and rolling together under the arc lamps in the constant noise of the generators that provided the electricity for the big shops, thanks to the inventive minds that are always trying to give the crowd new sensations.

Agnes, nibbling a piece of cheese, was thinking about the fair, about the stalls that sold nougat and cotton candy, about the wrestlers posing almost naked in the cold, about the even more deplorable displays of young girls at the strip-tease show or the freaks and the circus. Because there would inevitably be a circus. Agnes had seen it in the snow falling the night before, the first night after Claire's death. She remembered the name, glowing in neon: *Crucifer Circus.*

She thought about all this, even though she was in no mood for a fair under such sad circumstances.

The father, just to say something, talked about the nasty man who had made him such an indecent proposition. He got worked up talking about it, righteously angry, until the mother asked him to calm down and be quiet.

"You're going to make yourself sick, dear... and besides," she pointed to the room and sobbed, "think about her in there."

A heavy silence fell over the three of them for a while.

Agnes suggested again that they go to bed. The next day would be hard. Putting her in the coffin, the funeral, the burial... Not to mention the endless stream of people. The entire small town would be there. And it would start all over again. The consolations, the handshakes...

The father, more quietly, said:

"Guys like that should be hanged."

Agnes, still placating, explained that there were people who thought the opposite, and who took pictures of the deceased on their death beds. But she quickly added that she agreed with Claire's father, who had kicked out the strange man who had offered to take some photos of the poor girl on her deathbed. Wasn't that really a bizarre idea?

The parents said goodnight. They tried to resist, but were too exhausted. After one last short visit to the awful room, they went into their bedroom. Like every time they went to see dead Claire, they started crying again, and Agnes was worn out comforting them. But she did not let it show.

It had been agreed that she would call them at midnight. They would take the next shift and Agnes would go back to her house, her parents' house. But she knew that she would not have the courage to wake them up. Personally, she had made up her mind. She should spend the night near her departed friend and let the poor, grieving parents rest.

The mother had brought her a thick bathrobe, a man's bathrobe that belonged to her husband. It was huge, made of Pyrenees wool, and she could wrap herself up in it and hide from the cold. With her feet in foot-warmers, her hands inside the sleeves like a nun, Agnes curled up as comfortable as possible in a big armchair. As far as possible from the window. They had closed it to keep out the music from the fair and the noise being vomited out by the microphones from barkers trying to shout over one another.

There was nothing in the room but a small, flickering flame from a traditional votive candle. Agnes was dreaming as she watched the flame that was meant to keep away evil spirits. She got drowsy. The cold was doing its work. The young girl knew that the night would be long and hard, but didn't she have to watch over Claire and do something for her poor parents?

For them especially. We never do enough for the living. As for the dead...

Claire was there. Dead. Her pretty face had already taken on that serenity of those less tortured in the flesh, whose soul had been set free, flown far from the trials and tribulations that awaited human beings every morning.

Claire, with her blond hair that her mother had arranged to rest in waves around her shoulders; Claire, her hands folded on her white, summer dress; Claire, with the pearl rosary from her first communion. And flowers. All these flowers that cost a lot at this time of the year around Christmas. The florists in town had been in demand.

Agnes heard vaguely, very vaguely, the parents snoring in their room. They had boasted in all sincerity that they would not be able to sleep a wink.

Agnes knew that it would not happen, and here she had the proof. Now she was alone to watch over Claire.

Alone with the little flame. Fire. Life. A life that at the gates of death meant that everything surely did not end with this departure.

Agnes was feeling drowsy, but fought to stay awake. It would not be good. You had to watch over the dead, at least that was the tradition. And she was not doing this out of politeness, but for the great affection she had always felt for Claire, her childhood friend, whose side she had never left. And then the sickness had come, the sudden, deadly leukemia...

Claire, with her legendary beauty, with her golden hair, as they said, had only lived a few months after that. Soon, it was all over...

It must have been snowing outside. The fair was screaming. Fortunately, the big double curtains were drawn to keep out the glaring, colored lights that were an outrage to the pious glow of this chapel.

Agnes bit her lip. *I don't want to fall asleep*, she thought.

She reminisced about the photographer who had surprisingly tried to offer his services in such circumstances. Agnes wondered what had made the man do it. He was not from the town, for sure. A traveling photographer, probably, maybe with the fair? But these kinds of pictures did not seem to fit with those kinds of photographers. Ideas spun around in little Agnes' head, Agnes who did not have a keen sense of reality.

Between half-closed eyelids, she saw only the small flame dancing on the candle, which she would have to replace in an hour. There were nine others, set aside for this. Agnes knew where they were. What time was it? She had no idea.

Claire's parents were sleeping, overwhelmed with fatigue and sorrow.

It was cold, ever so cold now in the mortuary room. Agnes shivered inside her bathrobe. A shiver that shook her out of her drowsiness. She blinked. Oh, how the flame was really dancing now! Why? As if a draft was blowing through the room...

All of a sudden, Agnes became scared. She had no idea why. Scared because she thought of the stories she heard a long time ago, when they talked about the souls who came from beyond to accompany the departed who had just passed the great threshold.

The flame was dancing more and more. This was not a hallucination. And then there was the freezing cold...

Agnes looked at the window, the window she couldn't see with the big curtains drawn in front of it. Behind it was the square, the fair, the dark alcove behind the huge lottery stall that hid Claire's parents house. Agnes wondered if a gust of wind might have opened the window, which would explain the chilly air and the trembling candle flame.

She wanted to get up and go over there to check. Oh how tired she felt... and without knowing why, she couldn't do it.

In front of her was the big, white bed, and Claire's lily-white body, motionless, lying down forever.

Agnes was panic-stricken, but still did not move. Why did she want to spend the night of the wake here alone? Wasn't it too much for the nerves of a young girl?

She told herself, *Walk, go to the curtain, open it and close the window, if that really is the problem.* Such a simple action, but Agnes couldn't bring herself to do it.

Time passed. A minute. Hours. She had no idea.

She was hypnotized by the small point of fire, like a will-o'-the-wisp, which was strange in a room full of silence and death. Frozen—from the cold or from fear?—Agnes tried to fight, to get up, to react.

Call out to Claire's parents? But they were sleeping. So deeply that they would not hear her. Besides, she couldn't call out. Scream? There was a huge lump in her throat.

Silence in the room, noise outside. She suddenly realized that no, there was not total silence. She heard, a lot more clearly, a lot more loudly, the growl of the microphones, the cacophonous tunes of the various stalls, the cries of joy from the boys, and of false fright from the girls, on the rails or in the horror train.

The curtain had moved. She was sure of it. There was no doubt about it.

An instant of panic. Excruciating.

And then Agnes, being an intelligent girl, thought: *I'm being stupid... the curtains... it's the window. The wind opened it... I hear the rides, the fair, the people... I'm going to close it.*

Finally she was about to get up, but stopped.

A man had entered. He stood tall before her. In a manner of speaking, because he was pretty short. He told her, insistently, to stay quiet, by putting his finger to his lips. He got in through the window. He was there behind the curtain. He was carrying something, a kind of small black box that Agnes couldn't see clearly through her great fear.

He approached her. It was as if he was gliding. The girl, her eyes wide, her muscles tense, was about to get up and scream, it was obvious. More quickly, however, he was on her, pushed her back into the chair, and put his hand over her mouth. In his hand was a kind of soft cottony ball. That smell... a nauseating smell...

"Don't move," he whispered, "I won't hurt you."

The smell... tasteless and stomach-turning... Agnes felt paralyzed. Was it a sedative he was putting in her nose? Or only the fear, the awful sensation washing over her?

She stayed vaguely conscious but knew that she would not move, could not move. She felt as if she were going to die, like Claire who was already dead.

"I didn't come to steal anything. Or to hurt anyone, I swear. Don't be scared."

His words were contradictions in this absurd situation. They came through a fog. The fog was also before her eyes. But she still saw the flame dancing on the candle. And Claire. Claire lying here. Claire all white and beautiful, so beautiful!

A flash in the room. Another flash.

The man walked around the bed, holding up his box. He leaned over, moved his head, bent his knees, kept moving his box around.

Agnes, in the depths of her living nightmare, did not understand and told herself that there must be a simple explanation.

A flash. Another. Another. More and more.

The man left.

Agnes was again alone in the death room. Alone with Claire. Claire who was death itself.

It was cold. Agnes was numb with fear because the icy draft was still coming from the open window. Numb from the sedative also, light but effective, that had succeeded in neutralizing her.

The candle was dying since it had not been replaced. A mass of melted wax with the blackened wick in its death throes.

Outside, still a thousand voices were sounding their pleasure at the fair.

The man flew into the night, in the shadows of the house of death, toward the shack that casts a long puddle of black.

He disappeared after having taken 20 pictures of Claire's face.

Agnes could no longer hold on and passed out.

CHAPTER II

"You understand, Monsieur Verano. The situation is... so delicate that I had to resort to the grave digger without alerting the police. And I have to say that I was really embarrassed... as much as I was scared, maybe, if I wasn't lucky enough to know Dr. Sorbier..."

Teddy Verano smiled and nodded.

"I knew that you'd dealt with a similar case one or two years ago under pretty dramatic circumstances," Jean-Michel Lefort continued.

"That's right," the ghost detective said. "And that all started, in fact, in the same way. Or pretty much, since in the case of Cyrille Denizet's fiancée, the body had disappeared. When we opened the coffin, it was empty."

Jean-Michel shivered. He stood up, just to do something, and took the bottle of whiskey.

"Another drop?" he asked.

Teddy Verano held out his glass, not at all shy about it. He had nothing against Cutty Sark, and said so, lighting up a cigarette, which put him in the right frame of mind for his investigation. He took small sips, watching Jean-Michel, who had gone to the window and was watching the snow fall over Senlis.

He had sped over here on the highway.

"It seems to me that all we can really say is at this time is that it's a case of grave robbery."

"But of course," said Jean-Michel, turning around. "My poor love wanted only one thing before she departed: to be buried a dozen miles from here in that little rural cemetery. In fact, in the town where she grew up, where we know a lot of people. That's why, the day after the funeral, Old Flin, the road worker and grave digger, a jack-of-all-trades in the area, came to talk to me."

Teddy Verano thought about this with a sip of whiskey on his tongue.

Viviane Lefort had been brought three days ago to her final resting place, the victim of a heart attack. She had died at 30, her whole life spent with a fragile heart, and left behind a grieving husband. The day after the funeral, Old Flin had been embarrassed to tell Jean-Michel, who had gone back to the cemetery, that the dirt looked like it had been turned up during the night, right where the fresh grave had been laid. Jean-Michel did not want to believe it, but Flin showed him the traces, hard as they were to see in the muddy snow.

"I know my job... I know how to make the little mounds. Someone dug it, Monsieur Lefort. They did it during the night."

Jean-Michel tried to doubt it, at first. Then, he asked the man to check it out, in utter secrecy, after slipping him some money, and it was agreed that, during the sad, ugly day, under the gray sky threatening to snow again, they would dig the grave again, just to make sure.

No one came. It was the middle of the week and the townsfolk rarely showed up before the weekend. The two of them, therefore, shoveled out the pile of clayey soil covering the coffin in which Vivian Lefort rested. The deeper they dug, the more Flin was convinced that the ground had been disturbed.

"Me, I fill it in different than this."

As he made comments, Jean-Michel became frantic. His hands, blue from the freezing wind, clutched the shovel as it gouged out the earth, trying to find the coffin. He was thinking crazy thoughts. Although he was far from superstitious, not at all a believer, he wondered if some mad necromancer or some nefarious madman had not taken the remains of his wife.

The coffin looked intact, but Flin shook his head.

"They opened it. Look at this screw... Not tight..."

"But Flin... What you're saying... It's awful!'

"Monsieur Lefort, I don't get it. I've buried people here for 30 years and never once..."

Jean-Michel cut him off with a wave of his hand.

"We have to see for ourselves."

"See what?" Flin was alarmed.

"If she... if she's still here."

"Open it, you mean? I can't do that!"

Procrastination and discussion ensued. Flin's job was on the line and maybe criminal prosecution as well, if caught. It was crazy enough to do what he had agreed to do so far for Lefort's peace of mind, and in memory of his dear wife, but now... Wouldn't it be better to call the police?

But Jean-Michel Lefort was dead set on knowing the truth right now, and at any price wanted to avoid a scandal for the memory of his dear, departed wife. One extra reward and Flin finally took a screwdriver out of his pocket, grumbling that "it's not legal" and "this will all end badly." Jean-Michel did not care. Gritting his teeth, he watched the old man lift the cover that separated the living from the dead.

She was there, in her shroud, and he could now breathe freely. He had feared the most awful things, without knowing what they might be. He had to pluck up the courage to move aside the sheet and look at the still beautiful face of his Viviane.

In the meantime, Flin, suddenly aware of what he was risking, and of the madness they were engaged in, harassed him and begged him to finish up. They had to close the coffin, turn the screws, and put the soil back in place as quickly as possible, which they did as a few snowflakes started falling again. And they left the cemetery covered in its white blanket of silence.

But Jean-Michel could not sleep. He ran down to Paris, desperate to tell someone, but recoiling before the notion of talking to his family. So, his old friend Dr. Sorbier had listened to him attentively.

"My friend, I don't like this kind of story. But I agree with you when you say that you don't want the matter leaking out. Why not talk to a private detective?"

"Do you know one?"

"Yes, I do. And one that deals in matters other that the usual adultery trials and pre-marriage inquiries; he's a specialist in the Occult."

Jean-Michel was startled.

"The Occult? But I don't care about that nonsense, and when she was still with us, my wife took no interest in it either. She never went to a fortune-teller. as far as I know."

But Dr. Sorbier had his opinion. Jean-Michel finally took his advice and called Teddy Verano, who came to Senlis and listened to the long story of the ominous adventure.

"What do you think, Monsieur Verano? I've told you everything, and I don't understand a thing. I don't need to tell you that Dr. Sorbier trusts you completely."

"I'm grateful to him. Let's see... Above all, I'm thinking about what you said: although the coffin was opened, the body wasn't touched."

"That's right."

"But there was—as the grave digger was absolutely certain—a violation of the grave."

"Certainly. The ground had been disturbed, the screw loosened..."

"And you're sure that the... the body... was still..."

"...Intact? Indeed!"

Teddy Verano took another swallow of Cutty Sark while Jean-Michel added, almost mechanically:

"It was as if someone had wanted to open the coffin just to see her... to look at her again." He clenched his fists and groaned, "Oh, if only I knew who the bastard was!"

The detective lit a cigarette.

"Intact inside her coffin, you're sure? That's the main point. And those traces Old Flin talked about?"

"Oh, absolutely impossible to identify. There were a lot of people walking around, of course... After the ceremony, only the grave digger was there, and until the next day, nobody was at the cemetery."

"Except the guilty party," Teddy Verano mumbled.

"Yes, but he... Flin saw there were footprints that weren't his own. But it was snowing. It snows a lot nowadays, so..."

Teddy Verano waved it off. He realized that they wouldn't find any interesting leads there. Suddenly, an idea crossed his mind.

"I'm sorry. but I have to ask you a very delicate question… one that might offend you."

Jean-Michel replied clearly but in a slightly changed voice.

"Ask away. Anything you want. I want to know the truth and I'll do everything I can to unmask this wretch who opened Viviane's coffin."

"Imagine, Monsieur Lefort, that someone—a man, very likely—felt… something for Madame Lefort. This someone could have come secretly, driven mad by grief, to see her face one last time without anyone else… without you knowing."

He saw that Jean-Michel turned pale, clearly offended as he had feared. But Lefort controlled himself and did not want to break his word.

"You're right to ask this… bold question. But I'm sure that nobody, you hear me, nobody in our circle, nobody to my knowledge, could have done this." He shook his head and continued with deep sadness. "It's true that she was very beautiful."

He went to get a picture frame off the table where a bouquet of fresh roses was protecting it.

"Look."

Teddy Verano admired it. Viviane was indeed very pretty. He felt his heart skip a beat thinking that it would outrage any man to think that such a beauty's tomb could be violated.

"A madman," Jean-Michel said. "Just a madman."

"No doubt. But potentially, a dangerous madman."

Jean-Michel suddenly jumped over to the detective.

"Why? Do you have any idea?"

"Not yet. What if we went to the cemetery?"

"You think that…?"

"Oh, you've already done, or tried to do, the important stuff. A few days from now, the coffin will be sealed up for good, I imagine, and this will all be over."

"Not for me. Not as long as I don't know the truth."

"Of course, Monsieur Lefort. But I'd like to talk with Old Flin myself."

Half an hour later, in the glum and snowy Picardy countryside, not far from the highway, Teddy Verano's DS stopped near the cemetery where the unfortunate Viviane lay.

"That's the place."

Jean-Michel Lefort pointed at a rustic pavilion by a grove of trees, halfway from the town itself.

Flin was there. A short, young, chubby girl told them so. She ran behind the building right away. It was not hard to understand that she was feeding the chickens.

"That's Giselle, Flin's daughter."

"She's been crying. Her eyes are red and it was obvious she didn't want to talk to us for long in her state."

Jean-Michel shrugged his shoulders.

"She's all the old man's got, but he's no tender heart. They say he gives her thrashings."

Flin, a skinny but sturdy local man, gnarled and with a moustache, greeted Jean-Michel Lefort and looked awkwardly at his companion.

"Don't be scared," Teddy Verano said smoothly, "I'm not with the police. I'm just a friend of Monsieur Lefort. So, we've come to pay you a little visit and solicit your opinion...."

Flattered, Flin apologized. He talked about something else, about the girl who gave him so much trouble.

"That charming little girl?" Teddy Verano pretended to be surprised.

Flin shrugged.

"She's a tramp. She goes out at night. In this weather, I ask you..."

They brought him back to more pertinent matters. But they did not get much out of him. He stumbled over his words, saying that, after all, maybe he was wrong, maybe it was the wind that moved the dirt, and when it came to the loose screw, he said he could not remember this detail.

Obviously, he was scared.

The whole thing was going too far and he was sorry he had said anything, in spite of the generous tip given by Jean-Michel Lefort.

Teddy Verano realized that they were up against a wall of dishonesty and he found a way to say goodbye as soon as possible. On seeing that they were about to leave, the gravedigger became friendlier, but was still in a hurry to see them gone.

Outside, they found themselves in the half-light, in the wind, under a darkening sky where a few snowflakes still fluttered about.

"I don't understand," Jean-Michel said. "You wanted to see this guy, but we barely got anything interesting out of him."

"He has nothing to tell us because he doesn't want to talk anymore. Anyway, I don't think he knows much. However..."

He looked around, imagining more than seeing the cemetery and the small woods on the opposite side of the town.

"You want to go over? I think it's closed at this hour."

"Flin's in charge of it?"

"Yes. But sometimes he sends his daughter."

They started off in the snow toward the DS when they heard Flin yelling:

"Step on it, you little floozy! You close it up?"

The girl must have stammered something like, "Not yet."

Teddy Verano put his hand on Jean-Michel's arm.

"I bet this is the right time."

"Sure. Look who's running over."

Gisele was dashing through the snow, having put on her nice boots, which clashed with her cotton dress and apron. After tying a scarf around her head, she was going to close the cemetery gate like every evening.

"Let's go," Teddy Verano said.

They got into the car and, without saying another word, took off. Jean-Michel did not know what the detective was thinking, but Teddy Verano was already cooking up a plan.

Except he had a surprise.

They passed by Gisele, walking to the resting grounds, and she gave them a weird look as they went by. The silhouette of the girl had barely melted in the snowy night when the car drove around the cemetery and headed for the woods. But Teddy Verano, like Jean-Michel, had time to see the small Citroën 2CV parked along the cemetery wall.

Teddy Verano said nothing, did not even slow down. He kept going and entered the woods, which gave him complete cover. Then, he stopped, got out of the car and invited his passenger to follow him.

The other car was still there, lights off. Silently in the thick snow, that helped cover their advance, the two men made their way through the trees.

CHAPTER III

Gisele was still red from running, and her breath made small clouds around her mouth. She was having difficulty catching her breath.

Suddenly, an arm wrapped around her.

Gisele cried out in alarm, when a deep voice, trying to be as soft as possible, whispered in her ear:

"Dummy... It's me, you know it's me!"

Gisele pushed him back a little, in fun.

"You scared me."

"Well. that's new. If you're scared of me..."

The young man laughed hoarsely, but the sweet, round face of Old Fin's daughter did not brighten up.

"Do you always have to be so stupid?"

"Well, well," he was starting to feel his spirits rise, "if you're not happy, you just have to say so. I'll go and then..."

He pretended to back off but she grabbed his arm.

"No, don't go. Don't leave me all alone."

The boy was having fun and, with his thumb pointed to the cemetery wall behind him, where they had said they would meet as usual, observed:

"Is it *them* that give you the willies?"

Gisele shuddered, but not from the cold. Being a good country girl, she was not too sensitive to the snowy weather.

"Jean-Pierre, please." She suddenly hugged him close and whispered, "You know exactly what happened... the other night."

As clumsy as Jean-Pierre was, after first thinking that a gush of spontaneous tenderness had thrown Gisele into his arms, he knew now that, in truth, she was still terrorized by their previous date, three days ago, at 11 p.m., in this same place.

"You should stop thinking about that, Gigi. Look, we have better things to do than reminisce about such silly things."

It was clear that Jean-Pierre was ready to move on to "better things," but the girl did not yield to his ardent whisper in her ear.

"Please, I don't feel like it."

Jean-Pierre, therefore, had to give up the idea—only for the moment, he hoped—of going farther.

"OK, what is it now?" he grumbled. "Your father again?"

She moved her head in a way that said yes and no.

"It's not just my father."

"What then? Are you tired of seeing me?"

"No, I never said that."

Now Jean-Pierre was getting upset. He'd come all the way on his bicycle, and that was no easy feat. He had left it in the bushes to meet Gisele when Flin had sent her to close the cemetery. He had a motorcycle, but he did not use it to go to the rendezvous because it was too noisy and might alert the gravedigger.

It was for her that he'd ridden almost two miles in the snow at the risk of breaking his neck. She should have considered this. He complained a little about it before restarting his advances.

This time, Gisele put him swiftly in his place.

"Listen, we have to talk."

"That's what we're here for, doll," he said lovingly.

"Ah!" Gisele was fed up. "You boys only think about one thing... Don't you remember the last night we came here?"

Jean-Pierre pretended to think—he knew perfectly well what Gisele meant—and guffawed, a little forced, like anyone who wants to be tough and show no fear.

"Oh, yeah, the ghosts!"

"Jean-Pierre, be quiet."

"Say, it's not midnight yet. It's not their time."

"The other night, it was 11 p.m."

"Yes, sweetie, on the nose."

"You're an idiot. Those rays of light..."

"I told you it was lightning. Things like that happen."

"There was no storm. And it'd been snowing for eight days."

"Well, maybe it was will-o-the-wisps. They happen in cemeteries. I heard something about it. They even said that's what makes people believe in ghosts."

Gisele was not so easily defeated.

"When we saw those lights, you weren't so sure."

"Of course not. I was surprised. When you're busy having fun like we were, and then you see lights over the cemetery wall..." He waved his hand as if to chase off a bad memory. Coming back to his idea he continued, "Still, when we see each other, don't you have anything else you want to do?"

"Listen," Gisele said, "something happened that night."

"What? In the cemetery?"

"Yes."

And she told him about Old Flin's discovery, the desecrated grave, and the visits, first by the guy who must have been the dead woman's husband, and then, half an hour ago, by the same guy with someone else.

Jean-Pierre frowned and admitted:

"I don't like this at all."

His passion had suddenly vanished. He was wondering if, in case there was some dirty business, he would risk getting involved while in the middle of a passionate "conversation" with the gravedigger's daughter.

Not to mention that Old Flin was not particular understanding, especially when he had had a little to drink, and he suddenly felt it was his duty to protect the virtue of his only daughter, something which he normally took no interest in.

"Well, what I mean is…" Gisele started.

"You mean, we shouldn't see each other anymore?"

In spite of everything, he was already regretting her decision. Gisele, even being short and chubby, was attractive and, even with her father's outbursts, she already had some experience in premarital fantasies.

"No, I didn't say that. But we can't see each other here."

"So, where?"

They whispered about it, holding each other close.

Jean-Pierre, while talking, took the opportunity to become more intimate, but he could see that Gisele, such an expert in the game under other circumstances, was too preoccupied by both her father's occasional threats and by this story about ghosts or ghost lights that her naïve little soul could not sort out.

They did not hear the approach of the man spying on them from around the wall, using the stone as an excellent sound conductor that had allowed him to follow almost the whole conversation. Moreover, Gisele was starting to feel the heat of the boy's advances. She became all the more frightened when someone coughed nearby. She started to run away, and Jean-Pierre suddenly became a lot less manly; he was ready to do the same.

However, a man's voice, a little sarcastic, could now be heard after the short coughing fit, indiscreetly interrupting the lovers' intimacy.

"Excuse me, please. I might have disturbed you…"

Jean-Pierre was already feeling braver, knowing that it was not Old Flin who was barging in and making him feel inferior.

"Listen, you…"

"Don't get angry, Jean-Pierre… nor you, my dear Gisele."

"You know our names? That's too much!"

"But of course. It was a very simple thing. Don't try to figure it out. But above all, don't worry, I mean you no harm."

Jean-Pierre turned around and Gisele instinctively clung onto him, half-hidden behind him, which also warmed her up because it was getting chillier.

"Fine, but what do you want with us?" asked Jean-Pierre.

The boy stepped forward, self-confident, and raised his voice to boost his courage.

The man before him, handsomely dressed, watched him and smiled. In spite of the darkness, they could see his hazel eyes, a little mocking but not mean, and some silver hair around his temples. He was rather tall, in good shape, and pushing forty.

Gisele bit her lip. She had seen him before. She recognized him. It was…

Jean-Pierre was not very reassured. He knew that there were creeps around, lunatics who spied on lovers, and sometimes did more than just watch. More than one crime had been born out of such depravations, and, in spite of everything, in such a situation, nothing told Gisele's lover that this man's intrusion was innocent.

However, there was nothing threatening in the intruder's attitude. Moreover, Gisele and Jean-Pierre were both wondering how this guy had just showed up here. On a bike, like Jean-Pierre? Certainly not. His suit was not meant for bicycles, especially in the snow.

"Listen," the man said, "you won't say anything. And for my part, I won't say anything either."

"Say anything about what?" Jean-Pierre barked back.

"Well," the man smiled bigger than ever, "nothing to Old Flin, for a start."

Gisele started crying without really knowing why. Jean-Pierre wondered what this meant, and did not know how to react. This guy here was getting the better of him because he seemed to know a little too much.

"OK," the young man sighed, "let's get it over with. What do you want from us?"

"Good! It's very cold, so the sooner we're done, the better. Of course, I'd prefer to take you out somewhere for some grog, but I think the closest bar is in town, and you'd best not be seen together over there... Not to mention Papa Flin might end up wondering why is his daughter taking so long to close the cemetery, which she does almost every day at the same time."

Jean-Pierre was looking impatient. The man waved off what he was about to say.

"Let's drop it. I just want some information from you two, that's all."

"Are you a cop?"

"Not a stupid idea, my boy. But not exactly true either. What do I want? To know exactly what you saw over the cemetery wall three days ago—or rather three nights ago."

Gisele shivered, but one couldn't have told if it was from the cold or from fear. In any case, she was crying a little less now, more sniffling and listening carefully, waiting for what her boyfriend would say.

"What we saw?" he grumbled. "Uh, basically... What was it, Gisele? Not much really."

He wanted to challenge the interrogator and send him packing. But he told himself, not without some caution, that this man already knew a lot, and it would be better to deal with him than challenge him.

Gisele answered with only some kind of grunt.

"Charming language, little lady," the man said mockingly. "Except, I do want to know more... about the ghosts. What did they look like?"

Jean-Pierre quit stalling.

"They weren't ghosts. First of all, there's no such thing as ghosts."

"That's debatable, Jean-Pierre, but that's not the question. What did you see? Lightning? Surely not; we agree on that point. No snowstorm in the area since the beginning of the season. Will-o-the-wisps? I'd be surprised, at least if you stood right here… because you were on this spot?"

Jean-Pierre nodded.

"Very well. It's a nice spot… and warm, too, even with the cemetery on the other side. With this weather, not so much, but, hey, it seems to suit you two just fine. Yes, I know, Papa Flin, when the mood comes over him, can be very strict, and not much fun. Let's skip that bit. You were saying that you saw some lights. It wasn't lightning and couldn't be will-o-the-wisps for the simple reason that they come from swamps, bogs, rarely from cemeteries, and they couldn't be seen from this spot anyway. So, what was it?"

Gisele could say nothing, and Jean-Pierre was feeling increasingly embarrassed. In spite of everything, he now felt reassured. This man did not seem threatening, and his polite, even kindly, tone dispelled his fears.

"In truth, we don't know," he replied.

"But it was… constant… like a beam?"

"You mean, a beam like from a lighthouse or a headlight?"

"Good question. More precisely, was it from a car headlights or blinkers."

"Sort of."

"They were blinking?"

"No, it was more like flashes."

They were dancing around the truth.

Finally, Jean-Pierre, with Gisele hanging on, who had also regained some confidence, explained that they were brief lights, kind of bluish sometimes, and greenish white at other times. He really thought a snowstorm was coming. It was Gisele who saw them first, and got scared. He had to comfort her and it ruined their rendezvous.

They went over it again, and Gisele described what had happened so mysteriously in the cemetery. Then the stranger just wanted to know if they had seen someone, or heard an engine, or seen tracks or a parked car. Their answer led him to understand that they had, in fact, cleared out in record time and only saw each other again half an hour ago.

Therefore, he said farewell, thanked them, and said they had nothing to fear, that neither Old Flin nor anybody else would know anything at all about this meeting. After a grand tip of his hat to Gisele, he left, disappearing around the corner of the wall.

Jean-Pierre remained silent for a moment, and almost wanted to follow him. He was furious, feeling like he had just been played for a fool. Suddenly turned tough guy, he grumbled:

"I'm going to show him, that bastard…"

Gisele clutched his arm.

"No, please, stay. You never know."

Deep down, Jean-Pierre was only half-convinced that he should have run after the stranger to make him pay.

They whispered together for a little while, frightened by the encounter, then decided to choose another place to meet. It would not be easy. They left each other after a quick kiss, but their hearts were not in it.

Gisele went back home, where she got a good thrashing for being late.

"You were with that pig, Jean-Pierre, again, for sure! You tramp!" screamed old Flin.

She listened to the string of curses as he swore that the boy would never marry her, but dump her after knocking her up.

While Gisele was thus being "educated" in this special fashion, Jean-Pierre pedaled to the nearby town, cursing the snow that threatened to make him crash, cursing girls, fathers, and all the perverts who bust in on romantic trysts, cursing the ghost lights, and everything else.

Passing by the woods, he heard an engine and caught sight of a car heading toward Senlis.

CHAPTER IV

Jean-Michel Lefort opened the curtain in the living room and trained his empty eyes outside, seeing nothing but the dark night and the inevitable snow falling.

"That damned fair is finally over."

"A county fair?" Teddy Verano asked.

"Yes." Jean-Michel sighed. "During the... the tragedy... Viviane's final days... and the funeral... all that infernal racket. It was awful."

He came back, glass in hand, to the detective. Teddy Verano was trying to put on a good front, but he saw his client was upset. The investigation was apparently getting nowhere.

"Nothing. This weird lightning in the cemetery... what does that prove?"

"Oh," the detective responded, "it doesn't seem to prove much yet, Monsieur Lefort, I agree, but..."

Jean-Michel spun around and faced him.

"But what?"

"I told you. You have to be patient in these kinds of cases. It's obvious that our visit to Old Flin and the conversation I had with his daughter and her lover don't seem—I say seem—to have, as you say, 'proven anything'."

Lefort bit his lip. He was thinking he had already gone too far.

"Sorry. I'm in such a state since... since I lost Viviane."

It was the day after their trip together. Teddy Verano, as agreed, had returned to his house in the evening. Being a man of the world Jean-Michel Lefort served some port and was already letting his irritation show too much.

Teddy Verano could have said all kinds of things: especially, that poor Viviane was in no more danger, and that her grave, if it had been opened, seemed to be free of any real desecration, as her bold husband had himself seen.

Calmly, he put down his glass of Cintra and took out a piece of paper from his wallet. He saw Jean-Michel suddenly perk up, guessing this was something interesting.

"I have collaborators," Teddy Verano said. "My wife Yvonne and my stepson, an ardent young man who wants to follow in my footsteps and is doing so little by little. You know that I often take on several cases at the same time. I'm doing just this now. I have to protect certain important people, so I can't do everything myself. So, I asked Yvonne to go through my files and she has compiled a little press book by clipping out everything in the press that might bear any relation at all to your case..."

He held out a small notebook. Jean-Michel instinctively held out his hand, but Teddy Verano pretended not to see the gesture.

"My wife and her son were looking for, amongst other things, anything unusual that has happened lately, in and around Senlis. At first glance, any minor news items we might find might only seem vaguely connected to your case. But sometimes..."

He lifted the paper in his hand and continued.

"Ten days ago, or rather ten nights ago, in Péronne, which is not too far from here, a young girl was watching over her deceased friend. Yes, a childhood friend had passed away prematurely. In the morning, the parents of the deceased found the poor girl passed out by the bed. At first, they thought it was from emotion or fatigue. Not at all. When she came to, with a little help, she showed signs of the most violent terror. Trembling and disoriented, she told them that a man had come in the night and used chloroform or something like that on her."

"And then? Did he steal something or what? Desecrate the dead?"

"Nothing like that. Everything was normal except for the open window."

Jean-Michel got excited.

"A man... in the night... around a dead girl... Yes, you're right. There could be a connection."

Teddy Verano held back a smile. He saw that, this time, his client was not going to complain about the investigation stagnating. But Viviane's husband reflected:

"Are there any other details?"

"Not much. The police investigated. Pretty routine, I have to admit. And except for the local press, they're not talking much about it."

"Did they say if they found anything? I don't know, maybe what he used to put the girl to sleep?"

"No. The papers lack details. But it's obvious that they're not taking this too seriously. They think it was a fit of nerves."

"The open window?"

"No traces of anyone climbing in. Besides, the room was on the ground floor and easy to access. And what does a window prove? She could have opened it herself."

Teddy Verano paused before whispering softly, waiting for Jean-Michel's reaction, prolonging the effect because it amused him a little to see someone questioning his abilities.

"The young girl in question had a nervous breakdown after a local paper, the only one to our knowledge, continued to investigate this apparently innocent story. They didn't get much... except she kept repeating, 'the flashes... the flashes'."

"What?"

Lefort had jumped and his face suddenly turned pale, showing the high degree of his emotion.

"Flashes! Flashes... Then you've found the clue we were looking for!"

"Oh," the detective spoke calmly, "it's not magic. Everybody reading the paper, particularly the ones from the Oise and the Somme, could have come to the same conclusion you did… if, of course, they knew what the Flin girl and her boyfriend saw."

Jean-Michel was pacing the floor, suddenly losing his self-control, which was not surprising for a man who had not slept in a few days.

"Flashes… The Flin girl saw flashes, and in a death room, flashes too. And this happened the night after my wife's burial. Now, they opened my wife's coffin, I'm sure of it, and these two witnesses saw the same phenomenon: flashes."

He came back to Teddy Verano.

"Excuse me. It's true I'm…"

"Yes, yes," the detective cut him off. "You're putting your trust in me, and I know it. Only, you wanted us to go a little faster. Well, here's a result."

"Flashes? What could it mean?"

"I can't tell you yet."

"Photos? Films? But why?"

"That's the mystery I'd really like to clear up. We're living through something like a pulp novel, Monsieur Lefort. Except that, in this case, I think this stranger taking pictures of a dead girl on her death bed and—I'm sorry—of another in her coffin is not an ordinary criminal. It seems to me that I smell sulfur behind all this."

Jean-Michel looked at him, but once again Teddy Verano spoke before he could.

"You're thinking that, because of my specialty, my research into the Occult, I'm wandering off. Possibly, but what professional photographer or rather, as I'd like to believe, what kind of amateur, and for what particular purpose, could take these kinds of morbid pictures?"

Lefort raised his hands in ignorance.

Teddy Verano stood up.

"I propose we go to Péronne?"

"Péronne? Yes, of course! On the motorway, it'll take less than 30 minutes. You want to question that girl?"

"Yes. I don't think it would be a waste of time?"

"You're right. I agree!"

They left and, once again, Teddy Verano took Lefort in his DS. He always preferred to drive himself. He knew the region well enough and their trip would be brief.

On the way, he kept an eye on the posters still up on the side of the road, advertising the fair that had lifted anchor 24 hours ago. He glanced at the names, one of a fortune-teller, which brought back a flood of memories, and of a circus too…

They were in Péronne soon, getting information at the police station. Teddy Verano introduced himself and gave out his business card. It was not very hard for him to get the address for the Percheron house, the parents of poor Agnes.

The policeman had been the one who had answered the call. His advice was clear:

"It's nothing to make a fuss about. At least, at first, because now…"

"Now? Young Agnes isn't doing well?"

"She isn't getting over it, Monsieur. I mean, who would think of leaving a girl alone all night with a corpse! She got scared, the poor girl. Since then, she's been living a nightmare. They're taking care of her, but I doubt you will be able to see her. It seems she's lost a few marbles, and all she talks about is flashes of lightning or something. Like, she could have seen lightning flashes on a night like that!"

"Come on! In the middle of the night, in Péronne, there couldn't have been a lot of people outside."

"That day, or rather that night? Well, as a matter of fact, there was a bunch of people around. You see, there was the fair…"

"Right," is all Teddy Verano said, while Jean-Michel Lefort, making the connection, furrowed his brow.

Outside, they saw the posters, still hanging and not yet ripped off by the wind and melting snow, or covered over by other posters and municipal decrees. They found the same names again, the fortune-teller and the Crucifer Circus…

At the Percheron house, they plainly refused to let them enter.

"More journalists!"

"Not at all, Monsieur…"

"Are you doctors?" Claire's father yelled. "Only doctors see my daughter, get it?!"

They did not press him. Pretending to be from the police would not do much good either. They were stuck.

Before leaving for Senlis, where Teddy Verano would continue on to Paris, they went to drink a whiskey in the local bar. They talked with the charming lady who owned the place, who apparently knew all about Agnes' adventure. She knew the girl well personally, and thought their nerves were shot from the night of the wake.

"And then," she added, "the people from the papers came on a bit too strong."

"Oh," Teddy Verano remarked, "you mean, outside the local press?"

"Yes, but it was more than enough. There was a good deal of publicity the first day, but since the police said that it was all in her mind, the big papers let it drop. But there's this little guy going around, doing some local reporting and he wanted to keep it going, to give the story a boost, to make it into a scoop. So he tried to get into the Percheron's. He convinced the mother, but the father arrived and threw him out. Just then, the idiot tried to snap a picture of poor Agnes. What a drama!"

"Why? For a photo?"

"Of course. Agnes—I have to tell you she's been in bed ever since that awful night—started screaming. That's when Monsieur Percheron threw that young reporter out."

"Poor kid! She must have been scared."

"Yes. She's still talking about the flashes that scared her. You think the other guy, with his flash, would have known better…"

Teddy Verano knew how to hide his satisfaction, just like his disappointments, behind a friendly smile that said nothing. Jean-Michel looked annoyed and gulped down his Cutty Sark.

Teddy Verano chatted a while longer with the likeable barmaid who, thinking maybe he had other intentions, encouraged him. They talked about the fair. Yes, the house where Claire had died was located next to the fairground. The detective finished his drink, paid and left, dragging Lefort out and getting from the owner a "see you very soon" look full of innuendoes.

Jean-Michel wanted to talk, but Teddy Verano stopped him.

"I told you that we're hot. In a manner of speaking, because in this weather… Let's return to the house of the dead girl."

Even at night, they spotted it easily again. They searched for traces of the stalls from the fair, but the snow had already covered all the tracks.

"This is useless," Teddy Verano said. "We must talk to Agnes."

"Yes, I agree, but how? She's sick, very sick, as I understand it. You want to bring the police into it?"

Teddy Verano turned to him in the shadows, silently holding out a cigarette.

"You could have brought the police into it yourself, Monsieur Lefort, but your concern was, and still is, to avoid any scandal. You wanted everything to stay quiet about Madame Lefort's grave."

"Yes, you're right. That is my concern."

"You wanted to trust me, and I thank you. Therefore, until further notice, we must act alone. However, I will tell you that it's not impossible that, at some point, I might find it necessary to inform a certain chief of police who is a friend of mine. Then you'll have to accept my decision. Understood?"

"You're clear as a bell, Monsieur Verano."

"I don't like blunders. I'm starting to think none of this is terribly abnormal, but it is peculiarly upsetting. I don't like necrophiliacs and I suspect that's what we're dealing with here—a jerk like this is the lowest of the low among criminals."

"You told me two hours ago that you were thinking of some kind of sorcery."

"And for you, that's all make-believe, right?"

Jean-Michel nodded.

"I'm sorry to have to tell you, but you don't know the subject very well. Just like you, I think that there's nothing that is truly supernatural in nature, which would be a contradiction, but there's certainly many things around us, influencing our lives, that we don't or can't see. Certain people, since the beginning of the world, have tried, and often succeeded, in taming these forces and using them for their own benefit. They are usually dangerous. Their applied form of science, that they make up, is what we usually call magic. It's empirical science but science all the same."

Jean-Michel opened his eyes wide.

"What about my poor wife?"

"Well, there are all kinds of vampires, from the traditional ones who feed on blood to survive, all the way up to the ones who steal bodies or souls. In this case, we may be dealing with a new kind of vampire, a vampire photographer if you will. Yes, I know, it sounds like a joke. Monsieur Lefort, an old ghost-filled castle, a romantic setting, a haunted house, an alchemist's crypt, are all a little outdated when it comes to horror. But these people still exist. Now they have modern laboratories, they make movies, they do… God knows what? But they are here, in our lives, around us, next to us, with us. And believe me, they are no less dangerous than before."

Jean-Michel Lefort, the rationalist, the man of the mechanical world, said nothing. But he felt shivers run down his spine.

CHAPTER V

The fair had moved on to Montdidier. That was where Teddy Verano found it.

What was he going to be looking for?

He did not know himself. He did not even really know what its connection was with the case, but he felt there was some link between the two affairs: both had taken place while the fair was nearby, or at least in the vicinity. Péronne, Senlis. And now Montdidier.

It had not been very hard for him to follow the tour. There were colorful posters up almost everywhere trying to advertise the stunning program of all the attractions. He gave another case, the job of tailing a candidate for divorce, to Gerard, his stepson, who was more than ready to give up his studies to start working full-time as a private detective. He also neglected to recontact Jean-Michel Lefort. Sometimes, Teddy Verano preferred to work alone. And he did not know what lead to follow yet...

But what did it matter! What he needed was to soak himself in the environment of that fair, which seemed to be connected to two strange cases, each one concerning a dead young woman and a mysterious photographer.

In less than an hour and a half, as always on the unavoidable motorway, he had reached the town of Montdidier, sitting on a little hill for centuries, proud to be the birthplace of Parmentier.[8] The sky was gray and the ground muddy where the last snowfall was melting, waiting for the next. Teddy Verano parked the DS and headed for the field of stalls where he trudged around for most of the day.

He had an idea, a very vague idea. Fairs usually travel with photographers. He found two, watched them for a long time, and challenged his professional conscience to the point of getting his picture taken. He talked a little to the photographers and, with two horrible pictures in his pocket, he had to conclude that he had drawn a blank. The two photographers, one of which was woman, seemed perfectly harmless, neither one being anything like a necrophiliac.

Of course, he would have been a pretty mediocre detective to linger over such appearances, but, after all, the trail of intrigue would have been too obvious if it had brought him straight to the guilty party.

He hung around the displays, dreamed a little in front of a futuristic railway from the year 2000, the haunted house, and the flying saucer bumper cars. He gave a look of brotherly sympathy to the strip-tease show and declined an offer from an old, obese coach looking for a sparring partner for the pseudo-

---

[8] French pharmacist Antoine-Augustin Parmentier (1737-1813), mostly remembered today for his outspoken promotion of the potato as a food source for humans in France and throughout Europe.

wrestling matches. While two "plants" in the crowd took up the challenge that they were paid for, Teddy Verano, listening with one ear to the growls coming from the animals, ended up at the Crucifer Circus. One show had ended and another one was about to begin.

The circus was a small one. The train of caravans of yesteryear had been replaced by half a dozen huge, well-kept trailers bristling with television antennas. Behind the canvas tent, he saw the animals, off to the side, and the boards flapping in the icy wind, sometimes giving a peek at the cages where the Bengal tigers were pacing.

Among all the hollering, he heard to a barker, a long-winded clown who had replaced the portable megaphone of old with an electric microphone, an instrument that had to be credited with the power of rendering the human voice totally unintelligible.

Teddy Verano was starting to get bored. He wandered between the circus rings and found himself near the platform where the performers went back inside to prepare for their acts and where the barker was inviting the public to "squeeze into the best seats."

Teddy Verano followed the crowd, paid an ageless cashier with outrageous make-up, who was already shriveling up and whose clothes, like all "beauty" tricks, tried desperately hard to claim that she was born beyond the Pyrenees. He was nice, as always, with the fair sex, and received a killer wink in return. Then he climbed into the stands, on the third row.

The barker showed up, doubling as the Ringmaster. He was assisted by a traditional little clown in a bright red suit full of sequins. It was a small, bent gentleman, who seemed to limp, and "fix" himself constantly to stand straight.

Teddy Verano watched this scarlet clown and his very talented tumbling, although the jokes shouted at him by the Ringmaster sounded more like swipes from an outdated almanac. Under the white and red-striped mask, the clown's ugliness was striking. His eyebrows and the section around his eyes were all the color of fire, which made him look more disturbing than funny.

The Ringmaster's body was hidden under layers of plastering but, on closer inspection, Teddy Verano decided that he, too, was little favored by nature.

Now he became struck by all the faces of the artists who made up the troupe. The face of the amazon could have been slender and pretty, but was marred by an interminably long nose. The two acrobats were a well-built couple, but the man had a horrible lazy eye, and the woman a birthmark that covered half her face. Such as it was, they were talented, and their trapeze act was dizzying.

Teddy Verano, who loved artists, gave them a roaring applause along with the rest of the audience, who knew a quality act when they saw one.

Quality was also present in the magic act. The magician, dressed in a dinner jacket, had a jutting chin and big lips; his assistant was none other than the cashier, whom Teddy found even more wilted, more ravaged than before, despite her age when the women of our time are in full flower. They gave a curious exhibition of mental telepathy and Teddy Verano thought, not without surprise, that outside of the tricks, the well-known "keys," this woman seemed to possess authentic powers of divination.

The Ringmaster and the scarlet clown continued their pranks between the acts. They also played a kind of sketch, of questionable taste, making fun of doctors. The Ringmaster, of course, played the patient, and the scarlet clown used the most scatterbrained means to try to heal him of an imaginary sickness; he got huge laughs from the audience, but not from Teddy Verano. In the forced comedy, he saw a deep sadness and he could not stop watching the little figure who looked like a bouncing flame, and the face which must have been hideous in its natural state, whose make-up only rendered more frightful. When the clown passed close to the stands, on seeing his face up close, a child started howling, and its parents had to take him out.

Kids have these instincts..., Teddy thought.

He was no longer having fun and no longer applauding.

Next, he saw a family of acrobats, father, mother and two children. Dreadful faces, a totally bald man with the face of an albino who managed to find a one-eyed wife and give birth to an ugly girl, whose outlandish features, combined with her father's pale skin, excluded her from any desire, and a boy who alarmingly combined the features of both parents and his sister. Talented, for sure, spinning, leaping, flying around, forming anatomical spindles and human pyramids with mastery. But ugly, very ugly, hopelessly ugly.

Teddy Verano had no desire to joke about it, even being alone. His usual good mood melted away before these aesthetic disasters.

A real museum of horrors. As if the circus owner did it on purpose.

Then, the performers set up the scene for the big act, the star attraction, namely the exhibition of big cats presented by the "world-famous" tamer, Crucifer himself.

Since this was the name of the circus—Teddy remembered seeing the posters in Péronne and Senlis—he must certainly be the boss of the troupe.

The stagehands set up the cage. Then, led by the inevitable Ringmaster and scarlet clown, came all the others who had quickly slipped on appropriate outfits. There was the gorilla-chinned magician, the lazy-eyed trapeze artists, the albino acrobats, father and son, completely hairless and their heads glistening in the spotlights.

The hideous group disturbed Teddy Verano. He tried not to dwell on it, listening instead to the small orchestra playing *Les Saltimbanques*. It was the right choice. Teddy Verano remembered seeing the comic opera at the Porte-Saint-Martin theater, with unforgettable performers; he smiled at the happy memories to dissipate his unease.

All of a sudden, he scolded himself. Was he here to lounge around or to find a clue about the photographer of the dead?

He examined the orchestra, or rather the young woman, whose only job was to start the turntable. He was not surprised to see her thin shoulders holding up one of those angular faces, completely chinless, that make the male sex flee at first sight.

There's certainly no one here pretty enough to compensate for the others.

For the men, it might have been acceptable; but this was the first time that he attended a circus performance of any kind with such a festival of ugly women.

When the Ringmaster, who had amused the public with some lame jokes while the cages were set up, announced the great Crucifer and his partner, Miss Mahlia, he finally hoped to see a pretty girl.

Crucifer entered and, at first, Teddy Verano thought he was a rather handsome man. Tall, solid, with a hard profile, a little gypsy-like with his curly black hair. But when Crucifer walked around the tent in the traditional blue uniform with gold buttons, boots and a whip, the detective saw his other profile. Furrowed with horrible scars, likely the remains of some savage attack by one of his favorite cats. The eye had been spared, but it opened in a marred, tortured flesh that was gruesomely swollen with deep, red ravines.

And then, there was Miss Mahlia.

One of those stunning silhouettes of women. In a sequined black tutu, she was led by the scarlet clown who, fighting the sway of his twisted legs, and with his weird make-up, looked like some cheap Quasimodo presenting a genuine Esmeralda.

With her beautifully styled blonde hair (could it be a wig?) the ravishing Miss Mahlia came forward. The gossamer tights highlighted the splendor of her legs, and the very low cut corset revealed a chest of classic beauty. Her graceful arms and elegant neck, slightly tilted, helped create an aura of desire in idealization.

Only, she wore a mask—and for Teddy, the reason was obvious.

If she doesn't show her face, even when the act is finished, it's because this Venus must really be a monster.

He thought of nothing but this during the show: two lions and two tigers together "for the first time in the world," as the Ringmaster announced.

Crucifer forcefully controlled the movements of the rather cranky animals that must have been suffering from the cold. They responded to his orders without much enthusiasm, but the gladiator stood firm.

And during this time, Miss Mahlia performed under a spotlight. A fairly boring dance made up of a simple series of pretty poses. But the incomparable beauty of the woman's body, drifting among the massive bodies of growling flesh, had a striking effect.

The chinless girl stopped her "orchestra" while Miss Mahlia leaped onto a stool that Crucifer invited the beasts to surround, placing their monstrous paws around her graceful legs.

At that moment, Teddy Verano looked to see who was working the spot-light. He saw the scarlet clown, adding this other job to that of official joker. In spite of the shadows around the improvised technician, the detective was struck by the glare of his eyes. The gruesome figure was ogling Miss Mahlia, whom he was in charge of lighting up, and all the passion that an abject man can feel towards a desirable woman shone through his pupils.

Well, well... Maybe that proves that Miss Mahlia may not be as hideous as I thought...

The act went on. Teddy Verano noticed nothing more of interest. He did not particularly admire Crucifer's agility, Miss Mahlia's grace, or their courage. He was eager for the show to be over, and get back to work. Luckily it did not take long. The final applause died out as the crowd poured out into the chilly air. Teddy Verano slipped around by the trailers.

Night had fallen. It was cold. The wind was blowing again and flapping the canvas tents. In their cages, the wild cats growled, angry at being cold.

CHAPTER VI

One after another, the stalls went dark as the interminable garlands of lights went out, as well as the colored neon tubes and arc light that just a minute before were stabbing through the cold and sad night.

Teddy Verano walked noiselessly around the Crucifer Circus, in this part of the fairground where only the carnies roamed; they had not really stamped down the snow, so there was enough of it to muffle the sound of his footsteps.

As he approached the trailers, he had the weird sensation of seeing huge puddles of darkness forming before his eyes. This phenomenon was due to the gradual disappearance of the bright zones, as the stalls switched off their garish lights. After the sparkling, artificial warmth of the fair, here was the triumph of the night and cold again.

Teddy Verano raised the collar of his overcoat. He thought, for an instant, of going back to where he had left his DS, near an intersection that sloped down into the town itself.

Forget it. I'll only be here for a few more minutes.

If it worked... What he intended to do was quite simple. He just wanted to try to get a closer look at the private life of the circus people. There had been nothing out of the ordinary, however, during the performance. Not the least incident, the slightest clue, nothing that seemed to have any connection to the fatal night when poor Agnes in Péronne had lost her marbles, or to the violation of Viviane Lefort's grave.

And what if tonight, something happened?

He pictured them all. He thought about them. About their faces, their mutilated, ugly, deformed faces, about this carnival of monstrosities that the strange Crucifer seemed to maintain around him for some kind of dark purpose.

Ugly women and hideous men. And Miss Mahlia...

Mahlia, whose gorgeous body gave a glimpse of the forbidden fruit, and who made a little knot in his throat with her black tutu and sequined corset. Mahlia, whom the scarlet clown, chasing her with the spotlight, had spied on with his greedy eyes. Mahlia, who wore a mask...

But her figure...

Teddy Verano shrugged. He had seen so many pretty women in the course of his career! And although he had been faithful to Yvonne since he had married Gerard's mother, he had still added a few pretty numbers to his collection. And yet, deep down inside, he could not get rid of the image of Miss Mahlia dancing among the wild animals; he tried, in vain, to find what this vision conjured up for him...

It had not struck him at first, but the more he thought about it, the more he was convinced he had seen Mahlia before, Mahlia in her black diamonds, Mahlia the partner of the disfigured lion-tamer, Mahlia, who...

Idiot! You've never seen this girl before.

He smiled silently to himself.

But right now, you're going to see her again!

He heard the muffled roaring nearby, behind the flapping canvas. He was in the very center of the group of trailers making up the Crucifer Circus. But he saw nobody. The fair was staying for two or three more days, and since they did not have to break down the tents, the performers must have gone back to their respective trailers, which was normal in this weather.

All of a sudden, he jumped. Over the deep growls of the wild cats, still moaning and crying out their nostalgic rage in this freezing world so hostile to them, a loud argument had broken out, coming from one of the trailers.

Instinctively, Teddy Verano flattened himself against the nearest one, that was dark and quiet, and then clearly saw, right across from him, another trailer, whose small window was lit up. A dark figure crossed it. The figure of a man, all worked up and shouting.

Teddy Verano had a hard time understanding him. As always, he was consumed by the imp of curiosity. It was his nature, even before being a detective, and no doubt, the former had pushed him into the latter.

The man was arguing, obviously with a woman. The woman passed by the makeshift screen of the window, displaying a brief shadow puppet show that made Teddy flinch.

It was Miss Mahlia.

But Miss Mahlia was not her name; it meant nothing. It was an unremarkable, vaguely artistic, stage name. A name that hid her real name, like the black mask in the show was hiding a face that Teddy Verano would have paid dearly to see. Not only because what he had seen of the woman left him to imagine what beauty her face might have once possessed, but also because a dim memory was floating deep in the depths of his mind, and he could not manage to grasp it clearly.

However, right under the window now, he could not just see them but he was starting to hear them better. They were indeed quarreling.

"...forbid you, get it? You can't waste your time watching this rubbish TV show!"

"So I can't even watch television now? That's too much!"

"There are better things to do."

"I work here, don't I? I risk my life every night."

"And me? Don't I risk mine?"

"You're the tamer, that's your job."

"And yours is to..."

There was silence and Teddy Verano knew exactly what it meant.

A man is furious with a woman. They argue… and then, at a certain moment, exasperated, the man gives in to the brute and lets himself be won over by the woman's seductive charm, becomes enchanted by the woman he desires. Therefore, Teddy Verano easily guessed what might be happening.

"Oh, leave me alone, please."

"What's wrong with you?"

"You want me to rest, Cruci."

"You're angry because I wouldn't let you watch that show? Listen, Mahlia, it's for your own good. What's the point of stirring up old memories?"

It sounded like Mahlia sighed. Teddy Verano supposed it more than he heard it. Now Crucifer became gentler, more insinuating.

"Mahlia, for now, it's not possible… and it's better for you to not look back into the past. But soon, soon, when he's found it…"

Mahlia laughed briefly, insultingly and, at the same time, bitterly.

"If he ever finds it!"

"You don't believe anymore?"

"Since he first promised us…"

"Mahlia, you don't believe in… certain things. But you used to."

She suddenly became angry.

"Yes. But you know what it cost me. That's what got me… where I am today…"

"Mahlia, Mahlia… Soon, Mirk will succeed. He's working hard on it, you know that. And it'll be for you and for me… for both of us. Back to a normal life. Oh, Mahlia, on that day… What revenge ewe shall have!"

Mahlia jeered. Her voice was beautiful, but dark. Teddy Verano suddenly shuddered on hearing certain modulations.

"On that day! Supposing that this demon gives us what he promised… Do you think that all women will be yours, tamer of my heart?"

"All women…" Crucifer's voice became more savage and more sensual than ever. "On that day… No, not all women. What do other women matter to me? Only you, Mahlia, only you! And it will be you who will inflame me, who will make me crazy, with your beauty…"

"No, not that word!" she almost screamed.

He gave in.

"Don't be so tense, please. We can but hope…" He paused, before saying quietly, "We have paid the price. These things are bought and they don't come cheap. We're risking a lot, but for such results… you and I, both of us… the best circus in the world, with the prettiest girls and the most magnificent men. Oh, Mahlia, do you think that what we're trying to do isn't worth it?"

There was a short pause before Mahlia lets out a little cry.

"Don't touch me. Not the mask, Cruci! Please, not the mask!"

Teddy Verano listened to all this and wondered what it meant. With his remarkable professional training, he did not try to analyze it right away, or make any connections. He filed it away, that was all. He filed it away, thanks to his naturally active memory that had been firmly disciplined by a few simple and effective tricks, like memorizing Henry VIII's six wives or the 33 plays of Corneille.

He filed it away, recorded it. Later, he would process it.

He heard Crucifer scolding Mahlia again, a little angry, a little menacing, which made the detective shiver, despite the tones of voice he heard.

"He'll find it. It'll be for you, Mahlia. And for me, too, so that I won't be repulsive anymore. He'll find it, otherwise…"

"Cruci, Cruci, be careful! You said so yourself: Mirk is devilish."

"I know," the lion-tamer barked. "If he didn't traffic with who knows what powers, he couldn't succeed…" He paused and lowered his voice, so that Teddy Verano could barely hear him. "If it's true, if he's not bluffing, if he can really give us what we lost… Oh, Mahlia, you'll be beautiful again, and I won't sicken you anymore."

"Cruci, I never said that. Besides... (the young woman's voice sounded horribly desperate, which made Teddy Verano feel bad) ...am I any better than you? Aren't we in the same boat? Like all the others? Poor Fever Blister, at her age… a shriveled up old woman at thirty. And if they call Arsène Lack-o-Luck, it's only for his poor face. And the Ziganos, you think they're beautiful? What a family of monsters! And the others?"

"Patience, Mahlia."

"Yes... But Mirk must keep his word."

"If he doesn't keep his promise, I'll feed him to my lions."

She must have shrugged while saying:

"Don't be stupid, Cruci. Anyway, listen… I'm scared."

"Of that runt? You make me laugh."

"No, no, please, Cruci. Watch out. He's stronger than you."

"You're joking, Mahlia."

"But don't you see what he's capable of?" she exploded. "If what you say is true? In any case, we can't know if he'll go all the way, if he'll finish what he promised. But what he's already done… We can't…"

"He, too, signed with…"

"Be quiet! Be quiet! You know we can't talk about that."

It sounded to Teddy Verano like Mahlia was crying. Crucifer tried to soften his harsh voice that was used to giving orders to his huge wild animals.

"Mahlia, magic or not, the result is what counts. What does it matter to us! Everyone here knows what was promised. They're waiting. Believe me, if Mirk double-crosses them, they'll get their revenge." His voice rang out like a toll bell. "It's awful to live with faces like ours. So, whatever it takes to get out of this… Whatever it takes. Even what Mirk is doing. Afterward, we won't care."

217

It was snowing again. The trailers were silent and Teddy Verano, alone, pressed against Crucifer's rolling home, forgot about the biting cold, wrapped up as he was in this conversation that he was in the perfect place to hear.

He would have given anything to be able to "read between the lines." But what did it matter! He would remember everything. Later, he would make the connections, gather up the various clues, and the puzzle, which he was already convinced was real, would come together, piece by piece, before his eyes.

Suddenly, he saw something moving in the shadows. A weird shape hiding in the night that suddenly sprang out and a raspy voice shrieked:

"What are you doing here?"

Teddy Verano was more annoyed than surprised, because he wanted to hear more and this intrusion was messing up his plans. But he had anticipated this situation and prepared, for all practical purposes, an explanation to justify being here among the trailers.

"Oh, sorry. I guess you're with the Crucifer Circus?"

He saw, through the murky veil of snow, a skinny little man, bent and twisted, whose eyes seemed to glow strangely.

"Yes, I'm from the circus," the scratchy voice said. "But you... you'd better explain yourself. You can't come in here. Unless..."

Teddy Verano could not react this time. The gnome pulled something out of his pocket and the detective got a full shot of light directly in his face.

It went out right away and everything faded to black again.

Despite his usually quick reactions Teddy Verano realized that he had just been seriously thwarted by the scarlet clown.

CHAPTER VII

It was him. There was no doubt about it. Without his thick, red and white make-up, he was absolutely hideous. In the dark, his face took on an eerie, dazzling aspect. And with his skinny, twisted body, he came out of the shadows like some unreal creature in the thick curtain of glistening snow surrounding the trailers.

Teddy Verano recognized him. Without any problem. But he was upset at being surprised by the bright flashlight that let the other see him clearly, which was exactly what he always tried to avoid in these situations.

"Why'd you come here?" the raspy voice asked.

Teddy Verano opened his mouth to give his carefully prepared explanation. The other did not give him time. He piped up again right away, and it seemed to the detective that it was more for him than for Teddy Verano himself.

"Why'd you come here? In your condition, it'd be totally useless. You don't need to be among us."

It was a pretty enigmatic statement, but Teddy Verano did not get flustered.

"Monsieur, pardon my indiscretion but…"

Once again, the clown without make-up cut him off.

"I saw you. You're normal. I can even say that you're not bad looking. More than one man would probably not mind having a face like yours. And I'm sure that more than one woman has said so, that they're not very cruel to you."

Teddy Verano swallowed hard and tried to find something to say. Now he was starting to get puzzled and not really understand anything.

"So," the clown continued, "you're not here for that reason. You're not a monster, not even an ugly man, not hideous. Therefore, you can't come among us. There's no point."

This time, he made a direct reference to the repulsive circle of unfortunate carnies. But it seemed like a thorny subject to dwell on, and Teddy Verano, as much as he wanted to find out more, and know why the gnome talked openly about such things, thought it better to change the subject.

"I'm very glad to find you here. There's no one around. With this weather, I'm not surprised. In short, I'm being indiscreet. Sorry, but it's my job. Basically, I do a little reporting on the side, and after seeing the Crucifer Circus put on such an interesting show this afternoon, I wanted to interview some of its performers around the caravans… well, the trailers, I guess... It's more modern. I'd also like to take a picture or two."

"A picture! Pictures!" the little man suddenly looked scared. "Why are you talking about taking pictures?"

"Why not? To illustrate the newspaper article; it's totally normal."

219

"No, no, no more mention of that."

"OK, but you know that readers are hungry for them."

The gnome seemed to hop because he was swaying and bobbing in a weird way. He could not seem to stay put, probably due to his deformed hips that must have caused him constant pain, and that he tried to hide just like in the ring with all his different pranks.

"I know newspaper readers. They're like everyone else. They love people who are beautiful, Monsieur. Pretty girls. In all the papers, the movies, on TV, that's all they see. Beautiful girls. And it's understandable. But the others… No, Monsieur, nobody's interested in the others."

"Allow me," Teddy Verano said softly, finding this man weirder and weirder, both in his behavior and his speech. "Maybe you could provide me with just one picture. I don't know, how about the most attractive member of the Crucifer Circus, Miss Mahlia, for example."

The gnome jumped like he had seen a lizard.

"Miss Mahlia… You said, Miss Mahlia? You want a picture of Miss Mahlia?"

"Sure. What's so strange about that? She is an artist. All the artists in the world carry pictures with them taken by professional photographers. They have them for the press, for reporters… and for admirers. I have to admit," Teddy Verano laughed, "that I'm not embarrassed to include myself among the latter when it comes to Miss Mahlia."

The longer he talked, the more he saw the scarlet clown cringe, as if what he said was torture to him.

"You're an admirer of Miss Mahlia? And you want to publish a photo of her?"

He was staggered, as if someone had announced some scandalous absurdity.

"No, Monsieur. No! Don't talk about that. Get away from here, that's my advice."

Teddy Verano had made up his mind to hold his ground, to play it cool despite the ludicrous and disturbing attitude of the other.

"But since she appears with a mask, can't I get a picture of her face?"

This time, the clown almost somersaulted.

"Not that! No, not that!" He was literally gasping. "Her face… the face of Miss Mahlia… But Miss Mahlia has no face!"

"No face?"

Now the gnome sobered up a little. He got a hold of himself and must have realized that he was going to regret what he had just said.

"I mean… No, it's impossible."

"But, there must be a reason."

"A reason? Yes… yes…"

Clearly he was searching for one. Teddy let him "swim." But the scarlet clown was already talking again.

"A reason? Yes… jealousy."

"Ah-ha! And who was the jealous devil?"

"Crucifer, Monsieur! He's terrible. Nobody except for him can see Miss Mahlia face to face. It's weird, I know, but what can you do? They're both like that."

"And she accepts this situation?"

"She does."

"Does she have a choice?"

The gnome thought twice before answering.

"Monsieur, you're asking too many questions. Listen, you'd better just give up the whole idea. Leave us alone. We're honest carnies and we're not hurting anyone. We go from town to town and…"

"That's exactly why it would be interesting to write an article about the Crucifer Circus."

"No, Monsieur. We don't need the publicity and…"

Something creaked and a big rectangle of light suddenly cut through the night. A rectangle that carved out, like a huge shadow puppet show, a figure whose outline was all that could be seen, all black on the yellow screen of the trailer door.

And a hoarse voice that Teddy Verano recognized right away rumbled:

"Mirk! Is that you? Who are you talking to?"

Very quickly, the clown pulled Teddy Verano behind another trailer.

"Hush! It's him. Can't let him know we're talking. He'll be furious… and he'll take it out on me."

"Mirk!" Crucifer's booming voice called out.

Teddy Verano made a quick connection with the conversation overheard between Crucifer and Miss Mahlia. Mirk, therefore, was just the scarlet clown. He realized that, during the show, the Ringmaster had, in fact, presented all his fellow performers, except for his partner.

Mirk—it was obviously him—looked scared to death. He pushed Teddy Verano as far back as he could, left him and walked forward.

"Mirk!" the gladiator shouted for the third time.

In the light coming from the trailer door, Teddy Verano saw Mirk advance, pathetic, hard to watch, while the gigantic outline of the lion tamer, made even bigger by the optical effect, looked terrifying.

"Is that you, you little runt? What are you doing? I heard you talking… who with?"

"Don't be angry, boss."

"Come here, moron!"

From his hiding place, Teddy Verano could still see them; behind Crucifer, he made out an elegant, female form. It was obviously Miss Mahlia, but he saw her against the light and could not tell whether or not she was still wearing her mask.

Crucifer was in shirtsleeves, despite the cold. He had taken off his dolman jacket but was still wearing his leather pants and boots. He let loose a flood of curses upon the scarlet clown, who stood there, looking like a frightened child in front of some torturer.

Teddy Verano watched the woman's shape, her very beautiful lines in some kind of tight-fitting bathrobe, reach out and put a hand on the lion-tamer's shoulder.

"Let him be, Cruci."

Teddy Verano remembered. that Miss Mahlia had been scared of Mirk. Why? This was baffling.

Miss Mahlia kept trying to calm him down, but Crucifer kept threatening Mirk, saying that there was someone here, that all intruders should be chased away, and that if Mirk brought in strangers, he would introduce them to the end of his boot.

"You're making me get cold, you wreck. Why'd you come over if there's nobody here? Do you have something to tell us? Have you found another one?"

"No, boss. I haven't have time to work. We just finished the show."

"Of course, he's right," Mahlia jumped in, clearly trying to patch things up.

Teddy Verano thought that she was less afraid of Crucifer's anger at the scarlet clown than the retaliation of the latter, undoubtedly believed to be mysterious and dreadful.

However, Mirk stayed at the bottom of the small stairs leading up to the trailer like in an old caravan adapted to modern use.

The lion-tamer jumped down and grabbed his collar.

"You haven't found anything, have you? Well, some advice. Find something... fast. Do whatever you want. All means are acceptable, you know. But I'm warning you not to waste time, or you're in for a licking."

"Hey, Cruci, enough!" Mahlia intervened.

She went down the three steps and, in the process, passed through the light coming from the lamp inside. Although she was out of her uniform, Teddy saw that she had kept the black mask on, and Mirk's incomprehensible comments sped through his mind.

However, the lion-tamer was back to his initial suspicions.

"You didn't come here for nothing, for the fun of it... You have nothing new to tell us... So, I know you were talking with someone."

Mirk started to deny it, but Crucifer seemed to be particularly irritable and Teddy Verano easily imagined that this strong man, who was probably very handsome before being mauled by some wild animal, must have seen his personality deteriorate afterward—and likely, it probably wasn't very easy-going to start with.

"You're going to talk, right?"

Teddy Verano was starting to feel uneasy. His story was a total lie. He had tried to fool the gnome with his tall tale of an article, photos, and an interview, but this would probably not hold up with a brute like Crucifer.

On the other hand, if Mirk apparently had accepted without question what Teddy Verano had told him, it was because he seemed to be not normal, mentally speaking, but he had responded with strange ramblings that the detective was still waiting to sort out, seeing that it only added to the mystery that he felt was looming over this circus haunted by monsters.

Crucifer belched out some words that got lost in the wind, which had started whistling again around Montdidier. The detective saw the poor clown literally lifted off the ground with one hand by the animal-tamer.

"Are you going to answer me?"

Mirk talked, terrorized, hanging above the snowy ground, struggling to get free and nodding his head in Teddy Verano's direction. The detective knew that he had been made.

Scared by the heavy hand of the lion-tamer, the clown, with no costume or make-up, the miserable human waste, gave up any thought of defense and admitted that somebody had come and this somebody was still close by.

Crucifer let go of Mirk, who rolled in the snow, and barked:

"Photos! A guy who wants photos! I'll give him some photos of Mahlia!"

He leaped, pushed the young woman back, forcing her to scramble up the stairs, and forced her back into the trailer. In the process, Teddy Verano saw her once again, in full light this time, with her silken bathrobe clinging tightly to her body. Thus, for a second, she looked almost nude, which shook him up. Because it reminded him of a distant memory of a naked woman... but who?

Crucifer reappeared, slamming the door on Mahlia, crashing down the steps and running into the snow, still in shirtsleeves like he was laughing at the cold, the wind and the snowflakes fluttering around him.

In a mad rage he kept shouting:

"Photos! The swine! He's gonna see..."

Teddy Verano thought he could stand up to him, physically. But practically speaking, he was in the wrong. He did not belong to the police department and, in any event, no police officer would be allowed to question a suspect at such late hour.

His only choice was to disappear, which he would have done willingly if he could have gotten his bearings. But the night was dark, and the blinding snow and cold wind were not very encouraging for an honorable retreat.

"Hey everybody!" Crucifer rumbled. "Come over here! Zigano! Lack-o-Luck! Wildor! Everybody come here! There's a guy who wants pictures of us. Ha, ha, ha!"

His raucous laugh rang out louder than the snowstorm and, for a brief instant and he punctuated his call with a particular sound: despite being troubled, the detective recognized the crack of a whip. The expert tamer had grabbed his work tool and was searching for him, tracking him like a wild beast.

Yvonne's husband quickly thought, *What nest of vipers have I gotten myself into?*

He could have asked himself another question: Was all this of any use to his investigation? Had the things he heard between Crucifer and Mahlia, and from the mouth of the scarlet clown, any connection to the macabre adventure of young Agnes or the violation of Vivienne Lefort's grave?

But this was no time to ask himself such questions.

In the snow falling onto the fairgrounds, in the middle of the Crucifer Circus, people started popping up.

Dragged out of their sleep, dark shapes appeared in the black and white night; everyone in the troupe, those hideous people, frightening to look at, those ugly freaks, answered the call of the disfigured lion-tamer to began the hunt for their prey.

CHAPTER VIII

The smell was enough for Teddy Verano to know where he had just run to: the animal cages. The musty smell of straw and the huge animal bodies, in spite of the chill, smelled strongly. The detective had slipped under a canvas sign, being especially careful to stay out of sight, helped by the dark night.

Except that, now, he was here.

A faint rumbling could be heard nearby. He figured that he was too close to a cage and moved away. Not only was he aware of the danger, but he also felt completely ridiculous. And he was furious. He thought about Gerard, his stepson, his protégé.

If he saw me in this bind, he would crack up. Teddy caught in a trap... now, that's funny. I can hear him already.

The big cats were rolling around in their beds of straw that their keepers had piled into the cages to protect them from the cold. On passing by, two or three times before, Teddy Verano had felt the aura of heat from the infrared lights, which cast red splotches in the darkness, and sometimes sparkled off the eyes of the lions and tigers who were arranged in couples in two different cages. It was very dim, only a relative light; Teddy Verano preferred the dark. This was no time to get spotted.

He could still hear Crucifer screaming outside, and other voices answering. They had called out and yelled, and with the rumbling storm, it all melted into a muffled cacophony that was broken every now and again by Crucifer's whip lashing at the wind, or the muted curses of crowd, or the soft roars of the wild animals being disturbed in their tranquility, smelling the stranger and crouching in their cages.

Mirk had collapsed in the snow. Crucifer had tossed him there, but now the runt, obviously aware that he could not avoid the madman's anger (which was why he had changed his mind and ended up confessing that there really was a visitor) had decided to give up the intruder. Finally, he scrambled to his feet and started searching with the others around the trailers.

In fact, they found little evidence of the detective's presence. The snow and the wind had covered his tracks within seconds. Moreover, the members of the troupe all arrived at the same time, only adding to the general confusion, which allowed Teddy Verano a few seconds' headstart that he used to sneak a little blindly, under the canvas.

He now was with the animals, but maybe they were not as dangerous as these weird people in the Crucifer Circus. Besides, as he moved forward, just feeling his way, instinctively avoiding the dim light of the infrareds, it sounded like the muted thunder of voices being carried away by the snowstorm was coming closer, louder, more intense.

He understood. He had no other choice.

Very agilely, even with his overcoat, Teddy Verano rolled under one of the cages that was sitting on its wheels and sealed with hay underneath to resist the cold. He huddled up there and did not move, suffocating in spite of the cold, very uncomfortable, bothered by the hay that tickled his ears and crept into his sleeves and pant legs. But as it was, he was nearly invisible.

Crucifer and the others barged in and Teddy Verano, lying on the ground, saw in the vague red light a strange merry-go-round of the performers. They were dripping with snow and shook it off. They were not completely dressed, but wrapped up enough, except for the lion-tamer who seemed unmindful of the cold.

They were here, led by Crucifer. The entire Circus except for one person—Mahlia.

Despite his position, that was as awkward as it was ridiculous and dangerous, Teddy Verano thought again of the beauty who always wore her mask, a mask that she even refused to take off for Crucifer, a mask that hid...

...What kind of face?

"Miss Mahlia has no face."

Crazy words from an even crazier creature. Mirk, the scarlet clown, had spoken this nonsense and Teddy Verano believed he was saved by this eccentricity. Except that the idiot, under Crucifer's threats, had betrayed him and thrown the gang of ugly misfits on his trail.

He saw them and wondered how long they would continue searching for him. But, all of a sudden, they changed their attitude. They started laughing in a weird way and shouting at each other so loudly, so noisily, that with the background of the storm and the roaring of the animals fed up with the disturbance, not much of what they said could be understood.

Teddy Verano, however, could make out that they were talking about him among other things. He heard:

"Photos... get out of here... scared... photos... he's crazy... no right... photos... forbidden... photos... beauty..."

The word "beauty" had suddenly rang out and everyone repeated it continually.

"Beauty... beauty... beauty..."

Teddy Verano breathed deeply, but with great caution, because he did not want to be caught.

They were talking and laughing, laughing hysterically, especially the women, which was painful. They made jokes, which caused more laughter. But everything was as painful to hear as it was to see. For Teddy Verano, even in his awkward position, could see them.

Every man and woman, surrounding Crucifer, who stood beside the sinister gnome who turned into a scarlet clown for the shows.

The fat man with the swollen, lipless face and huge ears, who was horribly ugly, was the Ringmaster; both he and the ludicrous clown introduced the shows. Teddy Verano had imagined his ugliness before, but now, without make-up, he saw him as a tragic horror. The Ringmaster, a monstrous swine...

And that deformed, endless nose like a trunk... That nose marring the face of a woman, whose melancholy eyes were not without beauty, and whose mouth remained sensual. The amazon, who had so nimbly jumped through the paper hoops. This poor woman was good-looking, but could easily be made fun of, which had probably happened far too often in her life.

And the Zigano family... the hideous one-eyed woman with her husband and son, the albinos whose bald, repugnant heads glistened in the infrared, making them look like ridiculous demons. And the couple's daughter, so poorly favored, this awful girl with the lunar head, maybe a half-wit, whose squat body, all muscles, looked like an athlete's seen in a concave mirror, with no traces of femininity...

Here was the magician without his top hat, without his make-up and novelty tie, which had half-hidden his face during the show, looking horrendously ape-like.

And his partner—Teddy Verano guessed that she was the one called Fever Blister—whom he had smiled at, who looked horribly ravaged, with her skin all wrinkled and folded, shriveled up, but with younger hands than he could have imagined, affected by some mysterious sickness that made her a kind of living mummy. Without make-up she, too, came out of the dark and recalled some spectral apparition.

All the acrobats were there. The woman with the awful birthmark; the man with his lazy eye stuck in a corner of the socket, so that you did not know whether to laugh or be scared at his terrible face.

All of them were there... and now, they seemed to have forgotten that they had left their trailers because Crucifer called them to search for the crazy guy who wanted a photo of Miss Mahlia. A photo of a member of this grotesque band.

Crucifer suddenly shouted:

"Be quiet!"

And he cracked his whip.

Overhead, Teddy Verano heard the animals rumbling and the heavy foot-steps of a digitigrade echoing on the planks. The wild cat was pacing, not happy. He heard it moving around the straw. But the whip cracked again and even the lion quieted down.

Teddy Verano wondered what all this meant, and inevitably thought of the wake in Péronne, and the opened grave near Senlis.

Little by little, he sensed that this gathering of the circus freaks held some-thing mysterious. They were already forgetting about the intruder who had snatched them out of the beds. Since Crucifer had called them, they had come, but they were happy to have an excuse to come here. For what purpose? That was another question...

Impressive, with his whip in hand, Crucifer managed to quiet them down.

Teddy Verano was still hiding, awkwardly, scratched and pricked and annoyed by countless needles of hay. He squirmed around and strained his neck to the breaking point in order to see. The frightful faces, emerging from the night in splotches of dark purple zones, looked almost supernatural in the startling décor.

The lion-tamer's fist seized the little man called Mirk by the collar. He pushed him roughly into the middle of the circle formed by all the ill-fated, either from birth or from some unfortunate accident.

The tamer moved around and appeared sometimes with his good profile, which showed him off, or sometimes with the opposite side, and the awful scars in the infrared glow that made him more hideous than ever.

"Mirk promised!" he roared. "You know what he promised us!"

A kind of muffled clamor came out of the mouths of all those present. And the inarticulate voices expressing some weird feelings, maybe of desperation or of anger, maybe of hope or of repressed, hysterical madness, echoed through the wild animals and stirred them up. Teddy Verano shuddered on hearing them above him, very close, separated only by the wooden planks of the cage that shook under their powerful paws as their huge claws scraped dreadfully, making him break out in a cold sweat, even though he was safe from their attack and the men might be more dangerous.

Crucifer jumped, cracked his whip, and made the big cats move back, growling but obeying.

Mirk had not moved. Obviously, he was scared. Teddy Verano saw that the gnome was trembling, but, at times, the detective glimpsed the nasty look on the scarlet clown's face. And he understood Miss Mahlia's fears.

In his eyes, those strangely bright eyes, Mirk had a real glimmer from Hell. The little man, no doubt, hated the lion-tamer. He could have hated him for a number of reasons, but the main thing (it was not hard to guess) was the privileged situation that he had with the masked dancer.

After controlling the animals for the moment, Crucifer stormed back into the circle, shoving the performers in the process. But nobody said a word. It seemed that, in the weird Crucifer Circus, the actions and the will of the boss was law.

Teddy Verano had seen many fairs in his lifetime, been friends with many performers in the ring and in the music hall, but he was thinking that he had never seen an ambiance like this. Where was that famous fraternal solidarity among travelers, always ready to help each other and never leave a comrade in trouble? Here, he figured, these people were brought together and held together by some infernal pact, by some dreadful power.

"Mirk promised," Crucifer resumed. "He came to see me tonight. He still hasn't found it but…"

Everyone started fidgeting again and talking at the same time. The commotion lasted 30 seconds before Crucifer ended it with a crack of his whip.

"Mirk knows. Mirk's got the secret. He can give you… give us what belongs to us by natural right. We must all benefit from his aid." Another crack of the whip cut through the murmuring and he continued. "Tell them, Mirk. Tell them what you're going to do."

The gnome looked up and his face rose directly into the infrared glow. Even though he was in regular clothes, with nothing special about them, and had no make-up on, Teddy Verano thought he was seeing the scarlet clown again. But not the funny, friendly performer, amusing children and young souls. No, something like a demon, god-awful ugly with eyes spitting flames and a body that more than ever recalled the nightmares of Hoffman and Grimm.

"I'm working on it," his thin voice said. "I'm working for you, for all of you. For you, Crucifer, for you, Wildor, and for you, Vera Zigano."

He turned and pointed to each of them in turn. Nobody said a word and, in this movement, the terrorized runt suddenly took on an authority that he had lacked so far.

"For you… for you… for you…"

He stopped. The big cats were growling in the shadows. Teddy Verano held his breath.

"I asked for you help. So far, you've done what I asked. Oh, I know, Crucifer blames me for not succeeding yet. But be patient! I tried to snatch away from life that beauty that you're all dreaming of. I wasn't able."

He paused before continuing and his voice squealed unpleasantly. He was panting, but he shouted, which would have almost been funny if it were not so frightening.

"I sent you out to look for death. I went myself. Neither life nor death has yet delivered to me the secret of true beauty, of living beauty."

It looked like Crucifer was about to do or say something. The scarlet clown stopped him by raising his hand.

"I know… I believe I know what it takes. To satisfy all of you, to satisfy you, Crucifer, so that Mahlia can be what she ought to be, I'm going to try something else… I'm going even farther."

He hiccupped and you could not tell if the sound coming out of his mouth was laughter or moaning, threats or cries of terror.

"Yes! Even farther! Since life and death haven't given me what I want, I'm going to catch it in between. Do you understand?" He clenched his small, thin, knotty hands and pronounced, "In between… life and death."

His words fell in the silence. Crucifer did not move, as if subdued. He stood there with arms crossed over his whip. The hideous carnies encircling him in the red glow looked frozen but their eyes were alive, intensely. Even the wild cats were quiet.

In between life and death... What does he mean? Teddy Verano, captivated, panicky, asked himself.

Mirk suddenly stood as tall as he could.

"But you have to obey me."

With one voice the men and women yelped:

"We will obey you."

"You have to go farther than I have pushed you so far."

"We will do it."

"We will do it!" Crucifer barked. "We will do whatever you say. But watch out! I warn you. You've jeopardized us. You've demanded outrageous things. You're going to incur the wrath of the authorities. We've already had to make good an escape a few times. We'll do anything for what we want, but you're forewarned—you'd better not deceive us."

He stood up straight, magnificent, his arms still crossed over his whip.

The runt had regained his confidence and seemed to challenge him.

"I understand, Crucifer. But this time I'll do it..."

Then all the poor deformities almost chanted:

"Beauty! We'll be beautiful. All of us beautiful. Mirk... Mirk... Whatever you want. Crucifer, we have to help him, to obey him... Beauty. Beauty!"

Mirk gestured with his thin hand asking for silence, but it was Crucifer who got it with a crack of his whip.

"A man came here just now."

"Was he beautiful?" the amazon asked innocently.

The question sounded absurd to Teddy Verano who, under different circumstances, would have burst out laughing.

"A pretty handsome man," the gnome said, his face twisting into a ghastly smile. "But what was he doing here? Enemies are threatening us..."

The carnies growled like the wild animals echoing them.

A whiplash. Silence. Mirk continued:

"These people have no business here. I'm telling you, we have no time to lose."

"You're the one wasting time, blabbermouth."

Crucifer was getting angry again. The scarlet clown gave him a dirty look.

"Do you think that invisible forces obey just like that, Crucifer? You can train and tame lions and tigers, but not spirits."

"Go to Hell!"

"Don't say that!" Mirk howled, losing control.

A shiver ran through the circle. A woman dared to raise her voice:

"No, we can't talk about that. We have to understand Mirk. He's risking a lot for all of us..."

"We're taking risks, too," the lazy-eyed acrobat said.

"But it's worth it," the Zigano son piped up, nodding his bald head.

"Listen," Crucifer said, "this has lasted long enough. I give you three days. No more. After that…"

"In three days, I'll have succeeded."

Then they all let loose. They started laughing again, shouting, talking at the same time and the word "beauty" was the only clear word in the cacophony.

Crucifer cracked his whip, but this time, he could not get them to stop, as if the scarlet clown's promise gave them some kind of demented hope, beyond nature, that surpassed human limits…

All of a sudden, in the middle of the circle of ugliness made more ugly by the infrared light, between the cages where the animals continued growling, someone showed up. Someone whose appearance made them all shiver.

Mirk curled up, like a toad wanting to jump away, but denied by nature. Crucifer made an angry gesture and the others backed away. In his hiding place, Teddy Verano also shivered without knowing why, maybe for the suddenness of the intrusion.

Still in her close-fitting bathrobe, and wearing her perpetual black mask, Miss Mahlia had made her appearance. In a changed voice she said:

"You say that you're going to succeed, Mirk? I heard…"

The scarlet clown saw her look at him with eyes that flashed as much desire as diabolical fury.

"I will succeed, Mahlia. For you."

Crucifer glanced sideways at the clown.

But Mahlia moaned and her voice broke.

"Well, hurry up. Hurry up, Mirk. I can't stand it any longer! I can't stand it!"

CHAPTER IX

"Be strong, Mahlia! I told you I'll succeed... We're all working on it... We're all taking a great risk, but afterward... what a result!"

The gnome had jumped toward Mahlia and was now on his knees before the splendid creature. He talked and talked, stumbling and stammering, almost comically, as Teddy Verano had already noticed.

The others were seized by a kind of frenzy. The closed ranks and their hideous faces lined up in the infrared.

"Yes, Mahlia... We'll do whatever Mirk wants. We have to..." And they tirelessly resumed their mantra. "Beauty... Beauty..."

Crucifer, who was obviously not happy with the scarlet clown's attitude, grabbed his arm, forced him to his feet and pulled him away.

"Enough of this nonsense. Action!"

"You gave me three days, Crucifer."

"This is your last chance," the lion-tamer threatened.

The runt straightened up on his twisted legs and challenged the giant.

"You say, *my* last chance, but it's yours as well."

The women got involved. The amazon, the acrobat, the contortionists, the fortune-teller, all suddenly cried out hoarsely:

"Our last chance! Our last chance, our last chance..."

They started laughing again and shrieking. The men chimed in. The wild animals started growling again and the tamer yelled for silence, banging his whip furiously.

Mahlia straightened up.

"I hope you told the truth. It's necessary, Mirk. We aren't sad because you're going to give us..."

"Beauty... Beauty... Beauty..."

Teddy Verano thought he heard someone in the chorus say three simple words:

"At any price!"

What price would it take, in fact, to transform all these creatures and make them normal? It was not plastic surgery, of course, *because their ugliness seemed to have different origins.*

"We have to laugh! We have to hope!" Mahlia cried out, getting carried away now with the others.

"Yes, yes! Let's laugh and sing!"

The ringmaster with the pig face shouted:

"Dance, Mahlia, dance our joy!"

They all echoed him in a frenzy:

"Dance, Mahlia, dance!"

Zigano, the head of the acrobatic family, hooted:

"It's all the same to you, Crucifer, if she dances for us?"

Crucifer had a kind of insulting laugh.

"I keep her face. No one has the right to see it."

"Mahlia, no face!" a sexless voice yelled, which Teddy identified as the young Zigano.

But the carnies started singing a kind of loud, monotonous chant and clapping their hands. Mahlia started moving in the infrared that served as a bank of lights.

The magician stepped forward and, in the red glow, his face looked like a nightmarish King Kong.

"You're beautiful, Mahlia, beautiful like we will all be. You're beautiful."

"Ha, Lack-o-Luck is losing his mind," the Ringmaster jeered. "Fever Elister is going to get jealous."

The small woman who looked like a mummy grimaced under her make-up as the amazon replied:

"Jealous of a beautiful male like that, I can understand."

"No jealousy!" a few voices cried out. "Crucifer's not jealous."

"No!" the tamer growled. "Not jealous. Except for her face. The rest... Hold on! The proof..."

Mahlia danced and her supple body in the silken robe created a suddenly sensual ambience that clashed with the demented, disturbing circle and made the ghastly spectacle even more dizzying.

The lion-tamer joined action to his words. He cracked his whip toward Mahlia with such skill that the cord wrapped around the young woman without lashing her, like a snake coiling around her slim waist and shoulders that one imagined were as graceful as possible.

One could only imagine.

With unbelievable skill, Crucifer pulled the whip and tore off her bathrobe.

A clamor arose among the carnies, but they did not stop their rhythm, beating out Mahlia's dance with their hands, a kind of cadenced movement that was like her performance among the wild animals.

Under the cage, in an awful position, bothered by the hay that choked and pricked him, Teddy Verano felt his heart jump in his chest. Mahlia naked, caressed by the soft light of the infrareds, was unquestionably a statue of flesh carved by an incomparable artist. But although this beauty, flecked with dark spots that accentuated the coppery tint of her skin, flustered, the detective also felt something else. This magnificent body, this shameless woman—he knew them both from before.

He remembered now. He had believed it only a resemblance upon first seeing the masked dancer in the ring. He had felt some dim memory awaken in him when he was crouched by the trailer, freezing in the snow, and listening to her conversation with Crucifer. But Mahlia's voice had been muffled, distorted.

Now, in all her flesh, he could swear he could identify her.

In the shadows, his mute lips pronounced a name.

But he stayed there, motionless, numb, luckily protected from the cold by a layer of hay, sometimes hearing the heavy paws of the big cats pacing on the planks right over his head.

Naked, provocative, sensual, troubling Mahlia kept dancing. Crucifer stood stiffly, whip in hand. Without a doubt, he would lash to death anyone who tried to lay a hand on her.

And Teddy Verano saw the leering men and the grinning women.

What was hiding behind this mask that she apparently never took off? They did not know.

At least, she could, without shame, exhibit her impeccable body, both finely and solidly built, that stirred up dreams of Eros.

They sang for a long time. Then the chant came to an end. Crucifer threw the bathrobe over Mahlia's shoulders and they left. One after the other, the rest of them left, too. The crazy party was over. Mirk the scarlet clown was the last to leave.

Teddy Verano waited for a minute before slipping out of his hiding place, more than happy to be able to stretch a little.

Bloody hell, my legs and arms are falling asleep!

Now, he had to get out of there as quickly as possible. He shook the hay off himself and, with this, attracted the animals. One of them came right up to the bars, which they had not done while Crucifer was there. And the beast, a magnificent lion, roared and shot out a menacing paw.

Teddy Verano swore again. *Bloody hell!* And he figured it was high time to beat it. He hurried to the door of the huge trailer holding the animals. He was starting to get familiar with the place with the help of the infrared lights casting their purplish glow. Except that he was in for an unpleasant surprise: the door was locked.

Teddy Verano broke out in a cold sweat.

This is completely stupid. I get stuck under the cages and watch the lunatics' Sabbath... I escape from them, or they forget me in their nonsense, and now, here I am, trapped like a rat!

He raged. To no avail. It was locked tight. The lion roared again and the tigers, who had been calm so far, started to get worked up.

This time, I'm screwed. They're going to hear the animals and come back. A guy like Crucifer must sleep with one eye open.

Then, he heard the click of the lock. He jumped back, causing another roar, luckily more quiet, from the lion upset with his presence. He dashed to the back of the trailer, but found no exit. There was only one solution: to get back into his original hiding place.

He had never felt so ridiculous.

But someone was coming in. Maybe it was whoever took care of the cages, probably one of the performers. In principle, wild animals had to be watched very carefully.

The stranger passed by, but Teddy Verano was not so well positioned to see this time. He felt his heart stop when he realized that the person who had entered was bending over to look under the cages.

He heard a voice whisper:

"Come out. Don't be scared. I know you're there."

This time, he was suffocating and decided to do what it took to get out of this completely absurd situation. He started crawling out of the hay. An action that once again made the big cats roar.

But a hand appeared, came closer and grabbed his own. A wrinkled hand, like that of a very, very old person. A woman judging by the size. Almost a doll's hand, but a 100-year old doll.

At the end of his rope, Teddy Verano crawled out and shook himself off, scorning the animals' bad mood this time.

"Well, yes, here I am!"

"I knew it. I saw you come in and figured you were under a cage. But they're all so stupid! They aren't thinking about you anymore. They think you got away."

He saw the small woman, knee-high to a grasshopper, ravaged and shriveled up, but fighting against it with theater make-up, wearing a veritable mask of putty and pencil marks under a coating of ocher powder. None of this, however, could hide the horribly dried out skin, the reptilian neck and the aged hands. Only her eyes looked young, even mischievous, and he saw the smile from when he had entered the circus.

It was the cashier-cum-fortune-teller, the assistant of the ape-faced magician whom they called by the odd name Lack-o-Luck, she who in the Crucifer Circus was known as Fever Blister.

She smiled at him, a sad smile, more depressing in trying to be alluring.

"You're going to leave and run away... very far away," she said.

"Yes, yes." Teddy Verano answered passively, dazed as he was by this unprecedented night and his absurd situation.

She led him out. He was back in the wind. A little less snow but the ground was covered.

"Why?" he murmured. "Why are you doing this?"

He saw her shrug her tiny shoulders.

"Because earlier when you entered the circus you looked at me... like men look at a woman... not at a freak."

"But... you are a woman."

She took his hand again and he felt her little nails bruising his skin.

"I was pretty once. Yes. And then... premature aging. A rare disease, I'm told. I'm an old carny... at 32."

He almost cried. She looked twice her age, and how many 60-year olds of the fair sex in our world try to look their best...

"You're doing this for me. How can I...?"

"Don't bother! Get going!"

"You don't even know what I'm looking for here."

"Surely not the same thing as us. You're too handsome. They only accept monsters here... or near-monsters."

"You're exaggerating."

"Maybe you're with the police. I don't care. Anyway, I think it's all going to end badly. So..."

This statement struck Teddy Verano. Yes, the eccentricities of the Crucifer Circus were covering up something insane, something terrible, he felt it. Poor Fever Blister was not fooling herself.

He looked at her kindly, gallantly, with a hint of sensuality in his smile that belonged to men of a certain class, who knew how to keep lewdness out of it. Fever Blister, the living mummy, had been deeply moved by this smile and thus was willing to betray her friends. Monsters, she thought them...

"Go now! Get out of here!"

"I want to thank you. You might be risking..."

She laughed sadly.

"The others? They're exhausted from all their crazy chanting. They're already dreaming about Mirk's promises. Beauty... Ha!"

"You don't believe him?"

"Mirk is just a sham wizard. Like Arsène, the magician, at best."

"Arsène? Your partner, right?"

"Yes. If they call him Lack-o-Luck, it's because he earned it... with his mug."

"What if he sees you're gone?"

"Him? He doesn't give a damn about me. He's Bertha's lover, the amazon... the one with the trunk of an elephant, like at the Bouglione's Circus."

It was 2 a.m. Teddy Verano knew that he would never be so lucky again. Fever Blister was helping him, but afterward...

His head was full of everything he had seen and heard. He told himself that there was some link with the sinister mysteries in Péronne and the cemetery next to Senlis. A link that he had to find, to connect, but it was there.

Therefore, he leaned over and, in the cold night, placed his lips on the withered lips of poor Fever Blister.

She stood there for a minute, without moving, watching him vanish in the snow. His head was already on fire when he jumped into the DS and set off toward Paris.

236

CHAPTER X

"Gerard! Are you there? Where's the TV guide?"

Teddy Verano shouted through the half-open door of the bathroom. He had woken up at 7 a.m.—even though he had arrived home at 4 a.m.—and gone to bed after a quick shower, without telling everything to Yvonne and Gerard despite the fact that they had wanted to be brought up to date after being woken up.

Thus, the whole Teddy Verano agency, including Gerard, which he called his "family" as a joke, had been mobilized since dawn. Gerard, in pajamas, was brandishing the newspaper. He ran to the bathroom, peeked out and said to his stepfather:

"Here you go, Teddy. We've got to give you that rag to read in the shower now? That's something new."

"Don't be stupid. And give me my bathrobe... Yeah, that one."

Yvonne hastily prepared some coffee while in her bathrobe. She saw her husband come in, wrapped in his robe, his hair wet and mussed up, flanked by his stepson who was amused by the situation.

"Our great ghost detective is in a big hurry this morning. Watch out, ma, sparks are going to fly!"

"Hold on there, young fool. Look, yesterday evening, Thursday, at 8 45 p.m.... What was on TV?"

The three of them sat before their steaming hot cups and Yvonne gave the men a plate of toast.

"Oh, Teddy, you should have dried your hair. You're going to catch a cold."

"If you only knew, dear, what a night I had! I should have caught ten colds, a good case of jaundice, and who knows what else."

"Swell!" Gerard said. "The illustrious Teddy Verano is going to tell us all about it, I can feel it."

"You'll know what I did last night when you've given me the information I asked for."

"OK, OK. Channel one: Sports, the horses."

"Give me that if you can't read a paper."

"Allow me, Teddy. That was only Channel one."

"And Channel two, you, little monkey, what was on Two?"

"I should have told you first, Teddy. We watched it together... a new show."

"Oh, yeah? That's it. What was it?"

"*The Grave Opens at Midnight*... with one of our most charming acquaintances... the most famous client of Verano & Co."

"Edwige, right? Edwige Hossegor?"

"None other. Yes, a new success for our great star and friend, the unforgettable Mephista."

"Oh, Teddy, what's wrong?"

Yvonne, ever the devoted wife, came with a towel to rub his head and try to dry his hair.

Teddy Verano, who was starting to sip his coffee, literally choked. Gerard rushed over and offered him a napkin, still laughing.

"And a bib for little Teddy."

But the detective expressed his satisfaction.

"Great! Not only do I think I know the vampire or vampires who are photographing the dead but also why… So she is still alive?"

"Who?"

"Mephista!"

"Our dear Edwige? Of course, Teddy. Before the first episode of this new series—it wasn't bad by the way, pretty funny in parts—they interviewed her. She looked great."

Teddy Verano swallowed some coffee, put down his cup.

"When I said 'Mephista,'" he said, "I wasn't talking about Edwige but the *other one*. Not she who created the character for the screen, but… the entity itself… the Mephista born from the diabolical schemes of the mad genius Jules Verrier, who later seemed to incarnate herself in another woman…"

"Ah!" Gerard and Yvonne said together. "You mean Olga Mervil?"

"Yes," Teddy Verano said. "I think I've found Olga."

"But she's dead. She died in the fire at the Porte des Lilas when the red mass ended so tragically."

"Obviously not." Teddy Verano replied. "Don't you remember afterward, when they tried to identify the bodies? Some of them were almost completely charred. In spite of the efforts of Chief Farnese and his department, it was impossible to know exactly who was there at that sacrilegious ceremony of Satan worshippers."

"And you believe that Olga escaped the fire?" Yvonne asked.

"Yes, because of the fact that she wanted to watch this 'rubbish' TV show, and certain other things Crucifer said. But you don't know what I'm talking about. Listen…"

He finally told them about his extraordinary adventure in Montdidier and then, finishing his coffee, he sighed:

"I've got a migraine."

"That doesn't surprise me. You got almost no sleep. And after all that excitement. Go back to bed. Do you want some aspirin?"

"No, I hate drugs. Besides, I have to work… and you, too, Gerard. The tape recorder, go get it."

Teddy Verano, still in his bathrobe, settled into his comfortable armchair and was pampered by Yvonne. Gerard set up the tape recorder and grabbed a notebook and pencil to take notes.

"Let's see," the detective began. "I'm going to try to remember everything that seemed weird in the conversations last night. Crucifer and Miss Mahlia, Mirk and me, the hysterical shouts of that gang of lunatics…"

"Do you think," Yvonne asked, "that they're more unfortunate souls who believe in the devil and worship him?"

"It's a possibility. Except for that poor Fever Blister, who's more reasonable and sees things more clearly than the others… but let's get started."

He started the recording. Teddy Verano talked while Gerard took notes on the salient points that his stepfather indicated. The detective sighed and frowned. He had to make an effort to remember everything. There were so many details!

Finally, when he had finished his account, Gerard reread his notes.

"Here are the important points: Miss Mahlia, because of her beauty, that Monsieur Verano got a peep at, is like Olga Mervil, a.k.a. Mephista. Don't listen, ma, or you're going to get jealous."

"It comes with the job. Keep going, you idiot."

"Crucifer said 'Go to Hell' and it terrified everyone… meaning, these are people who are afraid that this might really happen."

"A good point, Gerard. What else?"

"The so-called Mirk, alias the scarlet clown, is doing some kind of research. He said that 'all means are acceptable,' that they have to 'obey him,' and they're 'taking great risks.' Finally, there's was also the gorgeous Fever Blister, who earned a kiss from our illustrious detective."

"Part of my duty, moron. I'd like to see you in my place."

"Hush, dirty old man! I'm sure that she was, indeed, a most seductive creature."

"I'll introduce you and you can judge for yourself. Go on."

"Let's see… Ah, yes, very important! Mirk said his research was going to take him 'in between life and death… What does this mean?"

"In between? In my opinion it would be the very moment that we call death. When the soul detaches from the body. This weird and disturbed individual is going to experiment on someone… when they're just between life and death…"

Gerard shivered.

"Oooh! Scary!"

"If you're scared, don't read horror novels and don't play detective. Stick to books about romance and history."

"Teddy, duty above all else. I continue: They're all freaks… meaning all kinds of ugliness. No beautiful girls or handsome men (referring to you, boss) in that circus. And you think that they have a plan: to become beautiful again by some kind of infernal pact, is that right?"

"Yes."

"Another important detail: Miss Mahlia 'has no face.' Which means?"

"I asked myself the same question. Perhaps she, too, is really ugly, deformed, which would explain why she always wears a mask, and why this other madman Crucifer, out of sadism, showed off his mistress in her birthday suit while refusing to show her face. The scarlet clown seemed to be madly in love with her, and ready for any kind of devilry in order to get what he wants. But since he wants to succeed, 'especially for her,' we must conclude that she, too, needs a new face."

"But then, Teddy, it can't be Mephista, because Olga, you remember, was a stunning beauty."

"Yes, yes..." Teddy Verano thought of something. "We'll have to see. But it doesn't change the situation."

"We know that," Gerard went on, "according to Mirk, these people are 'risking a lot' on the one hand, and are going to do 'terrible things' on the other. And after Crucifer's threats, it's all going to happen in the next three days."

"The next three days," the detective mumbled. "Today is day number one. If only we could find out..."

"Teddy, let's return to the topic at hand. The connection between your visit to the circus last night and the Lefort affair."

"The violation of Viviane Lefort's grave? And the mysterious photographer breaking into Claire's death room? I have some ideas... but they're still very vague."

"Also, what would Mephista be doing there?"

"I don't know yet, my boy," replied Teddy Verano, jumping up. "But right now, I don't really care. What a night! Your mother's right, I'm going back to bed."

"Beddy-bye, big Teddy? Do you need to be tucked in?"

"A right uppercut and a left hook, how would you like that? Would it put a damper on your funny bone?"

"Teddy, Teddy, be careful... You gave me lessons in boxing and judo and I..."

"I'm going to bed. You can sort the notes and also follow up on the Rensen case. You know, the good lady who thinks her husband is cheating on her with two secretaries at the same time. We have to think of that, too."

"A far less interesting case than that of the vampire photographer... and the return of Mephista... Good night, Teddy. Or rather, good morning."

Teddy Verano slept until noon while Gerard rushed through the current caseload of the Verano Agency, overexcited by the avalanche of mysteries and thinking of the unforgettable Olga, whose photos he had kept in the archives.

A doll like this... True, she sold her soul to the Devil and her movie debut started with a flood of disasters. That chick was crazy. Like Teddy always say, if you touch that kind of girl, you get burned badly.

He daydreamed for a moment.

If it's her, if she's escaped the red mass... why the mask? Why live with the carnies? So she won't be recognized? That's most likely. Condemned to hide her beauty that was already making heads turn before she finished her first film... Fate is funny! But then again, maybe it's not her. Teddy could be wrong.

He reread his notes and listened to the recording.

He raised an eyebrow on hearing this:

About this project, the collective hope of the Crucifer Circus, the project headed by Mirk the clown, who also said: These things can be bought.

Gerard thought again about the two previous Mephista cases.

Dangerous people... and a clown like this... I can't say he makes me laugh very much.

At lunchtime, Teddy Verano woke up and, right away, called Gerard, who had sorted out his notes, photos and everything he could pull together about both the very boring)Rensen affair, and what the Verano Agency was presently calling the Lefort affair, before (or so Gerard thought) having to refile it in the already thick Mephista file.

"Gerard, are you there?"

"Yes, boss."

"I have an idea."

"Bravo! I'm all ears."

"You're going to enter the ring."

"Me? Does that mean that I have to get in touch with the Crucifer Circus as soon as possible?"

"Exactly."

Suddenly, Gerard stopped smiling and joking. He knew that, this time, his stepfather was serious. Very serious. Teddy Verano often got ideas from his sleep, and had often found inspiration and the key to more than one mystery while dozing. Now he was about to entrust an important mission to him.

Indeed, the detective took him aside in the room that served as the annex office in their home on the Rue d'Enghien, while Yvonne, vaguely worried, prepared lunch.

The next morning, very early, the telephone rang. It was Jean-Michel Lefort.

"Monsieur Verano, do you have any news?"

"Nothing solid... at least no solid connection to... the affair that interests you. But a bunch of really interesting stuff. And today, I attack... or anyway, my partner and stepson, is going to attack the case under another angle, and, hopefully, make a big splash."

There was a pause as Jean-Michel Lefort seemed struck by such a direct answer.

"OK. I'd like to see you."

"Naturally. Ten o'clock, Rue d'Enghien, is that all right?"

"Excuse me… Could we do it right away? Have you heard the radio this morning? Although I don't know if all the stations are talking about it… After all, it's just a local crime."

Teddy Verano, who was still lying in bed, jumped up.

"A local crime…Of interest to us?"

"Yes. A kidnapping."

"What?"

And the troubled voice of Viviane's husband explained:

"Agnes Percheron has disappeared. Last night. Kidnapped no doubt."

Teddy Verano sat speechless for ten seconds before swearing:

"Bloody hell! You're right, Monsieur Lefort. Come. Come right now."

Fifteen minutes later Jean-Michel arrived at the Verano Agency. In the meantime, the members of the family were ready to see him. Teddy Verano had been thinking all the while getting dressed.

Agnes Percheron, the young lady from Péronne. Agnes who had watched over poor Claire during that frightful night. Agnes, the first witness of this sinister affair. Agnes, laid up in bed or screaming since the drama, who was scared of flashing lights because she had seen the visitor from hell take pictures of the dead…

Jean-Michel had learned about it from a telephone call from a friend. The disappearance had not caught the attention of the national media, but in the region, they were talking about it, and Lefort's friend, knowing that Jean-Michel was involved in the drama, had telephoned him.

When he arrived ,they talked for a long time.

A knock at office door made Jean-Michel's heart stop for a second.

A man entered. Young, there was no mistaking this by his silhouette, and pretty well built, but his face was in such a state… One of those poor deformed men with twisted, swollen features, and badly healed scars ravaging his whole face.

Jean-Michel forced himself to stay calm and was very surprised to see Teddy Verano laugh.

"What do you think of my monster?"

"I'm sorry... what did you say?"

"Yes, my dear Monsieur Lefort, I'd like introduce you to my stepson Gerard, my right hand man. Don't worry, he's usually not a bad-looking kid."

Teddy Verano got up to get a picture in a frame.

"Here, look. This is his natural state."

Jean-Michel could not get over it. The detective waved Gerard over.

"Look up close. You'd never know it, eh? It's make-up. Yes, right out of movies and television. But on closer inspection… With certain modern appliances… Latex, Monsieur Lefort, latex! And then, an old trick: a nut in the nostril that totally deforms the balance of the face… You see the result."

Jean-Michel, a little relieved, looked closely at the incredible work.

242

"Great! I'd swear the skin had been…"

"Eaten away by acid? Gerard is going to Amiens. That's where the Cruci-fer Circus is performing, starting today. But listen now to what I have to tell you."

Jean-Michel could not stop looking at the surprising vision fabricated by the skill of an expert make-up artist while Teddy Verano started telling him about all the curious goings-on around the trailers of the circus of the animal-tamer Crucifer, the lover of Miss Mahlia, who might very well be Mephista.

CHAPTER XI

The municipal circus in Amiens stands like a huge polygonal cheese dish cover, enormous and solid, Second Empire style, on the outskirts of the city. That is where traveling circuses perform, so that they do not have to set up their own big tent. It was there that Crucifer and his people settled for three days while the rest of the fair scattered around the area. The trailers were parked nearby and, as usual, the carnies saw Crucifer's performers stay a little apart.

It was already an established fact among them: Crucifer was a strange man who did not participate very much in the famous fraternity of the business he was nevertheless dependent on. No one disputed the quality of the attractions he presented, or the artists he hired. And it was just as true that, on the administrative level, he formed a clan apart, infinitely less easy-going than most of this world that gave so much pleasure and entertainment to the people.

Could this be blamed on the particularly unpleasant appearances of his performers? Most people believed this. They figured they could explain this by mentioning his own case. This beautiful young man, once reputed to be quite a seducer, had been mauled by a wild cat and his face had retained the cruel traces. Now, he seemed to be careful to surround himself with performers with more or less damage to their faces.

And Miss Mahlia, his mistress and partner, was seldom seen, except by the Crucifer troupe. Gossip ran rampant about her, but they knew nothing more. Miss Mahlia lived behind her mask.

It was there, near the Amiens circus, that a young vagabond was found roaming around. It happens a lot at fairs: homeless tramps wander around, a little bleary-eyes, looking for work sometimes, or pursuing some mysterious, indefinable goals...

It was the young Zigano girl who had seen him first. Short, horribly masculine, built as poorly as a girl could be, knotty and muscular, with a flat face, the acrobat had spotted the young man right away because of his frightful face. They had talked about the adventurous life in the circus, about his checkered past and dead-end present.

The Zigano girl had called over her one-eyed mother. She, too, examined him with curiosity. Soon the two women were calling out to their circus partners.

"Come! Come and see this!"

Teddy Verano's stepson (for it as he) felt ill at ease. He had played his role well enough to take the first step. With a girl, it was not hard when one is over 20 years old and not a complete beginner at this kind of thing, as was his case. But in this situation, he had to pass himself off as a misfortuned soul and, especially, keep them from scrutinizing his fake scars too closely, even if it would have taken a good doctor to spot the fraud.

Of course, to talk with the Crucifer people was his goal. It started off nice and easy for him, once he got used to the particular ugliness of the Zigano girl. After he had impressed her, all the women, with the obvious exception of the invisible Miss Mahlia, surrounded him.

Bertha the amazon, with the elephant nose; Lise Wildor, the acrobat whose face was eaten away by a birthmark; the shriveled up little mummy whom Gerard knew had helped Teddy escape, the melancholy but reasonable Fever Blister, who worked as the cashier as well as being the fortune-teller and the assistant for the indefinable Arsène, with the funny nickname of Lack-o-Luck.

Gerard was a little dizzy. The women were all there, looking at him and their disfigurements made him sick. Unpleasant on a man, sad on a child, these kinds of ugliness on a woman turned into a permanent tragedy, a genesis of woe.

Gerard pitied them, but the Crucifer women showed no discretion.

"The poor boy! What happened? He wasn't born like this... An accident? Fire? Or what?"

All eyes were on him, and the young Zigano, instead of keeping their bit of flirting to herself, seemed very proud of discovering this new monster and showing him off to her mother and partners in misery.

"I'm the one who found him... I'm the one who found him..."

She repeated this endlessly. Gerard, who had realized in 30 minutes of conversation, that he was dealing with somewhat of a half-wit, dreamed up some sad predictions for the poor girl's future.

Nevertheless, they pressed him with frank questions that are generally not asked of people with any kind of physical defect. He, however, acted shy, overwhelmed, remembering Teddy Verano's advice after he had so carefully drawn up this plan, based on his observation of these people's reactions that he had seen in the raw during that unforgettable night.

Gerard, in this small group of circus women, was already feeling the wave of hysteria that his stepfather had witnessed during his adventure. They were getting worked up, shrieking and shouting, all asking him questions at the same time.

The little Zigano, starting to demand her rights of discovery, stamped her feet and pushed away the encroaching shrews, continuing her chant:

"I'm the one who found him... I'm the one who found him..."

Fever Blister stood as tall as she could and stretched out her hideous, pathetic little hands of a withered doll and, in a sharp voice, said:

"Shut up already! Don't you see that you're hurting him?"

They quieted down, but their glistening eyes stared at Gerard in a way that made him turn pale under his plastic make-up. '

Bloody Hell, as Teddy would say, *are they going to end up seeing that it's fake?*

But Fever Blister seemed more humane than the others. She asked him kindly:

"Tell us, my boy, what happened to you?"

Gerard repeated exactly what Teddy Verano had told him. He sighed, turned his head away and in carefully chosen voice, designed to break their hearts, he murmured:

"A woman."

"What? A woman? What did he say?" Mother Zigano, who shined no brighter than her daughter in the realm of intelligence, started waving her arms.

The amazon cut in:

"Be quiet! Let him talk."

Fever Blister, as usual, saw more clearly:

"A woman did this to you?"

"Yes," Gerard sighed, playing his role of victim.

And he pronounced the word, the keyword that, if Teddy Verano was not mistaken, would open him up to all the sympathy of the Crucifer Circus:

"Vitriol."

The furies cried out, started talking together again, while Gerard nodding his head when the miniature mummy said:

"Jealously, eh? You cheated on her?"

He answered only with sighs. Finally, he talked a little, said that he was "out of work" and had wound up in Amiens, not knowing what to do.

Bertha—being close to the Ringmaster—mentioned that, at least in Amiens, they needed some laborers. Although there was no tent to set up, the carnies had other problems, faced with their responsibility of the building made available to them by the city. The others agreed and they decided to hire him on the spot, even just for a few days.

Gerard was dizzy. It was too perfect, going too well and too fast. But it was true that Teddy Verano had prepared a good plan. A monster had every chance to be welcomed quickly into such a society.

Afterward it was easy. The Ringmaster with the pig face hired him officially, not without visible sympathy. Other members of the troupe whom he helped right away with cleaning the stands and the ring also scrutinized him. He recognized them just as Teddy Verano had described them. He found them hideous and understood how right the detective had been. They had taken good measures because he, too—at least in appearance—was facially handicapped.

He saw Crucifer, who looked him up and down, said little, but approved his verbal hiring by the Ringmaster.

He did not see, at least right away, Miss Mahlia, who seemed to stay in her trailer all the time, coming out only for the performances. And this was just fine with Gerard. He had no desire that Miss Mahlia show the same interest in him as the other members of the troupe.

Because, he told himself, *if she really is Mephista, as Teddy believes, won't she be a little suspicious?*

Of course, Gerard had never met Olga Mervil when his stepfather had sided with Edwige Hossegor in the duel of the two Mephistas. But, in spite of everything, he knew he would feel uncomfortable in her presence. This woman had claimed to have commerce with the Devil...

With broom in hand, he was trying to prove his helpfulness when he heard a thin little voice call out:

"Hey you, new guy!"

Gerard held his broom and turned around. Being informed in detail by Teddy Verano, he recognized Mirk. This small, crooked man could be none other than the strange, sinister scarlet clown. Teddy's stepson was more disturbed than ever, horribly ill at ease.

The gnome was exactly as Teddy Verano had described him, swaying on his twisted legs and watching Gerard closely.

"Very good," he said, "very good."

Gerard kept the attitude he had adopted, that of a man struck down very young by bad luck, becoming clumsy, awkward, shy and not very talkative.

Mirk looked very satisfied with the new recruit of the Crucifer Circus.

"You did well coming to us. I'm sure you'll get along just fine here. What's your name?"

"Jacques."

It was the name he had told the Zigano girl. Afterward, they had hired him verbally and, in theory, for a few days. There had been no question of legality. Moreover, if they wanted more information, or asked to see his identification, he had papers in his pocket drawn up at the Verano Agency that gave him a false identity with a social security number and everything.

"Well, Jacques," the scarlet clown went on, "you'll be very happy with us."

The false Jacques figured it good to say something anyway.

"If you decide to keep me. If Monsieur Crucifer needs me when you leave Amiens."

"What's that?" Mirk shouted. "Let you go? A guy as *interesting* as you. Don't even think about it. Crucifer and I and the others are adopting you. You're one of us now."

The diabolical little eyes twinkled and Gerard felt them boring into his skull.

"One of us, you hear? You deserve us. But don't worry, you won't be unhappy. Quite the contrary. You're going to discover such joys among us! Listen, listen good..."

Gerard felt the twisted fingers of the little man crushing his flesh when he grabbed his arm.

"You like girls, right? Beautiful girls?"

"Yes... yes," Gerard said quietly, more and more worried, on the verge of nausea.

"Sure, I know. They tell me a girl made you what you are. But you'll get your revenge. You'll make her suffer... and you'll make others suffer too, because you'll soon become the most beautiful boy... you'll make the girls die for you. You'll become a new Apollo."

Gerard/Jacques was having a hard time playing his role, but once again, he figured he had to respond.

"You're funning with me."

"You don't believe me? I understand. But here, everyone gets it, everyone believes. They know. I'm going to give them beauty. And I'll give it to you too. Do you trust me?"

He hopped around bizarrely and Gerard felt more nauseous.

"Tonight... tonight... I'll tell you... I'll show you. You, just you, because you're nice to me."

Gerard's head started spinning when he heard this.

"Are you telling me the truth?"

"You'll see... you'll see. After the show, I'll take you. But hush!" He looked around and then squeaked, "Don't say anything to them... to these cursed females."

And he disappeared.

Leaning on his broom, Gerard was stunned. The Ringmaster yelled at him because he was not working. He got back to work in a flurry, but thought fast. What did this mean? Was Mirk suspicious of him? Did he know who he was? This could all be a trap!

But when the wine is open you have to drink. In for a penny, in for a pound. *But maybe I could learn something important, and then Teddy will be happy.* He thought about him, and about his mother who, at least in part, knew about his mission and must have been going crazy with worry.

The day seemed to go on forever, only broken by a short meal. Everyone, except for Crucifer and the invisible Mahlia, was there. These carnies, it was obvious, were not your normal carnies. During their meager fare, they broke out in laughter, fought, but immediately quieted down, then laughed hysterically again.

The little Zigano girl near Jacques/Gerard kept reminding everyone that she was "the one who found him."

Bertha wanted to touch his so-called wounds. He felt himself turn pale under his make-up but, once again, it was Fever Blister who yelled that "they should leave him alone," and they dropped the sick idea.

He had a sigh of relief when they asked him to go and clean the cages. He was less afraid of the wild cats than of this band of lunatics. Besides, he was happy to work around the homes of the ferocious animals, empty out the dirty hay and put in some fresh one. The Ringmaster and lazy-eyed acrobat were responsible for entering the cages themselves.

They showed him a corner, where he understood he was to sleep that night. Thus, he would be "well protected from the cold." And he could watch over the big cats because there could always be an accident, a fight among them, and they would have to be alerted right away.

The false Jacques accepted everything passively and spoke as little as possible, just saying that he was satisfied with his lot. He did not even try to roam around the trailers too much, because he did not want to raise any suspicions.

He wondered, however, what all this was hiding as he pursued Teddy Verano's investigation on his own, waiting for something to happen. He would have liked to find out about the enigmatic Miss Mahlia, but it was obvious that Crucifer was the only one who could enter the manager's trailer. Sometimes, Fever Blister or Mirk did, but only very rarely.

Anyway, his mission had a specific goal, at least at the start, that took priority over anything else: Yes or no, was Agnes Percheron, who had vanished 24 hours ago from her parents' house, at the Crucifer Circus?

Gerard noticed that the carnies often listened to their radios, especially at the news hour. They all listened to RTL, France-Inter and Europe 1. Furthermore, the television antennas on a few of the trailers led him to believe that, in spite of their attitudes of hysterical savages, worthy of the Middle Ages, the Crucifer performers were up-to-date.

Were they watching the news to know whether the police was still looking for Agnes?

Gerard had listened carefully to Teddy Verano. Something was supposed to happen at the circus *within three days*. Mirk had one last chance to "find it," to "succeed." Did this have something to do with Agnes' kidnapping?

If a girl is being held prisoner in one of the trailers, I'll find out pretty quickly.

Were Crucifer, Mirk and company guilty?

Like Teddy Verano, Gerard leaned toward the affirmative. But why did they take her was another question entirely…

This could only be the result, logical or not (whatever logic there was), of the violation of Viviane's grave and the photos taken against all decency of poor Claire's body.

This very painful day was finally coming to a close for him. He found Lack-o-Luck, the ape-faced magician, pretty friendly, as well as Wildor the acrobat. He drank some hot grog with them. They tried to get him to talk, but he shook his head sadly when they continually brought up how he had been transformed into a monster by sulfuric acid.

Now it was time for the show.

After putting on a kind of crazy uniform with ornamental braiding, the so-called Jacques helped in the ring, carefully rolling in and out the carpets, making noise behind the big cats, helping set up for the acrobats, bringing various props for the magician Harsen (or Arsène, a.k.a. Lack-o-Luck) and the great fortune-teller Madame Vassia (a.k.a. Fever Blister).

Finally, he saw Miss Mahlia, exactly as Teddy Verano had described her.

He was breathless. Not only because her body would, without question, affect any man, but also because, as secretary general of the Teddy Verano Agency, he was the one who took care of all the files. He had handled all the studio photos of Olga Mervil, the girl who had just missed becoming the biggest international star ever, whom Teleor and Hollywood had showered with money, who was supposed to dethrone Edwige Hossegor, the first Mephista, and who had, they believed, come to a tragic end in the fire during the red mass of the Satan worshippers.

Mephista...

It was her, he was sure of it. Even more sure than Teddy Verano.

At the end of the show, the scarlet clown, whose buffoonery had made no one laugh, came up to him and grabbed him with his bent hand.

"When you're done with your work, come and see me."

A little later, after the public had left, the animals were back in their cages and the carnies in their trailers, the clown, now out of his costume, waved to Gerard. Yvonne Verano's son told himself that he was about to strut into the lair of this new kind of sorcerer.

250

CHAPTER XII

"Come on... come on."

Mirk entered the trailer. It was exactly like the others. On its white side, the words "Crucifer Circus" had been painted in red.

Gerard had only been in one trailer, that of the Ringmaster, because that was where they all ate together. In that trailer, he had seen all kinds of Gypsy junk, Spanish carpets, dolls, old costumes, photos signed by the great stars of the music hall and circus, etc. A charming, warm chaos, impregnated with the odor of make-up and powder since the trailers also served as their dressing rooms.

In Mirk's, at first sight, it was the same thing, the kind of studio/dressing room/living quarters that one expects to find in such places. But the scarlet clown took him to the back, lifted a colorful curtain, and pushed him inside.

Gerard shuddered. From this moment on, he felt like everything was happening too easily, as if they were making Teddy Verano's meticulously prepared investigation as smooth as possible.

To leave was out of the question, so Gerard tried to call up all the reserves of self-control that he could muster. He thought about his lessons in boxing, judo, karate and wrestling either with Teddy Verano or his friends when the detective had gone back to train with specialists and brought his stepson as his partner.

Because behind the richly brocaded curtain that closed off the back of scarlet clown's trailer and separated it into two, he was in a very dark room, entirely decorated in black. He noticed right away that black drapery made the place unpleasant and created complete darkness in the frightening space. He felt more uncomfortable than ever, wondering if they were not about to jump on him, tie him up, or just kill him outright.

The truth was completely different.

"Wait here. I'm going to give us a little light."

Mirk fiddled with something in the dark. There was a click and what lit up the room was not exactly a glaring headlight, but just a kind of night-light, more like a funeral lamp.

The so-called Jacques blinked, which made Mirk giggle.

"You're a little surprised. Yes, you can't see too well yet, but you understand that here we don't need much light. *They* are so fragile! Bright light hurts *them*."

Who or what was he talking about? False Jacques thought it best to be cautious until further notice, so he asked no questions. He figured that he was going to be told everything, and he was not wrong. As if the new member of the circus had really become a great friend, the scarlet clown gave him the honor of seeing this unusual room.

"You see... no, you don't see well... Wait, I'll show you. (He lifted up the lamp). These photos... they're going to give you some idea of what I am, of what I'm looking for... what I've almost found for the happiness of those who believe in me... for your happiness, too, since God—and when I say God I might mean someone else—has led you to us just when I'm about to succeed."

He swung the lamp with his scrawny arm that floated in the sweater he had put on after taking off his sequined, scarlet costume. More than ever, he looked like a gnome out of some fantasy story. Gerard saw, with a knot in his throat, the individual photographs that were stuck to the walls on the black background.

Faces...

Men, women, children...

But all of them had been taken with a flash after death had already closed their eyes.

There was no mistaking it. These people, of all ages, but mainly young men and women, some very young, had their lips shut tightly, their noses pinched, their facial muscles relaxed, all the typical symptoms of death. The choices must have been carefully made, because, in spite of the Grim Reaper's touch, they had all been very beautiful, even the oldest ones, when alive. A few had their eyes or mouths slightly open, making it even more dramatic. All of them, however, in this carousel of death, formed a creepy circle, a morbid, unpleasant atmosphere and Gerard found it harder and harder to breath.

Nevertheless, he forced himself to murmur:

"I... I don't understand."

"Patience, my boy. You'll get it when I've shown you the other thing. But do you see here the choice? People who are no longer part of this world and whose pictures I could get. Beautiful faces, right? Enough beauty to give to all those like you, like our friends in the Crucifer Circus, like so many others throughout the world who have been afflicted either from birth or by accidents."

He raised his crooked fingers and Gerard shivered with terror and disgust when he felt those nails graze his fake scars.

"Don't be scared, my lovely," the gnome giggled. "I'll get rid of all this when the time's right. An Apollo, I told you. That's what I'm promising you will be."

Gerard had stopped himself from moving away because it was absolutely necessary that the scarlet clown, or anyone else in the Crucifer Circus, not realize that he did not want them to touch his supposedly mutilated face.

Mirk, however, did not press on and went instead to dig around in a corner. It was so dark that Gerard could not see what he was searching for. He saw him pick up something that looked like a big book and that turned out to be a photo album. Gerard was not surprised when the gnome opened the album, after putting it on a table, and he saw a series of small snapshots, all very eerie, taken on death beds or in some morgue.

Mirk turned the pages lazily showing him certain images of young men.

"You see, you can choose."

"Choose?" Gerard was choked up.

What monstrous choice was he talking about?

As if it was the most natural thing in the world, the scarlet clown replied

"Well... yours... whatever you like."

"No, I don't..."

"Oh, don't be stupid, boy. You were probably not bad-looking once. You became ugly because a girl was jealous. What wouldn't you give to become beautiful again like before, eh?"

His little laugh squealed.

"A beautiful boy... who will make the girls swoon. Because right now, to tell you the truth, unless you meet some perverted hag, I don't think the chicks have any desire to roll around with you."

Another unpleasant laugh while the gnome continued thumbing through the album, stopping at the pictures of young men around Gerard's age, except that they had been photographed dead.

"So, my boy, are you with me? Do you want me to make you beautiful again... with one of these?"

Gerard did not fake his shudder. In this situation, in this place, he forgot poor Jacques and became Gerard, lost on an adventure that was more frightening than he had ever been on with Teddy Verano.

"But how? How is it possible? I'm..." Instinctively, not playing a role, he brought his hand to his face.

"How?" Mirk giggled. "Ah, that's the snag. Patience and you'll understand."

He started ferreting around in the shadows. While his back was turned Gerard, whose eyes were getting used to the darkness that the meager lamp barely dispelled, noticed different shapes and vaguely glistening things like big, dislodged eyeballs. He knew. They were cameras. Mirk must have had a nice collection of cameras, and these weird eyes were just the flashes.

The whole room was apparently devoted to photography. But what kind of photography?

There was no doubt about it. Mirk was the one who had photographed young Claire's corpse in Péronne. Mirk had opened the coffin of Viviane Lefort to take pictures of her face. Mirk had committed such crimes ten times, a hundred times over.

Had Mirk kidnapped poor Agnes? That was still to be proven, but everything pointed to it just as Teddy Verano had expected.

"Here we are," Mirk said.

He was panting, carrying a huge chest as black as everything else.

"Help me! Watch out, it's fragile... very fragile!" He kept repeating under his labored breath, "Fragile... Fragile..."

As the fake Jacques gave him a hand to put the big box on the table next to the morbid album, he explained secretively:

"*They* are so delicate, aren't they?"

Gerard did not ask anything this time. He was about to find out.

The scarlet clown stretched his crooked hands over the chest, which was at least three feet long and half as wide and deep.

"My boy, you who are a monster... like us, all of us... you who deserve beauty... beauty that gives everything... life, women... you're about to see something you've never seen before, something few living people can say they've ever seen..."

He started fiddling with the lock.

"*They* are alive, you hear. *They* are alive... Oh, not yet like I want and that's why everything's failed so far. Crucifer's threatened me. Crucifer is impatient. The others too... and Mahlia... They thirst for beauty, for a newfound life and I'm going to give it them."

He straightened up a little and when he looked at Gerard his beady eyes glowed like never before.

"Life... But I know where I went wrong. I was stuck on death when there's nothing there... From now on, I'm going to work on those *who are just about to die*. Do you follow me?"

Yes, Gerard could have asked him a thousand questions. But he did not dare. He no longer knew what to say or ask... Besides, wasn't it all totally useless?

His thoughts were speeding by, very fast, through his feverish brain. In these apparently insane words of the scarlet clown, he saw what his stepfather had gleaned among all the crazy shouting during that insane night at the Crucifer Circus.

Had not Mirk promised menacing Crucifer that he would succeed by getting it "*in between*" life and death? Mirk's last statement put such assertions in an eerie light.

Once again, he felt the repulsive contact of the gnome's twisted hands tugging on his arm.

"Come. Don't be scared. You're going to see *them*. The living... no, the *almost*-living. And when I've succeeded to perfection... *living*. Like you and me."

In spite of his nauseating disgust, Gerard let himself be pulled closer. He was scared, terribly scared. He had the feeling that he was about to see something atrocious, abominable. And yet, even if he were free to run away, he could not do it. He wanted to see, to know. He had reached a point where the horror itself was fascinating, where man refuses to flee so that he can go all the way to the deepest depths of this exquisite horror.

Mirk threw open the chest. Gerard leaned over in the dark room and looked...

The dim glow from the lamp heightened the unusual, funereal aspect of everything. However, what was in the chest needed no special lighting to strike the imagination. Gerard saw masks. Anatomical masks in perfect relief lying against a black background, carefully placed on the bottom of the chest.

Mirk's squeaky voice came to him like the icy breath of a ghost.

"They're going to be alive."

Gerard thought, *they already are alive.*

What were they made of? He could have sworn that it was human flesh. In any case, it was synthesized to perfection. And one could think that if one touched these face masks they would really be human. But humans who had already stopped living, and Gerard felt horrible shivers run down his spine.

"Touch," the scarlet clown whispered.

He had grabbed Gerard's wrist to feel the young man's pulse.

"Going all the way. It's for you. For you to become as beautiful as before... Better even, since you'll choose the face you wish to wear. But I know what you're thinking... You have to know... the whole thing."

He pulled his wrist and Gerard clenched his teeth. He got control of himself in time, although he felt the strong desire to grab the scarlet clown, whack him on the head, destroy everything in the infernal room and, in his nausea, smash the chest containing the death masks.

But he thought about his mission. Teddy Verano had initiated him into his business, into his duty. Like him, he had to fight evil. Not only common criminals but everyone using the Occult, the mysterious forces of the world, for wicked and harmful ends.

Gerard knew how to control himself. He let his hand go and almost closed his eyes when Mirk put his fingers on one of the weird faces. He shuddered at the touch, but was not surprised to feel the typical coldness of death.

Mirk let go of his wrist and Gerard, with a kind of sigh of relief, pulled back his hand, but he had the awful feeling that the tips of his fingers still clung to that horrifying chill that opens to the beyond.

"You understand... they have to be alive. I haven't got there yet. But tonight, you hear, tonight..."

Gerard heard nothing more in his fog. Looking more closely, taming his emotions, he had just seen, among the synthetic faces—was this really the right word?—in the black chest, two masks that looked familiar. Two faces. Female faces. He had not recognized them right away because death had changed them peculiarly. Now, he knew, and everything that Teddy had investigated and corroborated came together in his mind. He who had sorted the files, asked for photos, studied and compared them, knew who these faces belonged to, these death-frozen faces that the demon clown said he could bring back to life.

This woman, whom life had abandoned too young, this woman who must have been very beautiful, was Viviane Lefort, whose grave had been violated in the small Picardy cemetery.

And this girl, so young that she looked like she was sleeping, the icy fore-head that Mirk had made Gerard's trembling fingers touch, was it not young Claire, whom poor Agnes had been watching over when the monster showed up with his horrible camera?

He got dizzy. If Mirk seemed to be talking pure fantasy so far, he wondered now what was true and what was not. He found himself on the borders of reality and nightmare, when everything impossible was starting to appear possible to him.

Abruptly, he noticed that, in the black room full of photos of the dead, he was no longer alone with Mirk. Two people had come in, silently.

A man and a woman.

Crucifer, with his half-lively and beautiful face, half-gashed permanently by the claws of a raging wild beast. And a woman wearing a black mask that hid her face. Or what passed for a face. A woman with voluptuous curves in a dark, shiny dress.

Gerard did not even think of Miss Mahlia. He remembered their past adventures and saw only... *Mephista*!

CHAPTER XIII

With a cigarette between her lips, she came forward, a smile on what could be seen of her face: a gorgeously shaped mouth, sensual and spiritual, but with that crease of callous irony that marked ambitious women who were rarely given to sentimentality.

For all practical purposes, Gerard nodded a greeting to which Miss Mahlia did not respond. She stood in front of him for a minute, smoking, and through the holes in her mask, he saw an unusual glimmer in her eyes.

Gerard had no doubt about it.

In spite of the carefully arranged mask covering her face from the base of the nose up, he could swear it was really *her*.

Crucifer was still standing by the wall of drapes. He, too, was looking at Gerard. A Gerard feeling more and more uncomfortable, and who would have given anything to feel next to him, even among these disturbing people, the reassuring presence of Teddy Verano, who had promised to act on his own. But when?

Miss Mahlia, or maybe Mephista, carelessly blew smoke into his face as he forced himself to put up a good front and act like a real numbskull.

Mirk did not move a muscle. Crouching by his weird chest with its even weirder contents, the scarlet clown was the perfect image of a spider waiting in its web, hiding there, both out of fear and to prepare its next attack.

Finally Mahlia went and sat casually on the edge of the table near the chest.

"Cigarette?" she asked.

Gerard was not expecting this. The masked woman kindly offered her pack of cigarettes. Teddy Verano's stepson was stunned for a split second, but reacted quickly and accepted.

It was Crucifer who held out the lighter. Right next to his face, he could see the hairy, powerful hand of the lion-tamer and also his face, bizarrely half-normal and half-awful, in the glow of the little gas flame.

"So, this is our new ring boy," she said. "Hmm! He won't spoil the collection. What do you think, Cruci?"

The tamer laughed sharply.

"If he spoils it, he won't spoil it for long, I swear. I'll put him in a state that will give Mirk another nice subject to experiment on."

Mahlia broke out laughing. A pretty, female laugh full of charm... But what kind of charms... All the sensual spells, all the fearsome magic a creature is capable of when she uses her beauty, her natural gifts, to do what it takes to reach her goal, no matter what that goal is. Yes, there was no mistaking it. The laugh, the mouth, the body, the voice, these eyes could belong only to Mephista.

Mirk's raspy laugh echoed the beguiling laugh of the magnificent dancer.

"Are you happy here with us?" she asked.

"Yes. Oh, yes, Mademoiselle."

"Did Mirk tell you what's awaiting you?"

"Yes… he did… he told me…"

"He showed you the masks? Come on, look at them with me."

She hopped down, grabbed Gerard's arm, pulled him close to her in front of the eerie chest and forced him to lean over with her. He felt the body contact against him, the quivering flesh bursting with a thousand desires, from which emanated an unbelievable aura of exquisite delight.

Gerard, who had followed the Mephista adventures every step of the way, understood why, when it was necessary to find a starlet to replace Edwige Hossegor, no one had hesitated to choose this girl who, from the start, had turned all heads, but whose budding career had been so tragically interrupted.

She was here, with him, next to him, alive, and suddenly fascinated by the masks of the scarlet clown.

In her company, Gerard looked at them again, as if trapped by a lover, no longer able to stop gazing at them. They scared him and they attracted him irresistibly. Mahlia/Mephista also seemed under their spell. She was devouring them with her eyes and he saw her lips part, whispering something under her breath. He felt her trembling with a strange joy, a joy that made him even more scared.

"You know now, boy… You know what you wanted to know…"

"I…. I didn't know… I wasn't looking for…"

"So then," Crucifer's hard voice cut in, "you take us for a bunch of idiots?"

He did not say much, but it was full of meaning.

Gerard's heart froze. Mephista's hand clasped his.

"You're shaking?"

"I… I…"

Crucifer approached them and gripped Gerard hard by the collar.

"Women like to play games. Cat and mouse. Very nice and all, but me, I have no time to waste."

"Monsieur Crucifer…"

"Shut up and answer my questions! Who sent you?"

Despite his dizziness, Gerard was perfectly clear-minded this time, and knew that everything was ruined, that the play was over, and was about to turn into a tragedy.

"This curious little… What a pity! He was charming." Miss Mahlia was back on the edge of the table, taking out a cigarette. "A light, Cruci?"

Without taking his eyes off Gerard, still holding him by the collar, Crucifer turned slightly to her, held out his lighter, flicked it and then put it back in his pocket. In this movement, Gerard could feel the incomparable strength of the lion-tamer. A Hercules. And he, in his youth, despite his muscles already trained by Teddy Verano, he knew that he was no match for him.

"Are you going to answer?"

"But... I don't know... I'm telling you..."

Play stupid all the way to the end. That was his plan. His stepfather had lectured him in case it came to this. Keep your secret as long as possible. Gain some time in case of a heavy blow.

The heavy blow had fallen. Hard.

Gerard wanted to fight back. He was suddenly thrown down on the table, crushed by Crucifer's strong hands, right up against the box of masks, his head resting on Miss Mahlia's fleshy thigh. As she watched the scene, her eyes sparkled with interest behind her mask.

"Mirk, give me something to tie him up."

Gerard struggled.

"But I don't want this! I protest!"

This expression made she whom he believed was Mephista break out laughing.

"He protests. Really, did you hear that? Oh, the boy's a comedian."

Mirk brought what was asked and Gerard, in a heartbeat, was tied up by the lion-tamer and the scarlet clown. Now he could say his melancholy goodbyes to the glory that crowns the mission of every good detective. He was caught like a rat in a cage and if Teddy Verano did not intervene in time...

At any rate, he had failed and there was no help coming from his stepfather in this adventure.

"What were you doing here?" Miss Mahlia asked, smoking elegantly, with a certain nonchalance that suited her to a tee.

"He's curious and me too. I'll show him what Mirk promised to do for us. He'll watch the experiment because it's tonight, right, Mirk?"

"Yes," the diabolical clown said. "We can't wait any longer. Especially since the main ingredient are in our hands."

"He's curious and me too," Crucifer repeated. "So, he'll tell us... everything he has to tell us."

"But... I have nothing to tell you," Gerard protested, still playing innocent.

He got a couple of hard slaps.

"Enough! You'll talk when we tell you to. Mirk, are you ready? Can we start?"

Miss Mahlia hopped onto her feet again.

"Mirk! Mirk! Is it true? You found it? Are you sure? You can do it?"

"I promised you Mahlia. You'll be beautiful! The face I chose will be yours... Alive! And no one will believe that you weren't born with it. And you'll be another woman, even more beautiful, more desirable, more..."

"Shut up!" Crucifer barked.

There was silence. The lion-tamer stepped up to Gerard, grabbed him like a sack of potatoes and threw him over his shoulder without too much effort it seemed. Gerard's upside down head, however, could still see what was happening.

"Well? Are you ready, Mirk?"

"One second... I have to wake up my treasures."

He brought out a weird, deformed flask made of some indefinable material. He leaned over the chest and sprinkled it over the masks like he was blessing them.

"They're fragile... so fragile. You have to take care of them, preserve their life, otherwise death will come back."

Crucifer obviously gave in to such good reasoning because he said nothing. Nearby, however, Miss Mahlia looked like she was burning up with impatience.

"I want to see... to know... to experience..."

Once the action was complete, Mirk closed the chest and put it back in a corner with extra special care, covering it right away with a black cloth.

"The mask?"

"It's over there. Lina has prepared everything."

They left the black lair and walked out of the trailer. The night outside was cold. Gerard thought of yelling and screaming, but he was in the middle of the fair, surrounded by the trailers of the Crucifer Circus. His voice would be lost and then...

In any event, his mission was to go all the way to the end.

Gerard knew that the crazy experiment that Teddy Verano suspected was about to take place. By some unknown process, Mirk claimed he could give beauty to all the monsters of the Crucifer troupe. And he was starting with Miss Mahlia.

Mephista.

But if she was really the beautiful Olga Mervil, why did they need to resort to such procedures? Gerard still had the pictures of her bewitching beauty in his head.

The walk was not long. From the chilly dark, where a few snowflakes drifted down, they went into another trailer. It looked no different than the others. All were white with "Crucifer Circus" in big red letters on the side, and all had television antennas. In this trailer was a woman whose profile was a wreck, her mouth and neck joined into one. Lina, in charge of the circus music, whom Gerard had seen only during the performance.

"Is it ready?" Mirk asked.

"Your orders have been carried out."

"The subject?"

"At your disposal."

"Did she scream or cry?"

"Of course. I did what I could to calm her down, telling her that she would be free soon."

"You said the right thing," the scarlet clown grimaced.

Gerard had already guessed what they were talking about when Crucifer threw him roughly on the ground.

"Why him?" Lina asked, apparently unsurprised.

For sure there must always have been strange things happening at the Crucifer Circus.

"He sought to know too much. He'll be a witness to the experiment."

Lina leaned over Gerard and he soaked up all the ugliness of the poor girl. Another one worthy of Crucifer's tragic parade.

"Yes, the Wildors and Fever Blister told me about him. Vitriol, right?"

"At least it's a good likeness."

Mirk came up and with his knotty, tortured fingers touched the make-up of Teddy Verano's stepson.

"The latest products. Wonderful! Biological latex... It would fool anyone."

"Fever Blister wasn't fooled," said Lina. "She sees. She sees. Can't get the better of her. 'Danger is on the prowl' she said. 'He's coming... with a false face... He's very close. . he's here!' She told us as much..."

"Fever Blister is a precious friend, a true medium," Crucifer cut her off.

Mirk was still grotesquely caressing the fake face of Gerard who felt like he wanted to throw up.

"Fever Blister put us on the trail and we caught the prey. He'll watch my triumph. But before that... Look how well this is done... so meticulously done... Of course, not like the masks of Mirk the Scarlet... Because those are life itself, and no one will be able to tear them off the faces upon which they will be magically grafted. This one is a technical miracle, but only technical, not true magic. And now, this miracle is going to disappear before our eyes..."

Gerard cried out in pain. Mirk had just torn off some of his plastic swelling allegedly caused by sulfuric acid. The scarlet clown held it up in his crooked fingers squealing more than ever.

Lina, Crucifer and Miss Mahlia leaned forward too and Gerard saw, above his face, their horrible, hostile, menacing faces. And he screamed. He screamed like an animal while the scarlet clown, with precise, inescapable movements, tore off the shreds of make-up painstakingly applied by Teddy Verano.

CHAPTER XIV

The screams woke Agnes from her slumber.

She had ended up dozing off, dazed by horror, fatigue and the excessive nervousness that had assailed her since the tragic night when she had agreed to watch over poor Claire. It had been a constant nightmare since then.

They had taken care of her, but she remained in shock after the wake. With the slightest glimmer, with the faintest glint of light, she kept seeing the crazy flashes that had captured the face of the deceased. They had interrogated her. Then her furious father had ranted against everyone. Doctors, journalists and even the police. Agnes, with her health shaken up, her mind shaken up, experienced all this in a kind of constant horror. Until last night...

Lying in bed, she had smelled that same strange odor, just like when the photographer of the dead had broken in. Then, nothing.

Until she woke up in this weird room, draped in black, with the permanent odor that she did not recognize, but was obviously chemical. She had seen only one person: her jailor, the chinless woman.

To her questions, the bizarre creature had given curt answers. She had simply said that "this would not last long," that "they needed her," and that she ought to "stay calm." Otherwise, she just kept watch over her, giving her something to eat twice a day.

Agnes, however, had barely touched her food. She was not hungry, only thirsty. They let her have some fruit juice and she lived off the Pam-Pam for now. Finally, she was able to get a little rest until the man had started screaming.

In her nightgown, Agnes curled up on the bunk she was on.

"I'm scared... I'm scared..."

The poor child, feeling her mind waver more and more, wondered what this all meant.

The chinless woman showed up, but this time, she was not alone. A man was with her. A small man. A twisted man. Very ugly ,with extremely bright eyes. Moreover, his fingers were stained with blood.

When she saw him, Agnes opened her eyes wide and from her throat sprang out a loud cry of horror:

"Him! Him!"

She recognized him. In spite of her confusion, the poor girl had no doubt. She had seen this gnome only once before in her short life, but under such circumstances that his face could never be wiped from her memory: he was the cursed photographer who had bombarded Claire's remains with flashes.

The chinless woman never showed any emotion. Her ravaged, dismal face and her toneless voice expressed no hint of humanity. She did not look at all troubled by Agnes' attitude. She came forward holding out her hand.

"Come with us," she ordered.

"No!" Agnes screamed without knowing why.

She did not know. She no longer knew. She would never know anything. She was living in fear, that was all.

The woman and the gnome looked at each other. They stepped forward together and grabbed her as she screamed louder.

"Leave her alone, you idiots. Don't you see you're scaring her."

They moved away and Agnes saw who had just spoken. She came in, looking very beautiful in her blonde wig and black mask hiding her face. She smoked a cigarette as she walked, swaying her hips, perhaps well practiced but perfectly delightful.

"Leave me alone with her for a minute. I want to talk to her... so she'll understand."

The hideous creature and the dreadful little man disappeared. Agnes saw nothing in front of her but this beautiful woman who was, unfortunately, masked. The stranger came and sat casually on the edge of the bed.

"Come on, Agnes..."

Agnes was not screaming anymore. She was taking short, tense and troubled breaths, feeling captivated by the charm that emanated from this newcomer.

"Agnes, I hope that *I* don't scare you. Let's make a little effort. Just say so..."

With her mouth open, Agnes watched this woman who was trying to be so friendly, but she could not believe that she was any more humane or less harmful than the others, since she was apparently living with them.

"Agnes..." Her voice sounded sweet and the pretty, sensual lips smiled, almost mimicking a kiss. "Agnes, you have to come with me. And obey me."

The young woman made an effort to talk.

"I... But what do they want with me?"

"I need you, Agnes."

"Me? But I'm nobody."

"I need your beauty, Agnes."

The pretty, long, slender hand reached out and caressed the poor girl's face, but she recoiled.

"So beautiful, my pretty. Am I really so repulsive?"

"No... no...."

"Well? Your beauty, Agnes, your beauty does not belong to you alone. Think, Agnes, think about the women who are ugly... like the one who just left... Think about so many others who don't have your luck to be so pretty. Don't you want to share a little with one of them?"

In spite of her confusion and her naivety, Agnes found these words frightening.

"But it's... it's not possible. I can't...." she stammered,

"You can, Agnes. You can give away your beauty."

Instinctively, without understanding, Agnes cried out:

"I don't want to!"

The masked woman had a big smile.

"Selfish little girl... you want to keep all your beauty to yourself."

Agnes was trembling. Now this seductive woman was starting to make her even more scared than the two others.

"I want your beauty, Agnes. I want your face. No, I'm not mean... and I want to be even better. I'll wear your soul on our face. If I had a face like yours, Agnes, I'd be good, very good..."

She reached out her hand, affectionately, over the bed and touched Agnes' knee, but she recoiled again.

"Come on. Let's go and get this over with."

"No, go away!"

"I'm staying, Agnes. Because you have to give me your beauty so that I can become better. Don't force me to repeat this."

"But," Agnes cried out from the depths of her despair, "if you want to be good, it doesn't have to be difficult."

"Humans live with their masks of flesh, Agnes. Your mask is beautiful and good. Give it to me and I'll be beautiful and good."

"Then you're not?"

The innocent cry came from her heart. The masked woman's smile grew bigger, turning it into a grimace.

"I'm not. Although, through you, I will become so."

"But who are you then?"

She bounded to her feet, straightening up her magnificent body in front of Agnes.

"Who am I? You want to know?"

Leaning forward she raised her hissing voice.

"I was beautiful too, once. I wanted to play with my beauty and control the world. For this, I signed the most terrible of all pacts. I played... and I lost. But I can still win another round. Who am I? *I am evil.* I was beauty and I became the beauty that destroys... and then... But what does it matter? You want to know my name? Poor little girl! If, like everyone else, you watch television... then you'll know my name: Mephista! *I am Mephista!*"

Stupefied, Agnes screamed:

"Mephista?... But Mephista is a character played by Edwige Hossegor..."

The masked woman laughed raucously.

"Idiot! Edwige Hossegor is but the actress who plays Mephista on the screen. Me, I'm not an actress, I am Mephista herself... *the true Mephista.*"

Agnes shivered, and told herself that one of them must have been crazy, if not both. She asked again:

"But why my face?"

"That's enough!" Mephista shouted.

With her strong grip, she grabbed Agnes and dragged her off the bed, but could not dodge her quick action.

All of a sudden the girl reacted unexpectedly and tore off the mask...

In the other part of the trailer, where he was struggling behind his gag, with his hands and feet tied, totally immobilized, no longer screaming, with all his clever make-up torn off, Gerard heard the pitiful cry of Agnes. He knew perfectly well that it was the kidnapped girl—it could be no one but her.

And he saw her enter the room, pushed by Miss Mahlia, or rather Mephista, a Mephista who quickly re-veiled her monstrous face that had been destroyed by the fire at the red mass, when Olga was punished for having made a pact with the Devil and had managed to escape the blaze, but by becoming this monster.

Lina, Crucifer and Mirk all grabbed the girl and laid her on a kind of ironing table covered with a big, white sheet. While the lion-tamer and musician tied her up and gagged her like Gerard, Mirk set up a system of mechanical arms over her, which, Gerard saw, held flash bulbs and cameras.

Teddy Verano's stepson had heard fragments of the strange conversation between Agnes and Mephista. Despite the missing pieces, despite his distressing situation and the presence of Mirk, Lina and Crucifer, he had been able to fill in the missing pieces of the puzzle, as his stepfather and boss would have done in his place.

Mephista. It really was Mephista.

And these lunatics, these fanatics, in some extraordinary ceremony that was both photographic and diabolical, now thought they could take Agnes' beauty and give it to Mephista, who no longer had a beautiful face and who wanted to change her soul by changing her face.

If Teddy Verano were here...

He, too, would have understood everything and instantly grasped the truth. He would have been especially useful in coming to help Gerard, whose face was bleeding. Even if the wounds were only superficial, they were still painful.

And coming to help poor Agnes even more. For Agnes was in danger. And what a danger!

The monsters were getting their victim ready. Gerard, on seeing this, was choking on his gag, twisting and turning on the wooden planks. To calm him down, Crucifer kicked him hard in the ribs.

The scarlet clown had a weird grimace on his face—his way of laughing.

"This charming young man whom our precious fortune-teller caught... He wants to know the truth. Now there's no harm in telling him what's going to happen."

"Hold on," the tamer said. "The girl... do we put her to sleep?"

Gerard got frightened when he heard these dreadful words:

"Put her to sleep? You're joking, Crucifer... I told you that I want to take her picture and stick it on the mask *at the very moment of her passing away.*

How do you figure on seeing this moment when a human being passes from life onto death if the subject is asleep?"

His squealing voice with horrifying undertones continued:

"She must be awake."

Gerard heard Agnes groan behind her gag. He knew that some awful drama was about to play out, that something abominable was being prepared. He wanted to react. He writhed in his fetters. But he could not do anything, not even scream out.

Who would come, anyway, except the circus folk around the trailer where the tragedy was unfolding? Monsters, all accomplices of the scarlet clown whom they hoped would redo their faces too, and for this, undoubtedly, they had helped him photograph Claire's corpse, dig up Viviane's coffin, and kidnap Agnes and bring her to this abominable laboratory.

Mirk flashed some bulbs, tried out different angles, and shifted the cameras. He came back to Gerard, leaned over and sneered:

"You wanted to know? Look!"

He showed him one of the wonder masks molded in strange material that he had taken out of the black chest. It looked like Agnes.

"Well done, eh? Lifelike... or almost. Thanks to the Polaroid, I can capture her features at the final moment of her life, and transfer it immediately onto the mask. *And it will come to life. It will have her life.* And I'll give the living face to Mahlia, who will become what she wants to be... another woman."

Gerard, half-suffocating, struggled in vain.

"Done talking?" Crucifer asked angrily.

Mephista stood motionless, chain smoking and staring at the face of poor Agnes, who heard everything as well.

Mirk went back to the deadly table and continued,:

"The big moment... the great passage... Let's get ready!"

Lina turned off the light. The inside of the trailer was only lit now by a small lamp tinted purple.

The scarlet clown announced:

"Silence! The technology that I'm using is fine... but, you understand, that it's not enough to capture a life that's in between two universes. I need... *something else, someone else...* I have to evoke *someone.*"

Gerard had difficulty seeing, but he glimpsed Mephista. She was trembling under her mask. No doubt this evocation of some kind of evil spirit was bringing back particularly terrible memories for the failed movie star.

Mirk was now making incantation gestures over Agnes' prone body. He was chanting words that Gerard could not understand, but that must undoubtedly have come from the kabbalah or other infernal dictionaries.

As Teddy Verano had told him, occultists turn insane easily when they begin to court infernal powers, summon evil forces that they think they can control, and, along with everything else, they lose their sense of the ridiculous.

266

But the ridiculousness of the situation did not make Gerard lose sight of the tragic side, especially concerning poor Agnes.

The scarlet clown must have finished his fiendish prayer. He said a few more words that Gerard did not understand, but the young man realized that, leaning over Agnes, Lina was cutting away the top of her shirt with a pair of scissors, baring the young woman's breasts.

Something appeared in Mirk's hands. Gerard was blinded. A cold flash. The glint of a long, steel needle.

Gerard heard the victim utter another otherworldly groan through her gag.

Crucifer, Lina and, above all, Miss Mahlia were holding their breath, gathered around the scarlet clown. Holding in one hand the knob that worked the camera, after adjusting it correctly, the little monster held the steel needle in the other, raising it up, pointing directly over Agnes' heart.

Then, he slowly lowered it.

The point touched the skin and punctured it.

A drop of blood bubbled out.

Agnes twisted in her straps, but they held her tight.

Gerard thought that he was going to die of horror. He guessed, more than he actually saw, but followed everything with a frightfully clear mind.

Suddenly, a racket sounded outside and they heard the wild animals growling and snarling in their cages, sensing danger…

CHAPTER XV

Fever Blister was fighting against her visions, and Arsène was scared, trying in vain to calm her down, to negate the effects of his mediumistic tricks. But the little mummified woman, endowed with exceptional sensitivity, marvelously prepared for clairvoyance, would not stay still.

"I see them... I see them... They're going to do something horrible... They're going to spill blood..."

At the request of Crucifer and Mahlia, Arsène had magnetized his partner and "Madame Vassia," docilely, had plunged into the arcana of the mysterious subconscious that clairvoyants possess. That was how she had detected the enemy presence in the circus. She had specified that he wore a mask, and it was not very hard for Crucifer, Mahlia and the scarlet clown to figure out that the young man, the so-called Jacques, the vitriol victim, was the prime suspect.

Now, it was well into the night.

Arsène, the magician Harsen, familiarly called Lack-o-Luck, watched in anguish, as he could no longer contain the visions that rushed faster and faster through Vassia. She was in a state of tension that worried him. It was impossible to put her into a normal sleep. With her eyes opened wide, she was describing the scenes she saw and predicting great calamity upon the circus troupe.

They were not alone in their trailer. Lise Wildor, Bertha, the Ringmaster, Vera Zigano and the others had all come to join them. No one at the Crucifer Circus wanted to sleep tonight.

They knew that Fever Blister, through her reliable instinct as a medium, had denounced the intruder who had deceived them, and who was now going through hell. They also knew something else: that Mirk the sorcerer, Mirk the scarlet clown, whom Fever Blister was the only who had not pursued, was about to try an awful experiment that he claimed was magic.

In fact, they were all here, ready for anything to get normal faces again, even accepting the terrible schemes exacted by the infernal gnome. Each of them had participated in the sinister adventure in Péronne, in the violation of Viviane's coffin, and in Agnes' kidnapping; this Agnes whom they knew was being guarded by Lina the musician; Agnes, whom they all thought, secretly, might bear the cost of the cursed scheme that was supposed—truth or illusion?—to give them new faces, a new existence.

Now, they were starting to worry. They all knew that Fever Blister, with her reasonable, sensible nature, did not usually shout out warnings in outlandish ways. They believed in Mirk and his magic, but they had much more faith in the talents of Vassia the medium.

Silently, their faces blank, but their eyes showing their anxiety, the carnies listened to the broken speech of Fever Blister who could no longer escape her invisible guides.

"They're spilling blood... The clown is red, more red than ever... and he's bringing calamity down upon us..."

"But the clown is going to free us!" Vera Zigano objected.

The clairvoyant's body twitched and jerked and she sneered:

"Free us? More like ruin us... and his promises... the masks... yes, I see them, the masks of flesh that he promised us..."

"Oh!" Bertha whispered. "Tell us, Vassia, tell us that he's going to save us, that we'll be different than we are... I want to be beautiful. I want to be like other women."

Leaning toward the medium they awaited her reaction.

The hideous little mummified face, squashed under make-up and rouge, tensed up.

"The masks... They're rotting... They're decomposing... It's death..."

She stopped talking, foaming at the lips, and fell backward, exhausted by the visions.

A mortal silence filled the trailer.

They were all gathered here, clowns, acrobats, jugglers. Only the quartet of Crucifer, Miss Mahlia, Lina and the scarlet clown were missing. What were they doing right now?

In theory, they were working to find the promised solution, but it could not be forgotten that they had two prisoners with them: little Agnes, snatched from her parents' house, heedless of all respect for humanity, and young Jacques, the fake vitriol victim, whose role in the Crucifer Circus was completely unknown.

The Zigano girl, who had come with the others, was sobbing, saying that she was scared and she did not want them to hurt Jacques "because she was the one who found him," which she repeated relentlessly.

Then the cursed carnies started talking together around Fever Blister. They sobered up. The collective hysteria, which had been cleverly maintained by both Mirk and Crucifer, was starting to dissipate and make room for reason.

Fever Blister's visions showed the future in a menacing light.

The Ringmaster grumbled:

"It can't go on like this. It'll bring trouble. The police. The cops aren't idiots. We can do whatever we want here... but we opened a coffin, took pictures of corpses... we kidnapped a girl! What else is going to happen to us?"

"I'll be pretty. Mirk promised me!" the Zigano girl wept.

She was answered with jeering laughs. They no longer believed. They were seeing clearly. It was not possible to live for long outside the law, to violate all the norms of life. The situation was going to hell and Fever Blister's warnings had to be taken into consideration.

Quickly, they put their heads together. Huddled up, whispering softly around Vassia, who was tired and said nothing, but watched them out of the small, black eyes in her mummy face, they made a snap decision, not well thought out, as crazy as every other decision they usually made together.

Meanwhile, two men in the chilly night were wandering around the circus in Amiens, sneaking among the stalls. They had come in a DS. They had alerted the police, but, according to the law, no search could be made before sunrise.

The police chief had told Teddy Verano:

"Monsieur Verano, I respect private detectives, but our officers are also on the trail. After all these weird stories, and especially after Agnes Percheron's disappearance, we've been looking at the strange behavior of the Crucifer troupe. At dawn, we do plan to search them."

But it was winter and the sun did not rise until 7:41 a.m.

Teddy Verano had thanked the chief. He already knew that he would have to act that very night, even if it was against regulation. Because Gerard was with Crucifer, and God knows under what conditions. And because Agnes must be there too, and the detective feared the occult madness that was spurring on the scarlet clown and his wretched disciples.

Someone was with him. Someone who knew everything and had offered to help, ready for anything to put an end to these people who had violated his wife's coffin. Jean-Michel Lefort.

The official police were not far away, certainly. It was 4 a.m. now, well into the night that surrounded the circus before the dawn. But what was happening there?

The two men were prowling around the trailers when they heard the tumult. And they witnessed one of those group events that seemed to strike up among the Crucifer people from time to time. They saw them marching in the snow, heading for one of the trailers, shouting, swearing, ranting, trying to break into it.

Teddy Verano came out of hiding, gun in hand, and rushed forward.

"Follow me, Lefort!"

He saw the carnies climbing up the steps to the trailer, banging on the door and the windows, shrieking and yelling for Crucifer, Mahlia and Lina, saying that they wanted in, that it had to end, and other things that made no sense.

"Let me through! Police!"

Teddy Verano had said this word, magic in its own way, that always deeply affected anyone whose conscience was not totally clear. They moved aside and, in spite of the darkness, he saw one of them smiling at him: Vassia, poor Fever Blister.

"I was expecting you," she said. "But the calamity is already here…"

"What's happening in there?" Teddy Verano raised his voice.

"We don't know," the Ringmaster said. "They won't answer."

"Who's in there?"

They were all talking at the same time, but neither Teddy Verano nor Jean-Michel were listening.

"We have to break down the door."

Wildor and Ziganc, the two big fellows, took over. It did not take long for the door to yield. They all rushed inside and, right away, screams of horror rang out.

In the dim purple light, they saw Agnes' almost naked body lying on a white table. It was not moving. It would never move again.

Like a frozen lightning bolt, a long, steel needle was sticking out of her heart and blood was flowing, flowing, a stream that formed a growing stain on the white sheet covering the death bed.

Teddy Verano turned pale and leaned over the poor girl, shaking his head.

"Dead, I'm afraid. Oh, the monsters!"

Jean-Michel's teeth were chattering. Teddy Verano turned to him and suddenly saw the frightened, frightening faces of the carnies.

"It's your fault too!" he yelled. "All of you! With your crazy ideas! You're guilty... guilty... You killed her! Killed her!"

They started babbling and shouting:

"No, not us... It was Mirk! Mirk! Mirk!"

They searched the trailer, but no one was there except for a man tied up in the corner, whom Teddy quickly freed with a sigh of relief. It as Gerard, safe and sound, apart from a few superficial wounds to his face.

"Teddy! Teddy!" he cried out when the gag came off. "It was her! It was... Mephista!"

"What happened?"

"They tried... some demented experiment. And they killed Agnes. They wanted to photograph her at the very moment of death. And Mirk yelled, 'For nothing! For nothing! She's dead for nothing! Everything's failed'"

"And then? After that? Come on, tell me..."

"They left. Mahlia, meaning Olga, and the lion-tamer, who seemed to have gone crazy, and the chinless woman..."

"Come on! Let's go, Lefort. We have to find them."

They ran across the grounds. The wild animals were starting to roar and the carnival around the Amiens circus was starting to wake up.

"Call the police!" Teddy Verano screamed to anyone listening. "There's been a murder committed at Crucifer's!"

Followed by his stepson and Jean-Michel Lefort, he searched the fairgrounds. They found Lina, lying senseless, obviously drugged, who couldn't tell them anything.

Then, they found another body, lying motionless in a trailer. It was Crucifer's. Understanding at last the worthlessness of the scarlet clown's magic, he had blown his brains out.

271

But there was no trace of Miss Mahlia, or rather Olga Mervil, Mephista, the disfigured Mephista, whom it would be hard to identity from now on.

Since the wild beasts were roaring more than ever, Teddy Verano and his partners headed over there just as the police sirens started wailing in the distance.

They arrived too late.

Raging mad, knowing that everything they had done was against the law, their delusions were over, the freaks of the Crucifer Circus, feeling cheated and betrayed in their insane hopes, guilty of various crimes at the behest of the scarlet clown, had tracked him down, accused him of being responsible for all their problems, and everything that would happen to them from now on...

They harassed him, slapped him, insulted him, hit him and hit him again and again... The women even more than the men unleashed their fury.

And Mirk screamed in horror as he was thrown against the cages.

A tiger's paw snatched him and broke his skull. He gasped and fell in a pool of his own blood, stomped by the angry carnies, while the wild animals, excited by the smell of blood, jumped around like lunatics in their cages.

The police arrived and several cars invaded the circus. They were going to do what they had to do, but, as always, Teddy Verano wanted to finish his investigation.

After he had been freed, Gerard had told him briefly what he had learned during his one day in the circus, and the events of the frightful night that followed.

They returned to the trailer that served as Mirk's lair. Lefort went with them. In the doorway, the three men were struck by a strange, sickening smell coming from the back of the room surrounded by the black curtains.

"That's awful! It reeks!"

"It's like... the smell of a rotting corpse."

They searched and found the black chest, the chest where Mirk the scarlet clown hid his famous masks that seemed to be made of flesh, made from photographing the dead, and that he claimed could replace the faces deformed by nature.

They opened it.

And they recoiled in horror at the vision, nauseated by the foul stench.

The masks of false life were now just masks of death, decomposing faces of flesh that were rotting away, as if they had really passed on from life to death.

They were all that remained of the demented experiment of the scarlet clown, the sad, foul-smelling testimony of the attempts of all these poor people who were willing, just like Mephista, to commit the worst crimes to get a new face, to try the impossible, to obtain an unattainable redemption...

The Man of a Million Words
Maurice Limat by Maurice Limat

My Childhood

I was born into a family of average workers. My dear mother would have also liked to become a writer, but never managed it. As for me, I wanted to write as soon as I began to learn how to read. I felt that I was destined to become a writer. After school, my mother, who had a certain literary flair, made me do dictations [9] drawn from the best literary works.

Between the ages of eight and twelve, my holidays were spent keeping an eye on the cows and turkeys in a farm in the Loiret region. My mother, who did not have much money, always managed to send me illustrated books and magazines which I devoured. I read *L'Intrépide* and the novels of José Moselli [10] and Jo Valle. Since my older brother worked in the newspaper business, I also received copies of girls' magazines, such as *Fillette* and *Lilie*, which included fairy tales, which I loved reading.

Three times a year, I worked on the farm, mostly daydreaming about the stories I'd read. If I was reading pirate stories, I imagined them cruising on the local lakes. I thought there were fairies, elves and wizards in the woods. I populated the countryside with all kinds of fantastic creatures. I read a lot of books while keeping an eye on the animals.

When I turned 14, I had to go to work. I was recruited by the Export Bureau. It was dreary work, and it lasted for my whole adolescence. I was scribbling a little here and there, short stories, embryos of plays, novels... I even tried my hand at poetry. I also was discovering many new authors. I joined the local library and I read Victor Hugo and Honoré de Balzac. At school, at age twelve, they'd made us read *Eugénie Grandet*, but it hadn't thrilled me. However, after I found a discarded copy of *The Splendors and Miseries of Courtesans*, I became a huge fan of Balzac.

I continued to scribble. My mother, who had been one of the first female typists in France, gave me a typewriter when I turned 18, so that encouraged me even more! I tried writing plays, then a novel... As my old master Chambreuil,

---

[9] French school exercise where a text is read aloud and the student must transcrbe it correctly.

[10] Black Coat Press published a translation of Moselli's *Illa's End*, ISBN 978-1-61227-031-9. Doc Ardan's forthcoming adventures *The Troglodytes of Mount Everest* and *The Giants of Black Lake*, were originally serialized in *L'Intrépide*.

of the Comédie Française,[11] would have said: "It's full of qualities and full of defects, but you should persevere!" So I did.

The Start of my Literary Career

At 20, my first novel was published. It was a very modest effort entitled *L'Aéronef C-3* [The C3 Aircraft]—an adventure novel. It was published in 1936 by Ferenczi as No. 24 in their imprint *Voyages & Aventures*. When it came out, I was a soldier, having been conscripted a fortnight before. While I was studying to become a corporal, I felt motivated to continue writing on the side. Then, Ferenczi decided to launch a new imprint, *Le Petit Roman d'Aventure* [The little adventure novel] to publish novella-length works of about thirty-two printed pages. They sent a memo to all their writers, and that's how I came to write *La Montagne aux Vampires* [The Mountain of Vampires]. I still remember it well: I wrote it during my evenings in the barracks, scribbling on the corner of a dining table. One night, I even had to write a chapter while another soldier was dancing on the table!

I sent the manuscript to my mother, who typed it, and my father went and delivered it in person to himself. I wrote about 20 novels under the same conditions during my military service.

Ferenczi wanted a healthy dose of realistic action in every book to satisfy their male customers, but we also had to include a little romance, for their female readers—but not too much, in order to not compete with their romance imprint. (I wrote a few books for that one as well.) One day, while I was on leave, I met their editor, who was a woman, and she said to me, "You're very good with the adventure novels; have you considered trying your hand at detective fic-

---

[11] Maurice Chambreuil (1883-1963).

tion?" I was 21 then, and followed her advice. So, I wrote *La Villa aux Squelettes* [The House of Skeletons], which was the first Teddy Verano novel.

After my military service, I was supposed to return to the Export Bureau, but I decided to take a chance, quit, and become a full-time writer. I began a career as a journalist and did very well, but then the war started, so I was drafted again and promoted to Lieutenant. Then I was captured by the Germans and ended up in a hospital in Koblenz. With false papers, I became a male nurse for a year. It did not bother me, because I liked caring for the wounded. Also, I spoke a little German, which helped. We set up a small amateur theater, for which I directed my first play, Moliere's *Le Medecin Malgré Lui*.

We reported people as being much sicker than they really were, so that the Germans would send them home. Once we even had a man repatriated who was a trapeze artist for the Medrano Circus! Eventually, I became really sick myself—nothing too serious, fortunately—and ended up being sent home as well. I returned to live with my parents, who, at the time, had been reduced to a state of abject poverty. To make money, I worked for a while with a friend of mine who was selling so-called pharmaceutical wine. I still managed to get three or four books out during that period. It wasn't much of a career, but it was fun. At the end of the war, I was able to resume my writing career full time.

Working for Ferenczi

It only took pocket change to buy any of the 32-page *Petits Romans*. The royalties they paid were equally small, but when one is 20, and earning the meager salary of a petty clerk in the Export Bureau, there is no pleasure comparable to holding one's own books between one's trembling fingers, no matter how little they paid.

I was very proud to be published in the same imprint that had already published such hallowed names as Jean de La Hire,[12] Max-André Dazergues, Sim (Georges Simenon) and Marcel Allain, the co-creator of *Fantômas*, as well as many more names now mostly forgotten, such as: Félix Léonnec, George Fronval, Albert Dubeux, Albert Bonneau, René Thevenin, and Marcel Priollet.

Ferenczi's father had started his company in 1879, with the notion of publishing small, inexpensive paperbacks. It was a great idea, which immediately sparked many imitators. Until then, popular novels were published in large formats, often as open-ended series. Ferenczi conceived of a cheap, small-sized, self-contained paperback, as a way to make popular literature accessible to everyone. The success of his formula lasted for decades.

Were they truly novels, or instead novellas? Did it matter? I remember having an argument with Léon Groc, another great popular novelist, who claimed that what we wrote was just overblown short stories, but I disagreed.

---

[12] The author of the Nyctalope.

Our stories were structured like novels, divided into chapters, with character arcs. They really were "little" novels.

Ferenczi asked all his authors to make a special effort to fit within the length of the new imprint. Obviously, he must have been pleased with my manuscript, since *La Montagne aux Vampires* was the first volume he released. *Le Petit Roman d'Aventure* normally retailed for the very low price of 25 centimes, but mine was sold, on a promotional basis, for five centimes! Ferenczi nevertheless paid me a bonus of 100 francs. I never knew how many copies *La Montagne* had sold, but sales must have been tremendous for him to pay me a bonus!

Ferenczi had at least a dozen different imprints—adventure novels, detective stories, romance... One of the editors in charge was a modest and simple lady named Mrs. Paulet. I can never repay her enough for her kindness. At the time, she was almost fifty. I never learned how she had arrived at her position. There was a rumor that he had once owned a hotel... She could make or break the career of a new author. Mrs. Paulet was gifted with an incomparable flair for sniffing out new talent, and remarkably sound judgment. She advised and guided the writers, asked them to cut or, on the contrary, add substance to a chapter, or make changes, and her requests were always justified and improved the books. She could take a half-baked, mediocre manuscript and turn it into a perfectly decent novel.

She read so many manuscripts that she ended up developing neuralgia in her face from the effort. She loved adventure novels and detective stories—but not the romance novels, which she found tiresome and repetitive. She was responsible for putting out ten books a week, which was a tremendous output. But if she was happy with a writer, she would send letters saying, "send us more books."

Alas! Even the best things must come to an end and the time came when the good Mrs. Paulet had to retire. Ferenczi replaced her with a Mademoiselle D*** who allegedly had a college degree, but whose first act was to reject a manuscript by Max-André Dazergues, one of Ferenczi's very best authors. I remember receiving a letter from a distraught colleague and friend, also very talented, who had in fact influenced me. He simply did not understand what was happening. It was the first time in thirty years that he had a received a rejection letter. Shortly thereafter, it happened to me, too. But the writing was already on the wall: romance magazines were stealing readers away from paperbacks, and other imprints were suffering from the competition with more hard-edged, longer books. Ferenczi floundered and the company folded two years after the death of Henri Ferenczi in 1964.

Other popular literature publishers

At Nicea, they changed their minds all the time. I wrote eleven *Dollar Dog* novels for them and I was starting on the twelfth, when I was told they were cancelling that imprint. The same happened with another series, *Antarès,*

Capitaine Corsaire; I had written seventeen of them when they suddenly decided to stop. I said, "Let me do the eighteenth book, because that will conclude the storyline," but they refused. It was a shame because I loved writing pirate stories. We constantly had to haggle over prices there. Normally, I would have been paid 5,000 francs for a short novel of this type, but they wanted to pay only 3,500 francs, so I had to turn down several other projects of theirs. When you write a lot of books, you want to write something that you would enjoy reading. That's the secret; you must love your job—and I really did. Passionately! I didn't become very rich, because one can't get really rich in this business. However, I had a lot of fun.

At the end of the war, I went to ABC editions, which published two or three novels of mine. Then, they became S.E.G. after they merged with another small publisher. I contributed to several of their imprints, with a lot of detective and espionage novels.

Their editor was Edward Brooker, a writer of English origins, already known in the business before the war. He had some tremendous ideas and started an espionage imprint. They were a series of twelve episodes in the magazine format, and he had made up the titles and commissioned the covers ahead of time. When I was asked to come in, there was a large board with all the twelve covers on it in his office. The first eleven episodes had already been plotted by Brooker. He said to me, "I'm not planning to stay in Europe because I think another war will start soon, so you'll finish the series." Then he left for Australia, and we never saw or heard of him again. So I wrote the twelfth episode based on the title (*The Mysterious Motorcar*) and the cover image.

The publisher was happy and asked me to continue, so we began a new series called *Secret Service*, and I wrote sixty-five episodes of it. Then I received a telephone call from a colleague of mine, Michel Lebrun, who told me: "Maurice, they're playing you for a chump. Do you have any ideas how many copies of *Secret Service* they sell?" So I asked two of my friends to check with the newsagents; they discovered that the book was selling out in 48 hours. The sales were averaging 50,000 copies, which was incredible!

Naturally, I had a shouting match with the publisher when I asked for a raise. They refused. So I killed off the hero—he got run over by a train—and wrote the words *The End*. That's why I moved to Grand Damier publishers. And from there, to Fleuve Noir. Once I was at Fleuve Noir, there was no reason for me to go elsewhere. They were wonderful, and our relationship lasted 28 years. I did not regret a minute of it.

My years with Fleuve Noir

I had already written a few short science fiction novels for Ferenczi: *Le mal des étoiles* [Evil from the Stars], *Les forçats de l'espace* [The Convicts of Space], *Le soleil de l'épouvante* [Star of Terror], *Courrier interplanétaire* [Interplanetary Courier]... Then, in 1955, I wrote *SOS Galaxie* for a short-lived publisher called Metal. It was my first "real" SF novel, in which I introduced the character of Captain Martinbras, whom I later reused in my Martervénux series.

The following year, I wrote *Monsieur Cosmos* for Grand Damier. It was very well received, so I followed it with two more novels, *Pas de planète pour les terriens* [No Home for Earthmen] and *La planète sans soleil*. [The Sunless World] But the publisher wasn't interested in SF. They cancelled their imprint, preferring to concentrate on detective and espionage novels. However, they were on friendly terms with Fleuve Noir, and they had the courtesy of sending one of my unpublished SF manuscripts to them.

Soon after, François Richard, who was then in charge of the *Anticipation* imprint, telephoned me to let me know that they had read my manuscript *Les Enfants du Chaos* [Children of Chaos], and decided to buy it. That was in 1959. It was the first novel of mine they bought. I was, of course, happy, especially after Richard told me: "There is no question of buying a single book; that's not what we want; we want an author, full-time; do you agree?" Of course, I did. So we signed a contract and I immediately gave him two more manuscripts I had waiting for a publisher. He asked me to do five books per year. I told him that when it came to SF, that wasn't so easy, and I negotiated him down to four.

Fleuve Noir also asked me to provide a sketch for the cover artist, the famous René Brantonne.[13] After the book came out, I had to pinch myself to be-

---

[13] René Brantonne (1903-1979) was one of the foremost French science fiction illustrators. Brantonne began his career as a commercial artist in the late 1920s, drawing French film posters for Paramount, MGM, Universal, Columbia, etc. and creating logos for Standard Oil (later Exxon). After the War, Brantonne began working as a comics artist on a number of adventure series for a variety of

lieve in my own luck! It was the same feeling I had twenty years before when my first novel had come out. This was totally new and exciting for me!

Océan, mon esclave [Ocean my slave] (1961) was one of the first novels I wrote for Fleuve Noir under my new contract. What was special about it was that before writing it, I dreamed it, in the truest sense of the word. I woke up one morning with the story already in my mind. That had never happened to me before. It's been one of my most popular novels ever since.

I have always felt that there are no limits to what one could write in science fiction, which is why I loved doing it. It was such a liberating experience! If you write a romance novel, you'll always end up with the same scenarios, good or bad. If you do a detective novel, you've got to be very careful with the clues, the science, etc. I had several policemen write to me to complain about some details I had gotten wrong. But with science fiction, your imagination is given free reign. It is not unlike writing poetry—SF is the poetry of the 20th century, and I hope of the 21st as well. Poetry has no limits, no boundaries. Why not poetic novels? I have always said that a science fiction novel is a poetic work.

Horror novels

Technically speaking, my first horror novel was *La Révolte des Spectres* [The Revolt of the Spectres], which I wrote in 1954 and which was published in a new horror imprint put out by L'Arabesque, another publisher with whom I

---

magazines: *Fulguros* and *Johnny Speed* for Artima, *Praline* and *Buffalo Bill* for Édition des Remparts. He even drew a short-lived French version of the American strip, *Brick Bradford*. During that time, he also became the cover artist par excellence of the Nyctalope novels and of the *Anticipation* imprint of Fleuve Noir, for which he drew over 500 covers.

worked in the 1950s. After I joined Fleuve Noir, I asked François Richard if there was anything else they needed. He suggested I write for their new *Angoisse* imprint, which they had started in 1954 and was short of manuscripts. So I penned *Crucifie le Hibou* [Crucify the Owl] (1961), which I dedicated to all those who fight against the suffering and death of animals. This was an expression of the remorse I felt, because when I was a kid on the farm, I was so bored that I wasn't always kind to frogs, moles and other field animals.

Of course, as a lot of other novelists like to do, I often use recurring characters. I had done this in my *Anticipation* novels, by introducing Robin Muscat, then Chevalier Coqdor. For *Angoisse*, I recalled my old friend Teddy Verano, P.I., back into service, and then I had the idea of creating Mephista, which was really two persons. There is this great actress, but also a starlet who looks like her and has made a pact with the Devil. I wrote thirteen volumes in the series and would have enjoyed doing more, but the publisher decided to cancel the imprint in 1970. That's a shame, because I really liked my two Mephistas.

The End of my Career

My last novel for Fleuve Noir was *Atoxa des Abysses* [Atoxa-of-the-Depths] in 1987. It was based on an idea that I had had in mind for some time, because I love stories of the deep. I created a romance between a young man and what he thinks is, at first, a mermaid, but who actually belongs to an aquatic race who are the descendents of Mû. For her love, my hero gradually undergoes a mutation, which normally would require thousands, of years, but which, in his case, occurs over the span of several weeks. He eventually becomes an aquatic creature and disappears into the ocean. His friends only find his clothes left on the beach. He has gone to join the beautiful Atoxa underwater.

This was the end point of my literary career. François Richard was gone and there were major changes in the literary direction that his successors at Fleuve Noir wished to take. They hired a whole new bunch of writers, but in the end, they could not stave off the decline. One after the other, all their once-wonderful imprints were cancelled. *Anticipation* lasted until 1997, but at the end, it was only a shade of what it had been.

My literary career spanned more than half a century. I'm happy because this was my childhood dream, and I achieved it. I never wanted to be anything but a popular novelist, and I became one. Sometimes, I think of all the people I must have touched, because I had millions of readers. These books that one could carry in one's pocket or read in the train, no longer exist today. Yet they entranced several generations. This form of literature is no more. To research it today is like doing paleontology. When I take a look back, however, I say to myself: I am a survivor, the last the survivor of a vanished world. I can look over my life now by looking over my books. I have lived halfway between dream and reality. But it's good to be able to realize one's dreams.

The Life and Times of Teddy Verano

Teddy Verano, a private eye who often dealt with mad scientists, robots, and demonic beings, was created by Maurice Limat in 1936 and made his first appearance in *La Villa aux Squelettes* [The House of Skeletons], when he was called to investigate what at first seemed to be a natural death, but in reality turned out to be the work of a madman who had learned to weaponize fear.

According to Limat, the first name "Teddy" was borrowed from the family cats who were named "Teddy" after the nickname given to the British soldiers who had fought alongside the French during World War I, and the surname "Verano" meant "Summer" in Spanish.

Verano's hair is brown; his eyes are identified as being hazelnut in color, and his kind but ironic smile is often mentioned in the books. Limat himself played the part of Teddy Verano when his mystery play *L'Ecole du Mystere* [The School of Mystery] was performed twice on stage, the first time in 1946 at the Jena Theater, and the second time in 1958 at the Coliseum Theater, both in Paris.

Verano returned in 1937 in *Le Mystère des Hommes Volants* [The Mystery of the Flying Men]. The following year, he freed Princess Sonia from a diabolical secret prison in *Sous la Cagoule* [Under the Hood] and narrowly escaped being decapitated in *La Guillotine Clandestine* [The Clandestine Guillotine]. He also appeared in the more conventional adventure novels *Radio Infernale* [Radio from Hell], *Mystère au Grand Large* [Mystery at Sea], *L'Enigme du Parachute*

[The Mystery of the Parachute] and *Le Puits de la Mort Lente* [The Pit of Slow Death].

Interestingly, the character of police detective Guy Farnese, who later returned as a supporting character in the Verano series, first appeared independently in *La Matraque du Fantôme* [The Ghost's Truncheon] in 1938 and fought the evil fortune-teller Demonia in *La Reine de l'Epouvante* [The Queen of Terror] in 1939. Farnese got promoted and eventually ended up Police Commissioner in the Mephista series.

In 1939, as Limat was drafted into the Army, Verano and Farnese had to take a back seat to their creator's military obligations and other, more fantastic works, although Verano still appeared in *On a volé un dirigeable* [The Stolen Airship], *L'Empreinte de la Panthère* [The Mark of the Panther] and *L'Espion invisible* [The Invisible Spy, 1940].

Verano made a brief appearance in the 1942 novel *Le Moulin Maudit* [The Accursed Windmill], but returned in full glory 1944 in *L'Ile Maudite* [The Accursed Island], followed by *Satanix*, in which he freed a young widow and her little boy from the threat of the eponymous madman. In 1945, Verano starred in *Mille et Une Blessures* [A Thousand and One Wounds] and *Meurtre en Serre Chaude* [Murder in a Hothouse].

In the following year came *Le Vase aux Sept Dragons* [The Vase with Seven Dragons], in which Verano had to solve the mystery of a pet kidnapper. The remarkable *L'Assassin est mort deux fois* [The Murderer Who Died Twice], in which a sea-horse is key to solving the mystery, was rejected six times, but, after it was published, was reissued nine times and won much critical acclaim. Also in 1946, Verano solved a traditional locked room mystery in *Le Manoir aux feu follets* [The Manor of the Will-o'-the-wisps] and defeated a mad scientist in *Le Meurtre d'un Robot* [The Murder of a Robot].

In 1947-48 Verano played sidekick to another hero, Marco, in a series of exotic adventures in which romance played a major role. This included a five-volume series-within-the-series subtitled *Les Forçats de l'Amour* [The Convicts of Love], followed by *La Femme à la Cape Rouge* [The woman in the Red Cloak] (1948), *La Nuit des Vaudoux* [Voodoo Night], *Cœur de feu, cœur de glace* [Fiery Heart, Icy Heart] and *La Déesse de Fièvre* [The Fever Goddess]. In it, Verano met a strange and fascinating psych medium, the beautiful Lionella, in what was his first venture into the Occult.

Verano still starred in more conventional mysteries such as *La Mort au cinquième acte* [Death in Act Five] (1947), the spooky *Le Club des Monstres* (1948), *Le Cercle de Minuit* [The Midnight Circle] (1949), *La Mort joue au billard* [Death as a Pool Player] (1949), in which Limat's billiard skills helped him craft an ingenious riddle.

In the 1950s, Teddy Verano's investigations, reflecting the mood of the public, began incorporating more fanciful elements, borrowed either from science fiction or horror tropes. Bloody murders were often hidden behind the trappings of fake science or bargain basement grand-guignol.

Verano appeared in *L'Assassin frappera le...* [The Murderer Will Strike On...] (1950), *L'Homme aux Aquariums* [The Aquarium Man] (1950), *L'Etoile de Sang* [The Bloody Star] (1952), *La Mariée Masquée* [The Masked Bride] (1952), *Du Tonnerre... le gars !* [By Thunder, What a Man!] (1952), a boxing mystery, *Le Serpent de Lumière* [The Snake of Light] (1952) about a Hindu death-cult, *Le Vol des Plans Z* [The Theft of Blueprints Z] (1953), an espionage novel with sci-fi overtones, *L'Etrange Supplice* [The Strange Torture] (1953), in which a madman used raptors to spread panic, *Les Morts-Vivants* [The Living Dead] (1954), another espionage thriller despite its horror title, and *Rue des Mauvais Garçons* [Street of Bad Boys] (1954) about the then-headline-making issue of juvenile delinquency,

Verano's first, true supernatural adventure was *La Révolte des Spectres* [The Revolt of the Specters], published in 1954). It was a herald of things to come, when Limat moved to Fleuve Noir in 1959. Meanwhile, Verano appeared in *Fais tes Griffes... Panthère!* [Sharpen your Claws, Panther!] (1955), *Bas les pattes!* [Hands Off!] (1955), *Meurtre d'un Vampire* [Murder of a Vampire] (1955), which was not about a supernatural blood drinker, but a murderer using vampire bats, and *On n'a jamais tué comme ça!* [They Never Killed Like That!] (1955), another thriller in which the gimmick is the use of carnivorous flowers.

By the time Limat started writing *Angoisse* novels for Fleuve Noir, Teddy Verano hadn't aged a day, even though he had been active in his mid-to-late 40ies since 1936. Since almost thirty years had passed, it is tempting to imagine that, sometime during the intervening years, the original Teddy was succeeded by a "Teddy Jr."

All the covers of the *Angoisse* novels were drawn by French illustrator Michel Gourdon, [14] justifiably famous for his pin-up art. Limat brought Verano back in *Le Marchand de Cauchemars* [The Nightmare Peddler] (N° 90, 1962) the third novel he wrote for the imprint, about an evil spell caster. Verano then appeared in most, but not all, of the succeeding novels, running through the gamut of supernatural themes: *Mandragore* (N°101, 1963), *Lucifera* (N°107, 1964) (about second sight), *Le Miroir* [The Mirror] (N°112, 1964) (schizophrenia), *La Prison de Chair* [The Prison of Flesh] (N°114, 1964) (hypnotism), *Le Moulin des Damnés* [The Windmill of the Accursed] (N°121, 1965) (evil mutations), *La Mygale* [The Mygalomorph] (N°123, 1965) (monstrous tarantulas), *Moi, Vampire* [I, Vampire] (N°127, 1966) (scientific vampirism), *Les Jardins de la Nuit* [The Gardens of Night] (N°129, 1966) (nightmare creating drugs), *L'Aquarium de Sang* [The Bloody Aquarium] (N°144, 1967) (more monsters), *En Lettres de Feu* [In Letters of Fire] (N°150, 1968) and *Amazone de la Mort* [Amazon of Death] (N°154, 1968) (the afterlife).

During the events depicted in *Mandragore*, Verano married Yvonne Parmier and adopted her son, Gerard, whom he trained to become his assistant and follow in his footsteps.

In 1969, Limat embarked upon the thirteen-volume series-within-the-series of *Mephista*, which is reviewed separately in our next article. After the cancellation of Angoisse, Teddy Verano made one final appearance in *Une Morsure de Feu* [A Fiery Bite] (N° 1063, 1981) in the *Anticipation* imprint, a tale about a Greek mythological monster which turned out to be the last survivor of a prehistoric creature.

---

[14] Michel Gourdon (1925-2011) was a renowned cover artist and the brother of another famous pin-up artist, Aslan (Alain Gourdon), with whom he shared to technique.

Whence Mephista?

by Artikel Unbekannt

Mephista was more than a femme fatale—she was *two* femmes fatales, as shown in the second novel of the series, in which the tragic figure of Mephista was split into two characters: (1) Edwige Hossegor, the kind-hearted actress who created the evil Mephista for the screen, and who remains plagued by visions, dreams and premonitions throughout the cycle, and (2) her evil, would-be replacement, Olga Mervil, who signed a pact with the Devil, and who, after being disfigured at the end of Volume 2, attempts to find some kind of redemption in the later volumes.

Throughout the series, these two women with their two nearly identical faces (Olga's, however, remained concealed behind her mask) remained separate, but complementary, incarnations of the same evil that is Mephista. Together, they form a powerful archetype, just as "forked" as the Devil's tongue is supposed to be, an evil entity lurking in the shadows, ready to reappear at any time.

For the pleasure of our readers, who may not get a chance to discover the latter volumes of the Mephista saga, here are brief summaries of the next ten volumes in the series:

4. *Mephista et la Lanterne des Morts* [The Lantern of the Dead] (N°190, 1970):
    Chantal and her companion, Claude, have a car accident. However, if the young woman manages to emerge unscathed from it, her friend dies in mysteri-

ous, frightening circumstances. Chantal eventually comes to believe that she is dead, too. Her parents call on Teddy Verano, who soon discovers that a strange witchcraft artifact, the so-called "lantern of the dead," is exerting a powerful occult influence on Chantal.

Teddy and his stepson Gerard investigate and find out that the sacred boundaries that separate Life from Death have been broken by Olga Mervil. However, this time, the evil incarnation of Mephista may find herself the victim of the forces she has unleashed, and she risks becoming lost forever between our world and the world beyond.

5. *Mephista et la Croix Sanglante* [The Bloody Cross] (N°197, 1971)

Liliane, the wife of the Jacques Valombré, is plagued by strange nightmares, identical to those suffered by a young woman from the local village a century ago. She believes that a vampire is lurking nearby, a belief strengthened by the discovery of a body with two bite marks on the neck in a local pond, seemed to be haunted.

As her husband is an old friend of Baron Tragny, Edwige Hossegor's companion, he comes up with the idea of asking Edwige to recreate the ancient drama, hoping to create a psychological shock that will free his wife from her frightful obsession. Edwige, a.k.a. Mephista, agrees to try to break the ancient curse, but her talent only causes the ancient vampire to rise from the accursed pond. Only Teddy Verano's intervention solves the mystery and banishes away the evil powers...

6. *Danse Macabre pour Mephista* [Dance Macabre for Mephista] (N°203, 1971)

Following several tragic accidents at the Monte-Carlo Opera, the dancer Rehann takes over the direction of a ballet adapting Edgar Allan Poe's *Masque of the Red Death*. But if the young man proves very gifted at directing his fellow dancers, his strange interpretation of what the ballet should be about starts having nefarious consequences on the mental well-being of the other dancers.

After more dramatic incidents, the Opera calls on Teddy Verano. The detective decides to enlist the help of Olga Mervil, who is being treated in a private clinic since the terrible events of Book 4. Verano plans to use the young woman's special connection with Evil to undo the spells cast by the malevolent Rehann.

7. *Mephista et la Mort Caressante* [The Gentle Death] (N°210, 1972)

Olga Mervil has not yet paid the price for the satanic pact that she signed in Book 2. She now falls under the sway of a strange, evil sect, the Servants of the Gentle Death, who uses special flowers, which emit a hypnotic smell, to disarm their victims.

Alerted by Olga's disappearance, Teddy Verano must act quickly to save not only Olga, but also his wife Yvonne, from the cultists who plan to sacrifice both women to their dark, demonic masters.

8. *Mephista et le Chasseur Maudit* [The Accursed Hunter] (N°219, 1972)

Diane, the wife of rich industrialist Hugues Dambard, seduces a young writer, Patrice Mazeuil, who has been hired by her husband to adapt a local legend into a film. But suddenly the events of the legend come to life. Diane becomes a huntress who drags Patrice into a spiral of debauchery, virtually under her husband's eyes. Hugues has vowed to save his daughter cursed with blindness. To do this, he does not hesitate to release the dark forces only hinted at by the legend.

Mephista, in the person of Edwige Hossegor, only makes a brief appearance in the novel, still plagued by her supernatural sensitivity to evil forces around her.

9. *Mephista et le Guignol Noir* [The Dark Guignol] (N°227, 1972)

A puppet show for children suddenly turns scary when the puppeteer is found strangled. Meanwhile, Edwige Hossegor is suffering from a mysterious illness against which the doctors are powerless. Teddy Verano and Gerard eventually discover a strange sculptor, Paul Setter, who has crafted a series of evil puppets, including a figurine of Mephista. Setter wishes to restore Olga's beauty.

Setter eventually captures Gerard, and his girl-friend Gilda, and forces them to attend a horrific underground puppet show that reduces them to the state of puppets themselves. But the evil that is Mephista is not so easily controlled ..

10. *Mephista belle à faire peur* [Scaringly Beautiful] (N°232, 1973)

Still seeking a cure for her "condition," Olga teams up with mad Doctor Brénon, who believes he can transfer the curse of Mephista into the body of one of his patients, young Sonia, who has just been dumped by her boyfriend, Francis. But at the last minute, Sonia has a change of heart and rebels; however, it is too late and she has now become a terrifying wraith-like monster who now pursues revenge againt Francis.

Using his occult knowledge, Teddy Verano plans to conduct a ritual to separate the intertwined figures of Sonia and Olga, but Mephista does not necessarily wish to abandon her new vessel...

11. *Mephista contre l'Homme de Feu* [vs The Man of Fire] (N°239, 1973)

Veronica, a starlet; Ghislaine, a sales clerk; Flora, a young widow. Three women who have met Thierry, a former stuntman, obsessed by an insane passion for fire, who seems unscathed by flames.

Edwige Hossegor, who wishes to help Veronica, decides to confront this dangerous man and goes to the river boat that serves as his lair. There, Thierry has surrounded himself with women, whom he calls the Devil's Vestals, and has learned to command the mystic properties of fire itself. A terrible fight ensues between Thierry and the Mephista...

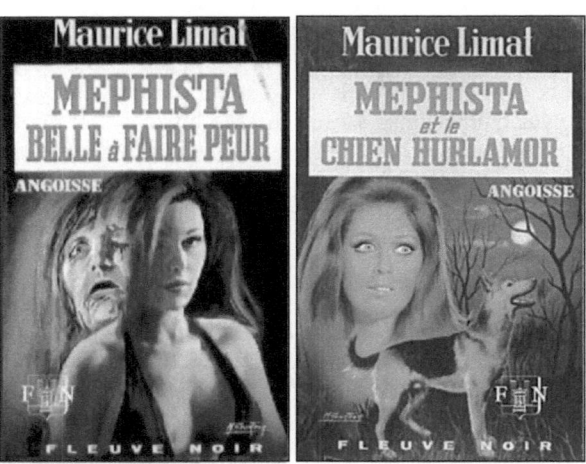

12. *Ton Sang, Mephista* [Your Blood, Mephista] (N°246, 1973)

Edwige Hossegor has agreed to play the part of a mother who, in order to save her son, must agree to sacrifice another boy. Meanwhile, young Luc is saved from death by receiving a blood transfusion from Hervé, another dying man. A series of sadistic crimes occur afterwad, for which Luc is the prime suspect, but he claims to have been compelled by Hervé's ghost.

What game are being played by the mysterious Dr. Macchi, who seeks to revenge himself on Edwige for her supposed past betrayal? Or Evelyn the nurse, Hervé's former fiancée? This time, Mephista must battle a psychic vampire in order to prevail.

13. *Mephista et le Chien Hurlamor* [The Howling Hound of Death] (N°252, 1974)

A dog, hitherto loyal and calm, starts howling at the moon. Young Victor Fleurion has his throat torn out, as if by a wolf, during a strange nocturnal hunt. Is a werewolf prowling the woods near the Chateau des Acacias, where Isabelle and her husband, the all too prone to anger Nicolas, are hosting a film crew that includes Edwige Hossegor.

The werewolf turns out to be a human being, heir of terrifying occult secrets, who can change into a beast at certain phases of the moon.

14. *La Maison du Frisson* [The House of Shivers] (*Mémoires d'Outre-Ciel* No. 24, Garry, 1981) (published under the nom-de-plume of Jean Scapin)

Luke and Gaëlle are a young couple returning from holidays when they are forced by a storm to find refuge in n old house. There, Gaëlle, entranced, is raped by a ghost, which leaves her with a bite mark. They then meet the owner of the house, the mysterious Clara and her pet snake, Baal.

Months later, Gaëlle discovers she is pregnant. Luke hires Teddy Verano (rechristened Aldo Vernon) to investigate. He does so with Edwige's help (rechristened Wanda and said to be Edwige's personal assistant on her TV show, *The Night of the Strange*).

Gaëlle is hospitalized, but disappears. She is the prisoner of Clara, who believes that if she can bend the restless ghost to her will, it will provide her with limitless magical power. Clara is convinced that the ghost impregnated Gaëlle and will return to take possession of its unborn child.

Teddy and Edwige arrive just in time to rescue Gaëlle. Edwige uses her acting skills to pose as another ghost and drives Clara insane. Gaëlle's pregnancy proves to be false; yet, the mystery of the bite mark remains...

(*Note*: Afer the abrupt cancellation of *Angoisse* by Editions Fleuve Moir, Limat resold this unpublished *Mephista* manuscript to another smaller publisher, merely changing the names of Mephista and Teddy Verano.)

Filled with references to classic works, such as *Judex*, *The Vampires*, *Belphegor* and *Fantômas*, Maurice Limat's *Mephista* series alternates between detective and horror fiction, without ever taking sides. And that is a good thing, because the two genres blend perfectly. Further, that subtle combination is what really defined Fleuve Noir's *Angoisse* imprint. Limat's books were unjustly underestimated at the time of their first publication. This new translated edition has enabled me to correct this injustice to a certain degree, and I'm very very proud to close this book on an acknowledgement of their visionary quality, still much alive today.

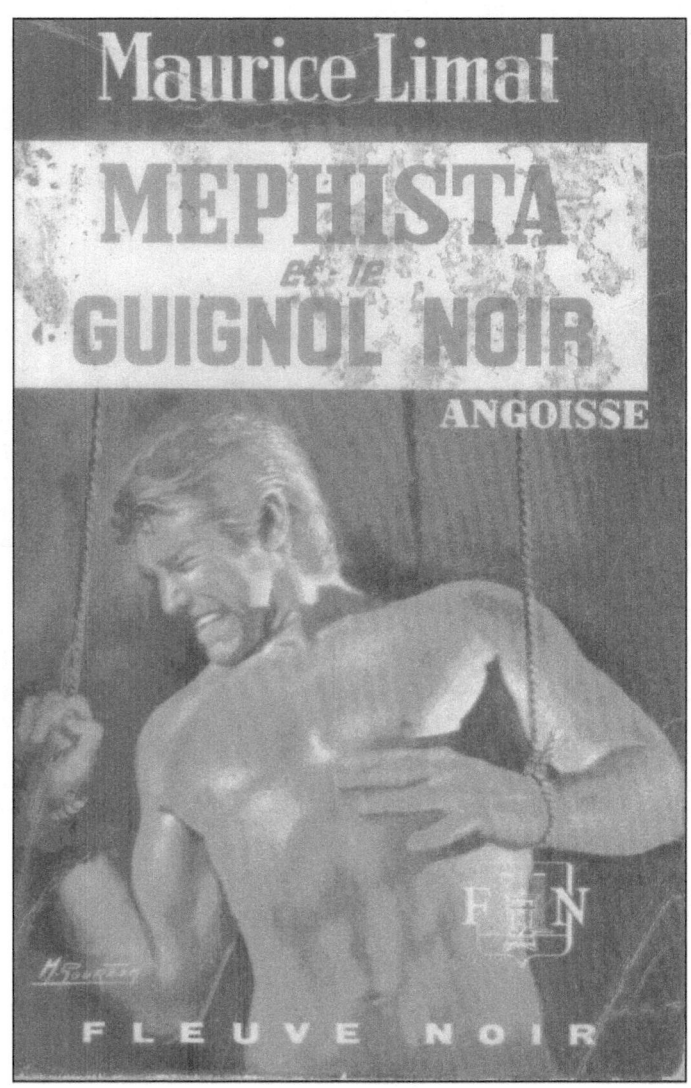

Teddy Verano as seen by M. Gourdon.

SF & FANTASY

Adolphe Alhaiza. *Cybele*
Alphonse Allais. *The Adventures of Captain Cap*
Henri Allorge. *The Great Cataclysm*
Guy d'Armen. *Doc Ardan: The City of Gold and Lepers*
G.-J. Arnaud. *The Ice Company*
Charles Asselineau. *The Double Life*
Henri Austruy. *The Eupantophone; The Olotelepan; The Petitpaon Era*
Barillet-Lagargousse. *The Final War*
Cyprien Bérard. *The Vampire Lord Ruthwen*
S. Henry Berthoud. *Martyrs of Science*
Aloysius Bertrand. *Gaspard de la Nuit*
Richard Bessière. *The Gardens of the Apocalypse; The Masters of Silence*
Chevalier de Béthune. *The World of Mercury*
Albert Bleunard. *Ever Smaller*
Félix Bodin. *The Novel of the Future*
Louis Boussenard. *Monsieur Synthesis*
Alphonse Brown. *City of Glass; The Conquest of the Air*
Émile Calvet. *In a Thousand Years*
André Caroff. *The Terror of Madame Atomos; Miss Atomos; The Return of Madame Atomos; The Mistake of Madame Atomos; The Monsters of Madame Atomos; The Revenge of Madame Atomos, The Resurrection of Madame Atomos; The Mark of Madame Atomos; The Spheres of Madame Atomos; The Wrath of Madame Atomos* (w/M. & Sylvie Stéphan)
Félicien Champsaur. *The Human Arrow; Ouha, King of the Apes; Pharaoh's Wife; Homo-Deus; Nora, The Ape-Woman*
Didier de Chousy. *Ignis*
Jules Clarétie. *Obsession*
Michel Corday. *The Eternal Flame*
André Couvreur. *The Necessary Evil; Caresco, Superman; The Exploits of Professor Tornada* (3 vols.)
Camille Debans. *The Misfortunes of John Bull*
Captain Danrit. *Undersea Odyssey*
C. I. Defontenay. *Star (Psi Cassiopeia)*
Charles Derennes. *The People of the Pole*
Georges Dodds (anthologist). *The Missing Link*
Charles Dodeman. *The Silent Bomb*
Harry Dickson. *The Heir of Dracula; Harry Dickson vs. The Spider*
Jules Dornay. *Lord Ruthven Begins*
Alfred Driou. *The Adventures of a Parisian Aeronaut*
Sâr Dubnotal *vs. Jack the Ripper*
Odette Dulac. *The War of the Sexes*
Alexandre Dumas. *The Return of Lord Ruthven*
Renée Dunan. *Baal; The Ultimate Pleasure*
J.-C. Dunyach. *The Night Orchid; The Thieves of Silence*
Henri Duvernois. *The Man Who Found Himself*

Achille Eyraud. *Voyage to Venus*

Henri Falk. *The Age of Lead*

Paul Féval. *Anne of the Isles; Knightshade; Revenants; Vampire City; The Vampire Countess; The Wandering Jew's Daughter*

Paul Féval, *fils. Felifax, the Tiger-Man*

Charles de Fieux. *Lamékis*

Louis Forest. *Someone is Stealing Children in Paris*

Arnould Galopin. *Doctor Omega; Doctor Omega and the Shadowmen* (anthology)

Judith Gautier. *Isoline and the Serpent-Flower*

H. Gayar. *The Marvelous Adventures of Serge Myrandhal on Mars*

G.L. Gick. *Harry Dickson and the Werewolf of Rutherford Grange*

Delphine de Girardin. *Balzac's Cane*

Léon Gozlan. *The Vampire of the Val-de-Grâce*

Jules Gros. *The Fossil Man*

Edmond Haraucourt. *Illusions of Immortality; Daah, the First Human*

Nathalie Henneberg. *The Green Gods*

Eugène Hennebert. *The Enchanted City*

Jules Hoche. *The Maker of Men and His Formula*

V. Hugo, P. Foucher & P. Meurice. *The Hunchback of Notre-Dame*

Romain d'Huissier. *Hexagon: Dark Matter*

Jules Janin. *The Magnetized Corpse*

Michel Jeury. *Chronolysis*

Gustave Kahn. *The Tale of Gold and Silence*

Gérard Klein. *The Mote in Time's Eye*

Fernand Kolney. *Love in 5000 Years*

Paul Lacroix. *Danse Macabre*

Louis-Guillaume de La Follie. *The Unpretentious Philosopher*

Jean de La Hire. *Enter the Nyctalope; The Nyctalope on Mars; The Nyctalope vs. Lucifer; The Nyctalope Steps In; Night of the Nyctalope; Return of the Nyctalope; The Fiery Wheel*

Etienne-Léon de Lamothe-Langon. *The Virgin Vampire*

André Laurie. *Spiridon*

Gabriel de Lautrec. *The Vengeance of the Oval Portrait*

Alain le Drimeur. *The Future City*

Georges Le Faure & Henri de Graffigny. *The Extraordinary Adventures of a Russian Scientist Across the Solar System* (2 vols.)

Gustave Le Rouge. *The Mysterious Doctor Cornelius* (3 vols.); *The Vampires of Mars; The Dominion of the World* (w/Gustave Guitton) (4 vols.)

Jules Lermina. *Mysteryville; Panic in Paris; To-Ho and the Gold Destroyers; The Secret of Zippelius; The Battle of Strasbourg*

André Lichtenberger. *The Centaurs; The Children of the Crab*

Listonai. *The Philosophical Voyager*

Jean-Marc & Randy Lofficier. *Edgar Allan Poe on Mars; The Katrina Protocol; Pacifica; Robonocchio; Return of the Nyctalope;* (anthologists) *Tales of the Shadowmen 1-11; The Vampire Almanac* (2 vols.)

Xavier Maumejean. *The League of Heroes*

Joseph Méry. *The Tower of Destiny*

Hippolyte Mettais. *The Year 5865; Paris Before the Deluge*

Louise Michel. *The Human Microbes; The New World*
Tony Moilin. *Paris in the Year 2000*
José Moselli. *Illa's End*
John-Antoine Nau. *Enemy Force*
Marie Nizet. *Captain Vampire*
C. Nodier, A. Beraud & Toussaint-Merle. *Frankenstein*
Henri de Parville. *An Inhabitant of the Planet Mars*
Gaston de Pawlowski. *Journey to the Land of the 4th Dimension*
Georges Pellerin. *The World in 2000 Years*
Ernest Pérochon. *The Frenetic People*
Pierre Pelot. *The Child Who Walked on the Sky*
J. Polidori, C. Nodier, E. Scribe. *Lord Ruthven the Vampire*
P.-A. Ponson du Terrail. *The Vampire and the Devil's Son; The Immortal Woman*
Georges Price. *The Missing Men of the Sirius*
Edgar Quinet. *Ahasuerus; The Enchanter Merlin*
Henri de Régnier. *A Surfeit of Mirrors*
Maurice Renard. *The Blue Peril; Doctor Lerne; The Doctored Man; A Man Among the Microbes; The Master of Light*
Jean Richepin. *The Wing; The Crazy Corner*
Albert Robida. *The Adventures of Saturnin Farandoul; The Clock of the Centuries; Chalet in the Sky; The Electric Life; The Engineer Von Satanas*
J.-H. Rosny Aîné. *Helgvor of the Blue River; The Givreuse Enigma; The Mysterious Force; The Navigators of Space; Vamireh; The World of the Variants; The Young Vampire*
Marcel Rouff. *Journey to the Inverted World*
Léonie Rouzade. *The World Turned Upside Down*
Han Ryner. *The Superhumans; The Human Ant*
Pierre de Selenes: *An Unknown World*
Angelo de Sorr. *The Vampires of London*
Brian Stableford. *The New Faust at the Tragicomique;The Empire of the Necromancers (The Shadow of Frankenstein; Frankenstein and the Vampire Countess; Frankenstein in London); Sherlock Holmes & The Vampires of Eternity; The Stones of Camelot; The Wayward Muse.* (anthologist) *News from the Moon; The Germans on Venus; The Supreme Progress; The World Above the World; Nemoville; Investigations of the Future; The Conqueror of Death; The Revolt of the Machines; The Man With the Blue Face*
Jacques Spitz. *The Eye of Purgatory*
Kurt Steiner. *Ortog*
Eugène Thébault. *Radio-Terror*
C.-F. Tiphaigne de La Roche. *Amilec*
Simon Tyssot de Patot. *The Strange Voyages of Jacques Massé and Pierre de Mésange*
Louis Ulbach. *Prince Bonifacio*
Théo Varlet. *The Golden Rock. The Xenobiotic Invasion; The Castaways of Eros; Timeslip Troopers* (w/André Blandin); *The Martian Epic* (w/Octave Joncquel)
Pierre Véron. *The Merchants of Health*
Paul Vibert. *The Mysterious Fluid*
Villiers de l'Isle-Adam. *The Scaffold; The Vampire Soul*
Gaston de Wailly. *The Murderer of the World*

Philippe Ward. *Artahe ; The Song of Montségur* (w/Sylvie Miller) *Manhattan Ghost* (w/Mickael Laguerre)

MYSTERIES & THRILLERS

M. Allain & P. Souvestre. *The Daughter of Fantômas*
A. Anicet-Bourgeois, Lucien Dabril. *Rocambole*
A. Bernède. *Belphegor*; *Judex* (w/Louis Feuillade); *The Return of Judex* (w/Louis Feuillade); *The Shadow of Judex*
A. Bisson & G. Livet. *Nick Carter vs. Fantômas*
V. Darlay & H. de Gorsse. *Arsène Lupin vs. Sherlock Holmes: The Stage Play*
Séamas Duffy. *Sherlock Holmes in Paris*
Paul Féval. *Gentlemen of the Night; John Devil; The Black Coats ('Salem Street; The Invisible Weapon; The Parisian Jungle; The Companions of the Treasure; Heart of Steel; The Cadet Gang; The Sword-Swallower)*
Émile Gaboriau. *Monsieur Lecoq*
Goron & Émile Gautier. *Spawn of the Penitentiary*
Paul d'Ivoi. *Around the World on Five Sous* (w/Henri Chabrillat)
Rick Lai. *Shadows of the Opera: Retribution in Blood; Sisters of the Shadows: The Curse of Cagliostro*
Steve Leadley. *Sherlock Holmes: The Circle of Blood*
Maurice Leblanc. *Arsène Lupin vs. Countess Cagliostro; Arsène Lupin vs. Sherlock Holmes (The Blonde Phantom; The Hollow Needle); The Many Faces of Arsène Lupin; The Island of the Thirty Coffin; 813*
Gaston Leroux. *Chéri-Bibi; The Phantom of the Opera; Rouletabille & the Mystery of the Yellow Room; Rouletabille at Krupp's*
Richard Marsh. *The Complete Adventures of Judith Lee*
William Patrick Maynard. *The Terror of Fu Manchu; The Destiny of Fu Manchu*
Frank J. Morlok. *Sherlock Holmes: The Grand Horizontals; Sherlock Holmes vs Jack the Ripper*
Jean Petithuguenin. *The Adventures of Ethel King*
Antonin Reschal. *The Adventures of Miss Boston*
Frank Schildiner. *The Quest of Frankenstein*
P. de Wattyne & Y. Walter. *Sherlock Holmes vs. Fantômas*
David White. *Fantômas in America*
Pierre Yrondy. *The Adventures of Thérèse Arnaud*

Victor Margueritte. *The Bacheloress; The Companion; The Couple*

SCREENPLAYS

Mike Baron. *The Iron Triangle*
Emma Bull & Will Shetterly. *Nightspeeder; War for the Oaks*
Gerry Conway & Roy Thomas. *Doc Dynamo*
Steve Englehart. *Majorca*
James Hudnall. *The Devastator*
Jean-Marc & Randy Lofficier. *Royal Flush*
J.-M. & R. Lofficier & Marc Agapit. *Despair*

J.-M. & R. Lofficier & Joël Houssin. *City*
Andrew Paquette. *Peripheral Vision*
Robert L. Robinson, Jr. *Judex*
R. Thomas, J. Hendler & L. Sprague de Camp. *Rivers of Time*

NON-FICTION

Stephen R. Bissette. *Blur 1-5. Green Mountain Cinema 1; Teen Angels*
Win Scott Eckert. *Crossovers* (2 vols.)
Jean-Marc & Randy Lofficier. *Shadowmen* (2 vols.)
Randy Lofficier. *Over Here*

ART BOOKS

Jean-Pierre Normand. *Science Fiction Illustrations*
Raven Okeefe. *Raven's L'il Critters; Rave's Faves*
Randy Lofficier & Raven Okeefe. *If Your Possum Go Daylight...*
Daniele Serra. *Illusions*
Randy Lofficier. *Over Here*

HEXAGON COMICS

Franco Frescura & Luciano Bernasconi. *Wampus*
Franco Frescura & Giorgio Trevisan. *CLASH*
L. Bernasconi, J.-M. Lofficier & Juan Roncagliolo. *Phenix*
Claude Legrand, J.-M. Lofficier & L. Bernasconi. *Kabur*
Franco Oneta. *Zembla*
L. Buffolente, Lofficier & J.-J. Dzialowski. *Strangers: Homicron*
Danilo Grossi. *Strangers: Jaydee*
Claude Legrand & Luciano Bernasconi. *Strangers: Starlock*
Thierry Mornet & Juan Roncagliolo. *Guardian of the Republic*
J.-M. Lofficier & others. *Strangers 0: Omens & Origins*
J.-M. Lofficier, M. Garcia, F. Blanco & J. Pima. *Strangers 1: Strangers in a Strange Land*

www.ingramcontent.com/pod-product-compliance
Lightning Source LLC
Chambersburg PA
CBHW030350020726
47493CB00003B/753